The Adventures of Laura & Jack

THE COMPLETE
LAURA CHAPTER BOOK COLLECTION

Adapted from the Little House books
by Laura Ingalls Wilder
Illustrated by Renée Graef and Doris Ettlinger

Laura # 1

The Adventures of
Laura & Jack

The Little House Chapter Books are written for children who want to share in the frontier adventures of the Little House girls Laura, Rose, and Caroline but who are not quite ready for the novel series.

The Little House Chapter Books are gentle adaptations of the Little House novels, enhanced by beautiful black-and-white illustrations.

US $4.25 / $6.25 CAN

ISBN 0-06-442045-0

LITTLE HOUSE

Laura #1

The Adventures of Laura & Jack

ADAPTED FROM THE LITTLE HOUSE BOOKS BY

Laura Ingalls Wilder

ILLUSTRATED BY

Renée Graef

HarperTrophy®
A Division of HarperCollinsPublishers

Adaptation by Melissa Peterson.

Illustrations for this book are inspired by the work of Garth Williams
with his permission, which we gratefully acknowledge.

HarperCollins®, ®, Little House®, Harper Trophy®, and The Laura Years™
are trademarks of HarperCollins Publishers Inc.

The Adventures of Laura & Jack
Text adapted from Little House in the Big Woods, copyright 1932, 1960,
Little House Heritage Trust; Little House on the Prairie, copyright 1935,
1963, Little House Heritage Trust; On the Banks of Plum Creek, copyright
1937, 1965, Little House Heritage Trust; By the Shores of Silver Lake,
copyright 1939, 1967, Little House Heritage Trust.
Illustrations copyright © 1997 by Renée Graef
Printed in the U.S.A. All rights reserved.

Library of Congress Cataloging-in-Publication Data
Wilder, Laura Ingalls, 1867–1957.
    The adventures of Laura & Jack / Laura Ingalls Wilder ; illustrated by
Renée Graef
    p.   cm. — (A Little house chapter book)
    Summary: Laura and her beloved bulldog, Jack, share some wild adventures
as the Ingalls family moves from Wisconsin to Kansas and later to Minnesota.
    ISBN 0-06-027130-2 (lib. bdg.) — ISBN 0-06-442045-0 (pbk.)
    1. Wilder, Laura Ingalls, 1867–1957—Juvenile fiction. [1. Wilder, Laura
Ingalls, 1867–1957—Fiction.   2. Frontier and pioneer life—Fiction.
3. Dogs—Fiction.] I. Graef, Renée, ill.   II. Title.   III. Series.
PZ7.W6461Ad   1997   95-26310
[Fic]—dc20   CIP
                                                                    AC

❖
First Harper Trophy edition, 1997

Visit us on the World Wide Web!
www.littlehousebooks.com

Contents

CHAPTER 1

Laura and Jack

As far back as Laura could remember, Jack was there. When Laura and Mary, Ma and Pa, and baby Carrie lived in the Big Woods of Wisconsin, they never had to worry about the bears and wildcats that roamed the forest. Jack stood guard every night. He was a watchdog, and it was his job to keep the family safe.

Jack was a bulldog. He had a stocky body and short legs. His light-brown fur was short, with darker-brown streaks through it. He had a large head and strong, square jaws. When he was guarding the family, he looked very stern and fierce. But with Laura and Mary he was always gentle.

Laura was a very little girl in those days. Mary was a bit older, and she was quiet and good. Laura liked to run and play with Jack. There were no other children living nearby—there wasn't even another house in sight. Just trees and more trees. Laura and Jack weren't allowed to stray into the woods, but there was lots to do right around the little house. Especially if you were a dog.

In the summer Jack had squirrels to chase and birds to bark at. At night he protected Ma's garden from the deer that lived in the woods. The garden was planted behind the cabin. During the day the deer wouldn't come so close to the house, but at night they got brave and jumped the

 2

fence. If it hadn't been for Jack, they would have eaten all Ma's carrots and cabbages. Jack ran after them and chased them out. In the morning Laura would find little hoofprints among the turnips, with Jack's pawprints right beside them.

In the fall Ma and Pa were busy storing food for the winter. They gathered the turnips and cabbages and beets and piled them in the cellar. Ma braided onions into long ropes and hung them in the attic above heaps of pumpkins and squash. Pa brought deer meat home to be smoked and salted. And when the weather was just right, he butchered a pig.

Butchering time was great fun for Laura, Mary, and Jack. Pa let the girls roast the pig's tail on a stick. It sizzled and gave off a delicious smell. When it was brown all over, Laura and Mary ate all the meat off the bones. Nothing ever tasted as good as that pig's tail! And Jack got his share, too. Laura gave him the bones to crunch.

In the winter the little log house was snug against the cold. Laura and Jack curled up by the fireside while Pa told stories and played his fiddle. Outside the wind moaned. Sometimes at night a wolf howled outside the walls of the little log cabin. Laura knew wolves would eat little girls. But she could look out from her bed and see Jack pacing back and forth in front of the door. The hair stood up along his back and he showed his sharp teeth. Pa had promised her that Jack would never let the wolves get in. Laura snuggled under the covers next to Mary, feeling safe and cozy.

One day, when spring was just around the corner, Pa made an announcement.

"I've decided to go see the West," he said. "I've had an offer for this place. We can sell it for enough to give us a start in the new country."

"Oh, Charles, must we go now?" Ma asked. The weather was so cold and the house so cozy.

"If we are going this year, we must go now," Pa said. "We can't cross the Mississippi after the ice breaks."

So Pa sold the little house. He sold the cow and the calf. He stretched a white canvas cover over the wagon. Soon everything was packed in the wagon and the little house stood empty.

Early in the morning the family climbed into the wagon. Laura wore her warmest clothes and her rabbit-skin hood. She and Mary held tight to their rag dolls while all their aunts and uncles and cousins kissed them good-bye. Pa picked up Mary and then Laura, and set them on the bed in the back of the wagon. Ma sat on the wagon seat next to Pa, with baby Carrie on her lap. Jack took his place under the wagon. He was going to walk all the way to the West.

At night they camped beneath the stars. And all day the wagon rolled on behind the horses. They crossed creeks and rivers. They drove through woods and strange, empty, treeless country.

One day Pa traded the tired brown horses for two black ponies. He told Laura and Mary they were called western mustangs.

"They're strong as mules and gentle as kittens," he explained. The ponies had big, gentle eyes and long manes. Laura and Mary named them Pet and Patty.

 6

Pa hitched Pet and Patty to the wagon, and they all traveled on together. They had come from the Big Woods of Wisconsin, across Minnesota, Iowa, and Missouri. And all that long way Jack had trotted under the wagon. It was a long trip for a little dog, but then Jack was not an ordinary dog.

CHAPTER 2

Jack and the River

One afternoon the wagon rolled to a stop. Laura looked out over Ma's shoulder. Ahead was a swift blue creek. They were in Kansas. They had left the Big Woods far behind them.

Pet and Patty dipped their noses to drink from the gurgling water. Jack followed them, lapping up the water with his red tongue.

"This creek's pretty high," Pa said. "But I guess we can make it all right. What do you say, Caroline?"

 8

"Whatever you say, Charles," Ma answered.

Pet and Patty lifted their wet noses. They pricked their ears forward, looking at the creek. Then they pricked them backward to hear what Pa would say.

"I'll tie down the wagon-cover," Pa said. Laura watched him unroll the canvas sides. He tied them firmly to the wagon box. Then he pulled on the rope at the back of the wagon. The canvas drew together tightly, making a round hole that got smaller and smaller. Laura watched Pa through the hole. First she could see his whole head, then just his face, then just the tip of his nose. At last the hole was too small to see through at all.

Mary huddled down on the bed. She did not like fords. The rushing water scared her. But Laura was excited. She loved the sound of the water splashing against the wagon.

Pa climbed back onto the wagon seat. "The horses may have to swim a bit in the middle," he told Ma. "But we'll make it all right."

Laura thought about Jack. "I wish Jack could ride in the wagon, Pa," she said.

Ma turned to look at her. "Jack can swim, Laura," she said. "He will be all right."

Pa eased the horses into the creek. Water struck the sides of the wagon, lifting it high. The wagon dipped and swayed. It was a lovely feeling.

All of a sudden the noise stopped. Ma said sharply, "Lie down, girls!" Laura and Mary dropped flat on the bed. Ma leaned back from the wagon seat to pull a blanket over their heads. It was stifling underneath.

"Be still," Ma warned. "Don't move!"

Mary didn't move a muscle, but Laura couldn't help wriggling a little. She wanted to know what was happening. The noisy splashing came back, and then it died away again. It felt like the wagon was turning in the water.

She heard Pa yell, "Take the reins, Caroline!" His voice scared Laura.

Then there was a loud splash beside the lurching wagon. Laura just had to see what was going on. She sat up, scrambling free of the blanket.

Pa was in the rushing water with Pet and Patty. All Laura could see was his head bobbing next to theirs. He was holding on to Pet's bridle, talking to the horses. Laura couldn't hear what he was saying; the water was too loud.

"Lie down, Laura!" Ma said. She looked scared. Laura lay down next to Mary again. She felt cold and sick. The ride wasn't fun anymore.

She squeezed her eyes shut, but she could still see the water raging around Pa's head. Her stomach felt sicker and sicker. Beside her Mary was crying without making a sound.

At last Laura felt the wagon's front

wheels grate against something hard. Pa gave a shout. They were on the other side.

Laura sat up again. She saw Pa running beside Pet and Patty at the head of the wagon. Water streamed off the horses' backs as they climbed the steep bank.

"Hi, Patty! Hi, Pet! Get up!" Pa called. "Good girls!"

Finally they reached the top of the bank. The awful water rushed on below, but they were safe. Everyone was safe—Pet and Patty, Pa and Ma, Mary and Laura, and baby Carrie.

Pa stood, panting and dripping, beside the wet horses. "Oh, Charles!" Ma said.

"There, there, Caroline," Pa said. He looked at the water. "I never saw a creek rise so fast in my life. Pet and Patty are good swimmers, but they wouldn't have made it if I hadn't helped them."

Laura knew that if Pa hadn't known what to do, they would have all drowned. The creek would have rolled them over and carried them away.

"Well," Pa said, "all's well that ends well."

"Charles, you're wet to the skin," said Ma.

And then Laura remembered. She cried out.

"Oh, where's Jack?"

They had forgotten all about him. They had left him on the other side of that terrible creek. He must have tried to swim after them, but they couldn't see him struggling in the water now.

Laura swallowed hard. She knew she was too big to cry. But there was crying inside her. Poor Jack! He had followed them all the way from Wisconsin, and

14

now they had left him to drown.

If only they'd taken him in the wagon! He had stood on the bank and watched the wagon going away from him, as if the family didn't care about him at all. He'd never know how much they wanted him.

"I wouldn't have done this to Jack for a million dollars," Pa said. He shook his head sadly. "I'd never have let him try to swim that creek if I'd known it would rise like that."

He walked up and down the creek bank, whistling and calling. But no dripping bulldog swam out of the water.

It was no use. Jack was gone.

CHAPTER 3

Eyes in the Dark

There was nothing to do but go on. They drove uphill, out of the river bottoms. Laura looked back all the way. She knew she wouldn't see Jack again, but she wanted to.

The river bluffs gave way to High Prairie. Tall wild grass swayed around the wagon. Far away, the sun's rim rested on the edge of the earth. Purple shadows began to gather over the land.

Pa stopped the mustangs. Everyone climbed out of the wagon. It was time to make camp. The wind made a mournful sound as it waved across the prairie.

Laura went to Ma. "Jack has gone to heaven, hasn't he?" she asked. "He was such a good dog."

Pa answered for Ma. "Yes, Laura," he said. "God won't leave a good dog like Jack out in the cold."

But Laura didn't feel much better. She watched Pa go about his camp chores. He didn't whistle as he usually did. Laura heard him say, "I don't know what we'll do in this wild country without a good watchdog."

Pa unhitched Pet and Patty. He put them on ropes so they could graze. Then he built a fire while Ma mixed up some corn cakes and fried slices of salt pork. Soon the family gathered near the fire to eat supper off their tin plates.

While they were eating, the purple

17

shadows closed around the camp fire. The vast prairie was dark and still. Laura and Mary began to get sleepy.

Ma was washing the dishes when a long, wailing howl rose up in the darkness. They all knew what that meant.

"Wolves," Pa said. "Half a mile away, I'd judge. I wish . . ."

He didn't say what he wished, but Laura knew. He wished that Jack were there. When wolves had howled in the Big Woods, Laura had always known that Jack wouldn't let them hurt her. A lump came into her throat and her eyes stung.

The wolf howled again. Laura jumped up and stared into the night. She saw something!

Two green lights were shining in the darkness beyond the fire. Two green lights close to the ground. They were eyes.

A cold chill ran up Laura's backbone. The green lights moved closer.

"Look, Pa!" Laura cried. "A wolf!"

In an instant Pa had his gun out, ready to fire at those green eyes. The eyes stopped moving. They stared at Pa in the darkness.

"It can't be a wolf," Pa said. "Unless it's a mad wolf. And it's not that." He pointed to the horses. They were still biting off bits of grass. If it had been a wolf, they'd have been nervous and fidgety.

"A lynx?" said Ma.

"Or a coyote?" Pa picked up a stick of wood. He shouted and threw the stick. The green eyes moved close to the ground, as if the animal crouched to spring. Pa held the gun ready.

The animal didn't move.

Pa began to walk toward the eyes, very

slowly. And slowly the eyes crawled toward him. Laura could see the animal now in the gray light beyond the fire. It was brown, with dark streaks.

Pa gave a shout and Laura screamed. The next thing she knew she was hugging a jumping, panting, wriggling Jack! He licked her face and hands all over. She couldn't hold him; he leaped from her to Pa to Ma and back to her again.

"Well, I'm beat!" said Pa.

Jack was very tired. He gave a long sigh and sank down next to Laura. Ma gave him a corn cake, but he was too tired to eat it. He just licked it and wagged his tail politely. His eyes were red, and his belly was caked with mud.

"No telling how long he kept swimming," Pa said. "I wonder how far he was carried downstream before he landed."

Poor Jack! He'd almost drowned, and then he had to track the wagon all those miles across the prairie. And when at last he reached them, Laura called him a wolf and Pa almost shot him.

"You knew we didn't mean it, didn't you, Jack?" Laura asked. Jack wagged his stumpy tail.

He knew.

CHAPTER 4

Jack and Mr. Edwards

In Kansas they found some good land with water close by. Pa built a little log house out of trees he hauled from the creek bottoms.

A neighbor named Mr. Edwards came to help Pa with the house. He was tall and thin and brown. He told Laura he was a wildcat from Tennessee. But he was very polite and always called Ma "ma'am." He wore a coonskin cap and high black boots. He could spit tobacco juice farther than

Laura thought anyone could spit. And he could hit anything he spit at, too.

When the house was finished, Mr. Edwards helped Pa build a stable for the horses. And the very next day, when Laura went to see the horses, she was amazed to find a long-legged, long-eared, wobbly little colt standing beside Pet.

Pa said it was a mule. Its ears were very long. They reminded Laura of a jack rabbit. They named the little colt Bunny.

The little house was nice and snug. There were holes cut into the walls for windows, and through them Laura could see the wide prairie. Before long, Kansas began to feel like home.

Summer passed and the weather grew colder. It was time for Pa to make a trip to town. The family needed cornmeal and other supplies.

He left early one morning before Laura and Mary were awake. He was headed for Independence, Kansas. He would be gone for four whole days.

Pa had hitched Pet and Patty to the wagon for the trip. Bunny was shut in the stable so that she wouldn't follow her mother. The trip was too long for a colt.

Laura and Mary stayed in the house with Ma. Outdoors was too large and empty to play in when Pa wasn't there. Jack was uneasy, too. He walked around the house alertly, watching for strangers.

At milking-time, as Ma was putting on her bonnet, Jack suddenly rushed out of the house. The hair on his back was bristling. Laura heard a yell and a scrambling, and a shout.

From outside the house they heard: "Call off your dog! Call off your dog!"

Ma and Mary and Laura ran out of the house. Hunched on top of the woodpile was Mr. Edwards. Logs shifted and groaned beneath him.

Jack had his paws on the woodpile. He was trying to climb up after Mr. Edwards.

"He's got me treed!" Mr. Edwards said. He backed along the top of the woodpile. Jack bared his teeth.

Ma could barely make Jack move away. His eyes were glaring red, as though he'd seen a wolf. He acted like he'd never met Mr. Edwards before.

Mr. Edwards climbed slowly to the ground. Jack watched his every move, growling softly.

"I declare," said Ma, "he seems to know that Mr. Ingalls isn't here."

"Dogs know more than most folks give them credit for," said Mr. Edwards.

He explained that Pa had stopped off at his place on his way into town that morning. Pa had asked Mr. Edwards to check on Ma and the girls every day while he was away.

Mr. Edwards was such a good neighbor that he'd come at chore time, to do the chores for Ma. But Jack had made up his mind not to let anyone go near the stable while Pa was gone. Ma had to shut him in the house while Mr. Edwards did the chores.

As he left, Mr. Edwards called out to Ma, "Keep that dog in the house tonight and you'll be safe enough."

The darkness crept slowly around the house. The wind cried and owls answered it with mournful calls. A wolf howled. Jack growled low in his throat.

Mary and Laura sat close to Ma in the

firelight. They knew they were safe in the house because Jack was there.

The next day was empty like the first. Jack spent the whole day pacing from the stable to the house and back. He wouldn't play with Laura at all. He was working, guarding his people.

Mr. Edwards came again to do the chores. And again Jack treed him on the woodpile. Ma had to drag him off.

"I can't think what's gotten into that dog," she said. "Maybe it's the wind."

The wind had a strange, wild howl in it. It tore through Laura's clothes as if they weren't there. And in the morning it was worse. It was so cold that Ma kept the door shut.

Mary and Laura stayed by the fire all day. They knew that Pa would have left Independence by now. That night he would have to camp on the prairie, alone with the horses and the cold wind.

The fourth day was very long. In the afternoon they began to watch the creek road through the window. Pa would be coming home soon.

Jack was watching, too. He whined to go outside. He walked all around the stable and the house. Sometimes he looked toward the creek bottoms and bared his teeth. The wind almost blew him off his feet.

When he came in, he wouldn't lie down. He paced about. The hair rose on his neck, flattened, and rose again.

He tried to look out of the window. When he whined at the door, Ma opened it for him. He trotted back to the stable to check on Bunny.

At chore-time Pa still wasn't home. Ma

29

brought Jack inside. She didn't want him to tree Mr. Edwards again.

When Mr. Edwards had finished the chores, he came to the house. He was stiff with cold. He offered to spend the night in the stable if Pa didn't come home. But Ma thanked him and said they'd be quite safe with Jack.

"I'm expecting Mr. Ingalls any minute now," she said.

Mr. Edwards put on his coat and mittens. "I don't guess anything will bother you, anyway," he said.

Suppertime came and went. Still there was no sign of Pa. Laura and Mary put on their nightgowns, but they didn't go to bed. Ma said they could stay up till Pa came home.

Jack stationed himself in front of the door. He paced up and down, and every

 30

now and then he growled. He would not rest until Pa walked through the door.

Laura and Mary yawned on their bench. Laura sat with her eyes very wide open. She was as determined as Jack. She'd stay up till Pa returned. But things began to sway before her eyes. Sometimes she saw two Marys, and sometimes she couldn't see anything at all.

Suddenly she heard a fearful crash. Ma picked her up. Laura had fallen off the bench, smack on the floor.

She tried to tell Ma she wasn't sleepy enough to go to bed. But in the middle of her sentence she yawned again, an enormous yawn that nearly split her head in two.

In the middle of the night she sat straight up. The wind gave a wild howl that rose and fell and rose again. Or *was* it the wind? Laura couldn't tell.

The door-latch rattled and the shutters shook. It was as if someone was trying to get in. But Jack wouldn't let anyone in, not even the wind. He rumbled low in his throat at the fierce howling.

And then Laura's eyes flew open. She had been asleep again. She looked at the fireplace, and there was Pa!

His boots were caked with frozen mud, and his nose was bright red. Laura ran to him, shouting, "Oh, Pa! Oh, Pa!"

Pa hugged her tight. He was so cold that Laura shivered in her nightgown. Pa wrapped her in one end of Ma's big shawl and Mary took the other end. Pa took them on his knees and they snuggled near the fire.

"I thought I never would get here." Pa sighed. He'd run into trouble with the wagon on his way home from Independence. Mud froze on the wheels until they wouldn't roll anymore. He had to climb out and knock the mud loose.

"And it seemed like we'd no more than started when I had to get out and do it again," he said. Then the horses had had to struggle against the wind all the way home. "Pet and Patty are so worn out, they can hardly stagger. I never saw such a wind!"

Ma brought him a steaming cup of coffee. He took a long drink and wiped his mustache clean. "Ah!" he sighed. "That hits the spot, Caroline!"

Pa showed them all the things he had bought in town. There was real glass for the windows. There was white sugar in a little paper sack. Mary and Laura each had a taste from a spoon before Ma put it away. There were nails and cornmeal, fat pork and salt, and all kinds of things.

33

Jack could relax now and sleep in his place by the door instead of pacing back and forth all night. He'd done his job well. Pa was home, and everyone was safe.

CHAPTER 5

Ox on the Roof

When Laura was seven years old, her family moved again. Once more they packed all their belongings into their covered wagon and set out on a long journey. This time they went to live in Minnesota. They lived in a dugout, a funny little house built into the side of a hill. The walls were dirt. The floor was dirt. The roof was grass that waved in the wind.

Laura and Mary could walk up a gently sloping path and stand right on the roof. Looking at the swaying grass, no one would ever guess it was a roof. "Anybody could walk over this house," Ma said, "and never know it's here."

Laura liked the new house. But she was sad that Pa had to give up Pet and Patty, the black ponies, and Bunny, the long-eared colt. He traded them for some oxen. Pa explained, "With those big oxen I can break up a great big field. I can have it ready for wheat next spring!"

The oxen were named Pete and Bright. Pete was a huge gray ox with short horns and gentle eyes. Bright was smaller. He had long, fierce horns and wild eyes. His coat was a bright reddish brown.

Laura looked the oxen over. Their legs were clumsy and their big hooves were split in the middle. Their noses were broad and slimy. They were nothing like Pet and Patty.

"Oh, Pa," Laura said. "I don't think I like cattle—much."

One evening Laura and Mary sat on a large gray rock out on the prairie. They were waiting for Pete and Bright to come home. Pa was working for a man in town, and Pete and Bright had no work to do until Pa was finished. They spent their days with a lot of other cattle, out where the grass was long and green.

Laura and Mary waited on the rock, just as they did every evening. Jack lay in the grass at their feet. He was waiting, too.

Suddenly Laura heard a great bellowing. The cattle were coming—and they were angry! When they reached the gray rock, the herd did not go by as it usually did. The cattle ran around the rock, bawling and fighting. Their eyes rolled. Their horns slashed at each other.

The air was choked with dust raised by their kicking hooves. Mary was so scared that she couldn't move. Laura was scared, too—so scared that she jumped right off the rock.

She knew she had to drive Pete and Bright into the stable. The cattle towered up in the dust.

Behind them ran Johnny Johnson. He was the boy who looked after the herd. Johnny tried to head Pete and Bright in the right direction. Trampling hooves and slashing horns were everywhere.

Jack jumped up. He ran toward the cattle, growling at their hooves. Laura ran, yelling, behind them.

Johnny waved his big stick. He managed to drive the rest of the herd away. Jack and Laura chased Bright into the stable. Pete was going in, too. Laura was not so scared now.

And then, in a flash, big Pete wheeled around. His horns hooked and his tail stood straight up. He galloped after the herd.

Laura ran in front of Pete to head him off. She waved her arms and yelled. Pete bellowed. He went thundering toward the creek bank.

Laura ran with all her might. She had to get in front of Pete again, to turn him back. But her legs were short and Pete's were long. The big ox raced ahead.

Jack came running as fast as he could. Pete ran faster and jumped longer jumps. And—*thump!* He jumped right on top of the dugout.

Laura saw one of his hind legs go down through the roof. That big ox was going to fall right on Ma and Carrie! Laura ran even faster.

Finally she was in front of Pete. Jack ran like lightning. He circled in front of the huge ox.

Pete heaved and pulled his leg out of the hole. Before he could do any more damage, Laura and Jack chased him off the roof. They chased him into the stable and Laura put up the bars that kept him inside.

Laura was shaking all over. Her legs were weak and her knees knocked against each other.

But no harm had been done. There was only a hole in the dugout roof where Pete's hoof had gone through. Ma stuffed it with some hay, and that was that.

Laura and Jack had saved the day.

CHAPTER 6

Cattle in the Hay

That wasn't the end of their adventures with the cattle. One day Pa and Ma hitched up the wagon and drove to town. They took baby Carrie with them.

Laura and Mary stayed home with Jack. They were old enough now to look after themselves.

With Ma and Pa gone, the prairie seemed big and empty. And there was nothing to be afraid of. There were no wolves here.

Besides, Jack stayed close to Laura. Jack was a responsible dog. He knew that he must take care of everything when Pa was away.

That morning Mary and Laura played by the creek. At noon they ate the corn dodgers and molasses that Ma had left for them. They drank milk out of their tin cups, then washed the cups and put them away.

Then Laura wanted to play on the big rock. But Mary wanted to stay in the dugout. She said that Laura must stay there, too.

"Ma can make me," Laura said, "but you can't."

"I can so," said Mary. "When Ma's not here, you have to do what I say because I'm older."

"You have to let me have my way because I'm littler!" Laura said.

"That's Carrie, it isn't you," Mary told

her. "If you don't do what I say, I'll tell Ma."

"I can play where I want to!" said Laura. She darted out of the dugout. Mary grabbed for her, but Laura was too quick.

She began to run up the path, but Jack was in the way. He stood stiff, looking across the creek. Laura looked, too.

"Mary!" she screeched.

The cattle were all around Pa's haystacks. Pa had worked for days cutting that hay and piling it into big stacks. And now those cattle were eating it!

They were tearing into the stacks with their horns. They gouged out huge chunks of hay and ate them. Hay flew everywhere, sliding off the stacks and spilling on the ground.

There would be nothing left to feed Pete and Bright and Spot, the cow, in the

wintertime. Without that hay they would starve.

Jack knew what to do. He ran growling down the path. Pa was not there to save the haystacks. Jack and Laura and Mary would have to do it. They had to drive those cattle away.

"Oh, we can't! We can't!" Mary said. She was scared. But Laura ran behind Jack and Mary came after her. They ran up onto the prairie.

The big, fierce cattle were very near. Their long horns tossed hay every which way. Their thick legs trampled and jostled, and they bawled with wide-open mouths.

Mary froze, but Laura was too scared to stand still. She jerked Mary along. She grabbed up a stick and ran at the cattle, yelling as loudly as she could.

Jack raced toward the cattle, growling. A big red cow swiped at him with her horns. He jumped behind her. She snorted and galloped.

All the other cattle ran jostling after her. But they didn't run away. They just ran around and around the haystacks. Jack and Laura and Mary couldn't chase them away.

The cattle tore off more and more hay. They bellowed and trampled. Hay slid off the stacks that Pa had worked so hard to make.

 46

Panting and yelling, Laura waved her stick. The faster she ran, the faster the cattle went. Black and brown and red cows. Striped cows and spotted cows. Huge cows with awful horns. All of them wasting Pa's hay.

Some of the cattle were even trying to climb over the toppling stacks. Laura was hot and dizzy. Her braids came undone and her hair blew in her eyes. Her throat was raw from yelling.

But she kept on yelling, running, and waving her stick. She was too scared to hit one of those big horned cows with the stick. But she waved it in the air and yelled with all her might. Jack jumped and growled and barked at the cattle.

Faster and faster the hay slid down. Faster and faster the cattle trampled over it.

Laura ran around a haystack and there

47

was the big red cow, heading right toward her. She couldn't scream now. The huge legs and terrible horns were coming fast.

Laura gulped. She jumped at that cow and waved her stick. She waved it as hard as she could.

The cow tried to stop. But all the other cattle were coming behind her and she couldn't. She galloped closer and closer.

At the last second she swerved. Laura found her breath again. The big red cow ran away across the fields. And all the other cattle thundered after her.

Jack chased after them, farther and farther from the hay. Laura and Mary ran with him. Far into the high grasses they chased those cattle. Pa's hay was safe.

Johnny Johnson rose from the grass. He was rubbing his eyes. He had been lying asleep in a warm hollow.

"Johnny! Johnny!" Laura yelled. "Wake up and watch the cattle!"

Breathing hard, Laura and Jack and Mary turned toward home. The high grass dragged at their trembling legs.

Laura was glad she and Jack and Mary had saved the hay. Now Bright and Pete and Spot would have plenty to eat in the winter. But she was even gladder to get to the cool, quiet dugout, where they could all rest.

But there was more excitement to come, that day.

CHAPTER 7

Runaway!

All that afternoon they stayed in the dugout. The cattle did not come back to the haystacks. The sun began to sink.

Laura and Mary wished that Pa and Ma would come home. Again and again they went up the path to look for the wagon. After a while they went up to sit on the grassy roof of their house.

Jack waited beside them. The lower the sun went, the more Jack's ears pricked up. He was watching for the wagon, too.

Finally Jack turned his ears toward the prairie. First one ear, then the other. He looked up at Laura. A waggle went from his neck to his stubby tail.

The wagon was coming.

They all stood and watched it come. When Laura saw the oxen, she jumped up and down. "They're coming! They're coming!" she shouted, swinging her sunbonnet. She could see Ma and Carrie on the wagon seat.

"They're coming awful fast," Mary said.

Laura stood still. She heard the wagon rattling loudly. Pete and Bright were running very fast. Too fast. They were running away!

Bumpity-bump! The wagon came banging and bouncing nearer. Ma was huddled in a corner of the wagon box. She was hanging on tight and hugging Carrie close.

Pa raced alongside Bright. He shouted and waved the goad at Bright. He was trying to turn the ox back from the creek bank.

But he couldn't do it. The big oxen galloped nearer to the steep edge. Bright was nearly pushing Pa over the bank. They were all going to tumble over, Ma, Carrie, and the wagon. They were going to fall all the way down into the creek.

Pa gave a terrible shout. He struck Bright's head with the goad.

In a flash Jack jumped up. He leaped at Bright's nose. Laura ran screaming beside them.

Pa shouted and Jack jumped. Bright swerved. The wagon flashed by with Ma and Carrie hanging on. *Crash!* Bright hit the stable.

Suddenly everything was still.

Pa and Laura ran after the wagon. "Whoa, Bright! Whoa, Pete!" Pa said. He looked at Ma in the wagon box.

"We're all right, Charles," Ma said. Her face was gray, and she was shaking all over. But she was all right.

Pa lifted Ma and Carrie out of the wagon. Carrie clung to Ma's neck, crying.

"Oh, Caroline!" Pa said. "I thought you were going over the bank."

"I thought so, too, for a minute," Ma answered. "But I might have known you wouldn't let that happen."

Laura hugged Ma tight. "Oh, Ma! Oh, Ma!"

"There, there," said Ma. "All's well that ends well."

Jack stood, panting, beside them. His green eyes sparkled. He knew he'd helped save Ma and Carrie, and he was proud.

CHAPTER 8

The Blizzard

There came another day when Pa took Ma to town. This time they decided to walk. It was winter, and the weather was beginning to turn cold. But this day was as bright as a spring one.

"Mary and Laura are big girls now," Pa told Ma. "They can take care of Carrie."

Ma put on her brown-and-red shawl. She tied her brown hood under her chin. She smiled up at Pa. Laura thought she looked just like a bird, with her quick step and bright smile.

When Ma and Pa had gone, Laura and

Mary did their chores. Laura swept the floor. Mary cleared the table and washed the dishes. After Laura dried the dishes and put them away, they had the whole day ahead of them to play.

For a while they played school, but soon the house began to feel too empty and still. The whole house seemed to be listening for Ma.

Laura went outside. There was nothing to do. She went back in. The day grew longer and longer. Even Jack was restless. He walked up and down before the door.

He scratched at the door, asking to go outside. But when Laura opened it, he wouldn't go out. He lay down and then got back up. He walked around and around the room. Something was bothering him.

He went to Laura's feet and looked up at her. "What is it, Jack?" she asked.

 56

He stared hard at her. He was trying to tell her something, but she did not understand. Jack gave a little howl.

"Don't, Jack!" Laura said. "You scare me."

"Is it something outdoors?" Mary wondered.

Laura ran outside, but Jack took hold of her dress with his mouth. He pulled her back inside. The air was bitter cold. Laura shut the door.

"Look," she said. "The sunshine's dark." The fine, bright day had disappeared.

"Maybe it's rain," said Mary.

Laura called her a goose. "It doesn't rain in the wintertime!"

"Well, snow then!" Mary snapped. "What's the difference?" She was angry and so was Laura.

They would have gone on arguing, but suddenly there was no sunshine at all. They ran to look through the bedroom window.

The sky was filled with dark clouds, rolling in fast. "A blizzard!" Mary said.

They knew about blizzards. Pa had told them. He had heard of some folks who were in town when a blizzard came up. They couldn't get back, and their children froze stark stiff because there wasn't enough wood in the house to keep the fire going.

Laura peered out the front window. Pa and Ma were nowhere in sight. Where were they? Surely it was time for them to come home.

Mary and Laura looked at each other through the gray air.

"The woodbox is empty," Laura whispered. She was thinking about those children in Pa's story. She started for the door.

Mary grabbed her. "You can't!" she cried. "We're supposed to stay in the house if there's a storm." She was right. Ma was very strict about that.

Laura jerked away.

"Besides," Mary went on, "Jack won't let you."

"We've got to bring in wood before the storm gets here," Laura insisted. "Hurry!"

They could hear a strange sound in the wind. It was like a faraway screaming. They put on their shawls and warm woolen mittens.

Laura was ready first. She looked at the dog. "We've got to bring in wood, Jack," she said.

Jack seemed to understand. He followed her out, staying close beside her.

The wind was colder than icicles.

Laura ran to the woodpile, with Jack at her heels. She piled up a big armful of wood and ran back to the house. Jack ran behind. Mary held the door open for her.

Then they didn't know what to do. Mary needed to help Laura bring in the wood. The storm was coming awfully fast. They couldn't open the door with their arms full of wood. But they couldn't leave the door open—the cold would come in.

Little Carrie spoke up. "I tan open the door!"

"You can't," Mary said.

"I tan, too!" said Carrie. She reached up both hands to the doorknob and turned it. She could do it!

Now Laura and Mary raced to bring in more wood. Carrie opened the door for them, then shut it behind them. Mary could carry bigger armfuls, but Laura was quicker.

Jack trotted behind Laura as she ran back and forth. Just as it began to snow, Laura and Mary had filled up the wood-box. But they didn't stop. They kept on dashing out for armfuls of wood. They piled it against the wall and around the stove. The piles grew bigger and higher.

The snow came down in a whirling blast. It stung Laura's face like grains of sand. When Carrie opened the door, it swirled into the house like a white cloud.

Bang! They banged the door. They ran to the woodpile. *Clop-clop-clop*, they stacked the wood on their arms. They ran to the door. *Bump!* it opened, and *bang!* it closed behind them. *Thumpity-thump!* they flung the wood onto the floor. And back outside they ran, panting.

They could hardly see the woodpile now. The snow was swirling all around them. The house was hard to see in the white swirl. Jack was just a dark blob running beside them. But Jack knew where he was. He wouldn't let them lose their way.

Laura's arms ached and her chest heaved. Words ran around and around in her head. "Where is Pa? Where is Ma?

 62

Hurry! Hurry!" The wind went on screeching.

The woodpile was gone. Mary took a few sticks and Laura took a few sticks and then there were no more. They ran to the door together. Laura opened it and Jack bounded in. Carrie was at the window, clapping her hands and squealing.

Laura dropped her sticks of wood. She turned just in time to see Ma and Pa burst out of the white blizzard. They ran into the house. They were covered with snow from head to foot.

Pa and Ma looked at Laura and Mary, who stood all snowy in their shawls and mittens. Mary said in a small voice, "We did go out in the storm, Ma. We forgot."

Laura looked at the floor. "We didn't want to freeze stark stiff, Pa," she said.

"Well, I'll be darned!" said Pa. "If they

didn't move the whole woodpile in. All the wood I cut to last a couple of weeks!"

There, piled up in the house, was the whole woodpile. Melted snow leaked out of it and spread in puddles. A wet path led to the door.

Then Pa's great laugh rang out. Ma's smile shone warmly on Laura and Mary. They knew they were forgiven for disobeying. They had been wise to bring in the wood, though perhaps not quite so much wood! And Jack had been there, as always, to help them find their way in the storm.

CHAPTER 9

Moving On

Life in Minnesota was hard for Laura's family. Every year Pa planted a crop of wheat, but the crops never thrived. One year a swarm of grasshoppers ate up all the wheat. Another year there was too little rain and the crops dried in the fields.

Pa decided it was time to move again. He had heard of a job far off in Dakota Territory. Once again the family got ready to move west.

Laura was a big girl now. She was excited to be traveling again. Laura was just like Pa.

65

She loved to see new places.

The bustle of packing began. Carrie was old enough now to help Pa load the wagon. Laura washed and ironed all the clothes. Food needed to be baked for the journey, and the canvas wagon cover had to be put back on the wagon.

Jack stood in the middle of it all, watching. Everyone was too busy to notice him, till suddenly Laura saw him standing between the house and the wagon.

She knew there was something wrong. Jack wasn't frisking about like he usually did, laughing and cocking his head. He stood still with his legs stiff. His forehead was wrinkled and his stubby tail was limp.

"Good old Jack," Laura said. But he didn't wag his tail. He looked at her sadly. "Pa," she called. "Look at Jack."

She stroked his smooth head. Jack

wasn't a young dog anymore. Years had passed since he had chased squirrels in the Big Woods of Wisconsin. His bristly hair was gray.

Jack leaned his head against Laura and sighed. All in an instant, Laura knew. Jack was too old to make the trip. He was much too tired to walk all the way to Dakota Territory under the wagon.

"Pa!" she cried out. "Jack can't walk so far! Oh, Pa, we can't leave Jack!"

Pa agreed with her. "He wouldn't hold out to walk it, that's a fact," he said. "I'll make a place for him in the wagon. How'll you like to go riding in the wagon, huh, old fellow?"

Jack wagged one polite wag. He turned his head aside. He didn't want to go, even in the wagon.

Laura knelt down and hugged him.

"Jack! We're going west! Don't you want to go west again?"

Always before he had been happy when he saw Pa putting the cover on the wagon. He had trotted under the wagon all the way from Wisconsin to Kansas and then to Minnesota. Every night while Laura slept in the wagon, Jack had been outside guarding it. Every morning he had been glad to begin a new day of traveling.

But now he just leaned against Laura and sighed. He nudged his nose under her hand so that she would pet him. Laura stroked his gray head. She could feel how tired he was.

"Good dog, Jack," Laura said. She gave him a good supper and then made his bed. He slept on an old horse blanket near the door. Laura shook the blanket out to make it more comfortable.

Jack smiled and wagged his tail. He was pleased that Laura was making his bed. She made a round nest in it and patted it to show him it was ready.

Jack stepped in and turned himself around once. He stopped to rest his stiff legs. Then he slowly turned again. Jack always turned around three times before he lay down to sleep. He had done it when he was a young dog in the Big Woods. He had

done it in the grass under the wagon at night. It was the proper thing for dogs to do.

He turned himself around the third time. With a bump and a sigh, he curled into his nest. Then he lifted his head to look at Laura.

Stroking his gray head, Laura thought about what a good dog Jack had always been. He had kept her safe from wolves and bears. He had helped her bring in the cows at night. He had played with her on the prairie and along the creek. When she went to school, he had always waited on the path for her to come home.

"Good Jack," she told him. "Good dog." He licked her hand with the tip of his tongue. Then his nose sank onto his paws. Jack sighed and closed his eyes. There was a long trip ahead, and he needed his rest.

In the morning when Pa spoke, Jack did not stir. Pa said that Jack had gone to the Happy Hunting Grounds.

Laura imagined Jack in the Happy Hunting Grounds, running gaily over a wild prairie. He would sniff the morning air and race the wind. He would spring over the short grass with his ears up and his mouth laughing, just as he used to.

"Good dogs have their reward, Laura," Pa said. And there never was a dog as good as Jack.

Come Home to Little House!

THE ROSE
CHAPTER BOOK COLLECTION

Adapted from the Rose Years books
by Roger Lea MacBride
Illustrated by Doris Ettlinger

1. MISSOURI BOUND
2. ROSE AT ROCKY RIDGE
3. ROSE & ALVA

THE CAROLINE
CHAPTER BOOK COLLECTION

Adapted from the Caroline Years books
by Maria D. Wilkes
Illustrated by Doris Ettlinger

1. BROOKFIELD DAYS
2. CAROLINE & HER SISTER
3. FRONTIER FAMILY

WAITING
for
SUNRISE

Other Books by Eva Marie Everson

Things Left Unspoken
This Fine Life
Chasing Sunsets

Books by Linda Evans Shepherd
and Eva Marie Everson

The Potluck Club
The Potluck Club—Trouble's Brewing
The Potluck Club—Takes the Cake
The Secret's in the Sauce
A Taste of Fame
Bake Until Golden
The Potluck Club Cookbook

a cedar key novel • book 2

WAITING
for
SUNRISE

EVA MARIE EVERSON

Revell

a division of Baker Publishing Group
Grand Rapids, Michigan

© 2012 by Eva Marie Everson

Published by Revell
a division of Baker Publishing Group
P.O. Box 6287, Grand Rapids, MI 49516-6287
www.revellbooks.com

Printed in the United States of America

Library of Congress Cataloging-in-Publication Data
Everson, Eva Marie.
    Waiting for sunrise : a Cedar Key novel / Eva Marie Everson.
        p.   cm.
    ISBN 978-0-8007-3437-4 (pbk.)
    1. Cedar Key (Fla.)—Fiction. I. Title.
PS3605.V47W35 2012
813'.6—dc23   2012002541

The internet addresses, email addresses, and phone numbers in this book are accurate at the time of publication. They are provided as a resource. Baker Publishing Group does not endorse them or vouch for their content or permanence.

12   13   14   15   16   17   18   7   6   5   4   3   2   1

Dedicated to
Sally E. Stuart
(our pal, Sal)
in honor of the years of tireless efforts she has given
for Christian writers
and the world that affects them.
Thank you, Sally! We love you!

Prologue

Spring 1964

Patsy Milstrap sat on the passenger's side of the jet-black '63 Ford Falcon Futura. Her husband, Gilbert—whose face seemed transfixed on the road before them—rested an arm over the steering wheel as though they'd not a care in the world.

Earlier in the drive from their South Carolina home to Cedar Key, Florida, and as the sun grew warmer, Gilbert had lowered the convertible top. It was now midafternoon. In spite of the scarf tied around her head and secured under her chin, Patsy's long hair had been whipped to a frenzy. Her face felt sunburned. She would ask Gilbert to raise the roof, but she couldn't find the energy to do so.

Besides, she liked knowing her body could still feel . . . something. Lately, she'd only wanted to slip between the sheet and the coverlet of their bed—the one she'd shared with Gilbert for nearly fourteen years now—cover her head, and sleep. Not her devotion to her husband nor her love for their children—five, ranging from four years of age to thirteen—could penetrate the pain she'd been living with since the first had been born.

Or had it been forever?

Clearly she was dying, she thought. Clearly no one could hurt this much and survive.

And the pain . . . so deep . . . maybe even Jesus couldn't reach it.

So deep . . . like the blue-green water on both sides of the road leading into Cedar Key, where Gilbert had rented a cottage for them. They would stay a week, he'd said. Just the two of them. The children could stay with his sister Janice and her husband. And their children. It would be like going off to church camp, he'd said, while Patsy and he would come for the arts festival he had heard about.

She liked art, didn't she? he'd asked.

And they would go boating. Take bike rides. Relax in the sunshine. It had rained so much in Trinity lately. It would do them *both* good.

Okay, she'd said. Okay.

"And maybe," he'd hinted with a wink, "we can snuggle like we used to."

Patsy closed her eyes at the thought. If she came up pregnant again . . . it would be worse than the other times. Every time, a little worse. Every time . . .

"We're nearly there," Gilbert chimed from beside her.

She opened her eyes, turned her head slowly toward him, and forced her lips to curl upward into a smile. She could do that much, right?

"Was that a smile I just saw?" he said. The deep dimple of his cheek came into view. "See there? One minute in Cedar Key and you're getting better." He squared his shoulders. "I knew this was a good idea."

Patsy looked back to the front of the car. A town—a little harbor town—was coming into view. Fishermen on a dock. Weathered hands pulling crab baskets from the water and into a boat. The scent of the marsh washed over her.

In spite of its pungency, she liked it.

"Are you hungry, Patsy? I'm ravenous."

She looked at him again, nodded. "Yes. A little."

The dimple returned. "See there?" he repeated. "Another good sign." The car slowed as they entered the city limits. "Let's get to the cottage, settle in, clean up, and find this place Walter told me about."

"Sikes?"

"Sikes's Seafood. I'll bet the food is about as fresh as anything you can get on the coastline."

Patsy inhaled deeply. She liked a good fried shrimp. And deviled crab. She hadn't had that in ages. That with a baked potato . . .

The cottage was everything it had been touted to be. The cottony-white walls, the dark, rich furniture, the white eyelet curtains and bed linens, and the polished hardwood floors helped Patsy begin to relax. To feel that maybe her life was going to be okay. Even if only for a week.

A week in Cedar Key.

Patsy unpacked their luggage while Gilbert showered. When he was done, she took a quick bath, worked the tangles out of her hair, then brushed it until it shone. She worked it into a long braid that snaked over her shoulder before dressing in a knee-length mint-green A-line skirt with matching sleeveless blouse. She wore no jewelry, no makeup. Only coral-colored lipstick.

The way Gilbert liked it.

"Will you put the top up on the car?" she asked as they stepped from the front porch of the cottage. "It took forever to get the rats out of my hair."

Her husband slipped an arm around her waist. "Anything for my lady."

She sighed as he opened the car door for her. Allowed her to get in gracefully. Closed it. She watched him sprint around the front to his side.

He is trying so hard.

A few minutes later they arrived at the seafood restaurant near the harbor they'd heard about from Walter, one of Gilbert's business associates. Walter had also told them about the tropical healing balm of the island.

Already a line was forming at the front door of the establishment. Patsy glanced at her watch. It was only five o'clock. She thought they would have been early enough. Maybe the food really was that good.

She waited at the end of the line while Gilbert gave the restaurant's hostess their name. He returned a minute later. "Fifteen minutes. That's not bad."

Over the fifteen minutes, she found herself drinking in the sights and sounds of Cedar Key. Already she liked it here. It called to her, like an old friend, and made her feel as though she'd been here before.

Seagulls soared overhead. Patsy craned her neck to watch them, then lowered her chin to view them through the glass walls of the restaurant as they dove into the rhythmic waves below.

They inched closer to the inside of the restaurant. Gilbert slapped his flat stomach, drawing Patsy's attention from the white birds to the pressed white of his button-down shirt. "I smell good ole fried seafood. I think I'll have shrimp. What about you?"

She strained to make the decision. "Deviled crab."

He wrapped his arm around her waist again and squeezed. "Somehow I knew you'd say that."

"You know me well."

"Since you were no more than a pup."

"Milstrap, party of two?" the hostess called over the heads of the few hopeful patrons left standing in front of them.

Gilbert raised his hand. "That's us."

They entered the restaurant, Patsy behind the hostess, Gilbert behind her. Sikes's Seafood was all wood and glass. The walls sported lifesavers and nets with shells caught between the yarn. Large mounted fish. Stuffed replicas of tropical birds perched on beachwood. It was typical tropical, and to add to the setting, the Beach Boys sang "Surfin' USA" from a jukebox.

The hostess stopped short before turning toward a man in dress casual attire. "Oh, I'm sorry," she said to Patsy and Gilbert. "Just a minute, please, while I ask my boss a question." She returned her attention to the man. "Mr. Liddle?"

At the sound of the name, Patsy felt the air suck into her lungs before she heard the intake of breath. Gilbert's hands gripped her forearms.

The man stopped. Turned toward them. Smiled briefly at them. "Yes, Brenda . . ."

How could it be, Patsy wondered. How was it that here, in Cedar Key, she stared into a face she hardly recognized.

And into eyes she would never forget.

1

Summer 1946

With the war a lasting memory and the manufacturing of appliances back in full swing, thirteen-year-old Patsy Sweeny and her thirty-year-old mother went to town to splurge on a new Maytag wringer washing machine. Not so much for herself, Bernice Liddle told her husband Ira—a man as tight with a penny as he was firm on her role as wife and mother—but to enable her to bring in other people's wash. It was for a good cause too, she'd told him, what with so many women still working outside of their homes.

"And goodness knows," she told Patsy as they drove to Gibson's Department Store—a place Patsy always thought smelled of new tires and cleaner—on the day of purchasing, "we could use the extra money." She cut a sharp eye toward her daughter. "You tell Mr. Liddle I said that and I'll deny it, you hear me?"

"Yes, ma'am," Patsy replied. She was smart enough to know the rules of the house. No one demeaned her stepfather. At least, not to his face.

"You're a good daughter," Mama said after several minutes.

Patsy knew her mother had been thinking. Thinking about what she'd just let slip. Thinking about what would surely happen if Mr. Liddle found out she'd said it, even to her own child. Her words of praise were no more than a line of insurance, but Patsy felt pleased to hear them anyway.

Patsy looked out the open passenger window of the oversized black 1936 Chevy coupe Mr. Liddle had purchased for his wife the year before. "To use when you have to do your shopping or if the kids get sick," he told her when he brought it home. "Not for any running around to visit with your friends."

As if Mama had many friends for visiting.

"Sure is hot out there." Patsy tilted her face toward the June sun then drew her head back into the car. "The beans are already near about drying up before I can pick 'em, and it's not even July yet."

"You just have to get out there earlier, is all."

Patsy's eyes scanned lazily from the side of the long dirt road they traveled to the woman behind the steering wheel. Mama was only seventeen years her senior, yet she looked and seemed so much older. Like a grandmother instead of a mother.

"Yes, ma'am."

They purchased the washer for $54.95 plus tax. As her mother counted out the last of the loose change, Patsy ran her fingertips along the wringers of the floor model. She listened when Mr. Gibson said someone would deliver it to the house within the next few days. Then her mother gave their address and phone number—931—and asked that someone call before they arrived. "To make sure we're home," she said, as though they had a busy social schedule.

Patsy looked up, wondering where else they'd be when

the washer came. She heard her mother whisper, "Will you let others know, Mr. Gibson, that I'm taking in wash now?"

Patsy walked away from the embarrassment of the moment. Not that she was ashamed of taking in wash; she merely felt the sting of her mother's humiliation.

But a week later, that machine became her own cross to bear. While her friends from school met at Cassel Creek on hot summer afternoons, Patsy stayed busy washing clothes for her family while her mother took care of what felt like the rest of Casselton, Georgia. Her days became endless hours of caring for her little brothers, five-year-old Harold and four-year-old Billy, picking and putting up vegetables from the dusty fields behind their two-story bungalow, and washing clothes.

The washing was one thing. The ironing and the folding and the putting them away was another.

They kept the machine next to the back door on the wide, screened back porch. Twice a week Patsy pulled the washer from the outside wall, ran the electric wire to a kitchen plug, added water and Duz detergent to the tub, allowed it to agitate for a few minutes, and added the clothes. While they washed, she ran clean water into a wooden rinse tub, which she then dragged to the back side of the washer. After flipping the chrome switch of the machine to the "off" position, she pulled the soapy clothes into the rinse tub, added another load to the wash, and began the backbreaking task of wringing the individual pieces.

When it was all done, she hung the clothes on the line before setting everything to rights on the back porch, including returning the Duz powder to its place under the skirted kitchen sink.

Oh, how her mother loved Duz. Their kitchen had been

furnished by the goblets, dishes, dishrags, and drying cloths that came inside each new box, which meant she didn't have to spend any extra of the allowance Mr. Liddle gave but could still have nice things.

On the days she wasn't washing the laundry, Patsy ironed it. And on the days she didn't iron the laundry, she dusted the house and broom-swept the carpets. Living on a dirt road, in a house that sat on a plot of land without a blade of grass, meant the house always stayed dusty and the rugs sometimes felt like a sandbox to bare feet. To keep from stirring the dust, she used the sprinkling bottle from laundry days and cast droplets of water on top of the worn wool before sweeping. She thought it a good idea and her mother had even praised her for it. Life was too hot and too busy. And her body ached at night from the stress of her labor, but in the morning she felt all right.

Then came a day in August.

Her mother had been overwhelmed with other people's laundry and two little boys who'd eaten too much of the taffy they'd pulled the day before. "Patsy," she called out the back door as Patsy walked up from the vegetable garden; a bushel of freshly picked field peas rocked against her hip.

Patsy shielded her eyes against the late morning sunlight and squinted to the back of the house. "I got enough peas to shell for a month of Sundays," she called back.

"Never mind that now," her mother hollered.

Patsy made her way to the unpainted wooden steps leading up to the porch before she set the bushel basket at her feet. "What do you need, Mama?"

"I need you to help me out here, clearly I do. I'm running back and forth with a chamber pot for your brothers and trying to stay on task with this wash here. Mr. Liddle will be home tonight from his sales route, and if he sees the dust that's built up in the house . . . well, you know how he gets. Go put on one of my aprons and get to work in the house, now."

Patsy ascended the steps and got right to it. Sometime later she went to the kitchen in search of her mother, finding her there stooped over the sink, wearing her old housedress and a pair of Red Goose shoes in need of resoling, washing the peas from the earlier picking. "Mama, I dusted the whole house except for your room."

Her mother glanced over her shoulder. Her eyes went first to the kitchen wall clock and then to Patsy. She raised her hand to press against the brush rollers that held her hair in tight curls. "Lord-a-mercy, I gotta do my hair, so go ahead and dust in there too."

Patsy did as she was told before her mother could change her mind. Oh, how she longed to be in that room . . . to touch the dainty items that rested atop her mother's vanity. She walked into the room as though entering a church—reverently, taking it all in. Every bit of furniture, every framed picture, every needlepoint pillow from her mother's hand.

She moved to the bedside tables, ever so careful to pick up the lamps, dust under them, and return them to the exact spot she'd found them. Patsy swallowed hard when she came to Mr. Liddle's chest of drawers. If he thought for a moment that Patsy—rather than his wife—had been the one to touch his things . . .

She drew in a deep breath, picked up each item one at a time—the brush and comb set, the matching lint roller, the small jewelry box placed perfectly in the middle. A library book—*Listen, Germany* by Thomas Mann—rested along one edge. Patsy picked it up to run the oily cloth over the wood. Thinking herself quite wise, she laid the book on the white crocheted bedspread her mother had made from a Star Book pattern so as not to get oil stains on the back cover of the book.

Her mother's vanity was neatly arranged. Her lotions, perfume, and dusting powder were to the left of the oval mirror. To the right, a faux gold filigree lipstick holder, with Cupid playing a guitar in the outside center, held four tubes of lipstick with the matching vanity set angled to the left in the center. Patsy glanced toward the opened door. With a captured breath, she removed each item and placed it on the padded stool at her knees. She oiled the wood until the patina reflected her image. Before replacing her mother's pretties, she pulled a dry cloth from the pocket of the apron and wiped each one as though she were drying a freshly bathed infant.

Before finishing the vanity, she inhaled from both the perfume bottle and the dusting powder tin and imagined herself getting ready for a fancy party, the likes she'd probably never see. When everything was as it had been before she entered the room, she straightened and smiled. She'd done a good job. Maybe good enough that Mama would let her do it again.

"Patsy?" The voice came from behind her; it was neither harsh nor gentle.

"Oh, Mama," she said turning. "You startled me."

"Hurry, child, before Mr. Liddle comes home."

Patsy crossed the room to where her mother stood framed by the doorway. "I did a good job for you, Mama," she said.

"I know you did, now come on. The boys need a bath and the dining room needs preparing and then I want you to comb out my hair."

The ritual was always the same. As soon as Mr. Liddle returned from his sales trips, her mother put away his traveling things. For a while, he played with his sons, then smoked a pipe and read the paper in wait for supper.

He never said a word to Patsy other than, "Girl, you been helping your mama?"

"Yes, sir." She tried not to look him in the eyes—they were steel gray and sharp as a shark's tooth. She just replied and then went on her way.

It had always been like that between them. He only spoke to her—really spoke to her—when he was giving her a whipping. On those occasions—not as frequent since her twelfth birthday—his words came in staccato beats. "What. Did. I. Tell. You. About . . ." Then he'd finish with whatever he'd told her about that she'd done or hadn't done to his liking. It made no never-mind. One time he hit her across the back so hard she lost her breath. That night Mama tucked her into bed, asked if she was all right, then said, "Just don't make him mad, Patsy, and you'll be fine."

He never hit the boys. For that, at least, Patsy was grateful. But he'd hit Mama a few times—most often a slap across her face. Those times he called her names like "stupid" and "worthless," said she was lucky he came along when he did to rescue her sorry self from "that pit five-and-dime and Mr. Harvey Jenkins."

Patsy didn't know what that meant exactly, but she knew better than to ask.

After supper—the night of the bedroom dusting and Mr. Liddle's return—Patsy said good night to her mother, who sat knitting in her overstuffed chair in the living room, the one Patsy had polished to a shine earlier in the day. She added a quick "Glad you're home safe, Mr. Liddle" to the man whose oversized frame filled the chair sitting catty-corner on the other side of the room, listening to *Abbott*

19

Mysteries on the Philco console radio between him and his wife.

"Good night, Patsy," her mother said.

"See to it that you check on the boys before turning in," Mr. Liddle answered as he shifted his pipe from one side of his mouth to the other. Even from where she stood, Patsy could hear the black Bakelite bit as it raked across his teeth, and it made her shudder.

She did as she was told—the boys were both sleeping in their upstairs bedroom, the one right across the hall from their parents'—and then returned downstairs to her own simple but comfortable room. She stripped out of the clothes she'd changed into for supper—they weren't fancy but they weren't ripe with the smell of field peas and lemon oil either—out of her underthings and into the pretty, thin pink cotton gown Mama had made for her.

Sometime later—she couldn't be sure how long since she'd slipped between the cool sheets of her bed—she heard the racket coming from upstairs. Her mother's voice pleading. Mr. Liddle's voice demanding. She bounded out of bed and into her mother's cast-off slippers. Patsy was out the door and halfway up the stairs before she had time to think better of it.

"I've told you and told you," Mr. Liddle shouted. "Haven't I?" Patsy heard the slap of flesh against flesh. "Haven't I?"

"Please, Ira," her mother whimpered. "The boys . . ."

Patsy took a few more steps up the stairs and stopped. She hardly breathed, but her eyes blinked rapidly. She'd never interfered in her mother's fights with Mr. Liddle before, but this time sounded . . . different.

"A man has to know," Patsy heard him say as though spoken through clenched teeth, "that he can leave his home in proper order and come home to it the same way."

"And you have." Her mother's voice shook.

Patsy heard something—someone—stumbling across the room followed by the sound of something else dropping to the floor.

The book! She'd left it on the bed, had failed to return it to the chest of drawers.

"I expect that when I leave this house, you and you alone come into this room. Haven't I made myself clear on that issue?"

Mama's answer came in sobs. "But . . . if you knew . . . how hard today . . . has been for me . . ."

"Stop your nagging." He swore—using the "unpardonable sin" expletive, according to Patsy's best friend, Mitzy. He said it again and a third time. "I don't want the girl in my bedroom. And if I have to beat that into you, then so be it."

Patsy heard the sound of his belt buckle coming undone, the swish of it leaving the loops, the first smack of it against her mother. She fled up the remainder of the stairs, pushed opened the nearly closed bedroom door, and screamed, "Stop it! Stop it! If you're going to hit someone, hit me! I left the stupid book on the bed!"

She reasoned later that it had been the shock of seeing her standing there and of hearing her shouting like a mad-woman that stopped Mr. Liddle from hitting her mother that night. That it had been the sight of her nearly nude body silhouetted by the night's bright moonlight bursting through the gauzy drapes and open windows that caused him to stop seeing her as "the girl" and start seeing her as she soon was to be. A woman, fully budded. No longer did the gray of his eyes hold steel ready to rip her to shreds. Instead, they held something more monstrous than that.

Something she'd never witnessed before but knew to stay away from.

And—she knew—no longer did his hands itch to hit her, but to embrace her. To stroke her. To touch her in a way that would leave her permanently scarred.

2

Patsy loved riding the school bus. And why shouldn't she? It was there, squeezed together on the last seat to the right, that she and her best friends Mitzy Powell and Jane Cartwell shared the secrets and laughter that came from being thirteen. School had been in session only a week, and already it was unfolding to be a banner eighth grade year.

On that first Friday afternoon, the girls sat huddled together.

"How'd you do on the spelling test?" Jane asked Mitzy.

"I made a ninety."

Patsy looked at Mitzy. "Me too. What word did you miss?"

"Ominous."

Patsy smiled. "Me too. I forgot the last *o*."

The three friends giggled. "It's still *unbearably* hot," Mitzy said. She threw the back of her hand against her forehead, a dramatic flare she'd learned from hours spent at the picture show. Her dark curls danced about her face as the bus bounded down the rutted road outside Casselton. "I say we meet tomorrow afternoon at the creek for a swim." She looked from Patsy to Jane and her dimples deepened. "In?"

"I'll say," Jane said. Slender fingers raked blonde hair up

from her swanlike neck. "If it weren't for having to babysit my little sister this afternoon, I'd be there today."

For the last half hour, Patsy, who sat closest to the window, had felt sweat roll from her armpits down her sides. Her handmade cotton shirt became damp in places. She peered out the half-opened glass, watched the scenery go by in a blur of green. She held back the mousy brown hair her mother had trimmed just the night before—had insisted on it, in fact—with her left hand, keeping it away from her face and eyes. Turning to her friends with a shake of her head, she said, "I wanna go. Honest I do. But . . . Mr. Liddle returns tomorrow night and it will all depend on what Mama has for me to do." Her upper lip curled as she said, "I've got field peas to shell this afternoon too. Mountains of them. I declare, sometimes I think my fingers are going to fall off from all the shelling, and I'm sure she's going to have me picking more tomorrow besides."

Mitzy, who sat on the aisle side, leaned over Jane and rested her forearm on the seat back in front of them. "Sneak away, then."

Jane's eyes grew as large as Patsy's felt. "Why, she can't do that, Mitzy."

Mitzy's expression grew stern. "Why not? All she has to do is say she's picking the peas, which is pretty much all she ever does. We can meet up at the creek, swim, then go to the lower lot and help her gather a bushel." Her dark eyes darted up at Patsy. "We won't stay long, Patsy." She held up three fingers. "On my honor as a Girl Scout."

Tempting as it sounded . . . "I can't unless Mama says it's okay," Patsy said. "I want to. I do. But if Mr. Liddle found out I'd done anything without Mama's okay . . ." The memory of weeks earlier still seared her memory.

24

Jane crossed her arms over the schoolbooks resting in her lap. "I don't know how you stand living in the same house with that man."

"That makes two of us, Patsy," Mitzy added.

Patsy shrugged. "He's all right, I guess. He has his occasional outbursts, but he's been a good provider, and like Mama says, he took the two of us in when nobody else would have."

Patsy returned her attention to the world outside, drawing near the road where Mitzy and Jane would be dropped off to walk the rest of the way to their homes. Another mile or so down the road and it was Patsy's turn.

She hadn't told either of her friends about what had happened. Hadn't shared with them that she was doing everything in her power to avoid Ira Liddle. He'd almost cornered her once, since that night. The previous Saturday she'd been in the storage pantry, putting up mason jars full of green beans and fresh peaches she and Mama had canned that day. When she heard footsteps over the tune she hummed, she peered over her shoulder expecting to find her mother there. "I got it, Mama," she said. Then, "Oh. I didn't . . . I thought you'd gone to town, Mr. Liddle." If she hurried, she could be done with the chore and get out. Patsy reached toward the deep oval-shaped basket beside her feet where a few more jars stood at attention. "I'm just helping Mama . . . putting up these cans of beans and peaches."

Her hands shook; she could barely grip the jar's mouthpiece.

"You're a good helper for your mama, aren't you, girl." It wasn't a question. It wasn't even meant to be a compliment.

Patsy's insides churned. "I try, Mr. Liddle." She gripped the handle of the basket and then wrapped it in her arms, pressing it against her middle.

25

Her stepfather took another step into the room, his frame all but blocking the light from the kitchen. "Why don't you call me Ira, Patsy? I am, after all, your stepfather. Or, you can call me Daddy."

The churning stopped, replaced by a lack of any ability whatsoever to feel. She could only stare at the man. His face was shadow, his scent of pipe tobacco and some kind of pungent aftershave. Patsy tried to think of something to say, even as plans of escape tried to form. "I . . . I . . ."

Another step. He leaned against a shelf's frame to his right. Light broke from around his left shoulder. Now she could see the dingy white of his teeth, the hint of a smile.

The steel in his eyes.

"You know, Patsy . . . you and I . . . could be friends. Good friends." Beefy arms slid across his barrel chest. "It would make me happy and it would make your life a whole lot nicer." Another smile. "If you get what I'm saying."

Patsy took a step back, realizing with it that she had trapped herself. She had nowhere to go. If she screamed for help, her stepfather would only claim she was lying. Her mother would suspect her of causing trouble, perhaps. Her brothers—so precious to her—would see her as the source of problems in the household.

"Mr. Liddle, I . . ."

"Ira, Patsy. Call me Ira." Another step forward. "I think we should begin again, you and I. Shall we?" His arms stretched toward her. "Maybe start with a hug."

"I . . ." The basket toppled to the floor and rolled atop her feet.

"Patsy?" Her mother's voice rang from beyond the monster at the door. "Patsy!"

Patsy's eyes darted toward the light. "Mama, I'm in here!"

She gathered the basket and straightened as her mother stepped into the pantry.

"Oh, Ira," she said, coming up short. "I thought you'd gone to town."

Patsy's stepfather turned. "I was going to . . ." He nodded toward Patsy. "But your daughter needed some help first."

Patsy's mother looked first from her husband, then to her daughter, and back to her husband again. She smiled. Weak, but it was a smile nonetheless. "Oh, I see. How kind of you, Ira." Then to Patsy: "Child, the boys need their baths. See to it, will you?"

"Yes, ma'am." Patsy turned her eyes to the floor and willed her feet to leave the room as fast as they could. Passing Mr. Liddle, she heard him say to her mother, "Such a good little helper you've got there, Bernie. I don't know what we'd do without her."

The school bus screeched to a stop, jarring Patsy from her memory. Mitzy and Jane pulled books to their chests before standing and peering down at her. "So, are you in or out?"

Patsy nodded. "In. Meet me at one o'clock. That's when the boys go down for their naps."

Both friends smiled. Nodded. They ambled up the aisle, toward the front of the bus. Jane looked over her shoulder, mouthed "See you tomorrow," and then continued forward.

"See you," Patsy said to no one. She sighed, nervous at the thought of swimming before working. Wondering if Mama would allow it or if she'd have to sneak to the creek after lunch.

At least, she thought, Mr. Liddle wasn't home until tomorrow night.

When Patsy arrived home it was to find her mother standing on the front porch. She was dressed as if she were going to

27

town. Her dark-brown felt suit hat—the one with the single feather and a pearl flair on the front side—was cocked perfectly atop her head. She wore her matching dark brown gloves, a purse was draped across her forearm, and she wore a hint of lipstick from one of the tubes from the little cupid holder.

Patsy felt elation. If her mother had to go to town . . . and she needed her to help with her little brothers . . . maybe she'd be more apt to allow for swimming on Saturday. "Going to town, Mama? Do you need me to watch the boys?"

Mama came down all three of the concrete steps that led to the landing. "The boys have gone over to Mrs. Dabbs's house. She's watching them for me this afternoon."

Patsy blinked. She clutched her books tighter to where they rested low on her belly. "Are you okay, Mama? Are you sick?"

"No, Patsy, I'm not sick. But I want you to get in the car with me now." She took a breath, exhaled slowly. "We have to go somewhere."

Patsy looked from her mother to the car and back again. "Where?"

Mama inhaled deeply. "Just do as I say," she answered, walking past her daughter.

Patsy had never defied her mother, never argued with her about anything; she wasn't about to start now. Not today. She walked up onto the porch, placed her schoolbooks on one of the wicker rockers, and then skipped back down the steps and to the car, an embroidered purse swinging at her side.

They were halfway to town when Mama cleared her throat. Patsy thought she sounded like a little girl. "Patsy," she said. Her hands flexed on the steering wheel, then rolled—pinky to index finger—like little drumsticks. Another deep sigh slipped from her red-painted lips. "Patsy, do you remember . . ." Her mother swallowed.

Patsy tucked her left ankle under her right knee and swung around so that she could better see her mother. "Remember?"

"When you were a little girl . . . a very little girl. Do you remember your father? Your real father?"

Patsy nodded. "A little. Not a lot. I remember . . ." She peered out the windshield. "I remember the smell of him mostly." She smiled. "And sometimes I dream about him. I dream of him walking through a doorway and I run to him and he picks me up and swings me around and around." Patsy blinked. "And he sings . . ."

"Come, Josephine, in my flying machine . . ."

Patsy looked again to her mother, who looked at her child. Together they sang, "Going up she goes, up she goes . . ."

The older smiled at the younger before adding, "That was no mere dream, Patsy. That was a memory." Her gloved fingers drummed along the steering wheel again. "I'm glad you have it. It will keep you warm on cold nights as you grow older." She smiled weakly before continuing. "Do you remember anything else, Patsy? Anything about our lives together?"

"Sometimes I think . . . I think about a house. With a narrow staircase beside a paneled wall."

"That was our home. Anything else?"

Patsy shook her head. "Not really. There're little things, but I don't always know if they're real or imaginary."

Her mother stole a glance at her watch ticking silently at the hem of her glove. "We've time," she said, mostly to herself.

"Time?"

"Patsy," her mother continued. "Do you remember anything—anything at all—about me in those days?"

"Of course, Mama. I remember you being in the kitchen. I remember your laughter. I remember . . . Daddy coming home and the kiss he always gave you." Patsy squeezed her hands together in her lap, where they rested atop her purse. "You don't do that with Mr. Liddle, Mama. Why?"

Mama shrugged. "Ours is not a marriage born out of . . . passion." She looked at her daughter. "Ordinarily, these are not the kinds of things I would discuss with you, but . . . there are things I want you to know."

"Like?"

"Like about love. And marriage. And motherhood."

"Does this have anything to do with where we're going?" Patsy licked her lips as she looked out the windshield. "And can it possibly be to Slim's? I'm simply parched and absolutely dying for a Nehi."

Slim's Service Station served three functions. It was a place to buy gas and get your car fixed, a place to buy ice-cold sodas and snacks, and a place to stop along the new Trailways bus route.

Mama cleared her throat again. "Actually, that's exactly where we're going."

Patsy sat up a little straighter on the seat. "Really? Then can I? Can I have a Nehi Peach?"

"Yes, you may." Her mother smiled toward her. "But Patsy, I must talk with you first. And you must listen. Listen carefully."

"Okay, Mama. I'm listening."

Patsy noticed her mother's hands gripping the wheel tighter now, the outline of her knuckles nearly visible through the cotton. "Patsy, when your daddy died on that awful day . . . I was . . . expecting."

Patsy frowned. The forbidden topic. "You mean the baby."

"Yes. Your oldest brother."

Patsy stared beyond the hood of the car to the road before them. Stretched out like an old clothesline bobbing in the wind, dipping here, curving there. "My brother," she whispered. "But . . ." The *t* was stuck on the back of her front teeth. "I thought you never wanted to talk about him, Mama. So, I haven't."

"I couldn't take care of him, Patsy. My son. Not without your father. And both our families were struggling through the Depression, you know. No one could afford another mouth to feed."

Patsy could feel herself growing angry. Unsure. She turned her face toward her mother, whose face was streaked by silent tears.

"You can't begin to understand, Patsy. But I . . . I did what I thought best." She swallowed. "My parents had been against my marriage to your father, as you know. They'd given me a lovely wedding, but they'd made it clear we were on our own. I had too much pride to . . ." Mama's eyes batted back tears. "To go back and beg." She shook her head. "And, like I said, they were no better off than we, really. How could I ask them to take us back? Me, with a toddler and a baby besides."

"But they were your mama and daddy."

"You don't know them like I know them. As far as they are concerned, I have done the right thing. I found myself another husband, a man who provides well enough. A good man when you get right down to it. I've had more children. I run a good home."

Patsy frowned. *A good man*. Ira Liddle provided well, yes. But he wasn't *good*. At least not from what she'd seen over the years. But that wasn't the point Patsy wanted to focus on. "You are a good mama, Mama. You do run a good home."

Mama gave her a weak smile. "Let me finish, Patsy. I need to tell you now about your brother."

"Okay, Mama."

Another deep breath. Then, "The reverend—our pastor— knew of a couple in a place called Trinity. Trinity, South

31

Carolina. Buchwald is their last name, and they couldn't have children of their own. He made all the arrangements—"

At hearing their name, Patsy felt nausea wash over her. She'd imagined, at the very least, that the adoptive parents of her little brother had been friends. But strangers? "I knew you'd had him adopted, but I didn't know who to."

"Patsy." Her mother extended a hand toward hers, but Patsy slipped it away. Something was wrong. Bad wrong. She could see it in her mother's face.

She crossed her arms; her voice took a tone she'd never before taken with her mother. "What's this really about, Mama?"

"I don't have time for tantrums, Patsy Sweeny. You must listen to me now." Her chest expanded beneath her best go-to-town dress. "Yes, I gave my son to a nice couple to raise. I didn't know them personally, but the reverend did and he said . . . he said they were good people. Christian people. If that makes me a horrible mother, then so be it. God forbid you ever have to know . . . ."

The car slowed as they neared town, and Mama continued. "Before you go judging me, you should know I married Ira Liddle because I needed to put food in your stomach. We were hungry, and I can only pray that this is one thing you do not remember. We were hungry and I was working seven days a week for hardly enough money to put a roof over our heads. Making sure you were safe and sound was my number one priority." Patsy watched in earnest as her mother's chest heaved several times. "We're near the bus station."

"Slim's." The name came out like a prayer.

This time, it was Mama who licked her lips, a tiny pink tongue sliding over thin red. "Today I make another sacrifice, Patsy. Today, I'm putting you on a bus to go to the Buchwalds, to live with them and your little brother."

Tingling began at the top of her head, poured down her face, over her shoulders, and made its way along her spine. The whirring inside her ears kept her from hearing anything else her mother said, though Patsy could see her lips moving. "What?" she finally said. The car rolled to a stop in front of the small white brick building. SINCLAIR GASOLINE was stretched across the front—white over burgundy between two square columns—and, for some reason, Patsy's eyes moved upward until they fixed on the letters, tracing each one. S-I-N . . .

Her mother continued. "Mr. Liddle is—"

Patsy's head spun to face her mother. "An ogre!"

"Patsy!"

A knot formed in Patsy's throat as tears pushed their way from the corners of her eyes. She glared at her mother. "He is and you know it!" She clapped a hand over her mouth, if only to show Mama that even she was shocked at the way she was speaking. But Mama didn't seem upset with her. For a moment, Patsy felt they were no longer mother and daughter, but friends. If she were going to bare her soul, the time was now. "The way he treats you, Mama. The way he . . . the way he looks at me." Patsy pounded her palm against her chest in tiny staccato beats. "Don't you even see, Mama?"

Mama pulled her firstborn toward her, drawing her closer until they met in the middle of the front seat. "Hush now, child. Yes. Yes, I know. Yes, I see. Why do you think . . ." She kissed Patsy's hair, just behind her ear. "Why do you think I'm letting you go?"

Patsy was crying too. Her mother's hands held the sides of her head, pushed it back until their eyes—wet with tears—stared into each other's. "What do you mean, Mama?"

"The bus will be here soon, Patsy. Everything is set. I've called Mrs. Buchwald and I have a bag packed for you."

Something inside Patsy shook. This couldn't be happening. Mamas didn't send their thirteen-year-old daughters away.

Did they?

"Mama, don't do this."

"Patsy . . ."

"No." She felt her eyes go wide. "I know! Go with me." She grabbed her mother's shoulders, then jerked her head toward the backseat. "Harold and Billy. Where are they? Why aren't they here?"

"I told you, Patsy. They're with Mrs. Dabbs."

"Go get them. We'll all go . . . to Trinity, did you say? We'll be together, Mama. What will it matter that we've left home? I can get a job." Desperation rose within her. "I can help."

But her mother shook her head. Patsy took in the blue of her mother's eyes, eyes drowning in tears. "Don't make this difficult, Patsy. I cannot leave Mr. Liddle. Don't you understand? He will find me. He will come after me . . . for the boys. Besides, he's my husband. By God's law, I should stay."

"By God's law—" Patsy swallowed past the lump. "But if you send me away . . . what will he do to you, Mama?"

Mama looked down. "Whatever it is, I can bear it. As long as I know you're all right."

"Nooooo . . ." Patsy clung to her mother again, buried her face into the gentle curve of her neck, inhaled the scent of Coty perfume. "Mama," she whispered. "Don't . . . please don't. I'll do anything. I'll stay away from him."

"Patsy, don't make this more difficult than it already is."

Patsy opened her mouth, hoping for one more plea, one more argument. But before the words could tumble out, they were drowned out by the sound of the bus screeching to a stop.

3

"So many things," her mother had said she wanted to say. To tell her about love. Marriage. Children. In the end, there'd only been a half hour at best. From the descent of the first passenger alighting the oily pavement around Slim's to the moment Patsy became the last passenger aboard for departure. One half hour. Casselton was not an important enough stop, she wagered, to be more than that.

Patsy made her way toward the back of the red and white bus. The last seat on the right was empty, as though it knew this was where she liked to sit. But with her friends. Not alone. She faltered halfway, caught herself on the shoulder of another passenger—an airman who'd already closed his eyes for a nap. His face registered startled annoyance even as he gently grabbed her arm to steady her.

"I'm so sorry," she whispered.

"You all right there?" he asked simultaneously.

"Sit down, young lady," the bus driver called. "We've got a schedule to keep."

Patsy straightened. Looked behind her. "Sorry," she said. Then down to the soldier. "Sorry," she repeated.

"Don't make no never-mind," he said, adding a wink for good measure.

No one else sat in the backseat, and for that Patsy was grateful. She slid in, all the way to the window, straightened her school skirt over her knees, then looked to her feet. Her brown penny loafers were still dusty from her walk from the bus stop to home. She pulled a pink and lavender handkerchief from the small embroidered purse. She wiped the tops of her shoes, shook out the handkerchief, and returned it to join the few items resting among satin lining.

Patsy peered inside the handmade gift from Mitzy, who she wondered if she'd ever see again. Mitzy, who'd be waiting for her tomorrow down by the creek.

She peered out the window. Her mother stood not twenty feet away. Stood by the car, one gloved hand up in some lame attempt to say good-bye. Patsy was angry, but she wasn't hateful. She pressed a hand against the window and mouthed "Goodbye, Mama," as though Bernice Liddle would be able to see her.

And perhaps she could. In that instance, just as the bus began its roll away from Slim's, Mama blew a kiss and waved once more, now with gusto. As though Patsy were going off the camp. Or to see a fond relative.

Patsy rested her forehead against the window, and this time cried silent tears that wracked her body. When there was nothing left but a few dry heaves, she shifted her weight until she had snuggled into the back corner, closed her eyes, and slept.

Someone shook her shoulder.

"Sleepyhead . . . hey, you."

She blinked. Wiped her fingertips across still-moist eyelashes. "Where . . ."

"Hey there."

She looked to the seat beside her. The airman—the one she'd bumped into earlier—sat next to her, grinning. "Hi." Her voice sounded like a frog's, so she cleared her throat. "Hi," she said again.

"Hungry?"

The bus was no longer moving. Outside her window the world was dark. Only streetlights cast spotlights here and there. "Where are we?"

"Darien, Georgia. Pit stop. If you're hungry, now's the time to get something. We've got an hour."

Patsy held her purse tight against her stomach. She wasn't hungry, but she reckoned she might be later on. "Maybe a little something."

The airman slid out of the seat to stand in the aisle. "After you," he said, extending a hand toward the front of the bus.

They exited the bus together, clearly the only two left. "I must have been sleeping pretty hard," she said, looking toward the bus stop, which reminded Patsy of Slim's, the only difference being she could smell fried chicken coming from inside.

Her stomach rumbled. Maybe she was hungry after all.

She watched as the airman, dressed in a pressed blue uniform, methodically placed his cap atop his head, then adjusted it low on his brow. "Where you heading off to?" he asked as they started to walk together.

"A place called Trinity."

"You don't say. Well, how about that? Me too."

Patsy kept her gaze on her feet and where they were stepping. "Do you know the Buchwald family?"

He chuckled. "Everyone knows everyone in Trinity."

"Are they nice people?"

"Wesley and Phyllis Buchwald are the very fiber of nice.

37

Good people." When they came to the door, he opened it for her. "Restroom will be behind the building," he said as they entered. As easily as he'd earlier placed the cap on his head, he removed it and tucked it under his arm. "Unless it's an outhouse."

Patsy peered up at him with a frown. He was much taller than she, handsome in a boyish sort of way. He reminded her a little of Henry Fonda, the way he'd looked in *Immortal Sergeant*. Cleaned up, standing opposite Maureen O'Hara. Of course, Patsy was a far cry from Maureen O'Hara. Her hair wasn't that glorious shade of auburn Miss O'Hara sported; it was plain ole mousy brown. She twisted the knitted handle of her purse. "Do you think it is? An outhouse, I mean?"

"Probably not. With the new bus line, the stops along the way are trying to class up." His chin jutted toward a counter. "Bet we have to get the keys over there." He even sounded like Henry Fonda. So sure of himself . . .

They walked to the counter as if they'd done it together all their lives.

"Keys are with the other passengers," a short, balding man said to them from near the cash register. Stretched to the right was a counter full of people wolfing down fried chicken, mashed potatoes, and green beans. Patsy licked her lips. Yep, she was hungry.

The airman strained his neck to look over the room. "I see an empty table over by the window," he said. "If you don't mind sitting with a stranger, I'll hold it while you go freshen up."

Patsy found the restrooms. She stood fourth in line and tried to get her bearings. Foliage and dusk surrounded her. The airman said they were in Darien, Georgia. Before today, she'd not even heard of the place. Now she was standing behind one of its buildings, waiting for her turn at the bathroom, listening to crickets chirp and frogs croak. Must be a swamp around here somewhere, she figured. She shivered, hoping none of the nightlife was inside the bathroom.

Patsy crisscrossed her arms to rub them and wondered about the time. She touched the shoulder of the woman standing in front of her. "Excuse me, can you tell me what time it is?"

The woman gave her a cursory glance, peered at her wristwatch, and said, "Near about eight."

No wonder her stomach kept rumbling. "Thank you, ma'am."

When it was her turn in the restroom, she hurried, thinking the airman needed to do the same. He was holding a table for them, he'd said. She figured she'd be obliged to do the same for him while he came out back.

Inside the bus stop, Patsy found the young man sitting at the table he'd indicated before. His cap rested comfortably next to the wall and under the opened window. Two plates of steaming food had been served.

He saw her then, stood, and motioned for her to come. "Have a seat. I'll be right back." He reached for the cap. "Don't wait on me. Go ahead and eat," he said, "before it gets cold."

Patsy blinked as she sat. "Do you know how much this is going to cost? My mama only gave me two dollars."

He smiled at her; a deep dimple sliced into his right cheek. "Then you're in luck, little sister. It's a buck twenty-five."

Back in the bus, they took their original seats. Night had completely closed in; it was now after nine o'clock. Patsy shivered as she hunkered down, folded her hands together, and formed a makeshift pillow.

Mama . . . She'd be home now, sitting alone after putting the boys to bed. Had her brothers asked about her? If so, how had her mother answered? She shuddered thinking about tomorrow when Mr. Liddle arrived home, glad in an odd sort of way she wouldn't be there to witness it. Or to be any part of his homecoming.

Mama was right; even one more weekend would have been dangerous for Patsy.

Still, her tears resumed until sleep, once again, took charge.

Patsy woke with each new stop and start, but she didn't move from her seat. The young airman had been nice enough to come back and check on her a few times, even called her "little sister" again, but she didn't feel like talking much.

Her stomach turned as she wondered—really for the first time—about the family and the life she was heading toward. Ominous, she thought, arriving in the pitch black of night. A nice family, the airman had told her. Well, people thought Ira Liddle was the head of a nice family. Maybe the family was nice, but Ira Liddle sure wasn't.

Her mother hadn't given her any instructions beyond getting on the bus. Would someone be in Trinity to meet her? And, if so, how would they know her? Or her, them?

It was a little after midnight when she heard the bus driver call out, "Trinity, South Carolina."

"That's me," she said to no one.

No one responded.

She gathered her purse and shuffled up the aisle. A few people in front of her were also getting off, including the airman, but most of the passengers continued to sleep.

Patsy grabbed the chrome railing along the three steps. She took each of them deliberately, keeping focus on her feet and her still-dusty loafers. Only when she'd reached the concrete did she look up.

This stop was like all the others, except the one in Savannah, which had been an honest-to-goodness Trailways station. This was a Standard Oil station, painted white with wide windows across the front. All the lights except the ones under the covering for the pumps had been turned out. Over the door, in large red-painted letters, were the words "Milstrap's; Est. 1933."

Patsy tilted her head at the name; her gaze drifted to where the airman shook hands with an older man who then grabbed the younger for a tight hug. Another passenger—a young woman—was slipping into the gentle embrace of a man. An elderly woman stepped into a nearby automobile.

"Little lady, you wanna come get your bag?" she heard the driver say.

She nodded and fought back familiar tears before following him to the side of the bus and the opened luggage compartment. She pointed to her modest suitcase. "It's that one right there."

Patsy clutched the handle of her purse, took steady deep breaths, and waited for her luggage to be yanked from beneath two others. Just as the driver handed it to her, she heard a baritone voice say, "You must be Patsy."

She turned. Standing in the glow of the street lamps was a man head and shoulders taller than she. His square face was balanced by round specs and a gentle smile. He was neither fat nor slim and his hair was mostly white. He smelled like Mitzy's father. Like Barbasol.

"Are you Mr. Buchwald?"

He nodded as he reached for her suitcase, which she gladly turned over to him.

41

"Mama told me to make sure Mrs. Buchwald got my luggage before I unpacked anything," Patsy told him.

Wesley Buchwald's smile grew wider. "Then we'll make sure she does." He extended a hand toward a vehicle parked just beyond the gas pumps. Even in near-darkness, Patsy could see it was big. Well kept and clean, albeit a little dated. Painted on the side of the back window panel were the words "Buchwald Flowers."

"You own a flower shop?" Patsy didn't move.

"I do," the man answered. "Miz B handles the majority of the arranging and I take care of the business side of everything." He nodded just so. "Even during the war, we managed all right. Not rich, but not poor. The Lord is good."

"Oh," Patsy replied, then mumbled, "Yes, he is." She jumped when the bus coughed into gear and prepared to roll away from where they stood. This was her cue to walk to the car. The very thing that had brought her here was saying good-bye. Now was the time . . . time to shuck off the old and begin anew.

4

Phyllis Buchwald greeted Patsy with open arms in the foyer of a two-story farmhouse that stood in the middle of an open field about two miles north of Trinity. "Oh, you darling thing," she spoke against Patsy's hair. "I'm so glad to finally have you here."

Patsy stepped out of the woman's embrace. "Thank you."

Wesley Buchwald walked into the foyer through the front door, carrying her meager luggage.

"Hon," Phyllis said to him, "put that in our room for tonight."

Patsy noted the kind but unspoken words between them. Mrs. Buchwald didn't flutter about nervously and Mr. Buchwald didn't enter with the fearful presence of Mr. Liddle. The thought was fleeting, but it was enough to make her relax, even if only a little.

Mrs. Buchwald, a somewhat stout and handsome woman, wrapped stubby fingers around Patsy's arm. "We'll go through the dining room here," she said, indicating the darkened room to her right, the same direction Mr. Buchwald had gone, "and into the kitchen for a little hot tea before I show you to your room." Her words were whispers, soft and coaxing. "Didja eat?"

"Yes ma'am."

"Well, come on then."

Patsy didn't hesitate to walk alongside Mrs. Buchwald, whose fingers slipped from around her as she pushed open the swinging door between the dining room and a butler's pantry.

After they'd stepped into the kitchen, Patsy paused. The kitchen glowed from a Bakelite lamp perched atop an occasional table standing at the far side of the room.

"Go have a seat at the table. Right in there," the older woman told her, indicating she should continue on to the table in the nook. "I've got the water simmering on the stove top."

As Patsy pulled a chair from the table, she realized she still held on to her purse as though it were a life preserver. She also noted that the chair nearest the lamp, which was to her right, was already pulled away from the table and that a book was opened at its place.

Sideward observation told her it was a Bible.

She placed her purse in the chair to her left, leaving the chair to her right for Mrs. Buchwald. Moments later, hot ginger tea was served in delicate teacups. "Here you go," the woman said. "And here are some sugar cubes if you'd like."

Patsy removed small silver tongs from the matching sugar bowl before setting about preparing her tea as she liked it. "You have nice things," Patsy said.

"They were my mama's. Mama loved pretty things."

Patsy took a sip of tea, careful to place the cup back into the saucer without breaking it.

"You must be plumb tired out." Mrs. Buchwald sat next to her and immediately took a sip of her own tea. "I know I'd be if I were you."

Patsy inhaled a spicy curl of steam. She closed her eyes, thought of just how truly tired she was, and that—at this very moment—she was in the same house as her full-blood brother. She opened her eyes. "I don't know what to call you."

A firm pat on the hand and she looked directly at her hostess. "Oh, hon. You can call me anything you like. Now, your brother—you know about your brother, don't you?"

"Yes, ma'am."

"Your mother said as much, but I wanted to make sure." She took a sip of tea, returned the cup to its saucer. "Your brother calls me Mam. Don't ask me how it got started because I just can't remember. But he calls me Mam and he calls Mr. B Papa. I want you to feel free to do the same if it'll make things easier for you."

It seemed an odd thing to do, calling complete strangers by such endearments. "I'll try," she said finally. "I suppose anything else would be . . ."

"The only thing I ask is that you not call us by our given names. That wouldn't be proper."

Patsy took in the woman's features in the veiled glow from the light. Her dark hair capped her head in tight but soft curls. Her face was round, and she, like her husband, wore round frameless specs. Behind them were dark, kind eyes. Her forehead was high and—even at the late hour—her lips bore the stain of red lipstick. She wore a simple housedress. Not yet ready for bed, Patsy supposed.

She patted Patsy's hand again before adding, "Drink up."

Patsy did as she was told. A noise from the kitchen door diverted her attention, but it was dark and she couldn't tell what it had been.

"That's Papa," she heard. "He's in our room, right off

from the butler's pantry. Out back is our greenhouse and a small shop. We have a place in town now too. Had to give it up for a while, but things are getting better now."

Patsy finished her tea as the woman continued to fill her in on the way of things. "Now, I want you to feel free to sleep in as late as need be tomorrow. But your brother is an early riser so expect to hear him mulling around upstairs."

"Is that where we sleep? Upstairs?"

Mrs. Buchwald nodded. "Yes. And we have indoor plumbing up there, just across from your room. I'm sure you'll need to use the facilities before going to bed." Her face turned toward the dining room door. "Papa and I are right down here if you need us. Are you done with your tea?"

Patsy nodded. Together, they stood, both gathering up the dishes.

"On Sunday, of course, we go to church." Mrs. Buchwald placed her dishes near the sink, and Patsy did the same. "We're Methodists."

"Mr. Liddle is a Baptist, so we go to church there." Patsy grimaced. It felt like a stupid thing to say.

"Nothing wrong with that," the woman said with a squeeze of Patsy's shoulders. "Now, let's get upstairs. I took the liberty of shopping a little for you. Bought you a pretty nightgown and it's all laid out for you on the bed."

"Thank you." Patsy stalled. There was something she needed to ask. "Mrs. Buchwald? Mam?"

"Yes, darlin'?" From the look on her face, Mrs. Buchwald was pleased with the title coming so quickly.

"There is one thing you can help me with."

"Anything. Anything at all."

"I don't know my brother's name . . ."

46

Patsy was grateful Mrs. Buchwald had given her permission to sleep in late. In spite of being in unfamiliar circumstances, she'd slept soundly and—to her knowledge—without dreaming. She'd even been too tired to cry.

When her eyes finally opened, the room was filled with bright light. The lightly ticking Westclox on the bedside table told her it was after ten o'clock. She pushed herself up on the polished pine twin-sized headboard and adjusted the feather pillow to the small of her back before taking in the room.

It was simply decorated. The bed was covered in crisp white sheets topped with a thin quilt handmade from scraps of pink fabric. A mirrored pine dresser with three narrow drawers and a matching bedside table made up the remaining furniture save for a white wicker rocker in one corner. Atop the dresser was a small arrangement of summer flowers resting over a crocheted doily. Her luggage stood just inside the door, and she wondered when it had been placed there.

Patsy pulled herself from under the covers then slung them back over the mattresses before smoothing them with the palms of her hands. A fluff of the pillow before placing it at the headboard and she was ready to get dressed. It was then she remembered placing her traveling clothes on the rocker the night before. But they were no longer there. Mrs. Buchwald—Mam—must have taken them to be washed.

She had no idea what her mother had packed. She'd just as soon her new family not know she was awake, so she heaved the worn luggage up onto the bed and opened it quietly. Inside, she found several items of her favorite clothes including a pair of dungarees with red and white checkered cuffs. She pulled them from the suitcase along with a red short-sleeved sweater.

She'd used the bathroom the night before and was happy it was so close to her room. After washing her face and brushing her teeth, she dressed quietly. Opening the bathroom door to return to her bedroom, she gasped. Standing across the hall, leaning one shoulder against the wall and with a leg crossed over the other, stood a boy. His face was strikingly handsome—even for a lad of eleven—and he wore dungarees rolled up at the cuffs, a dark red and light blue horizontally striped shirt, and a worn red cap with a green four-leaf clover front and center.

He smiled at having surprised her. "You must be Patsy," he said, straightening. He extended a hand to her as though they were new classmates.

Patsy swallowed. "I am." She didn't move. "You must be . . . my brother."

His head bobbed once. "Lloyd."

Her head mimicked his. "Lloyd."

He glanced nervously toward her bedroom door. "So . . . you like your new room? Mam arranged the flowers, but I put them on the doily."

She smiled. "It's nice. They're nice. Thank you."

"Mam says we don't have a lot, but what we have is clean. Mam likes clean."

Patsy took tentative steps toward her room. Lloyd turned as though to follow. "I guess I missed breakfast." She stepped into the room, Lloyd right behind her. This was new; just as she wasn't allowed in her mother and Mr. Liddle's room, at home her little brothers weren't allowed in her room.

"Yeah, but Mam will make you something to eat. Mam loves to cook. She's good at it too."

Patsy sighed as if she'd been squeezed. "Oh yeah?" She looked around the room, not knowing where to put her new nightgown.

Lloyd pointed to a narrow door on the wall to her right. "It's a little closet, but Mam put a hook on the inside of the door just for your nightclothes."

Patsy blinked. "Thank you. Again."

She opened the closet door. High inside was a bar with a few wooden hangers. She took them down one at a time, then set about to the task of unpacking her suitcase. Lloyd was quiet while she worked. He sat in the rocker, elbows on his knees, hands clasped together, and when she'd finished he said, "So, you're my real sister."

Patsy whirled around. She couldn't answer; she could only nod.

"Well, then." Patsy watched as he visibly swallowed. "I guess you should go on downstairs and eat something for breakfast before it's time for lunch."

Little William Liddle—called Billy—was only four years old that September night in 1946, but he was old enough to know what was what.

He knew his sister Patsy had gone somewhere. And from the way his mama was acting, it had to be somewhere bad. He reckoned she'd done something awful. His daddy was always mad at her for one thing or another; she must have really done it this time.

He also knew Daddy would be fighting mad about it too.

They'd been put to bed early that night, him and his older brother Harold. Him and Harold had played hard that day, and Harold had gone right to sleep. But Billy couldn't find his way to dreamland. The air was stirrin' in the house, and Mama was nervous as a cat.

When he'd heard Daddy's car shut off in the driveway, he'd closed his eyes tight. Daddy was sure to look in on them, and he didn't want to be caught with his eyes open. So he rolled over on his side, pulled the covers tight up under his chin, and listened while pretending.

He heard Daddy walking in the front door. Mama said something to him, low and easy. Daddy said, "Where are my boys?" Daddy's voice always boomed when he came home from his workweek.

And Mama said, ". . . both so tuckered out, I put them to bed early." Footsteps headed up the stairs. The door opened, and even with his eyes shut, Billy could see the shaft of light from the hallway.

The door closed. Mama and Daddy heading back down the hallway, Billy figured to their own room.

"Don't you want your supper?" Mama was asking. "I kept it warm in the oven."

Daddy said, "What'd you make?"

Mama rattled off, "Meat loaf and sweet potato soufflé and tomato slices with some cukes and I made a nice pound cake. Came out real good."

Daddy said, "Where's the girl?"

He always asked like that. Never called Patsy by her name. Always "the girl."

Billy sat up in bed now. "Harold?" he whispered. But Harold didn't stir.

"I said, 'Where's the girl?'" Daddy said it again.

Boy, oh boy. Mama'd better come up with a good one or Patsy'd sure get it when she got home. Daddy would whup her like he ain't never whupped her before. And then Billy wondered why Daddy always beat on Patsy so. She was a good sister. A pretty sister. And seemed to him like she tried real hard to make Daddy happy.

"She's gone," he heard Mama say.

"Gone where?" And then Daddy used those words Mama said she'd best not ever hear out of Billy or Harold or she'd wash their mouths out with soap. ". . . better not be off spending the night with one of her girlfriends when she knows we got to get to church in the morning and you need her help with the boys."

There was a long sigh of quiet. Then Mama said, "I sent her off." Right out of her mouth like that.

"What do you mean you sent her off?" Daddy's voice was low and it scared Billy.

"Be mad if you want to," Mama said, her voice sounding all strong. Not like Billy usually heard his mama when she was talking to Daddy. She was bossy enough during the work week when Daddy was gone, but just as soon as he came home . . .

"Harold," Billy whispered one more time. Still nothing.

Mama kept talking. "Don't think I don't know the kind of looks you've been giving my girl. I sent her off somewhere you'll never be able to get at her. No more whippings, Ira. No more . . . *looks*."

Billy wondered what that meant. What was so bad about Daddy looking at Patsy? A man had to look, didn't he, if he wanted to talk to someone?

The bad words started again. And then the hitting. Daddy hit to keep Mama in line. That's what he told Billy and Harold one time when Harold had asked. Harold seemed okay with the answer. But Billy didn't much care for it.

"Harold!"

This time Harold opened his eyes. "Daddy hitting on Mama again?" he asked.

"Yeah."

"She musta done something to deserve it, then."

"Mama is good, Harold. She don't do things bad."

"Daddy says all the time he's gotta keep her in line. So I know. Now go to sleep, Billy. You know what will happen if we get in the middle of it."

Billy sure did. When Daddy had told him and Harold about keeping Mama in line, Billy had asked, "Do you spank her 'cause she's done something bad? Like sometimes Patsy does and you have to whup her?"

"That's right, boy." Daddy reached down and ruffled Billy's hair like he'd done something right. "And when I do, you best stay out of it or I'll wear your rear end out too."

Billy didn't want that. No-siree-bob.

"Mama's not fighting back," he now whispered to Harold. "Not even crying this time."

"Go back to sleep," Harold said. He flipped onto his side opposite Billy and pulled the bedcovers over his head before slipping the pillow out from under his head and bringing it down over his ear.

"Maybe we should pray for Mama," Billy suggested. But Harold was having none of his words.

Billy slipped back under the covers, mimicking his brother's actions. "Dear Jesus," he said, hoping it was loud enough for the good Lord to hear. "Please don't let Daddy hurt Mama too bad tonight." Curse words reached his ears again and he swallowed hard. "And be with Patsy . . . wherever she is."

5

To be situated in such a small town, Trinity Methodist Church certainly was a grand structure. A total of twelve red brick steps led to the four-columned portico and double doorway. Inside the vestibule, a wide mahogany and marble table displayed a large gilded Bible under a massive framed copy of Sallman's *The Head of Christ*. On both sides of the Bible were gold candlesticks holding thick, flickering candles and on both sides of the table were another set of double doors opening into the high-ceilinged sanctuary.

Patsy thought it the most beautiful display of Christianity she'd ever seen.

Immense stained-glass windows lined the sides of the room. At the front of the church, behind a three-sided pulpit, hung a cross so large, Patsy feared that should it fall, it would do considerable damage.

The long pews ran down the middle of the room with an aisle along both sides. Like the pulpit, they were made of mahogany. They sat hard, but it was a small price to pay, Patsy decided, after hearing the angelic voices of the choir and the inspiring message of the pastor, affectionately called Brother Michael.

"Fine service," Papa remarked to Mam as they exited the family pew.

"What did you think, sweetheart?" Mam asked as Patsy stepped into the aisle.

Patsy looked around the crowded room of strangers. "I think it was marvelous. If I lived here, I can't imagine ever wanting to attend another church."

Lloyd was right behind her. "You *do* live here, remember?"

"Lloyd . . ." Mam's voice held a hint of warning.

"Yes, ma'am," he muttered.

"Now then," Mam said, wrapping an arm around Patsy's shoulder. "Let's get you introduced to Brother Michael and to some of the girls your age. We skipped Sunday school this week—we wanted you to get your bearings—but next week you'll go with them to your class."

A hundred butterflies took flight in Patsy's stomach. Meeting new friends right now . . . tomorrow a new school . . . next Sunday a new class. She swallowed, then nodded. "Yes, ma'am."

After being proudly introduced to Brother Michael as "Lloyd's real sister who has come to live with us too," Patsy was led over to two girls who appeared to be her age.

Mam took charge of the pleasantries. "Sandra Bedwell," she said, pointing to a petite oval-faced brunette, "and Rayette Peachman." Rayette was a tall, slender redhead who reminded Patsy of a young Lucille Ball. Then to the girls, Mam said, "This is our new daughter, Patsy Sweeny. Now I want you two to help Patsy find her way around for me."

Both girls smiled, first at Mam and then at Patsy. "Yes, ma'am," they said.

Mam promptly left them to get to know one another on their own.

Rayette took charge. "How in the world do you get to be a new daughter at . . . how old are you?"

"Thirteen. You?'

"Fourteen. But Sandra here is thirteen like you."

"So, dish," Sandra said. "Is this like *Anne of Green Gables* or . . . what?"

"Oh, I love that book," Rayette said before Patsy had a chance to answer.

"Me too," Patsy said, unsure as to what to tell and what to keep private. But the look on both girls' faces told her they wouldn't be easily put off. "It's a long story." She shrugged. "Do you both go to the same school?"

Rayette laughed. "Honey, everyone goes to the same school. First grade all the way up. But it's not too bad. Hey, you should try out for our junior basketball team. You'd love it."

"Are you on it?"

"I am, but not our Sandra here. Sandra is a majorette." She winked. "Ra-ra-sis-boom-bah."

Sandra gave her friend a look that read "I can speak for myself." Instead she said, "There's a lot more to being a majorette than just that, you know."

"All right already," Rayette joked with a wave of her hand. "I guess you're coming to school tomorrow," she said to Patsy.

Patsy nodded. "I guess so." She attempted a smile, but she felt empty. Tomorrow her friends back in Georgia would go to school without her, she without them. And she couldn't help but wonder what rumors would be spread before the day's end.

"Hey, I know!" Sandra said, suddenly animated, making it easy for Patsy to see why she chose to be a majorette. She practically cheered, "Why don't you come to Janice's with us today?"

"Janice?"

"That's a superb idea," Rayette added. "Janice Milstrap. Her brother is home on leave from the Air Force and the family is throwing a barbecue for him and some of his friends. Naturally Janice got to invite a few of hers too. We're going. Why don't you come with us?"

Patsy looked over her shoulder, past the small clusters of people who gathered around, to where Mam was speaking hurriedly to a woman Patsy supposed to be one of her friends. "I'd have to ask Mam."

"Oh, she'll say yes," Sandra said. "I'm just sure of it. Everyone loves a war hero."

Patsy returned her attention to her new friends. "He's a war hero?"

"Well, he was *in* the war," Sandra said. "That's hero enough for me."

"Sandra is all goon-eyed over Gilbert Milstrap," Rayette said.

Sandra looked heavenward. "He's dreamy," she said, her shoulders swaying.

Patsy smiled. "Isn't he a little old for you?"

"Who cares?" she answered with a giggle, then sobered and looked Patsy directly in the eye. "Who said how old he is?"

"I've met him. We rode the bus into Trinity together the other night." She wasn't sure if she should admit they dined at the same table. The look on Sandra's face told her she could get mauled.

"Oh, wow . . . I wish *I'd* ridden the bus with him."

"I'm going to be positively ill," Rayette declared. She looked at Patsy. "By the way, the service station you stepped off the bus at? That's Gilbert's daddy's."

"I sort of figured that out the other night," Patsy said.

Rayette and Sandra looked at her with furrowed brows. She added, "Gilbert's name tag said Milstrap, and the name over the door of the service station was the same, so . . ." She shrugged before looking back at Mam, who was waving at her to come. "Anyway . . . I'll ask Mam if I can go. Umm . . . how do I . . ."

"Get there?" Rayette asked. "My sister is old enough to drive. Warning, though; she's 'in love' with Gilbert too." She laughed at her own words, then sobered. "I'll ask her to pick you up. But you'll need to be ready by three."

"Okay. I'll ask Mam. If I can go, I'll give you the nod."

She was allowed to go, of course. Mam was thrilled and Papa not too far behind that she'd already made friends with two of the young girls of Trinity. Lloyd seemed a little saddened that his sister would not be spending another afternoon with him—they'd spent the previous day awkwardly beginning to learn about each other. But her brother quickly brightened when Papa said the three of them could go for a Sunday ride.

Patsy had no idea what that was, but it seemed to lighten Lloyd's demeanor.

She had very few clothes to choose from. She hoped she looked all right in a simple flared skirt and white button-down blouse. She tied a little scarf around her neck and prayed she didn't look silly.

During the ride to the barbecue, Rayette's sister Paulette and Sandra talked nonstop about Gilbert Milstrap. So much so that by the time they arrived, Patsy felt she'd known him her whole life.

The Milstraps owned an out-of-the-way place on Fiddler's Creek, a narrow body of clear water that danced over river rocks in the afternoon breeze and glistened in the sun. Cars filled the front lawn leading to the sprawling clapboard house. Within eyesight but beyond the house, young adults sat in outdoor chairs or stood in clusters. They chatted while sipping on iced tea from mason jars or taking swigs from soft drink bottles. A few stood along the creek bank; Patsy heard their laughter, even from just outside the car.

The yard was canopied with tall swaying pines; their needles rustled and shimmied in the wind. Patsy stared into them, watching the sunlight wink between their clusters as she waited for Rayette and Sandra to get out of the car, and for Sandra to give her reflection a once-over in the back passenger window.

"Get over yourself," Rayette teased, and Patsy smiled. So far, making friends with Rayette and Sandra was happening naturally. They weren't Mitzy and Jane, but they made her laugh. And, even if only for a moment, to forget.

"No one is making you wait for me," Sandra said.

Patsy cleared her throat. "Um, Sandra . . . looks to me like your competition is already halfway to Gilbert by now." She pointed toward where Paulette made a beeline for the guest of honor.

"And from the looks of things," Rayette added, "Paulette isn't the only one vying to get his attention this afternoon."

Sandra threw her hands out; they fell along her sides. "Who am I kidding? I look like a kid next to these girls."

Rayette leaned over and spoke from the side of her mouth. "That's because you are a kid."

Patsy gave Sandra's arm a pat. "That's okay, Sandra. Our turn at the Gilberts of the world will come soon enough."

Rayette sighed. "Now you're both making me sick."

The girls started toward the festivities. Patsy inhaled the sweet scent of barbecue from an outdoor pit. "Smells heavenly," she said in an attempt to calm her nerves.

Meeting new people had never been one of her strong suits.

However, there was one who was not so new. And he recognized her, even standing in Rayette's shadow.

Gilbert Milstrap walked toward them, having dislodged himself from a small crowd of people—mostly female—whom Patsy assumed to be his friends. His head was cocked to one side. He wore a pair of what looked like comfortable baggy pants and a short-sleeved cotton shirt he'd rolled up around his biceps. "Little sister?"

Patsy had to admit she could see why so many of the girls were crazy about him. Even for an older boy, he was attractive in an offbeat kind of way.

"Yes, it's me." She put on her widest smile.

He grinned back. "Well, what do you know?" He turned to his friends. "Hey, everyone! Let me introduce you to a sweet young lady who had the misfortune to ride the bus home with me . . ."

And with those words, Patsy's acceptance into the world of young Trinity began.

Before the day was over, she'd met several of the boys and girls she would attend school with the next day and a few of the town's adults. The unasked questions—who was she and why was she coming to live with the Buchwalds—were written on all their faces. But no one outright asked, and Patsy didn't volunteer the information.

The day was fun, all in all. She played badminton until she was breathless. Enjoyed kicking off her shoes and wading in the shallow part of the creek. Threw away all notions of ladylike eating and ate mounds of barbecue and nibbled away at corn on the cob until she thought her stomach could hold nothing else. But then the ice cream churns came out and she ended up delighting in a large bowl of homemade peach.

On the way home she laid her head back against the seat and stared out the window at the graying sky. For the most part, the stars were not yet visible, but a slice of the moon could already be clearly seen. Just below its bottom tip, a lone star winked. She wondered if, maybe, her mother was looking up at the same sky, seeing the same moon and star. And she thought of her brothers, who were bathed by now and getting ready for bed.

"Had fun?" Rayette asked, her body twisted to face the backseat.

Patsy nodded. "A lot of fun. Thank you for asking me."

"One thing's for sure," Paulette added from behind the driver's wheel. "No one is a stranger for long in Trinity."

Patsy could see that. And she was pleased with it. Still, and in spite of having had such a good time, that night Patsy pressed her face into the sweet-smelling pillow of her new bed and cried inconsolably. The two nights before, when she hadn't been too tired to think, she tried to tell herself she was just away from home for a little while. That she was visiting relatives. Or at summer camp. And that soon enough she'd return to her mother and little brothers.

But that day, the mixture of having had such fun with her new friends and the questionable looks of the adult townspeople affirmed the sick feeling inside Patsy. She was never going home again.

This was home now, and this family—the Buchwalds—was her new family. And whatever it took to forget where and who she came from, she'd do it. Brick by brick, she'd build a new life for herself.

Here in Trinity, South Carolina.

6

Spring 1948

Life in Trinity came easier to Patsy than she could have expected. She made loads of friends at school, and her social life—centered mostly around the church on Sundays and Wednesday nights, matinees on Saturdays, and school activities during the week—kept her busy. Her home life was filled with warmth and laughter. Though she was not formally adopted, within months of moving in with the Buchwalds, she took their surname as her own. There had been no talk of it. No discussion whatsoever. After Christmas break and a return to school in 1947, Patsy simply signed her name on her first homework assignment as PATSY SWEENY BUCHWALD. She soon dropped the SWEENY, even though it remained on her report cards, which were filled with satisfactory marks.

No one in Trinity questioned her about the name change. She supposed that, to anyone who knew the family, it made sense. Who wouldn't want to be a Buchwald? Mam *loved*. She touched. She stroked Patsy's arm as she spoke with her and even held her hand when a word of discipline—though rare—was necessary. Papa was a firm force of strength and

61

a rock of faith. Patsy thought him the wisest man she'd ever known, yet deep inside him stirred gleeful fun and mischief.

And Lloyd, her full-blooded brother, held the personality of both parents. His adoration of his older sister could not be denied, nor his boyish charm and intellect. He and Patsy often took long walks down pathways snaking throughout their property, and it was during these times he shared with her his thoughts of being adopted and his dreams of the future.

"Mam says," he told her during one such walk, "that most adopting parents don't like to tell their children that they weren't born to them." He reached forward and snapped a low-lying twig barring their way, then proceeded to peel off its leaves, one at a time. "But Mam says that our house is never to have secrets. That secrets can destroy a home. A family."

"So you always knew . . . you've always known."

"Yep. As far back as I can remember." He pointed toward the straw-laden path. "Be careful right up there. There's a dip that can trip you up."

Patsy smiled at her brother. "You must have spent a lot of time in these woods."

He shrugged. "When you're an only child—or at least you might as well be—you tend to learn to play by yourself. And learn to like it too." He squinted up at her. "Tell me about my brothers. Our mother . . ."

The request was painful to fulfill, but Patsy complied. She always did when Lloyd came to her, wanting to know stories of their familial history. She told him what she knew—stories of their parents' love for each other, their father's death and mother's struggle afterward—and when he asked questions without answers, she stated simply, "That I don't know. I clearly don't."

It seemed to be enough.

Patsy turned fifteen in the spring of '48. Mam allowed her to invite her three best friends—Rayette Peachman, Sandra Bedwell, and Janice Milstrap—for a Friday night spend-the-night party. Papa grilled hot dogs, and later on around a bonfire, the girls made s'mores and drank Coca-Colas while Lloyd and one of his buddies pestered them mercilessly.

For the past year and a half, Patsy had done everything with Rayette, Sandra, and Janice. They weren't allowed to date yet—not even sixteen-year-old Rayette—but they spent plenty of time talking about the day when they finally could. That night around the bonfire was no exception.

"The spring cotillion is in two weeks, girls," Rayette announced. "Everyone got their dress?"

Patsy nodded. She and Mam had spent hours working on hers, sewn from a Butterick pattern, made with spaghetti straps and from the most baby of peach taffeta. The full skirt was tied off at the waist with a wide satin bow in the back; it made a lovely swishing sound when Patsy walked around the house wearing it and practiced her dance steps with Papa. "Mine is in my closet," she said. "I can show it to you when we go inside."

Sandra lay back on the grass and drew her knees toward her chest before crossing her ankles. "If only we were allowed to be invited by a boy to the dance. All this 'come alone, leave alone' stuff is so boring."

Janice giggled. "You are so dramatic, Sandra, if not totally boy crazy." Her wavy blonde tresses swung about her shoulders and she tipped her head sideways. "I know you've gotten over my brother—he told me he hasn't gotten a single letter from you in three months. So spill . . . who in Trinity are you hoping to dance with?"

Sandra cut her eyes teasingly at Janice. "Hmm . . . Donny West . . . Michael Donaldson . . . Marvin Coates—"

"Marvin Coates!" the girls all said at once.

Sandra pushed herself up and onto her elbows with her sneakered feet flat on the dark grass. "What?" She pouted. "I think he's cute."

"Cute?" Rayette spat with a roll of her eyes. "He's all . . . I don't know . . . brainy."

Patsy tucked her legs up under her, hating to see Marvin, who was certainly nice enough, being made a spectacle of. "But in an adorable Cary Grant sort of way."

"Thank you, Patsy," Sandra said with a nod.

"Well, if anyone is interested," Janice interjected, "my brother is coming home, and for good this time."

"Really?" Rayette said. "I'll have to tell Paulette. I mean, she's practically engaged to be married now, but her feelings for Gilbert very well could stop the wedding." She grinned. "Now wouldn't that be just the scandal of the year."

It seemed to Patsy she was always laughing when she was with her friends, and she did so now. "Oh, Rayette. Don't say such things. It's very obvious Paulette loves . . . what's his name, did you say?"

This time they all laughed until finally Sandra stood and said, "Come on, Patsy. Let's go inside so you can show us your dress."

They gathered their s'more-making supplies and kicked out the fire before heading toward the looming house, which had grown dark in the shadows of evening. Rayette and Sandra walked ahead of Janice and Patsy, who said, "When will Gilbert be home?"

"In two weeks. He's hoping to be back in time for the dance. Principal Marksfield asked Gilbert to come. Even though he's older and all, he thought it would be nice to have him as a guest of honor."

"Because he's a local hero."

"Mmmhmm."

"So what will he do now that he won't be in the Air Force anymore?"

"He'll go to work at Daddy's service station. Gilbert is a wonderful mechanic. You know that's what he did in the Air Force. Mechanics."

Patsy nodded but said nothing. Being a mechanic was an okay job, yet she couldn't help but think it was something of a letdown after being in the Air Force. Then again, she thought as she entered the back door and stepped into the kitchen still warm from the evening meal, maybe it would be nothing short of sweet relief.

———————

A major difference in living with the Buchwalds rather than with her mother was attending Miss Grace's School of Charm. Miss Grace Brindamour, who lived in the biggest and certainly the nicest home in Trinity, was not only the owner of the etiquette school but also a dear friend of Mam's. After Patsy had settled in, Miss Grace insisted that Mam enroll her. Not that Patsy minded; her new friends also attended the twice-a-week classes. There, in the heavily decorated Victorian rooms, they learned about poise and posture—how to sit, how to walk, how to stand—voice and diction, proper introductions, dance skills ("And none of that new swing dancing, boys and girls"), party and dining etiquette, and the loveliness of true, inner beauty. Though Miss Grace taught all the best boys and girls of Trinity, most classes were not integrated, male and female. The element of male to female charisma was not something Miss Grace liked to talk about, much less allude to. Occasionally, however, she ventured into the fragile territory of propriety, and when she did, she was clearly uncomfortable.

These lessons always left Patsy and her friends in fits of giggles the following day.

The spring cotillion was an annual event that brought Miss Grace's lessons of proper social event planning to the gymnasium for the middle- and upperclassmen of Trinity School. Months had been spent in preparation. Weeks were spent turning the athletic feel of the gym to a more subtle, romantic setting.

The young ladies of Trinity were expected to arrive to the cotillion in formal dress, young men in coat and tie.

While Patsy had been excited to go the first year, this year she was beside herself. She was nearly sixteen now, and Mam had said she could wear lipstick and a little of her perfume.

"Once you are dressed," Mam said the afternoon of the dance, "then you can apply the lipstick. But spray the scent while you are still in your slip so there's no chance of staining the material of your dress."

Lipstick and perfume . . .

She refused to have any thoughts of her mother. This wasn't about Bernice Liddle. It was about going to a dance wearing *Mam's* lipstick. *Mam's* perfume.

Butterflies skittered inside Patsy. She could hardly believe how happy she was. That afternoon, she took a leisurely bath and dusted herself with talcum powder. In Mam and Papa's bedroom, she sat on the vanity stool and worked her nylons up first one leg, then the other before clamping them with garters. She stepped into the nylon half-slip—the one Mam had bought just for tonight, peach with a butterfly embroidered at the hip and the chiffon crystal pleating from the calves to the ankles. That done, she called out to Mam, who was waiting in the hallway to take her hair down from the tight pin curls.

She faced the mirror. Mam hummed as she rhythmically worked each of the bobby pins from her hair.

Patsy blinked several times. Though she tried not to think of her mother, she couldn't help but know that Bernice Liddle had been robbed of this moment. This joy. This bonding of mother and daughter.

Not by Mam, of course. By Mr. Liddle. But Mama had allowed it to happen.

Patsy pushed a breath from her lungs.

She would not allow herself to think . . .

"Patsy?"

"I'm okay," Patsy said past the knot forming in her throat.

"There are tears in your eyes." She placed her hands on the round of Patsy's shoulders and squeezed. "You miss your mother, don't you."

Patsy nodded; it was the only thing she knew to do. She'd conditioned herself not to talk about it, not with words. She couldn't tell Mam—couldn't tell anyone—how she really felt, the anger with her mother . . . a woman she missed so much. A woman lost to her.

"It's normal, I think," Mam said with another squeeze. "Your mother should be standing behind you now, not me."

To some degree, Mam's sentiments expressed what Patsy had been thinking. There was not an ounce of jealousy in Phyllis Buchwald, and for that Patsy was grateful. Neither was there a hint of condemnation in her voice. She had always been completely comfortable in her role with her new daughter, albeit different from the role she played with Lloyd. From the moment Patsy moved into the Buchwald home,

Mam seemed to understand her every emotion. She never pushed Patsy to talk about them, never tried to sway her from one way to another. She was just there to listen if and when Patsy wanted to talk, which was rarely.

Patsy took in another deep breath, exhaled, and allowed her eyes to meet the large bespectacled ones in the mirror's reflection. "You are my mother, Mam," she said.

Mam squeezed again. "You are a dear," she said. She reached over her for the wide-tooth comb and began to style the swirls of hair sitting atop Patsy's head. When she was done, Mam retrieved the dress from where it lay across the bed and brought it to the vanity. Patsy stood, stepped into the dress, and held out her arms while Mam zipped and tied.

When they were done and the lipstick had been carefully applied, Mam led Patsy to where Papa and Lloyd waited. Lloyd gave a whistle but Papa said, "Well, aren't you a beauty."

Patsy felt herself grow warm under the adoration, but she turned a full circle so her brother and father could get the full effect of the dress.

"Yes, ma'am," Papa said. "A real beauty."

Mam draped a cream-colored lace shawl over Patsy's shoulders before handing her a small clutch. "There will be someone at the cotillion to photograph, Grace said."

Patsy nodded. "Well, I guess I'm ready."

Papa stepped toward her and extended his arm. "Shall we go, dumplin'?"

Patsy placed her hand lightly between his wrist and elbow, just as she'd been taught by Miss Grace. "Thank you, Papa," she said. She blew a kiss to her brother and mother and, with her father escorting her toward his car, left through the front door.

7

On the far side of the gymnasium, round tables covered in white linen were flanked by six chairs each. On the other side, an orchestra sat and played social dance tunes of the day, songs like Jo Stafford's "Ivy" and Doris Day's "It's Magic." Along one wall were tables dotted with small plates of even smaller delicacies and oversized bowls filled with dreamy punch. In center court, couples danced according to Miss Grace's rules and under the eagle eyes of a large number of chaperones.

Patsy couldn't remember ever having such a delightful evening as this one. Her dance card stayed full; even as she stepped lightly with one boy, another would politely step in. To her surprise, one of those interruptions was by none other than Gilbert Milstrap.

"I could hardly believe it was you," he said as he led her, step-by-step, across the floor. Nancy Roberts, a local songbird, sang along as the band played "Now Is the Hour."

Gilbert no longer wore a uniform. Handsome as he'd been before, he looked simply adorable in civilian clothes. His hair had grown longer than the last time she'd seen him, but the twinkle in his eye was the same.

"Janice said you were coming back," she said, "and that you would be working for your daddy."

"That's right."

"Does it feel funny? Leaving the Air Force behind and working for your father?"

"Not so funny that I'm not grateful."

"To be home and working or to the Air Force?"

"Both." His dimples deepened as his eyes scanned her face. "I simply cannot believe how much you've grown up."

She giggled; she couldn't help herself. "It happens, you know, when you leave and stay away for so long. Children grow up."

"That'll teach me not to stay away from home so long."

Patsy looked beyond the edge of his shoulder just as Nancy's voice crooned, "When you return you'll find me waiting here . . ."

"Looks like I have," he said.

Her eyes returned to his. "Have what?"

"Found you waiting here."

Patsy wondered if she blushed. She certainly felt that she should have. There was something in the tone of his voice that set her nerves on fire. She felt like both a silly schoolgirl and a near-woman all at the same time. Nervous, she glanced around, wondering if anyone at the dance was watching them. She hoped they were and worried they might be.

"Maybe you should . . ." She couldn't finish her sentence.

Gilbert peered down at her. "Maybe I should what?"

Patsy shrugged. No, she couldn't say it. Shouldn't say it . . .

He smiled broadly. "Go on. Say what you were going to say."

She took a deep breath. The song was over and the couples around them were clapping. Gilbert and she politely did so too.

"Ladies and gentlemen," the band leader announced, "we're going to take a ten-minute break. Enjoy the punch and other refreshments and we'll see you back on the dance floor in a few."

"Good timing," Gilbert said, cupping her elbow with his hand. "Let's step outside and get some air."

Patsy stopped short. "Oh, I couldn't. I mean, Miss Grace would have a hissy fit."

He spoke directly in her ear. "Believe me, Miss Grace has plenty of chaperones out there standing guard. The Air Force would do well to take notes from her." He paused long enough to look into her eyes. "Besides, haven't you heard? I'm a local hero; I can do no wrong."

Patsy glanced toward the door. Some of her fellow students were leaving, while others were making a beeline for the refreshment tables. "Well, since you say there are chaperones . . ."

"There are." He placed a hand over his heart. "My word as a gentleman."

They stepped outside to the grassy area just beyond the wide gymnasium doors. The cool air of night wrapped itself around her, traveled down her slender arms, and she shivered. "Here," Gilbert said. He slipped out of his suit coat and placed it gently over her shoulders. "Better?"

Patsy nodded. She looked behind where they stood and saw the watchful stares of three chaperones. She smiled; one of them nodded back. She laced her fingers together and allowed her hands to rest in the folds of her skirt.

"Are you going to tell me?" Gilbert asked from next to her.

She turned her face toward his. "Tell you what?"

"What you started to say in there?"

She shook her head before returning her attention to the dark grasses in front of them. "It's silly. I have no right to tell you . . . to say . . ."

71

Gilbert nudged her shoulder with his. "Just say it."

"I was just thinking you might want to dance with . . . I don't know . . . someone like Miss Brinson."

This time, he turned to face her. "Miss Brinson?"

She nodded. "Our home ec teacher."

"Yeah, I know who Miss Brinson is. I actually went to school with her. Played ball with her brother, Whitey. But why in the world would you think I'd want to dance with Loretta Brinson?"

She looked up at him. "Well, she's pretty."

"She's all right."

"And she's single."

"So is Miss Grace and you don't see me asking her to dance."

Patsy swatted at Gilbert's arm. "Shhh . . . Gilbert, that's not nice." But she laughed anyway.

He laughed along with her. "Okay. So aside from being a teacher and pretty and single . . . why, pray tell, should I want to dance with her?"

Patsy felt heat rise to her cheeks. "Well, she *is* more your age. Like you said, you grew up with her. This is her first year teaching, you know."

The playfulness in Gilbert's face fell away, and Patsy immediately regretted her words.

"I said something wrong . . ."

"Nah."

"Yes. Yes, I did. I'm sorry . . . I just thought . . ."

Then he smiled again. "Look, little sister, I think I'm old enough and I've been around enough to know who I want to dance with." He touched the tip of her nose with his fingertip. "And right now, I want to dance with you. I looked across that wide gymnasium, and not one girl in there can hold a candle to what I saw when I saw you."

Patsy's head tilted a little to the right. "Really?"

"So, do a war hero a favor, will you?"

Patsy nodded, too floored to say another word.

Gilbert reached for the dance card dangling from her wrist. He took a moment to study it before slipping it over her hand and then handing it to her. "For the rest of the evening, make mine the only name on this card."

Patsy felt she could have slept the day away, but it being a Sunday, she was "up and at 'em" by seven a.m. The breakfast table conversation included wanting moment-by-moment details of the previous night's events, but Patsy remained vague, saying only that it was "dreamy."

Mam and Papa smiled at each other, Lloyd shrugged, and Patsy sighed into her oatmeal. She couldn't wait to get to church. To see Rayette and Sandra. They would know right off if her dancing with Gilbert had caused a stir within their peer group. Or with the teachers and other adults.

And, heaven forbid, with Miss Grace. If that were the case, Miss Grace would make a beeline for Mam before Sunday school. Patsy would probably be forbidden from doing anything with her friends. Instead, she'd have to endure "a talk" with her parents. The very thought made her shudder.

"Patsy?" Mam said. "You okay?"

Patsy looked across the round table. "What? Oh. Yes, ma'am. I'm fine." She looked at the bowl of lumpy hot cereal sprinkled with cinnamon and sugar, raisins, and roasted nuts. "But not really hungry. May I be excused?"

Mam nodded. "Yes, you may."

A couple of hours later, Patsy met Rayette and Sandra outside the church.

"Spill, spill, spill," Rayette demanded as soon as they'd

73

pulled her from hearing distance of Patsy's parents and little brother.

She feigned ignorance. "There's nothing to tell."

Sandra folded her slender arms. "I should be furious with you, you know." Then she smiled. "But you're one of my best friends, so I'm choosing to forgive you."

Patsy smiled back. "I don't know what happened. He just asked me to dance and I—"

"Couldn't say no?" Rayette offered.

Patsy shook her head. "Could you have?"

"Probably not. But, as you said to Sandra once upon a Sunday not too long ago, isn't he a little old for you?"

Patsy glanced at her watch and thought back to the afternoon she first stumbled into Gilbert Milstrap. In those days, they were—she was—too young for a man Gilbert's age. But she was fifteen now. Barely, but she felt eons away from the little girl who'd sat crying on a bus headed for Trinity. "We'd best get moving toward Sunday school or Mam will want to know what's going on."

The girls started walking toward the large brick building.

"I take it," Rayette said, "that you aren't going to answer me about the age difference."

"Seven years, four months, twenty days." Patsy, who had been walking between her friends, stopped at the doorway to the Sunday school wing. "I did the math as soon as he told me he was a Thanksgiving baby."

"And when was that?" Sandra asked, opening the door for them.

The trio stepped through. A throng of other churchgoers were milling about the hallway. Patsy made a shushing noise before mumbling, "Last night. In between dances." She inhaled quickly. "Miss Grace just walked into her classroom."

74

She pulled her friends over to the left side wall for the smallest semblance of privacy. "Listen, you two, did you hear any mumblings from the teachers or Miss Grace last night?"

Rayette and Sandra exchanged glances before nodding. "Oh yeah. Miss Grace's frown was deeper than Old Coopers Lake."

It was Patsy's turn to frown. "Wonderful. I'm sure she'll speak to Mam. Mam will talk to Papa and Papa will tell me I can't see Gilbert again."

"Again?" The girls said in unison.

Rayette's face turned serious. "Patsy, you can't *see* Gilbert Milstrap."

"Why ever not?"

"Because, he'll tarnish your reputation," Sandra answered. "He's too old. You're too young. Besides, we're not allowed to date yet, remember? Do you honestly think a man who has been in the Air Force is going to be okay with doing stuff in groups only? Church socials and the like?"

Patsy hadn't thought that far. She looked at the toes of her black patent Sunday shoes. "Probably not," she mumbled as the Sunday school bell rang.

"Come on," Rayette said, pulling on her arm. "We've got to go to class." She looped her arm in Patsy's as they stepped toward the center of the hallway. "Listen, Patsy, don't worry about it. Miss Grace will talk to Mam, no doubt about it. You'll get a lecture and then it'll all be over."

Patsy looked up at the pretty redhead. "But what if Gilbert *does* ask me out?"

"Tell him you can't date. That simple."

But it wasn't that simple and Patsy knew it. If Gilbert asked her out, she'd *want* to go. Granted, she wouldn't be allowed to date him, but what *if* he wanted to do things with her and her friends? What *if* he was okay with church socials and school functions?

It was a big "what if," but . . . what *if*?

The big crisis of the day was not that Miss Grace told Mam about Patsy dancing with Gilbert; she never had the chance.

Gilbert Milstrap showed up at Trinity Methodist Church between Sunday school and church. As Patsy and her Sunday school classmates rounded the corner of the building in order to head up the stretch of steps to the sanctuary, Patsy spied him standing near the marquee. He spotted her too; he gave a quick wave, a deep grin, and walked right toward her.

She broke from her pals to meet him halfway in the midst of all the good members of Trinity Methodist, including Mam and Papa. Patsy threw a momentary silent prayer up to God, asking that nothing happen within the next few minutes to embarrass her.

"Hey, little sister," Gilbert said when she'd reached him. He looked handsome, dressed pretty much as he'd been the night before, in a dark blue loose-fitting suit, complete with a double-breasted coat.

"Gilbert," she breathed out. "What are you doing here?"

He continued smiling. "That's a fine way to welcome a visitor to your church."

"But you're a Baptist."

With that he nearly roared. One of her fellow church members walked over and shook Gilbert's hand. Patsy hardly noticed who it was. She heard, "Gilbert, how are you doing?" followed by Gilbert's answer, "Fine, fine," but her eyes never left the young man's face.

"Gilbert," she said again.

But before she could say another word, Lloyd was at her side. "Mam says come on in, Patsy."

Lloyd had grown a lot in the last two years; he and Patsy stood shoulder to shoulder now. Patsy turned to him. "Tell her I'll be right there."

Lloyd didn't move. He just stared from Patsy to Gilbert and then back to Patsy again.

"Go," Patsy demanded.

Lloyd scooted off and Gilbert chuckled. "Okay, so are you going to invite me in?"

She glanced toward the doors of the church. "Uh, yeah. But I can't sit with you, Gilbert."

They started toward the steps. Only a few stragglers remained outside, and most of them were staring openly.

"Why not?" he asked her.

"Because . . ."

"Do you sit with your family or . . ."

"Or. I sit with Sandra and Rayette and a couple of the other girls from school. You'd stick out like a sore thumb."

He nodded. They reached the top of the steps. After walking across the landing, he opened the front door for her, then held it for the others coming behind them. Patsy didn't wait for his chivalry to be over; she kept her path straight, walking through the swinging doors into the sanctuary and down the aisle to slip into the pew where her friends waited.

"What in the world?" Sandra whispered.

Patsy shook her head. "Shh . . . don't say another word." She stared straight ahead, painfully aware that her friends were looking behind them and that Gilbert's footsteps were shuffling up the aisle. "Oh, my goodness," she whispered.

The steps stopped short. A rustling in the pew behind her and the giggles of her friends told her that Gilbert was sitting there. For the remainder of the service, that knowledge was never far from her eardrum. She heard him as he sang the three hymns, the rich baritone of his voice. He sang as though he were projecting from the choir, drowning out everyone on the right side of the church. When the pastor prayed and had said his "Amen," Gilbert repeated the word. He recited the Apostles' Creed with boldness of conviction. When Brother Michael acknowledged his presence, Gilbert said, "Appreciate it, sir." And when the pastor gave his sermon, Patsy heard the rhythm of Gilbert breathing.

It was the most marvelously uncomfortable hour of her life.

When the service was over, Patsy stood, turned ever so slowly to say something to him, but he was gone. He'd walked halfway down the aisle and was shaking hands with her father. There was an exchange of words that left Mam looking positively grief-stricken. Lloyd's eyes were round and full of mischief behind her.

"What do you think he's saying?" Rayette asked.

"I have no idea," she answered, "but I'm sure I'll find out soon enough."

And she did. Gilbert asked Papa if they could speak outside for a few moments. Once outside, he asked if he could come by the house later that afternoon. When Papa asked what his visit was about, he valiantly said, "I'd like to spend more time with Patsy."

According to Gilbert's version, which Patsy heard sometime later, Papa expressed that he could see no possible reason for a twentysomething man just back from the Air Force to want to spend time with a fifteen-year-old child.

A child.

It was the last thing Patsy felt like, but everything she was.

Patsy spent that afternoon with her parents and brother, riding the dusty roads in the traditional Sunday ride. Along the way, Papa stopped at the same bus stop where she'd first encountered his kind face. He bought a banana popsicle for Lloyd and an ice cream sandwich for her. Patsy wasn't hungry for it, but she ate it to keep it from melting all over herself. All she wanted to do was go home, lie on her bed, and think this whole Gilbert thing through. To daydream her way into the fairy tale or to nap her way through the nightmare. Instead, she sat in the backseat of the car and watched as the Southern landscape passed by her window in a blur. By the time they'd gotten home, she'd pretty much figured that, considering Papa's firm countenance earlier, Gilbert would give up on seeing her again. After all, there were plenty of young women of a more suitable age who'd give their right arm to date Gilbert Milstrap.

That night, Gilbert showed up for Sunday night services.

8

If Gilbert was nothing else, he was persistent. Over the course of the next few weeks and months, whenever Patsy went to Saturday matinees with her friends (a favorite weekend pastime), Gilbert was there. During impromptu Sunday afternoon football games with the gang, Gilbert showed up. He naturally played quarterback (after all, if he could fight in a war, he could surely throw a football) and always for the team Patsy was on. During school events to which the public was invited, there he was. And in all this, he made no effort to hide the intent of his presence.

The more time that went by, the more comfortable Patsy became with each arrival. She found herself, by that fall, looking over her shoulder for him at football games. He didn't come to Sunday morning services after the first time, but he was there for evening services and Wednesday night suppers. Patsy saved him a seat each week. By the time Christmas of '48 rolled around, it was understood that if you saw one of them, you saw the other.

Except, that is, during school and working hours. Then, Patsy was evermore the proverbial student and Gilbert was

80

hard at work, mostly figuring out a way to make his father's business more successful than it already was.

"Remember," he said to her as they came out of a Saturday matinee showing of *Every Girl Should Be Married*, which finally made it to Trinity in January of '49, "when you and I rode the bus together. That first night when you came to Trinity?"

She nodded, squinting as her eyes adapted to the graying sunlight as the afternoon eased toward four o'clock. "I remember."

"And of course you know the station where the bus let us out is Pop's." He slipped his hands into his loose-fitting pants as he shuffled alongside her. The rest of the gang ambled together in small giggling clusters ahead of them. Patsy suspected Gilbert held back deliberately, for the sake of his much-sought-after alone time with her.

She clasped her hands behind her back. "Yes. From the looks of things, seems like y'all have been doing all right too." It was a natural reaction—whether in the school bus, with her friends, or riding along with Papa and Mam—Patsy's head turned toward Milstrap's. There were always cars waiting to be serviced, parked in the three bays to be worked on, and clusters of teens hanging around the soda chest outside the front door.

"We've been doing just fine," Gilbert said. "But, I've been talking to Pops about adding on to the station, you know. Adding a café like the one in Darien."

Patsy gave him a sideways glance.

"But the café wouldn't just be for the Trailways patrons. Oh no . . . Think about it, Patsy—if the soda in the chest outside draws some of the older kids to the station, what will the café do? I'll tell you," he said before she had a chance to react. "People get off the bus and they're hungry. But people in town are also hungry. If the food is good enough, it'll draw patrons from right here in Trinity."

They came to a cross street and stopped for traffic. A winter's breeze skipped around the corner of an Allied store. From down the block, the tantalizing aroma of burgers and fries found its way to Patsy; she naturally inhaled and smiled. "But there's already a café in Trinity," she said as she brought the collar of her cashmere coat toward her ears to ward off the cold. "Just smell."

The two stepped off the curb together as Gilbert continued. "Yeah, I know. But I've got a plan for more home-cooked types of meals."

"And doesn't the bus stop here near midnight? Who wants to eat then?" They stepped up and on to the next curb. Peripherally Patsy watched their reflections pass in the high display windows of Mullican's Jewelry Store.

"Oh, sure . . . on the way up, it does. But on the reverse route it stops at four in the afternoon."

"I forgot about on the way back."

"That's because by four in the afternoon, sweet thing, you're sitting at Mam's kitchen table doing your homework and eating oatmeal raisin cookies."

Patsy frowned. How could he possibly know that?

"I know," Gilbert said, as though reading her mind, "because that's what Janice is doing about that same time."

Patsy stopped in front of Dayton's Barbershop, just under the red, white, and blue spinning barber pole. She jumped as the bell jingled, the door opened, and Mr. Dayton stepped out carrying a broom and the strong scent of talcum mixed with aftershave. "Mr. Milstrap," he said to Gilbert. "Looks like you could use my services."

"Mr. Dayton," Gilbert responded as they shook hands. He cut his eyes toward the mop of curls falling over his forehead. "Yessir, I know I do. Been busy lately."

Mr. Dayton, an ironically mostly bald man with thick arched brows, turned to Patsy. "Miss Buchwald, how are you this afternoon?"

Patsy beamed. "Fine, Mr. Dayton. You're here late for a Saturday." She looked toward the way they'd come. "We were just leaving the movies."

"I work late one Saturday a month," he said by way of explanation. He held his broom a little higher. "Now I've got to get my portion of the sidewalk swept before I can go home to Mrs. Dayton and supper."

"We'll move along," Gilbert said knowingly. "Good to see you again, Mr. Dayton." He took Patsy by the elbow to guide her forward.

Patsy's heart sank and soared at the same time. Gilbert rarely touched her, but when he did . . . something magical happened inside her. At the same time, she hoped her simple explanation of having been at the movies would be enough for Mr. Dayton, who was known for two things: a good haircut and good gossip. Betty's Beauty Boutique had nothing on Dayton's Barbershop when it came to idle chitchat.

Gilbert's hand slipped from her elbow as he continued, "So, my thought is . . . hey now . . ." Gilbert stopped, pointed to the burger joint, and said, "I noticed some of your friends went inside while we were talking to Mr. Dayton. Want something to eat? Ice cream soda?"

Patsy wasn't hungry, really. The popcorn and cola in the movie had taken care of that. But she wanted to spend more time with Gilbert, even if it meant having to do so with everyone else hanging around. "Sure."

Add-a-Scoop Malt Shoppe buzzed with conversation running high above the jukebox against the far wall. Notes and lyrics from Glenn Miller's "Don't Sit under the Apple Tree" bounced between the parlor tables and sweetheart chairs and over the thickly padded dining booths. Rayette, Sandra, and the rest of their gang were sitting in the last booth on the right side of the L-shaped room. Rayette waved at them as though guiding them through the fog of a storm. Patsy took a step forward, but Gilbert stopped her by grabbing her elbow again.

"Can we sit somewhere else? Just the two of us? I'd really like to tell you what I've been thinking about."

Patsy's eyes searched his. They were usually so full of mischief, but right now they were intense, pleading. She took a risk if she sat with him. True, she was almost sixteen, but she had a feeling that even after her birthday, her parents wouldn't allow her to date Gilbert unchaperoned. But, what was the big deal? They were in a roomful of people, any one who could call Papa or Mam at a moment's notice. And if someone did, she was sure to be on restriction from the movies for a month of Saturdays.

Still . . . there were those eyes.

She nodded.

Gilbert's neck craned to look around. There were two bar stools free at the counter, but he seemed to ignore them. Just when Patsy despaired that he'd have no choice, a man and woman stood from one of the parlor tables in the center of the room. Gilbert quickly guided Patsy toward it, even as the busboy cleared it of thick white plates and tall soda glasses.

As Gilbert held her chair for her, Patsy caught a glance at Rayette. Her mouth hung open like it was catching flies but snapped shut when Patsy pressed her own lips together to keep from laughing.

After they'd ordered (Gilbert insisted on something more than just an ice cream soda), Patsy said, "Okay. So tell me what you're dying to tell me."

Gilbert leaned over, resting his forearms on the white wrought iron table. "I've been talking to Pops. We're thinking about—if I can convince him of the logic in all this—we're thinking about adding on to the station."

"A café?"

He grinned his toothy grin. "Yes."

"For the patrons of the bus company *and* for the people here in Trinity."

His shoulders squared. "Yes!"

"And it will be different from this place . . ." she asked, looking around, "how?"

"I told you before, Pats. What do you have here? Burgers. Sandwiches. Ice cream sodas. Right?"

"Right. And don't forget the fries and onion rings." She'd no sooner said the words than their sodas were brought to the table.

Gilbert shifted in his seat like an anxious boy. "I know this woman named Martha. A Negro woman."

Patsy cocked her head. "How is it that you know her?" Rarely did whites and Negros know each other, especially in towns like Trinity, unless, of course, Martha was the Milstraps' maid.

"Her son and I were in service together."

Patsy was truly stunned now. How was it that all she'd heard about was the hero Gilbert Milstrap since she'd moved to town, but not one word about Martha's son? "Is he . . . Did he . . . ?"

"Die?"

Patsy nodded.

"No." He raised a hand as the clatter of someone dropping dishes in the kitchen startled the entire soda shop. From the jukebox, Hank Williams sang "A Mansion on the Hill." When things returned to normal, he continued, "I'm not here to talk about Buddy, Pats, nor the injustices in the world."

Patsy felt like she'd been slapped. "I didn't mean . . ."

"I'm sorry," he said before she had a chance to finish and just as their plates of sandwiches, fries, and quartered dill pickles were served. After the waitress walked away, they stared at each other as if not knowing what to do. Finally, Gilbert said, "It's just . . . you're right. You hear all about the white boy being a hero but nothing about Buddy." He shook his head as though to free it of the notion. "Do you mind if I pray?"

Patsy sighed in relief. "Yes, please."

Gilbert blessed the Giver of their good fortune and food loud enough for her to hear, but quietly enough that no one else could. When he was done, he said, "Eat up. I'll talk." But he popped a hot fry into his mouth anyway.

While she munched on a greasy grilled cheese sandwich, he told her, "I've already talked to Martha. She's willing to be the head cook. Meanwhile, Pops is looking into building on to the back of the station as well as the side where the café will be."

Patsy gulped a tangy swallow of cola. "Whatever for? The back of the station, I mean."

"I'll live back there."

Patsy's glass came down onto the table with such force she was surprised it didn't break. "Whatever for?" she repeated.

He laughed then. "I want my own place, Patsy. It won't be much, but it'll be a start. And that way I can oversee everything happening, both in the bays, the office, and the café."

"Won't that be a lot for you?" Patsy felt the sandwich set-tling heavy in her belly. If—and that was a big "if"—Papa and Mam said she could date Gilbert after she turned sixteen, she wasn't sure he'd even have the time. Then again, she figured, perhaps Gilbert Milstrap had grown tired of waiting for her to grow up. Maybe his interest in her had only been that of "big brother" all along.

But just as quickly, she thought, definitely not. Not the way he looked at her, followed after her. He'd even given her a pretty handkerchief with a *P* embroidered on it for Christmas; it had come as a complete surprise to her. She'd not bought him a thing.

"A lot for me?" He shook his head. "No. I've got plans, Pats. Big plans. I'm going to get this station up and going and then I'm going to franchise. Do you know what that means?"

Patsy gripped the paper napkin in her lap and twisted it. "Open another station?"

Gilbert leaned over the table again. "It's like you read my mind."

It was her turn to laugh. "Do you have a timetable?" She brought her hands back to the tabletop.

"I do. I figure by the start of summer we'll have the café up and going. I'll be moved in, out of my parents' place. Then . . . next summer . . ." His voice faded as his smile broadened.

"Then next summer, what?"

He unexpectedly slid his hands across the table and slipped them over hers. She thought to move but didn't. "I'm a patient man, Patsy Buchwald. I'm also a man who knows what he wants. And I want you . . ."

"Me?"

"To be my wife."

Miami, Florida

Seven-year-old Billy Liddle hated Miami. It was hot—even in winter—and Christmas among palm trees didn't seem like Christmas to him, in spite of the Scrabble board game Santa had brought.

His brother Harold loved it though. But that was just like Harold; he always managed to settle right in, no matter where they landed. He made friends easily. Before they'd even unloaded the moving boxes from the back of the truck their daddy had rented, Harold was surrounded by a bunch of neighborhood boys his age and was soon off and playing.

Not Billy; he stayed and helped their mama.

Mama cried a lot since they'd moved, and Billy thought he knew why. For one, when Patsy came home, she'd not be able to find them. Billy knew Mama missed Patsy something awful. She kept a framed photograph of her hidden in the same drawer she kept her underwear. Billy knew, 'cause he'd followed quietly behind her once and seen her taking it out.

He figured Daddy didn't know about the picture or he'd for sure tear it up and throw it away. Then there'd be another fight between him and Mama and no telling what would happen after that.

Another thing was that Mama didn't know anybody in Miami. Billy had been able to make at least one or two friends at school, but Mama had no one. No one, she told him once, but him and Harold.

Harold was hardly ever home, though. He was always off with his friends.

Daddy wasn't home much either. He said his job kept him plenty busy. Billy could tell that Harold missed Daddy, but Billy more dreaded the weekends Daddy came home than looked forward to them. Daddy yelled and hit on Mama all the time, even when she *didn't* deserve it.

Sometimes Daddy would whip Mama for the things she did when he wasn't even home. Things Daddy shouldn't have even known about except that Harold was tattling on her. Telling Daddy about her crying jags and getting paid to do it too.

Jags. That's what Daddy called Mama's crying spells.

One time, Billy asked Mama why she didn't at least go outside a little and try to meet some of the other mamas in the neighborhood. Mama said she just didn't have the time, but Billy had started to wonder if, with all the bruises she'd been sporting lately, she was afraid for the other mamas to know how often she misbehaved and Daddy had to whip her. Billy also wondered why Mama didn't try to be gooder.

Harold got whupped a time or two for staying out too late on Daddy's weekends home. Sometimes way past supper. But even Daddy's belt didn't seem to stop him none.

Billy worked real hard at not misbehaving, and it paid off. Daddy hardly ever spanked him. Billy was determined to be a good boy. And one day, a good man.

He just hoped that when he got all grown up, he'd meet a woman as pretty as his mama . . . and that she'd try real hard to be good too.

9

Spring 1949, Trinity, South Carolina

Since turning sixteen, Patsy had been anything but still. Papa and Mam employed her immediately after she received her driver's license so she could drive the delivery truck, the ever-faithful 1939 Ford Papa had picked her up in years before. While she enjoyed being a part of the family business, she especially liked the getting paid part, which meant having enough cash to buy nylons to her heart's content, and pocket change for going to the movies or to Add-a-Scoop afterward. But she knew her parents' real intent was to keep her time so consumed, she didn't have so much as a minute for seeing Gilbert.

Fat chance.

If anything, the busyness only encouraged them to find more creative ways to see each other. They'd already withstood the sideward glances of Trinity's finest citizens and the hard stares down Miss Grace's prim nose. And Patsy had heard enough of the gossip and innuendos about the difference in their ages. So when it came to Mam and Papa's deliberate antics, she saw them as just another hurdle on the track field of love.

Not that Patsy wanted to hurt her parents; after all, they'd been good to her since her arrival three years earlier. But she knew, deep down, that in spite of the age difference, Gilbert Milstrap was the man for her. And needing a "real father" had nothing to do with it.

"Remember, Mam," she said one afternoon as Mam tried to dissuade Patsy from seeing Gilbert even in group settings, "that Laura Ingalls Wilder and her husband were years apart in age. And look how wonderful that turned out."

Mam, whom Patsy was helping pull fresh-scented laundry from the line, only frowned over a linen sheet in response.

Papa was a little more verbal. He reminded her that she'd been sent to them for safekeeping, that she'd been a model daughter and even in this she was respectful, but that he thought life had so much more to offer her than to be the wife of a grease monkey.

His words, not Patsy's.

"Papa, you may not know this, but my father—my biological father—was older than my mother. And my mother was just crazy in love with him. If he'd not died so young in life, I'm sure they would have grown old together, still just as in love."

Papa was sitting in his favorite chair in the parlor, chewing on the stem of his pipe. "Now, I'm going to say this as kindly as I know how, Patsy. Your parents, when they married—no matter how much in love they were—could not have predicted that your daddy would die young and that Ira Liddle would come into the picture. We plan one way, and sometimes life gives us something else."

Patsy knelt at his feet and cupped her hands—one on top of the other—over the pressed line creasing the pants at one of his knees. "That's true, Papa, but what about you and Mam? When you married, you were in love, right?"

Papa chuckled in answer.

"And you still are, right?"

Papa puffed a moment on the aromatic tobacco before saying, "I love her with all my heart, sugar foot. But we had a lot going for us from the start."

"Like what?" Patsy's curiosity piqued. Mam was very close-mouthed about her love story with Papa, always saying, "That's an old story for another day." But maybe Papa would give her even the tiniest of glimpses into what life and love had been like for them when they'd married.

"For one, we were the same age . . . or near about. We wanted the same things out of life." He tilted his head toward her. "We had the blessings of our families and friends. And we had a plan. Do you have a plan, Patsy?"

"Of course we do, Papa. Gilbert's work is going well. He's even talking about opening up a station and café in another town soon. And as soon as I graduate next year, we'll marry."

She watched Papa's chin rise in defense. "And reside where? In the back of the station?"

Patsy's shoulders sank. "Well, I figure by the time we say our 'I do's,' he'll have another place for us."

Papa's eyes held that all-knowing I've-got-this-one look. "And if he doesn't?"

Patsy felt herself grow warm with emotion. "Oh, Papa. I'd live in a paper bag with Gilbert, I love him so much."

She watched her father deflate. "Well, with that kind of attitude, what can I possibly say?"

"Indeed."

"However," he said, shifting and allowing himself one more puff of the pipe, "I will not give you my blessing, Patsy. I can't. It goes against everything I believe is right for you."

"Papa . . ." Her hands fell to the floor on both sides of her narrow hips. "You don't mean that."

He stood, towered over her. "I do. You won't get any sympathy from Mam either. She and I feel the same way. Gilbert is a good man, but he's not going to marry you come next summer."

The wedding was set for June 27, 1950, the last Saturday of the month. The weeks leading up to the day of their nuptials became a flurry of caps and gowns, followed by luncheons, teas, and bridal showers given in her honor. Mam had worked since February—when Gilbert placed a miniscule diamond ring on Patsy's finger—on designing all the floral arrangements, the bridal gown, and the bridesmaids' gowns, of which there were three: Rayette, Sandra, and Janice.

Mam created Patsy's gown from yards and yards of white on white Chantilly lace. The bodice featured a crossover style with gathered shoulders. The skirt was full—fuller than full—with layers of netting underneath, all settling in the newly popular tea length near her ankles.

Rayette insisted Patsy wear the highest high heels possible. "You're so short, after all," she said one afternoon during a planning meeting with the other bridesmaids, all gathered around Mam's kitchen table, with bridal and ladies magazines from DeSpain's Corner Drug fanned out before them. "We don't want to lose you in the crowd on your wedding day."

Patsy added high heels to her growing list of things to do and purchase. "Got it," she said. "I'll make sure Mam and I get them soon so I can break them in. I certainly don't want my feet pinched the whole day."

If Mam wasn't fully on board with the wedding, Papa barely hung on to the edge. But his firm resolve *not* to bless their union had been undone by Martha, Gilbert's cook, whose cuisine Papa had taken to for lunch and Saturday breakfasts with the church's men's group. "Not as good as my wife's, but close enough," he'd say.

Martha had become the happy couple's crusader. In her not-so-subtle way, she'd leave the hot kitchen for the back side of the serving counter just so she could give Papa her opinion.

"Whether I ask for it or not," Patsy overheard Papa telling Mam one evening. The two of them were enjoying an after-dinner cup of coffee in the living room while Patsy cleared the dining room table for Mam.

"And what does she say to you?"

Patsy lingered near the wide-open doorway leading to the foyer so she could hear as Papa humphed. "Just that 'those two young'uns are gon' do what they gon' do and you may as well give 'em yore blessins' or lose 'em in the process.'"

Patsy had to stifle a giggle at Papa trying to imitate the sassy old cook.

"'And when she brings those grandbabies into the world,'" Papa continued in his mimicry, "'then what you gon' do? Not see 'em? Pretends they don't exist?'"

"Martha makes a good point," Mam said. Patsy heard the gentle resting of cup against saucer. "Don't you think so, Patsy?" Mam asked, voice raised.

Patsy inhaled quickly, said, "I'm not listening," then moved along to the kitchen to finish her voluntary chores.

From that day on, Papa wasn't 100 percent pleased, but at least he wasn't hard-nosed against the wedding either.

To his chagrin, however, Patsy *would* be moving into the back of the garage with Gilbert. So, while Mam worked on the wedding dress, Patsy stitched frilly curtains and over-stuffed decorative pillows, hoping to change the four tiny rooms from a bachelor pad that reeked of motor oil to the sweet-smelling home of a young married couple.

A young married couple in love.

With the nuptials just two weeks away, Patsy sat cross-legged in the middle of her bed, staring at a lineup of the wedding party she'd jotted on a piece of paper and palm-pressed against the quilt.

Her maid of honor was Janice, of course, because she was Gilbert's sister. Gilbert had chosen his father as his best man.

Then came Rayette and Sandra as bridesmaids, with Terrance Swanson—an old classmate of Gilbert's—and Lloyd as groomsmen.

Papa, of course, would give her away.

Patsy closed her eyes and imagined hearing Brother Michael as he said, "Who gives this woman in marriage to this man?"

Her mother and I . . .

Her shoulders slumped forward. In the years since her arrival in Trinity, she'd become an expert of sorts at pushing any thoughts of her former life into the dusty corner of her brain, the one so perfectly shielded by a brick wall she'd created. She'd deliberately changed her name. She thought of Mam as her mother; Papa as her father. Lloyd, of course, was her blood brother, and while he'd asked a lot of questions in the beginning, he'd eventually let them fall by the wayside after reasoning—she supposed—that talking about her previous home and family was nearly more than she could bear. She'd done everything within her power to forget. She worked hard on her studies, was dutiful at home and at the floral shop, stayed busy with her friends and with Gilbert. Trinity was her hometown. Buchwald was her last name. She had only one brother . . .

Still, she mentally calculated: Harold was nine years old now, Billy eight. She relaxed her mind enough to wonder what they looked like. When she'd left, Billy looked remarkably like their mother. Dark hair, almond-shaped eyes. Although hers were blue and his were coal black.

Harold looked more like his father.

Patsy imagined them both, all filled out, freckles across their noses, feet growing out of shoes faster than Mama could work her fingers to the bone to buy more. She also wondered, with the nation's economy booming, if Mr. Liddle was doing all right financially. Maybe Mama didn't have to work anymore doing other people's laundry. Maybe she got to wear those pretty dresses she loved and had enough nylons to keep her socially in step with the other ladies in town.

Sometimes, when she tried—which wasn't often—Patsy thought she could still smell her mother's scent. And sometimes, when she was overly tired, she dreamed of Ira Liddle. Those dreams never came out right for her. Never. They left her frightened, a shell of the person she hoped to become.

Now she opened her eyes to the small room around her. Since her arrival, she'd made personal changes. She'd learned how to crochet in home ec and she'd made an afghan throw for the foot of the bed. When she and Gilbert married, she'd take it with her, lay it on their bed. The thought made her shudder with anticipation.

She'd joined the ladies of the church quilting bee. Three quilts, made from scraps Mam had been collecting over the years, were stacked in the rocker still in the corner of the room. The ladies of the bee had made a special wedding ring quilt with scalloped edges for her and Gilbert; she planned to use it as their spread.

Patsy had also taken up reading; it helped pass the hours

between being at school, being at work, being at church, and being with Gilbert. Papa insisted that she purchase her books rather than get them from the local library. He went out and bought a beautifully crafted claw-foot, oak case. He and Mam gave it to her for her sixteenth birthday.

It would also go with her to her new home.

Her new home . . .

She spread her fingers wide and stared at the ring hugging her left third finger. Compared to the one her mother had worn when Patsy was just a little thing, it was hardly worth gloating over. Les Sweeny had given his bride-to-be the ring his grandfather had given to *his* bride, Patsy's great-grandmother. It had been an unusual ring—perhaps that was why Patsy remembered it so—with intertwining diamonds and sapphires orbiting around a center round diamond. Patsy remembered how her mother pampered the ring, touching it lightly with her fingertips, refusing to take it off.

But at some point she must have.

"Patsy?"

Patsy jumped, turned her head toward the door to see Papa's large size all but blocking the view into the hall. "Hey, Papa."

He took a step into her room. "You look . . . have you been crying?"

She scooted until her back came to rest against the bed's headboard. She brushed her fingertips across her cheeks, felt the moisture, and said, "A little. Maybe."

He pointed to the foot of the bed. "Do you mind if I sit?"

She shook her head no.

His weight caused the springs to creak and moan. Patsy watched as he removed the round glasses pressed to the bridge of his nose. He made a show out of pulling a handkerchief from his front shirt pocket, then cleaning the lenses, one at a time. "Do you want to talk about it?" he asked.

Patsy fought past a knot in her throat. "I was just thinking, Papa," she all but whispered.

He grinned at her. "About changing your mind?"

She laughed lightly. "Oh no, Papa. That's not going to happen."

He took a deep breath, exhaled. "About your mother, I suspect. Your real mother."

Patsy felt her eyes widen. "How'd you—"

"I'm no mind reader, my dear. Mam has been worried." He cleared his throat, made a big show of that too. "She's had something . . . something your mother wanted you to have when you married. She just doesn't know how or when to give it to you. She doesn't want to make you sad." He shrugged almost imperceptibly. "And you know Mam. She's all-knowing, that one is. And she says she thinks you've been missing your mother a lot."

"Does it . . . does it hurt her?"

"Nooooo." He chuckled. "Mam knows her place, same as I do."

"But I . . ."

"Would you like to try to contact her, Patsy? Would you like to see if we can find your mother? Your brothers? Ask them to the wedding?"

At first Patsy shook her head, shook it so hard she heard the wind in her ears. But then she stopped. "Could we? I mean . . . should we?"

"We could and we should." Papa slapped his hands over his knees and left them cupped there. "Tell you what let's do. How about you and I head over to Casselton tomorrow?"

"But it's so far . . ."

"Doesn't matter to me. We'll get up early—Mam can cook us a good breakfast and make us a picnic of snacks for along the way. We'll be there by lunchtime, grab something, and I'll take you out to dinner. We'll head back home late and sleep in on Sunday."

"What about church?"

Papa stood, straightened the waist of his pants, and said, "Sometimes, Patsy, doing the Lord's work means going outside the church building and its meeting time."

Patsy looked past his bulk. If she said yes, by this time tomorrow she'd be in Casselton. She'd see her mother again. Her brothers. With any luck, Mr. Liddle would not be home yet. And she could see Jane and Mitzy again. If nothing else, that made the trip worth the trouble.

Now Patsy nodded. "I'm game if you are, Papa. What time should I plan to be ready to leave?"

He looked at his Timex. "I'd say three o'clock." His arm dropped. "I'll go tell Mam." He stepped toward the door.

"Papa?" Patsy said.

He stopped, looked over his shoulder. "Yeah, sugar plum?"

"Thank you."

10

"I've been thinking, Papa," Patsy said from the passenger's side of the 1949 Chevrolet Styleline DeLuxe 4-Door Woody Papa bought for the business after he declared Patsy "drove the tires right off the other one."

"About?"

"Well . . . about my mother and brothers and Mr. Liddle. They live way out of Casselton, down a long dirt road. I was thinking that if Mr. Liddle is there, we might run into trouble."

"You think I can't handle Ira Liddle?"

Patsy shifted in her seat, tucking her left foot under the bend of her right knee. She wore a green and white square front neckline dress. The belt, which fit snug against her narrow waist, had been pinching for the last half hour, making her more than ready to arrive in Casselton so she could stand and relieve the pressure. She fluffed the full skirt up and over her knees before answering. "I didn't say that, Papa."

"Trust me. I can."

Patsy watched as Papa's hands flexed on the steering wheel. "What does that mean?"

Papa drove in silence for a moment before answering. "I

never told you, never saw a need to, but Ira Liddle came looking for you about two weeks after you came to live with us."

"What? How did he . . ." She shook her head. "Never mind.
Don't answer that. If he knew where I'd gone to, it's because
Mama told him. And if Mama told him, it was because he'd
beat it out of her."

"I'm not going to play games with you, Patsy. Never have.
You're probably right. I don't know for sure. I can only tell
you that he came to the house one night when you were out
with your new friends. I told him that unless I heard directly
from your mother, you weren't going anywhere. I also told
him that if he tried to do anything . . . find you . . . hurt you
. . . I'd report him to the police. That I had a good idea how
he found us. And I knew enough to ask our local sheriff to
call the law down there in Casselton for them to look into
pressing charges."

Patsy was intrigued. "What else did you tell him?" A smiled
hinted from her lips.

Papa glanced at her before shaking his head. "That's between Ira Liddle and me. Look here, Patsy. I know men like
Liddle. I know how they think, how they behave. I know that
your mama was afraid of the man. More for you than for
herself. And I know why."

Patsy felt hot shame splash across her cheeks. For a moment, she remembered standing nearly naked at her mother's
bedroom doorway. As though it had happened yesterday, she
felt Mr. Liddle's eyes wandering down the length of her body,
saw the gray turn to steel.

A puff of breath slipped from between her lips. "Maybe
we shouldn't have come."

"Don't you be scared now, little one. We've come this far,
we'll take care of business and be on our way." Patsy watched

as Papa's chin jutted forward. "Look. There's the sign for Casselton, just up the road a piece."

Five miles later, Patsy's eyes took in the changes of her old hometown. Few, but significant. Nothing stood still, she thought. Not time. Not buildings. Not people. She hadn't. Why should they?

She gave Papa the directions to the house and sat with her hands clasped on her lap as she waited for it to come into view. At least the packed dirt lanes slicing across the country hadn't changed. Blackberry vines still grew wild and thick on rickety fences running alongside dusty ditches. She leaned her face out the opened window and smelled of their sweet perfume, imagining herself with Mitzy and Jane, picking enough for their mamas to make jam and popping anything extra until the juice trickled from the corners of their mouths and onto their clothing. Her hair whipped around her face. The noonday sun skipping between the pecan trees cast both shadow and light into her eyes.

She pulled her head back into the car. "It's not far, Papa," she said, pointing to the narrow dirt driveway of her childhood. "Just right up here."

Papa slowed to a near crawl as he twisted the wheel to the left. The car bounded over the ruts of the entryway, causing Patsy to hold on to the armrest with both hands, lest she fall off the seat.

The car stopped close to the house. It had been repainted since Patsy had last seen it. Still white, but fresh. A white picket fence ran across the front and about fifty feet down the sides of the backyard. Miniature red roses grew on new trellises on both sides of the porch. An old hound sprawled just above the steps eased himself up and woofed, announcing their arrival. Patsy watched as a young woman, no more than thirty years of age, pushed open the front screened door. She was tall and slender. Her hair cupped just under her earlobes. She wore a housedress and an apron, and her feet were bare. From the car, Patsy could see that her toenails had been painted bright red. She looked at Papa, then back at the woman who cocked her hip before planting a fist on it. "Can I help ya?"

"That's not Mama," Patsy whispered as she opened the car door.

"Want me to go talk to her, child?"

Patsy shook her head without taking her eyes off the barefoot woman and her old dog. "No, sir. I can talk to her." She stepped out of the car. "Will your dog bite?" she called.

The woman crossed her arms over her middle. "This old thing? He ain't hardly got teeth. Can I help you with something? Are you lost? 'Cause Lord knows it's easy to get lost around here."

Patsy took a few steps toward the porch. "You've got pretty roses," she said, pointing toward the right trellis.

"I like to garden. Flowers, vegetables." She smiled at Patsy as though they'd known each other their whole lives. "My husband likes to build, so when we bought this old place, he added the fence and the trellises."

Patsy cleared her throat. "Do you know . . ." She cleared it again. "Do you know what happened to the family who lived here before you?"

The woman walked down the steps toward her. "The Liddles?"

"Yes."

"You know them?"

"Yes, ma'am."

"Then you ought to know they left here back in . . . gosh, when was it? Late '46, right before Christmas, I reckon."

103

Patsy moistened her lips with her tongue. "Do you know where they moved to?"

"Goodness, no. My husband bought this place from Mr. Liddle and then brought me over from Columbus."

"Do you think your husband would know?"

"He might. But he's off in Korea right now, so I'm afraid I can't ask him."

"Oh." Patsy blinked. "Well, then . . . thank you anyway." She started to turn away but looked back. "I hope . . . I hope your husband comes home safe. And soon."

"Thank you much."

Patsy returned to the car to report what she'd learned. "Papa, can you drive me to my friend Mitzy's house? Maybe she knows something."

Minutes later, Patsy exited the car again, this time in front of a more familiar home. Before she got to the front porch steps, a grown-up Mitzy ran out the door, screaming, "Oh, my goodness! Oh, my goodness! . . . I don't believe my eyes!" She embraced Patsy, squeezing and rocking from side to side. Then she jumped back. "Oh! We have to call Jane. Oh, my goodness . . . Jane won't believe this."

Patsy laughed. "Mitzy, you haven't changed."

Mitzy threw her hands up. They landed with a soft slap at her sides. "*What* happened to you? *Where* have you been?"

Patsy turned toward the car and Papa. She waved for him to get out. "I want you to meet Papa. His name is Wesley Buchwald." Patsy watched with pride as Papa ambled from the car to where she and Mitzy stood, now shoulder to shoulder. She made the proper introductions before asking, "Mitzy, do you know where my mother is?"

Mitzy's smile faded. "Come on inside."

After Mitzy introduced Papa to her mother—who embraced Patsy as though she were her own long-lost child—and Mitzy's mother had poured coffee into thick café-style mugs for everyone to enjoy around the kitchen table, Mitzy said, "I don't know what happened to your mother, Patsy. One day you were here and then you were gone. The next thing I knew, they were here and then they were gone."

Elaine Powell wrapped her hands around her coffee mug. "Even Corinne Dabbs had no idea where they'd gone." Her fingers flexed. "There was talk . . . in town," she almost whispered. "Even at the church . . ."

"Talk? Like about what?" Patsy asked.

"People wondering what happened to you, of course." She frowned before taking a sip of coffee and swallowing loudly. "People can be vile, Patsy, when they don't know the truth of the matter."

"Did *you* know the truth of the matter?" Papa's voice resonated between the knotty-pine walls of the spacious kitchen.

Mrs. Powell's left hand came up to the buttons of her blouse. Her fingertips fidgeted with them long seconds before she spoke. "I had my suspicions as to why Bernice . . ." Her tongue darted to her lower lip to moisten it. "I assumed that . . ." She looked at Patsy, took a deep breath, and said, "If you were my daughter, Patsy, and Ira Liddle were my husband, I'd have sent you to live with family in another state myself."

"Did my mother tell you that's what she'd done? Sent me to live with family?"

"Not in so many words, no. But your mother and I were as good of friends as Ira Liddle would allow her to have." She looked at Papa. "We didn't speak in words, Mr. Buchwald. We communicated with our hearts. Mothers' hearts can do that, you know."

Patsy looked at Papa, who winked at her. "Believe me, I know," he said.

"Mrs. Powell," Patsy said, "did Mama say *anything* at all that indicated they were moving?"

"No, honey. I'm afraid not. Just like with you . . . they were here, they were gone. In fact, they could have been gone for a week or more before anyone even knew." She looked at Papa. "That's the problem with living so far out and staying out of touch with most folks. Bernice did laundry—I'm sure Patsy told you—for a good number of the well-to-do ladies of Casselton. None of them even knew that the family was leaving. I heard they found the laundry, washed, dried, and neatly stacked in baskets in the living room, once someone finally went out to check on things."

"That sounds like Mama," Patsy said. She pressed her lips downward. "Papa, it sounds like we came all this way for nothing."

He patted her small hand with his large one. "I wouldn't say that, sugar foot."

Jane came for a visit. The three young women sat in the front parlor and talked nonstop about the events in their lives over the last four years while Papa waited patiently. Patsy promised to send them invitations to her wedding, gave them her new address ("And after I marry, I'll make sure to send you the address of my new place"), and promised to write.

"And I'm sorry, truly sorry, for not writing before. It's just that . . . I needed to leave all this behind completely. If Mr. Liddle found me . . ."

"We understand," Jane said. "Truly we do."

Patsy didn't cry when they said good-bye nor on the way home. But once she was safe under the covers of her bed, she wept long and hard. For her mother. Her brothers. And even a little for herself.

But when morning came, another brick supported the wall around her heart.

Patsy ran the aerosol can of hair spray around her head one last time and stepped back to see herself from head to toe. Usually, a little rouge and lipstick were all that adorned her face. But for a bride-to-be, she thought she passed muster. She looked . . . close to pretty with her every hair in place and wearing the deepest shade of red lipstick that could be bought at the local F. W. Woolworth. She pressed her hands against the satin slip caressing her flat stomach and inhaled deeply, pushing her chest forward, exhaled.

And giggled.

Oh, heavens, how much longer before they left for the church? For the honeymoon?

A knock at the door brought her thoughts back to the bathroom. "Mam says you'd best get into the dress now," Lloyd said from the other side.

"Where is she?" Patsy called back.

"In her bedroom, getting all gussied up."

Patsy looked to the mirror, smiled at her reflection.

"Where's Papa?"

"In the living room, pacing."

This time she smiled at the door.

"Go away, then. I'm in my slip and my dress is in the bedroom."

She listened for the sound of footsteps descending the staircase before opening the bathroom door and tiptoeing across the hall and into her room.

A package sat atop her bed, wrapped in silver and white

paper and tied off with a white ribbon and bow. Patsy looked behind her as if to find the giver there, but she was alone. She closed the door, crossed the room, and picked up the gift. She shook it. It was heavy. Solid. She tore away the ribbon and the paper, exposing a small white box.

Patsy opened it and gasped.

It was the gold filigree lipstick holder, the one she'd admired so long ago on her mother's dresser, along with the used tubes of lipstick. "How did—"

Her bedroom door opened; Patsy swung around to see Mam dressed in a lacy mother-of-the-bride powder blue dress. "Your mother sent it with your things that night. That's why she wanted me to take the suitcase before you unpacked it." She extended her arm. Patsy followed the length of it until her eyes came to rest on a small envelope. "She left this for you too." Mam waited for Patsy to take the envelope before adding, "I have struggled with whether or not to give this to you . . . considering everything that happened a couple of weeks ago. But it is not my place to make this decision for Bernice. She entrusted me with two of her most precious gifts and she trusted me with this present and letter for you."

Patsy took the envelope, clutched it to her abdomen. "Mam," she whispered. "I can't open this right now. Not today." Today was supposed to be about happy, about sunshine and the daisies in her bouquet.

Mam nodded. "I wondered about that too. But Bernice asked that you be given this on your wedding day. She told me you used to like to play with it. Touch it. Pretend you were a grown-up lady." She smiled weakly. "And now look at you. You are all that and more."

Patsy laid the letter beside the lipstick holder deposited on the bed beside her. "Mam, do me a favor. Put this away for me. I promise I'll come get it when I'm ready . . . but I'm not ready for any of this right now."

Mam took a step forward. "Patsy, don't do this, child. Don't try to force away your feelings for your mother."

Patsy swallowed past a knot. "You know what, Mam? My mother left Casselton without so much as a word as to where she was going. Surely she knew one day I'd try to find her. No forwarding address, though, huh? Nothing but a house that looks vaguely like my old home and a woman who likes to grow flowers while her husband serves in Korea."

"God be with him."

"Yes. God be with him."

"But Patsy." Mam took a tentative step toward her. "Perhaps Bernice didn't know where she was going? Surely you've thought of that."

"She may not have known where she was *going*, but she knew where she was once she *got* there. And she knows where I am. I may not be a mother yet, but I know one thing: I'd never let a child of mine go and not connect with her now and again."

"Never say never. You don't know what this life has in store for you, child. Only the good Lord does. All we can do is pray for his mercy."

"Then God be merciful, Mam. God be merciful over Gilbert and me."

An unreadable expression passed over Mam's face. She said, "Let's pray then, Patsy, that you never have to face such a decision as the one your mother faced."

Patsy stepped to where her wedding dress hung from the top facing of her closet door. She unhooked the hanger before gliding the dress over to the bed. "I have to get dressed now, Mam," she said. "Gilbert is waiting for me at the church."

11

While the Buchwalds were paying for the wedding, most of Gilbert's money was being invested in business and the things a man needed to bring home a bride. Like decent furnishings in the service station apartment and the burgundy 1945 two-door Mercury coupe he'd bought used from a high school buddy. It wasn't new, and the paint had a few scratches, but under the hood was clean.

Before they married, Gilbert had leaned against the door frame of the tiny bedroom he'd soon share with Patsy. While he was painfully anxious for that first night with her, to hold and love her between the warmth of the sheets, he didn't want to begin their marriage within four walls reeking of motor oil and gasoline. But he also knew he had no money to take her anywhere for a real honeymoon.

When he shared his conundrum with his mother, she suggested he write a letter to Aunt Cecelia and Uncle John, who lived in nearby Charleston. They were, she reminded him, financially set. Their spacious and historic home came with a carriage house in the rear of the property, perfect for a honeymoon.

Gilbert had never been good at writing his thoughts. He

wondered if it might be best to place a long distance call. But money was too tight for that too. Writing the request took several hours over a period of days; he wrote between his time at work, his time with Patsy, and his time alone with his own doubtful thoughts. But after he placed a 3¢ stamp on the white letter envelope and walked it to the post office, he felt hopeful.

Aunt Cecelia responded almost immediately.

```
My exceptional great-nephew Gilbert,
   Of course, dear boy, you can come and bring
your beautiful bride. Uncle John and I received
our invitation to the wedding. We are most
pleased for you, although your mother tells me
that your girl is much younger than you. Don't
let that dissuade you! Your great-great-grand-
parents were nearly fifteen years different in
age but their love brought nine children into the
world.
   John and I intend to arrive sometime Saturday.
I have plans to speak with your mother about our
staying with them. This will allow you and Patsy
a chance to be at our home privately for a night.
   The carriage house is, as always, ready for
guests. Please don't feel this is the only time
you can come. We'd love to have you any time.
   Until I see you again, I remain your loving,

                    Aunt Cecelia
```

Gilbert breathed a sigh of relief; his future held the promise of a booming business, a new bride, and a nice place to spend their first days—and nights—as man and wife.

For the most part, the wedding was everything she could have hoped for. Everything she had dreamed of. The morning sky stayed a brilliant blue until just after lunch. Then an un-expected shower, which lasted less than an hour, rained down on Trinity. It eased the sweltering temperatures both inside and outside the church but also encouraged a few gnats and mosquitoes to join the sacred service.

Everyone made it to the church on time, including her Casselton guests, the Powells and the Cartwells. Patsy had remained at home until three-thirty when she, her parents, and Lloyd quietly got into the car and drove to the church. There, she managed to slip into the bride's room without being seen by anyone of old wives' tale consequence. At four o'clock, the ceremony began.

She clutched Papa's arm and walked toward her handsome groom, forcing herself to concentrate only on the moment. She would not think of her mother or her two youngest brothers.

She raised her eyes to Gilbert's; his eyes sparkled at the sight of her. Sweet, handsome, persistent Gilbert—standing with his father. She would not think of her father who died. Or the one who had driven her away from her childhood home.

She would only think of Papa, whose hand rested over hers as they stepped toward her future. Of Mam, who wept appropriately in the left front row. Of Lloyd, standing in the lineup of groomsmen.

Of Gilbert. When this hour was over, she would finally be his wife. He would be her husband. She would always love him; he would never leave her.

She felt a warm rush when her hand slipped from Papa's to Gilbert's. He winked at her; she squeezed his fingers and smiled. Together they turned toward Brother Michael, who then spoke about the sanctity of marriage.

Patsy tried to concentrate, to listen and pay attention. But she knew she'd not remember much of this moment. Only the most important things. Gilbert reciting his vows to her, his voice strong and sure. And that when it was her turn to do the same, how she kept focus on the dimple in his cheek. And she would laugh because she could only whisper her part, her voice was so shaky, barely audible.

When the last words had been spoken and Brother Michael pronounced them "man and wife," she stood trembling as Gilbert raised the short lacy veil from her face. It tickled her chin and cheeks and tugged at the crown of pearls atop her head. He laid it carefully over the back of her head and smiled. His eyes went to her lips. It was time for the kiss.

She closed her eyes as he sweetly pressed his lips against hers. She was keenly aware of both the passion within the moment and the crowd of family and friends around them. When the kiss broke, they both sighed so loudly, the congregation laughed.

They were introduced as Mr. and Mrs. Gilbert Milstrap.

Once again, life started over.

After the wedding and the reception and in a flurry of rice, Gilbert opened the passenger door of the Mercury. He watched his wife as she slipped in and tucked her tiny feet close to the seat. The skirt of her wedding dress trailed over the doorsill. Instinctively, he reached in to scoot it over, bringing his face in line with hers.

"Oh," she said, reaching for it. Her voice trembled.

"Nervous?" he said quietly so the throng around them couldn't hear.

"Yes," was all she said.

He grinned all the way to the driver's side. He couldn't help it. He was happier than a man had a right to be, and his life was all he'd hoped it could be. His business was going well, he was now married to the prettiest thing he'd ever laid his eyes on, and they had a place to go for the night.

He drove in silence to Charleston. Not five miles out of town and his new wife was sound asleep. Her head was pressed against the frame of the open window. The hot summer air whipped the curls of her Rosemary Clooney–inspired hairstyle away from her face. He reached over and let his fingers be tickled by the dark ends until he feared waking her. She was exhausted, poor thing.

After reaching his aunt and uncle's home without incident, he shut the car off. Patsy stirred, blinking. She looked from the gracious home to him and then back to the home again. "This is where your aunt and uncle live?" she asked.

"Yeah. It's something else, isn't it?"

"I don't believe I've ever seen anything like it. Clearly, I haven't."

"Wait till you see the carriage house. It's pretty as a picture." He couldn't help himself with the next line out of his mouth. "But not as pretty as you."

Patsy clutched her hands together and looked to her lap. "Gilbert . . ."

"Come here," he whispered, sliding toward her as she did the same to him. He wrapped her in his arms and kissed her until it was improper to do so. "I'd best get you inside," he said, "before the neighbors start to talk."

She pressed her fingertips to her cheeks. "Gilbert, you undo me."

"Good," he said with a laugh. He opened his car door then went around to do the same for her. As she stood and stretched, he dipped his hand into his pants pocket and brought out a key. "Uncle John gave me the key to the main house. Said for us to go on into the kitchen and get something to eat. Aunt Cecelia made us some sandwiches and potato salad."

"How kind."

"We'll eat and then I'll get our things out of the car. How does that sound?"

Patsy only nodded.

"Let's go on in, then," he said, and jiggled the keys.

Gilbert's aunt Cecelia had made two sandwiches from thick slices of ham and cheese, two more from fresh pineapple. All four were slathered in mayonnaise and wrapped in wax paper. The well-stocked refrigerator also offered them homemade dill pickles, the potato salad Gilbert told Patsy about, sweet tea, and an icebox cake Patsy swore she must have the recipe for.

They sat across from each other at the yellow vinyl and chrome kitchen table for their wedding supper. Gilbert took ownership of the ham and cheese while Patsy delighted in the pineapple sandwiches. Between bites he asked her if she'd ever been to Charleston before.

She swallowed a sweet bite of her sandwich. "No."

"Then tomorrow I'll show you around. There's a lot of history here, you know."

Her fingers danced around the soggy bread to keep the rest of the pineapple between the slices. "The old South." She took another bite.

"May she rise again," Gilbert said with a raise of his tea glass.

They laughed together. It was nonsense talk, really. She knew that. They were both a little nervous. She definitely more than he.

Patsy drained the last of the tea in her Tupperware tumbler. She was still thirsty so she poured herself another glassful. "I'll clean up in here when we're done," she said while doing so.

"You'll do no such thing." He looked to the door leading from the kitchen to the rest of the house, then back at her. "Tell you what. Why don't you put the things that need refrigerating back where they belong. I'll get our luggage from the car, take you to the carriage house in back, and let you get washed up . . . or whatever it is you gals do before bedtime."

Patsy thought she saw him blush, and it delighted her.

"While you're doing that, I'll clean up in here."

"You can't do that."

"Why not?"

Patsy straightened her spine. "Because, silly, I'm the wife. I'm supposed to clean the kitchen."

He laughed. "Where were you when I was on KP?"

She laughed with him.

"Besides," he added. "Who do you think has been keeping the kitchen clean at the station?"

She paused as though she were actually thinking. "Not Martha, I take it?"

"Martha handles the café kitchen. Not our kitchen."

Patsy reached for his empty plate and put it on top of hers. "I guess I haven't thought in terms of you eating in our kitchen." She sighed. "*Our* kitchen. Oh, Gilbert . . ."

"What?"

She felt herself growing warm inside. "I'm so happy."

Gilbert stood, walked to where she sat, bent, and kissed her. "Me too." He winked at her. "You know, this is the start of a whole new life. For both of us."

"Tell me again, Gilbert. Tell me what you see for us."

116

Gilbert pulled the nearest chair to him. He sat on the edge, one arm leaning against the table. One arm resting on the back of Patsy's chair. "You and me, Patsy. We'll have a good life. We'll have children, and they'll grow up to know how much they're loved. We'll make sure they understand the things of God and country."

Patsy nodded. "I like that."

"You'll be the heart of the home, Pats. And I'll be out there, every day, making sure the business grows. Making sure there's enough for you and the kids." His eyes registered surprise. "We've never really talked about that, have we? Children."

Patsy feared she'd blush to the point of death. "No. I just assumed . . ." She couldn't finish her thought.

Assumed we'd have many . . . and you will love me more with each one, and they'll love me, and we'll be happy as a family. Complete. Never apart from one another.

"How many, Pats?"

"What?"

"How many should we have? Children?"

Patsy pressed her hand against her chest. "Goodness, Gilbert. How should I know? We haven't even . . . I mean . . ." She shook her head as she looked to her lap. "You know what I mean."

Gilbert's right hand popped the table. "Well, then let's start at four." He burst out laughing.

She laughed with him. "Four? Not all at once, I hope."

Now he roared. "Oh, good heavens, no." He leaned over for another kiss, which she gladly provided. "And not for a while. I want you all to myself for at least two years."

His voice had gone smoky; his eyes bore into hers. "Hmm," she said. "I want you all to myself too."

They continued to sit and stare for a few moments before Patsy remembered to breathe. "Well, then, Mr. Milstrap. I guess you'd best go on and get our things from the car so we can start this marriage, huh?"

The right side of his lips curled upward. "I reckon so."

———

They lay on their backs in their marriage bed later that night, fingers entwined, eyes staring at the swirls in the ceiling. Gilbert whispered, "Will you do something for me, Patsy?"

She turned her head to look at him, breathed in his scent. "Anything."

"Will you never cut your hair?"

The fingers of her free hand ran through the locks at the crown. "Never cut my . . . why? You don't like my hair?"

Gilbert released her hand, shifted until he rested on his elbow, then pulled her free hand away from her forehead. With his own fingertips, he lightly brushed at the dark strands as he said, "No, baby. I love it. I just . . . my mother never cut her hair for Pops. She told me once he liked hair on the pillow, and . . . tonight when I saw you lying here . . . I understood what he meant."

Patsy grinned. "Queen Victoria of England liked to watch Prince Albert shave, did you know that?"

Gilbert ran a finger over her brow. "Where'd you hear that?"

"History class."

"Is that what they teach these days?"

Patsy shook her head. "More than that, silly. But it's interesting, don't you think?"

The finger trailed down her nose. "Does this mean you want to watch me shave?"

She grinned. "It's fair play, I suppose. I won't cut my hair and you'll let me watch you shave."

His hand fell to her shoulder. "Every morning? Promise?"

Patsy reached up and nibbled his chin, already in need of a razor. "For the rest of my life."

12

Summer 1954, Miami, Florida

Thirteen was no age to be moving, not to mention clear up the state.

At least, that was what Billy heard Harold say. More than once too, and in more than just the usual words and phrases. Ever since they'd been told about Daddy taking a similar job with another company, Harold and Daddy had a number of arguments about it, the last one being the worst.

This time, Billy and Mama stayed in the kitchen sitting at the table. Mama's hands wrapped around the coffee cup between them. The toes of Billy's right foot bobbed up and down; the rubber of his sneaker gripped the linoleum. For the most part, Mama's eyes stayed closed while Billy's focused on the faucet over the deep, white porcelain sink in front of him.

"Boy, I've let you get away with a whole lot since we moved here, but you're just about to cross the line with me." Daddy's voice boomed from the living room, just yards from where they sat.

Billy reminded himself to breathe.

Mama took another shaky sip of her coffee.

120

"Look, old man—"

"Don't you 'old man' me, boy. I've been turning a blind eye to your hanging around riffraff and this is what it's come to. I'm telling you now, I won't put up with you running roughshod over me."

"Oh yeah, Dad. You don't mind my running roughshod over Mama, bringing you information on all the goings-on around here, but when it comes to me running roughshod over you . . ."

Billy looked over at Mama; her eyes were closed and her lips were moving as though in prayer. "Mama," he whispered.

The sound of furniture being shoved across the floor came from the other room.

"Shhh." The instruction was soundless.

The tick of his leg increased.

"What are you gonna do?" Harold's voice cut through the air from the other room. "Huh? Hit me like you do her?"

"Boy!"

Billy folded his arms across the slick Formica of the table. His head fell atop them, sweaty flesh against sweaty flesh. He inhaled the pine-fresh cleaner his mother had used earlier. "No, no, no," he whispered.

The first blow, followed by another, and another. Harold's *whomp* against the wall. The apparent finding of his feet, followed by shuffled steps moving quickly across the floor. The sound of body against body.

"I'll beat you within an inch of your life!" their father bellowed.

Mama jumped from the table. "No!"

Billy's head shot up, his twelve-year-old hand quick to grab her thin arm. "Mama, don't."

Mama sat, blinked back tears. Her narrow fingers wrapped around the coffee cup again.

121

Billy heard the all-too-familiar sound of Daddy's belt being pulled from pant loops. He looked from the door leading to the living room to his mother and then to the back door with only the worn screen keeping the neighbors from knowing what was going on. "Mama," he said to her. "Let's go. Let's go."

Leather slapped against his brother's body. Words spewed. Words he'd never say, much less repeat. Words he couldn't imagine saying to his father, even hating him sometimes as he did.

"Mama." Billy's right hand encircled her left wrist as he stood. "The back door. Let's go." Harold was putting up a fight now. A mighty struggle of rebellion against authority. Billy's eyes traveled from the kitchen door to his mother's face. Her own eyes were full of tears and fear. "Mama!"

She looked up at him. "Run, Billy. Run."

His left hand reached for her right and upset the coffee cup in the process. He watched it rock then fall and roll to the floor where it shattered against the linoleum.

The scuffling in the other room stopped. His mother looked to the floor then back to her son. "Billy." She pulled her hands free of him. "Go!" she hissed. "Do as I say!"

Billy took two tentative steps backward. "Come with me," he whispered back.

Mama stood.

"What the—what the devil's going on in there?"

Billy watched the blood drain from his mother's face. "Now!" she hissed again.

Billy turned, pushed the screen door with the palms of both hands, and leapt over the threshold to the stoop. He whipped his head to the left then to the right, where the side yard led to the front and a long, newly poured sidewalk led out of the neighborhood. He sprinted for a few yards, then tore away, running as fast as he could, to . . . to . . . where he did not know. He only knew he was running for his life, for all the good it would do him.

Sooner or later, he'd have to go home again.

And face Ira Liddle.

It was nearly eleven before Billy returned to the concrete, flat-roofed house he'd called home for the last five years. Like most of the houses in the neighborhood, theirs was painted salmon pink, but in the shade of night, it came off looking like vomit yellow.

The air was thick with humidity and cicadas crying out against the dark.

He slipped between the moon-cast shadows of palm fronds along the front lawn.

To his left, a metal lawn swing creaked as it moved in the breeze. He whipped his head around. A little too quickly.

"Ow," he groaned as his long slender fingers wrapped around his neck.

He took a few steps backward, turned toward the house again, made his way along the right-hand side—retracing the very steps he'd taken hours earlier.

The tiny room he shared with Harold waited for him on the back right corner. If the window was up, he was home free.

So to speak.

It was. And the screen was off, resting just below the window, against the house. Billy peered inside the room, illuminated only by the moonlight. Harold was lying on his bed, flat on his back, ankles locked, one arm cocked behind his head. Sensing Billy at the window, his head turned. "Hey, kid." The greeting was etched in pain.

Billy blinked. "You okay?" He kept his voice low.

"Hoist yourself on in here and let's get the screen back up before you wake the ole man."

Billy did as he was told, careful not to make any loud thumping noises as his sneakers touched the tile floor. By the time he'd righted himself, Harold stood beside him, ready to lean out and retrieve the screen. Together they slid it into place then locked the metal rings around the knobs jutting up from the window's ledge.

His brother, older only by a year in age but seemingly so much older in stature. Billy swallowed hard at seeing the cut that sliced diagonally across Harold's lip, the dark blue shadows pooled under his left eye and cheekbone. "He did a number on you, didn't he?"

Harold shrugged. "It don't matter. Wasn't the first time, probably won't be the last." He returned to his bed, sat gingerly upon it, then rested his elbows on his knees.

Billy pulled off his shoes, set them oh-so-quietly at the foot of his bed, then sat next to his brother. "Did he notice I was gone?"

Harold snickered. "Oh yeah." His fingers laced.

"Mama?" Billy's voice cracked, even in a whisper.

Harold didn't answer.

"Harold? What about Mama? Did she get in trouble for making me run?"

Harold turned his head toward Billy, ran his tongue along the swell of his lip. "What do you think, Billy? You think Daddy's gonna let her get away with anything like that?"

"What'd he do?"

Harold turned his gaze to his feet. "Gave her the same belt he gave me, only not so hard."

Billy didn't know whether to be grateful or not. "Why's

he have to be so mean, I wonder?" he asked over the lump in his throat.

"'Cause that's just who he is."

"Is she all right?"

"Isn't she always?"

Billy didn't answer right away. "Why do you think she puts up with his hitting her?"

Harold looked back to him. "'Cause that's just who *she* is."

Billy sat silent, counting his breathing in and out, in and out. Then, "Are we really moving?"

"Looks like it."

"Did Daddy say to where?"

"Nope. Said we'd know when we got there."

"I'm okay with that. I never cared for Miami that much."

"That's because you didn't make friends like I did, Billy."

Billy nodded. "But they're not very good friends, Harold."

Harold swung around until he was lying on his back again, ankles crossed once more. "Go to bed."

Billy stood.

"And count yourself lucky that Mama took the belt for ya tonight."

They moved on a Tuesday, two weeks later. Daddy rented a United Van Lines moving van. Billy stood hidden at the side of the house, holding his new Whee-Lo and watched fascinated as four muscled men loaded up all their worldly goods like they were nothing heavier than papier-mâché. Once they were done, he knew, his role and Harold's would be to help carry the boxes—each marked with the black Magic Marker Mama had bought at the five-and-dime—from the house to the van.

All morning, Daddy stayed inside, bellowing out orders to

the men while Mama continued to box up the "little things," as she called them. Harold had made a final run to say good-bye to his friends. Billy had done that the night before. It took all of a half hour to mumble "so long" to the one person he felt close to in Miami. He and Johnny Carr had nodded at each other and given a loose hug before Billy had ambled back home.

"Billy!" Harold's voice now came from behind him. "You'd best get out of la-la land and get inside. Daddy says the men are just about done here."

The two brothers walked toward the rear of the house. "When'd you get back?"

"A minute or two ago. Came in the back way."

"Did you say your good-byes?"

"Yeah. You?"

"Last night, after you went out."

Harold opened the kitchen door for Billy and he walked in to find Mama sealing another box. "Good. There you two are. Your daddy says to start loading the boxes. He just walked out the front door to find you." She glanced at her youngest son's hand. "Billy, hand me your toy so it doesn't get broken."

Billy gave his mother the Whee-Lo, then hoisted the box on the floor at her feet into his arms. "Mama, how long's it gonna take to get to where we're going?"

"I have no idea, son. Harold, there are boxes in your room. You start there."

Without a word, Harold shuffled toward their adjacent bedroom.

Billy left the kitchen, moving into the living room and out the front door, where Daddy stood talking to one of the United men. "Daddy? Where should I put this?"

"Start laying them upside the furniture in the back of the van," his father said without so much as a glance.

On his way back inside the house, Billy asked the same question he'd asked of his mother.

"Well, son, if you quit talking and start packing, maybe we'll be there by sometime tomorrow."

Daddy wasn't far off. They got to the new house somewhere after midnight the next day. Billy couldn't tell much about it in the glow of the street lamps, but he liked what he saw.

This house made the one in Miami look like a matchbox. Even Mama was delighted. "Ira," she breathed out as they stood at the base of the semicircular driveway, next to a newspaper receptacle with the numbers 1711 attached to it. "It's like a mansion."

"Well, you know, Bernie, I like to provide as best I can, and I believe good fortune will smile on me here in Gainesville." Words spoken, Daddy did something Billy hadn't seen much of; he wrapped an arm around Mama's shoulder and kissed her at the temple.

The United truck was parked in the driveway, abandoned. "Daddy," Billy asked as quiet as he knew how, "what are we gonna do about the big stuff? Are the men who drove the truck sleeping in the house?"

"No, son. They've gone on and gotten themselves a hotel room. But don't you worry none." Daddy's broad chest bowed out. "Someone will be here in the morning. Meanwhile, boys, grab the overnight cases your mama had you pack and let's go inside." Daddy dipped into his front pants pocket and pulled out a silver key. It glimmered in the lamplight. "Come on in with me, Mama." With his other hand, he tossed Harold the car keys before they disappeared into the shadows cast by tall trees in the expanse of the front yard.

Billy and Harold pulled marbled-green suitcases from the trunk. "Hey, Harold," Billy said, easing the trunk down. "What do you think?"

"'Bout what?"

The brothers walked up the driveway, each carrying two pieces of the Samsonite luggage. "About this place? You think maybe it's a new beginning?"

"I guess so." Harold sounded doubtful.

"I mean, did you see the way Daddy kissed Mama?"

"What of it?"

"Well . . ." Billy stopped walking and Harold stopped with him. "Don't you think that makes everything look kinda promising here? Maybe it's like Daddy said. Maybe good fortune will smile down on us here in Gainesville. And maybe Daddy won't fight with Mama no more and Mama will make some friends. Nice ladies, like herself."

Harold blew air from his nose. "Yeah. Maybe." He shuffled toward the door.

Billy held back.

"You coming?"

"Yeah. Give me a minute, okay?"

"Just hurry up, Billy. It's late."

Billy watched Harold walk inside the door. He tilted his chin upward and looked across the blue-black sky. The stars were numerous; he could see the Big Dipper. Ursa Major, he'd learned the year before in school. The Great Bear. "God," he whispered into the warm, sticky air. "Thank you for bringing us here. And thank you for Daddy being nice to Mama." He blinked. His neck was getting tired so he straightened it. From where he stood, it looked like every light in the house was now on. Through the large picture window he could see Mama and Daddy, walking through

128

a wide doorway into another room. Probably the dining room, he thought.

"And God . . . if you can keep Harold out of trouble. I'd appreciate it."

He took a step. Stopped. "One more thing," he said, cocking his head to the right and upward. "A friend for me would be nice. A true friend. A forever friend. If you don't mind." He smiled. "Amen."

13

With two weeks to go before the start of the school year, Harold kept his standing as the "make friends" champion of the Liddle household. The furniture had scarcely been shoved into place, the linens draped over the beds, and new dining table Daddy had surprised Mama with, before Harold was out the door, scouting the neighborhood, buddying up with the other boys along Clinton Street.

Daddy stayed home one day after they'd officially moved in and then he was on a route again, though with the new job, he returned more often on Fridays instead of Saturdays. At first, Mama seemed out of sorts in her new home, what with all the extra space she'd not had before. And Billy never left her side, preferring to help her unpack the boxes, determine where the pictures should be hung, how the knickknacks should be arranged. Mama encouraged him to do like Harold, to go out and make friends. But Billy's first obligation was to his mother. To helping her.

After a week, Billy decided to try his hand at going door-to-door, looking for work cutting grass on Saturdays. He'd had his eye on a new bicycle—a Huffy Customliner he'd seen advertised in *Boys' Life*. In one day, he landed three customers, all on Clinton, one of whom was Mr. Herbert Stone, administrator of the local hospital. The day he knocked on their door, Mrs. Stone told him her husband wasn't home quite yet but that he would be shortly, if Billy cared to wait. Then she offered him cookies and milk at their kitchen table, which he readily accepted.

Billy immediately took a liking to Mrs. Stone. She reminded him of Katherine Hepburn, both in appearance and in character. She was a nurse, she told him, and she worked at the same hospital as her husband.

"Is that where he is now?" Billy asked. "At the hospital?"

Mrs. Stone slipped into a chair—chrome backed and thickly padded in red vinyl—at the end of the pink Formica table. Billy watched transfixed as she slowly crossed her legs, listening to the sound of her stockings sliding against each other. She rested against the chair, laid her hands in her lap. From where Billy sat, they seemed to disappear into the folds of her dress, which was nothing short of pretty, even to a twelve-year-old boy. "Oh no, no, no. He's made a run to the Piggly Wiggly for me."

Billy stopped munching on the bite of oatmeal raisin. "Your *husband* went to the Piggly Wiggly?" he asked around the cookie.

"Don't talk with your mouth full, dear," she answered.

Billy took a swig of cold milk.

"And, of course. Why not?"

"Boy, my daddy would never be caught dead in a grocery store, even if he was hungry, I bet."

Billy watched as Mrs. Stone's shoulders squared. "And why would that be?"

He took a final bite of cookie, chewed, swallowed, and drained his milk. "He'd say that's a woman's place," he answered, then swiped the linen napkin Mrs. Stone had placed by his plate over his mouth.

It smelled like warm sunshine.

Mrs. Stone cleared her throat as she leaned forward, rested her arms against the edge of the table, and said, "And just what is a woman's place?" She smiled. "According to your father, I mean."

Billy shuffled his feet back and forth as though his feet wouldn't quite reach the floor. "Well, um . . . let's see . . . the kitchen, of course."

"Of course."

"And the grocery store."

"We've established that."

"The laundry room, if you have one, and the laundromat, if you don't."

Mrs. Stone gave thought to her ponderings before asking, "But, let's say, what about before your father married your mother? Would he have just worn dirty clothes back then?"

Billy laughed at the thought. "Gee, Mrs. Stone. I never really thought of Daddy as not being married."

"But surely he was, at some point, an unmarried adult male." Mrs. Stone made a tap-tapping with the toe of her shoe, which Billy had earlier noticed to be high and pretty. And he'd noticed her big toes at the opening near the front of the shoe, her red nails through shimmery nylons.

Billy shrugged. "Not as long as I've known him," he said, to which Mrs. Stone laughed.

Billy couldn't wait for Mama to meet Mrs. Stone, and he said as much when he returned home a few minutes after Mr. Stone walked into the back kitchen door, carrying two sacks full of groceries.

"And Mama, she wears high heels. Even in the middle of

the day." Billy leaned an elbow against the kitchen counter and watched his mother slicing cucumbers and tomatoes on a cutting board. Cold fried chicken and biscuits from the night before were already on a platter at the kitchen table along with a pitcher of sweet iced tea.

Mama looked down at her feet and the no-nonsense flat house shoes she wore daily. At one time they'd been rich navy blue but were now faded to dark gray. "Well, Billy, maybe they're going out tonight, don't you think?" she asked, peering at her son.

"I don't think so. Mr. Stone had gone out to the grocery store to get some things she needed."

"The grocery?" Mama's concentration went back to the cutting board, the tomatoes and the cucumbers. "Well, maybe they're having friends over then."

"She's real elegant, Mama. And she smells pretty—"

"William Watson Liddle, what are you doing smelling Mrs. Stone?"

Billy felt his shoulders slump. "Gee, Mama. It's not like my nose fell off when I walked in their door." He shrugged. Stood straight. "She smells like you do when Daddy is coming home on the weekends." He looked around. "Where's Harold?"

"Who knows. Gainesville will be no different than Miami; I can see that now."

"Is Daddy coming home on Saturday?"

"No. He'll be home on Fridays now that we're in Gainesville. This is where one of the home offices is. You know that. He told us when he first talked about this new company."

Billy thought a minute longer before posing the next question. "Mama?"

Mama scooped up the peelings from the vegetables and

threw them in the trash can in the corner of the kitchen. "What, son?"

"When Daddy comes home . . . you always . . ."

She was washing her hands now, standing at the kitchen sink with water spilling over her fingertips. "I always what?" Question asked, she turned her head to face him, her chin gracing her narrow shoulder and the colorful material of her handmade crisscross house apron.

Billy crossed his arms. "Well . . . you always seem so nervous. You scamper to make sure everything is just perfect for him. When he walks in the door, you run to get his luggage. You make sure he doesn't have to wait for long before dinner is on the table."

"That's the way your father likes it." She turned off the water, reached for a drying towel off the three-tiered chrome rack hanging at her left, and added, "Why? What does Mrs. Stone do?"

Billy blew out a breath. The last thing he wanted was to upset his mother; he loved her too much for that. But he'd always been able to tell her how he felt about things, and this was weighing heavy on his mind. "See, when Mr. Stone walked in, Mrs. Stone got up real easy like. She said, 'There's the man you need to speak with, Billy' and then she just walked right over to him. Not in a fluster or anything. Just walked over to him. And he gave her the bags he was carrying and then . . . well . . . they sorta kissed a little, and then Mr. Stone asked me how he could help me." Billy blinked a few times before moving on. "That's when I told him about my lawn service and asked him if he needed any help with his yard work."

Mama didn't move for a moment. "I see," she said. And then, "Well, did he?"

"Did he what?"

"Need any help?"

"Oh, yes ma'am. He said I can start on Saturday morning. Eight o'clock. He'll be home then and we can talk over what he'd like me to do. But he's making me do it once without pay. Just to see if I'm as good as I think I am." Billy smiled at his mother. "Then he says that if I *am* as good as I think I am, he has friends around here who'd probably like the same kind of work done."

Mama pressed her thin lips together. "Well, that's just fine, Billy. Just fine. Your daddy'll be proud too, no doubt."

Billy didn't know whether to be happy about that tidbit of news or not.

Mama pulled dishes out of the overhead cabinet, white plates with a golden stalk of wheat running along the left side. "Son, why don't you wash up for supper."

Billy took a step before saying, "Mama? Are you upset with me?"

She held the three plates close to her breast. "Now whatever would I be upset with you for, Billy? You're my baby boy and I love you."

"For telling you about Mrs. Stone. And Mr. Stone."

"Of course not."

Billy nodded. "Okay then." He took another step. "You think Harold will be home in time for supper?" he asked, pointing to the plates.

Mama held the plates out, studied them, and returned them near her middle. "I figure he'll get hungry and come on home sooner or later." She smiled, but Billy could tell it was forced. "As soon as I get these cukes and tomatoes onto a plate, we'll eat, so run along now."

"Yes, ma'am."

He was at the door leading to the dining room when he turned around and said, "Mama?"

Mama sighed. "What, Billy?"

"I love you too."

Trinity, South Carolina

Patsy Milstrap felt the spindles of the colonial rocker dig into the flesh of her back, separated only by the thin cotton of her baby blue nightgown that fell to her ankles. Its lacy hem tickled the tops of her feet. The sweet scent of baby and bottled formula swirled around her. In the summer heat, her long hair wrapped around her neck as tightly as the little fist around the index finger of her right hand.

She hummed a nontune, keeping rhythm with the sounds of the creaking rocker and the suckling of a sleeping infant. Her toes dug into the cold oak of the floor beneath her feet, pressing back and forth, back and forth.

Night clung to the world outside the window by which she sat. Two rooms away, her husband snored, oblivious to this early morning feeding, as he'd always been. One room away, two more children—a son, age three, and a daughter, age two—slumbered. They, no doubt, dreamed of tomorrow's—today's—playdate in Aunt Janice's pool.

Patsy sighed. Looked down at the tender life cradled in her arms, tiny lips quivering just left of her heart. The rocking stopped.

In four years, three children. How in the world . . .

She knew how. Gilbert's enthusiasm for her was second only to his hunger for his work . . . to make more money . . . to buy a bigger house . . . "To provide for my family and all these little ones we keep making," he'd said as though they'd done something so awe inspiring.

Three babies in four years.

But, oh yes, Gilbert's business had most certainly expanded, not only in Trinity but to the several small towns beyond. Now he was talking about Charleston. He'd be gone more, he'd told her. Especially in the beginning. Weeks at a time, he said. But don't worry, he assured her; he'd be home on weekends.

Her breath caught in her throat. The bottle's slick nipple fell out of the baby's mouth.

He'd be home on weekends.

Just like Ira Liddle. Walking through the door on Saturday nights. Home in time for supper. A playful tussle with his sons. Leering glares at his stepdaughter. A night of sweaty passion—she could imagine it no other way, if she cared to imagine it at all—with his wife. Her mother.

Bernice.

No wonder she'd been sent away. One less child to deal with. No matter how hard she'd worked to help, it hadn't been enough for Bernice.

Work. Work. Work. There was always work. No more peas to pick, but . . .

Tomorrow—today—she had stacks of laundry to do. Diapers. Lots and lots of diapers. Toddler clothes with worn knees and grass-stained tops. Gilbert's uniforms, with shirts and pants that needed to be pressed just so.

The floors needed to be mopped. Swept first. Then mopped.

Sheets. When was the last time she'd stripped the beds? Maybe they could wait one more week.

And she'd promised Greg and Pam she'd take them back to Aunt Janice and Uncle Marvin's. Maybe they'd forget. No, they wouldn't forget.

Children never forget.

14

Gainesville, Florida

Mrs. Stone came to the house, carrot cake in hand, to meet Mama. The two women sat at the kitchen table, drank coffee, and nibbled on cake, chatting away like two old friends. Billy leaned against the dining room wall next to the kitchen, eavesdropping. He tried to keep his head down—somehow it made it easier to listen—but with nearly every word spoken, his chin shot up and his body flinched, as if the whole of him was stunned by what he was hearing. Witnessing.

Mama had never let anyone into her life the way she did Mrs. Stone in the hour they spent sitting at that table. Not even the women she'd known for years in Casselton. But then, he reckoned, she'd never met anyone like Nadine Stone. Somehow, Mrs. Stone drew things out of Mama, stories Billy had never heard before in his life.

She even talked briefly about Patsy and some boy named Lloyd, though he couldn't quite make out who *he* was to Patsy, Harold, and him.

Mrs. Stone told Mama there'd be a neighborhood party on Labor Day and that they should be sure to come. "It's a lovely addition to living here," she said. "Oh, and just wait till you see what we do for Christmas and Easter and . . . oh, Fourth of July. You'll love it here, Bernice, I just promise you will."

Later, when Mama told Daddy about the neighborhood "shindig" as she called it, Daddy said that yes, they could be a part of it. "Should be" were his exact words.

"We're part of this community, aren't we?" he said to his small family as they sat around the same table where Mama and Mrs. Stone had talked.

From directly across the table, Harold gave Billy a look that read, "Who is this guy?" but then said, "Pops, we should go to the meat market and get some steaks, you and me. You can show me how to pick out the best ones."

The meat market. Sure, Billy thought. The meat market Daddy would go to. He hadn't thought of that before, when Mrs. Stone and he were talking over cookies and milk. Then again, knowing Mrs. Stone a little better, he figured the whole subject may have been best avoided. Women, Billy had once heard Daddy say, had no idea what a really good steak looked like before it was cooked.

No, Mrs. Stone would not have taken to that. But never mind that; the Labor Day picnic was coming and they'd all be there and Daddy could meet Mr. Stone and maybe they'd end up being friends too.

On the first Monday of September 1954, with lots of new neighbors dashing about or standing under shade trees talking, Billy helped Mama put out potato salad and deviled eggs and three-bean salad while Harold turned steaks on a nearby park grill and Daddy got to know the men of the neighborhood.

"Billy," Mama said as she placed a gallon of sweet iced

tea on top of the white cement picnic table their family had snagged for their own. "Why don't you go mingle with some of the kids over there?" Her eyes darted to the collection of swing sets and monkey bars where about a dozen children who looked to be about his age and younger congregated.

That was when he saw her. Long dark hair glistening in the sunlight, sides pulled back to the top of her head and held there by a large red bow. She was smiling. Laughing. Pushing a boy in a wooden swing who giggled and threw his head back with each upstroke.

"Yes, ma'am," Billy said to his mother. At least he thought he did.

He walked on legs made of rubber toward the children, toward the one in particular who'd caught his attention. "Hi, there," he said when he came near enough to be heard. "My name's Billy. William, actually. William Liddle. But everyone calls me Billy. Billy Liddle." He swallowed past a new feeling in his throat. "I'm new here."

She looked over her shoulder. Moss-green eyes met his. "Hi, Billy Liddle." She smiled at him. Perfect white teeth behind rosebud lips.

Rosebud lips? Now where had *that* come from?

"I'm Veronica Sikes." She nodded toward the child in the swing. "This is my little brother Travis. Travis, say hello to Billy."

To which Travis only giggled harder.

Veronica's shoulders slumped. "Oh, don't mind this one," she said. "He's only five and thinks everything in life is funny. I also have a brother a year younger than me. Stanley." She looked around. "He's around here somewhere."

Billy shoved his hands in the pockets of his jeans; one of three new pair Mama had bought him to start school the following day. "Okay." He kicked at the sand with his Keds. He looked down to them, back up to Veronica, and down again.

"I like your shoes," she said. "They look new."

"They are." He nodded, squinting one eye and tilting his head as though it was all so matter-of-fact. "They're like the ones Timmy wears on *Lassie*." He cringed inside. What a lame thing to say.

Veronica pushed her brother as his bottom glided naturally into the cups of her hands. "I love that show." Then she whistled the theme song.

Billy whistled with her until they both laughed.

"So, do you know whose classroom you'll be in yet?"

Billy pulled his hands out of his pockets, folded his arms across his chest. "Yeah. Mrs. Stuart's."

"Me too. You'll love her. She's strict, but she's really nice too." She took a step back from her brother and the swing. "She and my mother are good friends. The best of friends, really. But Mama says I can't go around acting like that when I'm in school."

"Like what?"

"Like Mrs. Stuart is going to let me get away with anything."

"Are you a good student?" Billy asked just as Travis squealed, "Don't stop pushing me!"

Veronica pretended to be frustrated—Billy could tell it was all just for show—before stepping forward again to give another hefty shove. "Yes, I am. You?"

"I do okay."

"You'll have to do better than okay, Billy Liddle. Mrs. Stuart expects all her students to do their best."

He smiled. "Then I will."

"Are you walking to school or taking the bus?"

"Walking."

"Where do you live?"

He gave the address.

"You're practically behind my house. Maybe I'll meet up with you sometime and we can walk together."

Billy's heart skipped. He held his breath for a moment in an effort to regain composure. "Yeah," he breathed out. "Maybe so."

It took Billy several weeks to get his timing right, but once he did, he spent every weekday morning walking the pretty Veronica Sikes to school and, every afternoon, walking her back home again. Once he asked her if he could carry her books, to which she replied, "I'm not really interested, Billy Liddle." She held her books low and in front, and, it seemed to Billy, she clutched them all the tighter.

He had been kicking a rock up to that point, but with her words, he let it lay and walked right past it.

He turned to walk sideways so he could have a good look at her. She wore a blue and pink checked dress with wide front pockets and puffy short sleeves. Her shiny black shoes clicked along the sidewalk in rhythm to the shuffling of his Keds. "What does *that* mean?"

"It means that I'm not . . . you know . . . interested in being a . . . girlfriend."

He felt himself growing warm and turned to walk forward again. "What makes you think I was thinking about you being my girlfriend, Veronica? I was just asking to carry your clunky ole books. Trying to be nice, is all."

"Oh."

"Is that all? Just 'oh'?"

She swung her books up and held them tightly against her chest. "What else do you want me to say?"

"Well, don't get mad or anything."

"Oh, I'm not mad." She looked at him and smiled. In spite of the current swirl of emotions inside him, he smiled back. "It's just . . . my parents don't even really want me to have boy *friends*. But Daddy said you're different because you do a good job on our lawn and you're new and . . . Billy?"

"Yeah."

"Can I ask you a question?"

"Sure, I guess."

"Do you and your family go to church?"

Billy slowed and she slowed with him. To their left, the well-tended lawns sloped toward them from large homes. To the right, the asphalt of a barely used two lane glistened in the early morning sunlight. Before and behind them, neighborhood children kept a steady pace as they walked toward school. Somewhere behind him, Billy knew, Harold lollygagged with his friends. "We used to."

"But you don't now?"

"Not since . . . well, golly. I don't think we've gone to church since we moved to Miami. I kinda remember going when we were little, Harold and me. Daddy and Mama and . . . um . . . well, we'd get all dressed up on Sunday mornings and then we'd come home afterward and Mama would have a pot roast cooking already."

Veronica stopped. "Are you against going to church?"

"Gosh, no, Veronica. Who would be against going to church?"

"Then why don't you go?"

"I don't know." Billy glanced behind him and spotted Harold about fifty feet away. "Can we keep going now?"

They returned to their walking. "Would you like to come to church with me sometime?"

Billy didn't answer right away. If he went to church with Veronica on Sunday, then Daddy would know. He had a feeling Daddy wouldn't take to his going. And Harold was sure to poke fun. "You mean, as your friend?"

"Ha-ha, Billy Liddle."

"I'd have to ask Daddy."

Veronica brightened. "Maybe your whole family would like to come. It's a really nice church and oh! You know what? Mr. and Mrs. Stone attend, and your mother and father like them, don't they?"

"Yeah."

"So, then." Veronica sounded as if the Stones' attendance at her church settled the whole issue. "Maybe the rest of your family would like to come too."

The Stones' attendance notwithstanding, somehow Billy doubted it. "Yeah," he said. "Maybe."

With that, Veronica let the subject fall. But just for the time being.

She asked him about church again the next day, just as their feet hit the cement steps of the school. They walked up, up, toward the three sets of double doors that opened into the wide front hallway of their school.

"So? Did you ask your parents about going to church?"

Billy cut his eyes left and right. All around them, kids from ages six to thirteen. Maybe some at fourteen. He wasn't sure. The sound of shoes shuffling up the steps, the giggles, the conversations . . . these were all a part of his early morning routine. Being asked about church was not.

"Why are you asking me now? We're two seconds from

you going into the auditorium and me going into the gym and you pick *now* to ask me?"

"Well, what's wrong with that, Billy Liddle?"

"Nothing, I guess," Billy mumbled. "It's just that you aren't giving us a lot of time to talk about it."

They stopped at the top of the steps. Veronica shot Billy a look he had come to recognize. He'd made her unhappy. And the last thing he wanted to do was to make Veronica Sikes unhappy. "May I have my books please?" she asked, hands reaching toward his hip.

Other students weaved around them. Through the doors held open by the brass doorstops, Billy heard chatter from within.

"Don't be mad," Billy said, handing her the books.

Her chin jutted forward and Billy noticed the lone freckle that rested there. How was it that, after nearly a month of knowing her, he'd never seen it before? "Oh, I'm not mad," she said. She clutched her books against her stomach.

"You look mad."

"I'm not."

"It's just . . . I have to talk about this with *both* of my parents, and Daddy doesn't come home until Friday, remember?"

"Oh." Her face softened. "I forgot about that." She smiled. "I'm sorry, Billy."

Billy shrugged one shoulder. "Don't worry about it, Veronica."

They started toward the doorway nearest them. "But you will ask, won't you?"

"Sure. I said I would, didn't I?"

They neared the place where Billy turned left toward the gymnasium and Veronica went straight toward the auditorium. "I'll see you in homeroom, then?" she asked, so sweetly

Billy thought pure cane sugar would have a hard time standing up next to her.

"Yeah," he said, sounding sheepish, even to his own ears. "I'll be right behind you."

———

Billy decided that night to go ahead and talk to Mama about his going to church. They—the two of them—were at the kitchen sink. Mama washing, Billy drying. Harold had gone to his bedroom, supposedly to do his homework. Billy was never really sure what Harold was up to at any given time.

"Mama?" Billy took a clean plate, slick with water, from his mother's hand.

"Mmm?"

"Veronica asked . . . she asked me if . . . if I could go to church with her sometime."

"Church?"

"Yeah." He turned the plate first one way and then the other. "Mr. and Mrs. Stone go to the same church as the Sikes."

Mama laughed. "What do the Stones have to do with this?" She handed him another plate. Billy set the first plate on the countertop beside him and took the second.

"Nothing, really. I just wanted you to know." He swallowed hard. "And, of course, you and Daddy and Harold are invited too. Veronica said to tell you so."

Mama smiled at him. "You like Veronica, don't you, Billy?"

Billy dropped the second plate on top of the first before reaching for the last. "She's nice, I guess."

"Harold says you walk to and from school with her every day."

"She's nice." He dared to look his mother in the eye. "What?"

146

"What?" Her voice was teasing, something he hadn't heard in a long, long time.

"Come on, Mama. Why are you looking at me like that? Can I go or not?"

Mama sighed, looked back to the suds-filled sink, and dipped her hands beneath the cloud of white. "I'd have to talk to your daddy. We haven't been to church since . . . since Casselton."

"Why didn't Daddy take us when we moved to Miami?"

Mama didn't answer. She pulled a meat platter—one that matched the plates—from the steamy water and took her time to wash it. Billy waited without a word, both for the answer and the platter.

But only the platter came.

15

Two things happened that weekend.

Three, really.

The first was that when Daddy came home on Friday night, it was to a grim-faced Mama. Harold had gotten into trouble at school, back-talking a teacher.

Billy watched from two rooms away—the openness of the house plan allowed for that—as his mother met Daddy at the door. Hands wringing. Even from where he stood in the shadows of the kitchen, he could see the tension in his mother's shoulders. The light quiver of fear that ran up her spine.

She handed Daddy a cocktail—something he'd taken up in Miami—and the folded piece of white paper she'd kept in her apron pocket since three-thirty that afternoon.

She'd even called Mrs. Stone to ask how she should handle the situation. Apparently, Mrs. Stone had said that Mama should meet it head-on.

Daddy handed Mama his suitcase. Said, "What's this about?"

"Maybe you should sit down and drink your cocktail first."

Daddy's face looked angry even before reading what Principal Thompson had written after he'd had a "talk" with

Harold. And after the paddling. The one Billy had heard Harold just scoffed at.

Billy now pressed his lower back more firmly against the countertop. Looked down at his feet. The Keds on his feet. The ones like Jon Provost wore. He tried to whistle the tune to *Lassie*, at least in his mind. Not out loud. Not now.

And he wondered why he hadn't just gone to his room before Daddy got home. Or to the Stones'. Or to the Sikes's.

Anywhere but here.

"Am I going to need two of these?" Daddy asked, walking toward the sofa and holding up his drink.

"I don't know." Mama sat across from him, in the low-back chair with the deep cushion.

"Which one of the boys?" he asked, waving the paper. "No, don't answer that, Bernie. I know which one of the boys." He took a long swallow of the drink. "What I really want to know is why you can't seem to control him when I'm gone. Is it so hard to keep a thirteen-year-old boy in check?"

Mama didn't answer. She tucked her chin toward her throat; her hands clutched each other.

Billy cocked his head a little to the left, watching. Daddy had better not . . .

Daddy drained the amber liquid from the short glass tumbler, placed it on the coffee table before him, and unfolded the paper. Mama retrieved the glass, wiped the table where it had been with the palm of her hand, and then watched her husband as he read. She put the glass on the floor at her feet.

It seemed to Billy that it took Daddy a long time to read just a few words. Not that he knew exactly how many words were on the page, but it couldn't be that many. Then Daddy stood. Unbuckled his belt, slid it out from the loops as he turned toward the long hallway where the bedrooms and the baths were. Where Harold had been waiting since they'd returned home from school. Where Billy was now thankful he wasn't.

Daddy folded the belt. Slapped it against his leg. His ample middle quaked; Billy could see it. Nervous for Harold, he wiped the back of his hand across his mouth, the inside of which was already drier than dirt.

"I'd hoped the move would change all this, Bernice." Daddy sounded almost sad.

"I know." Mama's voice was no more than a whisper.

"Yep." Another slap of belt against leg.

Billy waited for Mama to look up at her husband, but she didn't. She just waited. Just like Billy waited. Waited for Daddy to take the first step toward Harold's bedroom. Waited for the beatings to return.

But then Daddy turned toward Mama, and the belt came down toward her. Mama's face fell to the now-upturned palms in her lap as the leather slapped against her back. Billy heard a muffled whimper and immediately dropped to a squat, wrapped his arms around his knees, and tucked his face in. *Stop! Stop! Don't hurt my mama!*

And, dear God, don't let him see me . . . Mama would be so upset.

Two more whacks. Daddy speaking between clenched teeth. "Your job, Bernice. Your job is to keep them straight."

Mama crying, "I know. I know. I'm sorry, Ira. I'm doing my best."

One final whack. "Your best is not good enough. Never has been. Never will be."

Billy heard the stomping of his father's feet as he headed down the hallway. "Boy!"

Billy looked up. His mother was looking at him now; he could see her between the legs of the dining room chairs that

150

kept them separated. She waved at him to go. Flee. One more time, to run. Before Ira Liddle turned on him too.

From the depth of the hall, Harold's door jerked open. "You comin' for me, old man? This time I'm ready for you!"

Mama stood. "No! Harold, don't!"

Billy scrambled to his feet. Took the necessary steps to make it to the dining room door. Braced his hands on both sides of the frame. Harold's shadow was cast at length before him. Holding something. What was it?

"You think I'm scared of a baseball bat, boy?"

Daddy shoved Harold into his room. Harold tumbled backward like a house of cards caught in a sudden windstorm.

Mama turned to Billy. "Go," she mouthed. "Go."

And Billy did what he'd learned to do best. No need in begging Mama to come with him; she never had. She probably never would. But if she'd failed at keeping Harold straight, she'd succeeded at keeping Billy safe. That much he knew.

He went out the back door, not bothering to be quiet. No need. Enough noise was coming from the other side of the house to silence his exit. Without thought, he ran to the road, turned right, and straight to the Stones'. Mr. Stone was squatting in the front yard, fiddling with the sprinkler. He looked up when he heard Billy's footsteps at the end of the driveway.

"Billy."

Billy stopped running. Started walking. What was he to do from here, anyway? Tell Mr. Stone that his brother was getting a beating for back-talking a teacher? Tell Mrs. Stone that his mother had just been whipped for not doing a good enough job at mothering? Tell them the kind of skewed existence he'd lived as far back as he could remember?

"What brings you over here this late in the afternoon? Hoping to get an early start on the yard work tomorrow?"

Billy reached the man, younger than his father by maybe ten years. A handsome man. Kind. Loving toward his wife. Not a father for whatever reason, but Billy bet he'd have made a good one. Billy rested his hands on his hips and panted a few times before saying, "No, sir." He blew out a long breath. "I just thought I'd stop by and ask about your church. I understand you go to the same place as the Sikes . . ."

The second thing happened about twenty minutes later when Mrs. Stone stepped out the front door with a glass of lemonade for her husband and the news that Billy's mother had called and supper was on the table.

"Yes, ma'am," he said before thanking Mr. Stone for the information on Mercy Street Baptist Church.

He turned on his heels and headed home, figuring if Mama had called him to supper, everything was okay. It was all right for him to return. The house was safe. For now.

Mama was putting a platter of meat loaf—glazed on top with tomato sauce—on the table when Billy stepped through the back door. "Go wash up," she said, her voice monotone. "Supper will be ready to eat in about five minutes."

Billy looked around the room, past the dining room and into the living room. His father sat reading the newspaper, legs crossed as though he hadn't a care in the world. And maybe he didn't. "You all right?" He spoke low enough that only his mother could hear.

"I'm fine." She now stood at the stove, spooning green beans into a vegetable bowl; Billy thought he saw the handle tremble. Maybe it was the weight of the pot. Maybe it was everything else.

"Harold?"

"He'll be all right. Now go."

Billy walked straight through the kitchen. As he reached the dining room door, he heard his mother say, "Be sure to greet your father."

Which he did.

"Where ya been, son?" Ira peered over the top of the paper.

"Went to see Mr. Stone. To ask him about something." Billy started toward the hall doorway but stopped when his father spoke again.

"What do you need to ask Mr. Stone about?"

Billy walked to the chair, the same chair his mother had been hit in the hour before. He sat, placed his elbows on his knees. Cracked his knuckles. "Oh . . . see . . . they go to the same church as the Sikes . . . and Veronica Sikes asked me if I'd like—*we'd* like—to come to services this Sunday . . . and I thought I'd ask Mr. Stone what he thought about it, is all."

"Church, huh?" Daddy folded the paper—folded it and folded it—until it was a neat rectangle of small black-and-white print. "Might be something we ought to do."

Billy blinked at the words. "Really, Daddy?"

Daddy leaned forward. Reached for a new drink sitting on the coffee table. "Well, you know, son"—he took a swig, grimaced slightly, then swallowed—"one of the company home offices is here in Gainesville—the one for the southeast region—and how I look in this community is important. Going to church should be a part of what we do here as a family."

A mixture of excitement and dread poured through Billy's veins like honey from the plastic bear Mama kept on the kitchen table. He wanted to go to church with Veronica—shoot, he was even happy to be at school with her. To sit behind her. To breathe in the flowery scent of shampoo from her thick dark hair.

But another part of him didn't want his daddy and

153

mama—and especially Harold—coming if it was only to pretend to be some great family. Like Daddy was the great father of all fathers. Like he didn't hit Mama. Or Harold. Even when Harold deserved it.

Billy cracked his knuckles. "So does that mean we can go?"

Daddy took another sip of his drink. The liquid was drained from it. Ice clinked along the sides of the glass on their way back down. The smell of whiskey reached Billy where he sat, and his nose twitched. "You tell your little friend that we'll be there on Sunday morning. I assume services begin at eleven?"

"I think so."

"Then we'll be there." Daddy laughed as he sat back, unfolded the paper, and returned to reading. "With bells on."

And so, the third thing was that the family attended Mercy Street Baptist. Not just that Sunday but as regulars. Every Sunday as a foursome. Every Wednesday, just the three of them.

Billy liked going to church. Mama seemed to relax when they were there. Daddy acted like he was on a first-name basis with God, but at least he was pleasant. Harold made fun of it; his complaints started on Saturday evenings and lasted all the way to the door leading into the vestibule. But Billy didn't care. He got to see Veronica, to hang out with other friends from school, to listen to the Bible stories, and to go to activities the church had set up for the kids.

When he was honest with himself, which came only every so often, he admitted that he was getting excited about *just* being at church and all that went with it, even if Veronica wasn't there. True, true . . . Veronica being there was a plus. A definite plus.

But then there was everything else, like being away from home without being at school. And the church had a youth softball team, which he had joined. Turned out, he had a pretty good arm for pitching. He'd not known that before. When the time came for his Sunday school class to hold elections, he'd been nominated president and no one ran against him. Veronica was the class secretary-treasurer; she took up the offering, kept diligent records of how much the class had collected, and then gave the money to the Sunday school teacher, who put half in a churchwide fund and used the other half for class outings.

Like the hayride, and then a month or so later, caroling from door to nearby door and then returning to the church for hot chocolate topped with whipped cream. Or the Valentine's Day banquet, when they all dressed up in their Sunday best and had a nice dinner by candlelight. They'd not been allowed to so much as pretend to be sweet on each other, but Veronica had allowed him to sit next to her.

For that he was more than grateful.

The other thing he liked about going to church was Daddy's behavior before and after. He was only home Friday nights through Monday mornings anyway. And sometimes he didn't come in until Saturday and sometimes he left early Sunday afternoon. So, the little bit of time he *was* at home was spent in a new kind of peace for their family.

Harold never got into it; not at all. But he knew enough not to back-talk Daddy about it anymore. That was another thing Billy was grateful for. Daddy and Harold were fighting less. Mama and Daddy weren't fighting at all. And Mama was growing closer to Mrs. Stone, who was leaving quite an impression on Mama. Sometimes, Billy actually thought he saw her backbone straighten when she confronted Harold.

Still, unless she had to, she never told Daddy anything else about Harold's misbehavior.

Then again, maybe things weren't changing so much after all. Now, instead of being verbally and physically beat up by Daddy, she was being verbally beat up by Harold. Harold never knew when to see the glass as half full.

So really, nothing had changed, had it?

Except . . . maybe . . . the way Billy had learned to look at it.

16

Spring 1958

Three months after his sixteenth birthday, Billy knew he was in love with Veronica Sikes—which he'd suspected for some time. He also knew no other girl would ever have his heart the way she did. Ever.

Sadly, it appeared she did not feel the same way. Or maybe she did, he sometimes thought, and she just wasn't letting her heart and mind connect on the subject.

So on that one particular Saturday in late April of 1958, Billy decided everything would change. It was the night of the church youth spring fling, complete with carnival-type games, bobbing for apples, a booth that sold cotton candy, and horse and buggy rides for fifty cents per one mile out and back again.

With the amount of money Billy had made with his lawn business, he could afford to purchase not only the bike he'd bought three years ago, he could also afford to buy the horse, the buggy, and he'd still have enough left over to take Veronica and him to Orlando and back.

If she'd let him.

157

Veronica—Ronni, he now called her—continued with her "no boyfriend" clause. Not Billy and not any other boy. Which, of course, was just fine with Billy.

Jesus, Ronni said, was her passion. Her *passion*. Her word, not Billy's. And maybe that wasn't even a strong enough word. She loved the Lord so much, if she were Catholic, Billy feared she'd become a nun. What had started to worry him some was that she might want to become something like a missionary in some foreign, underprivileged country. Billy knew he'd follow Ronni *anywhere*, but he also knew he didn't have the calling to be a missionary. Just what he had the calling to be, he didn't know, but he knew it wasn't to be a missionary.

Sometimes Billy asked her what she wanted to do with the rest of her life. Every time, she'd reply, "I haven't thought that far ahead, Billy Liddle."

The answer always perturbed Billy. How was he to make *his* plans if she wasn't making hers?

So he'd say, "But everyone needs a goal, Ronni."

To which she'd shrug and say, "I guess I'll just stick with my plan to work for Daddy until God tells me what it is he wants me to do then." Then she'd look at him and smile that perfect, wonderful smile of hers and say, "What about your goals, Billy? Have you settled on one?"

"Sort of," he'd mumble, to which she'd just giggle.

But tonight, Billy decided, it would all change.

On that Saturday afternoon, Billy stood before the mirror over his chest of drawers and vigorously rubbed Brylcreem between his palms and fingers. "Well, Miss Veronica Sikes . . ." He ran both hands into his thick hair, which he then combed back. "You may not have a plan . . ." He dipped the side of his right hand into his hair to help create a wave. "But tonight I do."

158

He leaned over, grinned at his reflection so as to look for anything between his teeth that didn't need to be there. All good. He'd already applied aftershave and he smelled right nice, if he said so himself.

Billy shuffled his feet, left to right, right to left. "All right then," he said. "I think you'll do, Mr. William Liddle." He sighed. "Now let's hope Miss Veronica Sikes does too."

Billy left his room and started toward the living room, where Daddy was waiting for him with the keys to the car he was allowing Billy to drive that evening. "Billy," Harold's voice barked from the hallway's end, the bedroom directly across from Mama and Daddy's. Billy stopped, turned on a heel, and walked to the doorway, which was half open.

Or maybe half closed.

He rested his hands against the frame. At sixteen, he was now over six feet tall, slender, and he thought—for the most part—that he made a rather impressive picture when he stood like this. Sort of like the late James Dean, looking cool. "Yeah?" He pushed the door the rest of the way open with the toe of his right suede shoe.

Harold was sprawled on his bed. He wore a pair of white skivvies, no shirt and no shoes. Just skivvies. He looked like a soldier resting on his bunk. "Where ya off to all dressed up in a suit and tie?" He inhaled deeply. "Smell good too. Can smell you from all the way over here."

Billy frowned. The way Harold was about anything to do with the church, he didn't really want him to know. Then again, he probably already knew and this was just a setup. "Spring fling."

Harold sat up. "Oh yeah . . . yeah . . ." His hands pressed against his knees. Billy watched Harold's feet bounce, like they wanted to go somewhere but the rest of the body was

159

unwilling. "Going with Veronica, I bet." He grinned at his little brother, but it wasn't to be kind.

"Yeah." Billy pushed away from the door.

"Hey, where ya running off to?" Harold snickered, forcing Billy back to where he'd just been.

Over the past four years, Billy and Harold had grown anything but close. But Billy knew enough to know that Harold wasn't really all that interested in a brotherly conversation. "I gotta go, Harold. I told Ronni I'd pick her up by six and it's quarter till now."

Harold stood, walked over to the wooden chair pushed against the small bedroom desk near the window. A plaid short-sleeved shirt was draped over it. Harold jerked it off, swung it around his muscular frame, and dug his arms into the sleeves. "Ronni." He turned fully toward his brother. Harold reached for the pack of cigarettes on his desk, shook it, pulled one out, and slipped it between what appeared to be dry lips. "Let me ask you a question." He reached for a book of matches, struck one, and held the flame to the end of the cigarette.

The smell of sulfur and burning tobacco reached Billy before Harold had a chance to exhale.

Harold held the pack toward Billy. "Want one?"

"You know I don't smoke, Harold."

"Oh yeah . . . forgot."

Billy leaned against the door frame, watched his brother fiddle with the small buttons on his shirt, all the while the cigarette dangled from between his lips. Every so often he'd inhale, eyes squinting, exhale again. A thin veil of smoke now separated them. "If you've got something to say, say it so I can go, okay?"

Harold's head popped up, eyes flashing something Billy

didn't like seeing. Shirt buttoned, he pulled the cigarette from his mouth. "Just wondering . . ." He stepped over to the desk, knocked ashes into an already overfilled ashtray etched with "Holiday Inn" on the bottom. "Just how close are you and . . . what do you call her now? Ronni?"

Billy looked at his feet. "She's my best friend. You know that."

Harold snickered again. "I'm thinking there's something more." Billy's eyes locked with his brother's. Ten seconds of staring before Harold reached for a pair of pants hanging on the footboard of the bed.

"What are you doing?" Billy asked. He didn't like the feeling coming over him.

"Dressing. I got plans tonight too."

The feeling turned to dread. "Now look here, Harold. Don't go messing things up for me. Not tonight."

Harold adjusted the pants around his narrow waist. "Why? What's tonight?"

Billy felt himself grow warm. "Nothing."

Harold drew on the cigarette again, long and hard. While blowing a cloud of gray and white into the air, he stubbed the remainder into the ashtray. Old butts spilled onto the maple desk. "Tonight, huh?" He nodded. "Okay, okay. We've now established something special is happening tonight, and you don't want me to mess it up for you." He rested his hands on his hips. "We're brothers, Billy. What makes you think I'd do that?"

Billy stepped fully into the room. "'Cause you've gotten mean enough lately, Harold. You and all your friends think it's funny to do some of the nasty things you do. Me and my friends, we're just good kids wanting to have a good time without getting into trouble. Don't mess that up just to get your kicks."

Harold sat on the bed, reached under, and pulled out a pair of Hush Puppies loafers. "Don't worry, kiddo. I'm not gonna bother you and your little friends. You're all right there."

Billy watched as his brother pulled a pair of socks from inside the shoes, dug his feet into them. "So was that it? Are we done?"

Harold looked at Billy again. "Yeah. I just wanted to see what you'd be up to tonight."

Billy nodded once. "Okay, then. Sure. See ya tomorrow, I guess."

Thanks to Harold, Billy was five minutes late picking up Ronni. A fact that Mr. Sikes pointed out as he opened the door for him.

"I know, sir," Billy said. "My brother and I were talking and . . ." He stopped with his explanation when he realized Mr. Sikes was smiling at him.

"Well, come on in . . . come on in. Have a seat and let's you and me talk for a few minutes while Veronica does that last-minute fixing up girls do."

Billy liked Mr. Sikes. He was well-groomed. Handsome, even. He had an easy way about him. And he loved his family. He was a successful restaurateur, firmly established in the community and the church. He was someone Billy aspired to be like. Certainly more than his own father, whom they'd seen less and less of lately. Seemed to Billy he was coming in more on Saturday late mornings and leaving more on Sunday early afternoons. Which, in a lot of ways, was just fine with Billy, even if it wasn't with Mama.

"How's the lawn business, Billy?" John Sikes pointed to the sofa before sitting in what Billy knew was his favorite chair.

Billy sat. "It's good. Starting to build up again after the winter months."

"Not a lot of winter here in Florida."

Billy shook his head. "No, sir. But instead of cutting lawns once a week, I don't usually go but once a month or every three weeks, and that cuts into my income."

Mr. Sikes leaned back in his chair, crossed his legs. "Tell me something, Billy. Do you get paid by cut or do you have your customers on a payment plan?"

"Not sure what you mean, sir." Billy scooched back on the sofa, the one matching the chair.

"Well, see . . . it's just good business sense. Take the number of times you cut a customer's lawn in a year. Multiply that by what you charge. Then divide by twelve. Give your customers a monthly rate—which will be less in the summer months for you, but will sustain you all year-round."

Billy scratched at his temple. "I'd not thought of that."

John Sikes chuckled. "I'm a businessman, Billy. I have to think of things like that." He shifted in the chair. "Brings me to a point I'd like to make. How'd you like to work for me a couple of nights a week?"

"At the restaurant?" *Where Ronni works?*

Mr. Sikes grinned at what Billy knew was his naïveté. Of course, at the restaurant. "Where else, Billy?"

"I'm sorry. Not thinking, I guess. I know Stanley cuts your lawn, but you've never mentioned anything before about . . ." Billy laughed at himself. "Yes, sir. I'd very much like to work for you at the restaurant."

Mr. Sikes laughed with him. "Aren't you even going to ask what I want you to do for me? It could be pure grunt work."

Billy rubbed his hands together. "I'm good with whatever

you'd have me do, Mr. Sikes." From somewhere in the back of the house, the phone rang.

"That's what I like about you, son. You're willing and able."

Billy felt himself grow warm at the endearment. *Son.* Maybe one day . . .

A delicate clearing of the throat brought Billy's attention to the wide doorway leading into the Sikes's foyer. He jumped up while Mr. Sikes stood slowly. "Hey . . ." Billy breathed out.

She was a sight, all right. Cottony white blouse. Pink skirt with lots of—what did his mother call those? Accordion pleats?—that fell over what Billy thought must be a mountain of petticoats. She wore nylons too. And satiny baby pink heels. Her hands were hidden by little white gloves. She wore her dark hair scooped up and twisted around in the back with curls around her forehead. A small gold cross winked at him from her naturally tanned skin.

Billy Liddle counted himself the luckiest boy alive. "You look nice, Ronni."

"You look nice too," she said with a smile from lightly painted pink lips.

Something passed between the two of them. Billy felt it. Did she?

John Sikes clapped his hands together, breaking the moment, just as Harriett Sikes walked into the room behind her daughter. "Hello, Billy," she said.

Mrs. Sikes was as pretty as her husband was handsome. She looked at her husband. "Sweetheart, Vera just called from the restaurant. She wants to know what time you're planning to come back."

Everyone in the room turned to the man of the house, who glanced at his watch. "Just as soon as I see these two out," he said. He walked over to Billy, slapped him on the shoulder, and said, "Sorry Mother and I can't join the festivities tonight." Another slap.

"What about your parents, Billy?" Mrs. Sikes asked. "Are they going to the spring fling? Having a date night?"

A date night? His parents? Not hardly. "No, ma'am. Daddy said I could use the car and he and Mama would sit this one out." He smiled, hoping to keep Mrs. Sikes from asking any other questions about his mother and father. "But thank you for asking."

Mr. Sikes barked in laughter, gave Billy one final pat on the back as he said, "Now you take good care of my little girl."

"Daddy . . ."

"And have her back by . . . what time, Mother?"

Billy looked to Mrs. Sikes, who said, "We agreed ten o'clock."

Billy returned his attention to Mr. Sikes. Ten o'clock. His brain began the calculation. They'd arrive at the church by six-forty-five, seven at the latest. That gave them three hours. Three hours wasn't a long time . . . not a long enough time . . . but it would have to do. "Ten o'clock, Billy," John Sikes said. "Not a minute later." He raised a finger. "Not one."

"No, sir."

"Daddy, we're just friends, for heaven's sake."

John Sikes gave Billy a look that read "But not in this boy's mind." Billy grew warmer than before.

"I'll have her home by ten, sir," Billy said. He looked to the girl who owned his heart. "Come on, Ronni. Let's get to the church."

17

"Norma told me the other day that Brother Ralph said we could play music from the sound system at the spring fling," Ronni announced from the passenger side of Ira Liddle's yellow and white Chrysler Windsor. She fluffed her skirt over her knees and gave him a smile.

"I thought we always had music," Billy said, looking forward. He gripped the wheel until his knuckles turned grayish-white.

He didn't have to see to know Ronni rolled her eyes. "Not *that* kind of music. *Real* music."

Billy turned the wheel, making a sharp right. "You mean, like *our* kind of music?"

"Mmmhmm. Norma said she was bringing her Pat Boone albums and Jerry said he was bringing the latest Everly Brothers he just bought at Woolworth's." She sighed. "The Everly Brothers . . . just think."

"You think someone will bring Elvis?"

From the corner of his eye, he watched as she clutched gloved hands. "Oh no . . . no one is *that* brave, but Norma also said that she was going to try to slip in Buddy Holly."

"That would be boss."

"I know."

Ronni sounded happy, and nothing made Billy happier than Ronni sounding happy, so . . . so far, the evening was going well. He turned the wheel again, forced himself to relax, and the car bounded into the far side of the church's parking lot. Most of it, along with the church's property—not the side with the graveyard—had been converted into a carnival.

"Oh, Billy, can you believe this? I love the spring fling so much."

Billy parked the car. "Stay right there," he said. He opened his door, tumbled out, slipped the keys into his pocket, and then ran around to the passenger side to open Ronni's door for her. "Madame," he said, making a grand gesture.

She giggled. "This is why you're my best friend," she said, swinging her legs out of the car and planting her feet onto the pavement. "Looks like we've already got quite the crowd."

Billy shut the door behind her before falling into step with her. "Hey, Ronni?"

"Yeah?"

"Um . . . I just wanted to say . . . you look . . . very pretty tonight."

Veronica stopped. Turned to look at him. He noticed how her index fingers laced each other, as if they were pinky swearing. Her head tilted to one side. "Thank you, Billy Liddle." Her voice was whisper soft.

He sighed. Contented. So far, so good. "You're welcome." Then he smiled his best lopsided grin. "Hey, I hear Connie Francis singing. Wonder who brought her?"

"Maybe Jean. She loves Connie Francis." They continued to stare at each other before she finally said, "Well, let's go, okay?"

Billy bought her cotton candy. Pink, to match her dress.

He won a blue and white teddy bear for her by throwing darts. They played the cola-ringtoss—Ronni won—walked the cakewalk—this time Ronni won a cupcake, which Billy ate—and took part in the square dance competition, where they were the third to be voted off the stage.

But they laughed about it, all the way through.

For a while they watched Brother Ralph—a powerhouse of a man—challenge carnival guests to a round of arm wrestling. It cost twenty-five cents to enter, the money going to missions. Ronni asked Billy if he wanted to go hand to hand against their pastor, but Billy declined. No need in being totally humiliated on the night he hoped would end with Ronni seeing him as boyfriend material.

When the sun had nearly set, Billy suggested the horse and buggy ride. Ronni seemed relaxed and in good spirits when he asked; the success of his plan was now all the more promising. "I'd like that," she said.

So they walked to the large live oak standing sentinel at the back of an open field, the loading and unloading station . . .

Where about twenty other couples appeared to have the same idea.

"Oh . . ." Ronni drawled. "Do we really want to wait for this?"

"Sure we do." But he looked at his Timex just to make sure. They'd spend more time standing here than he'd counted on, which would leave them with precious little time before Billy had to get her home. Still, for his plan to work . . .

Patti Page crooned "Let Me Call You Sweetheart" from the sound system.

Billy slipped his hands into his pockets, all the while his mind scrambling for something to say. He cleared his throat. "Is it all right with you, Ronni? To wait, I mean?"

She looked around, as though she were not sure. Or like she was looking for someone else to be with. He'd counted himself lucky that she hadn't run off with any of her girl-friends already. "No . . . no. This is fine." They took a step up. "Looks like there's more than just one horse and buggy, so maybe this won't take *too* long."

Billy felt defeated. "Look, Ronni. If you're going to have that attitude . . ."

Veronica's green eyes grew wide. "What attitude? What's wrong with you, Billy?"

He shook his head. "Nothing." He looked down at his shoes, which had grown dusty by fine grains of sand. The night had gone so perfectly; he didn't want anything to spoil it for them. *Him.* "Sorry."

The sound of tires squealing in the parking lot stopped him from saying anything more. He turned, as did everyone standing nearby, and, he figured, everyone within a mile ra-dius. He felt his brow furrow.

Harold's car—a '56 Chevy convertible—was among the half dozen skidding dangerously close to other parked cars, the start of the carnival booths, and the tree line on the left side of the church property. Instinct raised Billy's right arm, his hand gripped Ronni's, and he pulled her behind him just as Harold's car jumped a curb and tore across the open field. Billy saw one of his brother's hands on the steering wheel, one holding a beer bottle. It was raised in some sort of mock salute.

The other cars followed close behind. Someone shouted "Holy rollers!" Someone else laughed.

Engines revved. People screamed. The two sounds became feverish. Billy heard a whinny. He turned to see a carriage filled with four of his fellow church youth, eyes wide at the cars barreling toward them. The horse—an impressive flaxen-maned brown quarter horse—reared, his front hoofs rising two feet from the earth. It pitched forward; the carriage jerked and then sped behind the spooked animal.

Others around them ran, but Billy pushed Ronni against the tree, wrapped himself around her, his back to her front, his arms straining to keep her safe. His eyes locked with Harold's just as the car started to skid.

Billy knew his brother; Harold was going to fake them out.

He was going to come dangerously close to him and Ronni. He was going to dare them to run like Billy always did. And if they did, he'd laugh. And he'd do it again and again.

Dust had kicked up behind the Chevy, leaving the others in a brown cloud. Billy heard Ronni scream; he pressed himself even tighter against her, keeping his eyes in perfect line with his brother's, daring him to kill them both if he thought he could. Anything less from the younger, and the older would torment them for life. Billy couldn't let that happen. Not tonight. Not that he truly believed . . .

Harold threw back his head and laughed. He flipped the wheel to his left until the rear of the Chevy pushed its way toward them. Calculating the velocity, Billy realized that the speed had been too fast, braking had come too slow, and his brother's face now registered surprise. Billy screamed "Run!" even as his left hand grabbed Ronni's right wrist and pulled. The sound of others—the cries of both young and old in realization as to what was about to happen—filled his ears as quickly as the dust and grit sanded his eyes. He jerked the girl whose face was paralyzed in fear, threw his arms around her, then fell to the ground and rolled.

The thud of metal against tree trunk, the bending of one against the other, rushed over him.

Ronni cried his name from beneath. He scampered to stand, yelled, "Harold!" before hobbling toward the wreckage. Fearing the worst and seeing nothing close to it. The car was beyond repair, but Harold sat with only a trickle of blood dripping from his nose to the front of the shirt that had earlier hung on the back of a chair.

Harold took a sip of beer, the bottle still clutched in his left hand, and said, "I thought we'd join you."

Billy wasn't sure when the other cars had stopped. He wasn't aware of the moment when the adults who'd been attending the spring fling ran onto the scene. He didn't hear the police sirens shrieking in the distance. He only felt the hot chrome of the driver's door in his hand, the cotton as he clutched the front of his brother's shirt and pulled until Harold was out of the car, lying facedown in the dirt, struggling to stand. Billy kicked him, swore words he'd promised never to use.

From deep within a tunnel, he heard Ronni yell his name as she always did. "Billy Liddle." In spite of the obvious pleading in her voice, he kicked again. This time Harold rolled over, laughed at him, causing the anger that had been boiling inside him for so long to explode. Something guttural escaped from deep within his gut, and he fell on top of his brother, ready to beat the life out of him, if he had to.

But before Billy could make matters worse, Brother Ralph's muscular arms encircled his waist and pulled him up, then pushed him toward Ronni. Her slender arms slid over his shoulders and encircled his neck. He felt the strength of them. Her face buried itself into his neck, the moisture of her tears slid down his flesh and into his shirt. "Ronni . . ." he breathed.

She tilted her head back, looked into his eyes. "Are you okay?" she asked.

"Me? I'm okay. Are you?"

She didn't answer but instead looked over his shoulder. The look in her eyes told him he should too. Behind them a short line of police cars were entering the church's property. Billy looked to where Brother Ralph had helped Harold to his feet and held him, waiting for the police to arrive.

"The others have disappeared," Ronni said, her eyes scanning the grounds.

"Cowards. They left Harold to face this on his own."

With her fingertips pressed against his chin, she turned his face to hers. "Don't tell me you're going to feel sorry for him, Billy Liddle. He practically tried to kill us."

He shook his head even as he wondered if she felt his shiver. "That wasn't what he was doing." Billy became keenly aware of the people gathering. "Come on," he said, drawing her away from what he knew would be a spectacle. "Let's go over by the candy apple booth."

"But what if the police need to talk with you?" she asked.

His hand reached for hers. He wanted to protect her, to guide her, to tell her everything his heart had hoped to say. Gratefully, without hesitation or another question, hers slipped into his, allowing him a moment of gallantry. "I'm sure they will. But I'd just as soon not be a spectacle." He gave her a lopsided grin. "Well, no more than I already am."

They moved against a stream of curious onlookers but made it to the booth unnoticed. Billy turned to face the scene of the crime, keeping her face toward his. When he was needed, he'd know it. Until then, precious minutes were slipping away.

"Look, Ronni . . . there was something I . . . when we were going to be out there with the horse and carriage. I had something I wanted to say."

"Billy? You look ashen. Are you going to be sick?"

"No."

"Because if you are, I wouldn't blame you. After all that just happened."

Billy shook his head. "You don't understand, Ronni. This kind of stuff . . . *This* is what I've grown up with. This isn't new to me. Harold's got bad blood running through his veins, you know that."

She blinked. "I know you don't like to talk much about things at home. That you'd rather be with me and my family than with yours."

"For good reason." He took both of her hands in his. "Things in my family have not always been . . . have never been, really, like what you think. Not like what Daddy and Mama make them out to be when we're at church. Do you understand what I'm saying?"

"Not really, no."

Billy looked back at the scene. The police had made it to Harold. He had been handcuffed and was being led toward a squad car. Brother Ralph's neck was craned, his eyes roaming about the grounds. "Brother Ralph is looking for me," he said.

"Then we'd best go back."

Billy squeezed her hands. "No, wait. Wait until I say what I have to say."

"Okay." She sounded timid and afraid.

"Ronni, you've been my best friend since we moved here."

"And you're my best friend, Billy Liddle." The green in her eyes intensified.

"I've done all right here. First pitcher for the church team—"

"No one pitches like you, Billy."

"Sunday school president every year and I'm on the youth group leadership team."

"I know." Pink lips broke into a smile. "I'm so proud of you."

"My business has been successful, Ronni, and now your dad has asked me to work for him."

"I know that too."

He pressed his forehead down on hers. "Don't be mad, okay?"

"Billy?" He could smell her breath, they were so close. Cotton candy and sweet candied apples. "Why would I ever be mad with you?"

"Because . . . because you're always so focused on God and you say we're best friends."

"We *are* best friends."

"But I want more than that, Ronni. We're not twelve anymore. We're sixteen and—"

She pulled her head away from his. Their eyes met. "I feel the same way too," she whispered. "But Daddy really doesn't want—"

Billy laughed. Felt the first flight of hope rise up inside. "Your daddy knows, Ronni. He's reading me like a book." He squeezed her hands again. "But I'm more than happy to speak with him. To tell him my intentions. To promise him to respect you and not do anything that would make him ashamed."

"Or God."

"Or God."

She took in a breath through her nostrils then back out before giggling just enough to set his heart to flight. "So what are you asking me, Billy Liddle?"

He peered over her shoulder, past the multicolored and striped curtains and awnings of carnival booths, to the field now covered in the gray of late evening. Brother Ralph had

174

spotted them and was walking to where he'd hoped to hide. His time was more than precious now. "Be my girl?"

Ronni rose slightly on her toes, kissed him gently on the cheek, and whispered, "I've always been your girl, Billy Liddle. I suspect I always will be."

18

Trinity, South Carolina

Patsy wiped down the kitchen counter in her new home for the third time since washing, drying, and putting away the breakfast dishes. Behind her, at the kitchen table, Mam folded a load of towels she'd just hauled in from the indoor laundry room.

"How in the world one family can dirty this many towels is beyond me," she said in her best "I do declare" voice.

Patsy pretended to be amused as she laughed and said, "You *do* know how many children I have, don't you?" Sponge clutched firmly in her rubber-gloved hand, she leaned against the countertop to face her mother. The scent of Pine-Sol wafted around her.

Mam plopped another tri-folded towel on top of a short stack. "Four and counting."

"Not on your life. Four and *stopping*."

Mam reached for a hand towel, one of the new ones Patsy had just ordered from the Sears catalog. Suez Tan, the color was called. One of their newest colors. To Patsy it looked like another form of pink just with a prettier name. "I can't help but say I'm glad to hear it, Patsy."

176

"I told Gilbert, 'Enough is enough.'" She turned to the sink, dipped her hand and the sponge into the scalding water, brought it up, and squeezed. It splattered against her cotton shirt and denim pedal pushers as she went back to wiping down the counter.

The fourth time.

"Aren't you afraid you'll take the color off the kitchen tiles that husband of yours paid so much for?"

"I'm not sure how to take color off of cream-colored tiles, Mam."

"I'm talking about the pink ones."

Patsy turned again to her mother. Mam was placing the folded laundry into the wicker basket perched at the end of the old farm table Gilbert had purchased for one of his station cafés but had decided to bring home instead. Together they'd sanded it before he'd headed back out again for another stretch of time on the road, managing Milstrap's now five locations.

The original plus one for each child, he'd joked.

Not funny, she'd said.

And then he was off again, leaving her to be both father and mother and table painter. Nurse and teacher and housekeeper.

Part-time housekeeper. He had employed a woman who came in twice a week to help with the heavy work.

Like ironing, he'd said.

"Thanks, Mam, for coming over to help me today. Having the ladies from the church coming this evening is just more than I can deal with by myself. And with Ella Mae not coming until tomorrow . . ."

Mam hoisted the basket onto her ample hip. "What time should I come back for the young'uns?"

"Five-thirty?" Patsy threw the sponge into the water and

reached for the basket as she walked across the wide kitchen. "Want me to take that?"

But Mam was already heading toward the rest of the house. "I've got it, Patsy. I know how to carry a load of clothes and put them in the linen closet."

While Patsy waited for her mother to return from the far side of the house, she emptied the cleaning water, then scrubbed the sink down. That done, she peeled away the rubber gloves, which kept her hands soft but made her feel hot all over.

You should wear gloves, Gilbert had told her once as they lay in bed. Your hands are getting red and chapped.

She didn't mind so much, she told him, although she really did.

He kissed her fingertips, drawing each one into his mouth as he so often did to tease her, then turned her palms up and kissed them too.

But he minded, he said. He didn't want his wife to have the hands of a scullery maid.

A scullery maid, she now thought. If she *were* such, would she be as miserable as she was now? Would she have to pretend as hard that she wasn't?

"That's done," Mam said as she reentered the kitchen, startling her. "What can I do for you next?"

Patsy shook her head. Her hair was tightly bound by brush rollers and felt heavy. Other than a trim, she'd not cut it since before her wedding day. When Gilbert was on the road, she wore it in a ponytail or twisted behind her head. When Gilbert was home or she was attending special events or socials, she wore it down. Just the way he liked it. "Nothing," she said. "I'll finish up the house, bake the cake, and prepare the little finger sandwiches."

"Did you decide if you were going to have stuffed celery sticks?"

"I did." She walked over to the fat pink refrigerator and jerked the door open to reveal a covered platter full of them. "Ta-da."

Mam peered in. "Cream cheese and pineapple or pimento cheese?"

"Both."

Mam threw up her hands in mock praise. "You are a wonderful hostess, my dear. The ladies at the church will be talking about this for a month, I'm sure." She walked to a corner chair where her purse rested. "It's hard to believe she's only twenty-five, they'll say."

"An old twenty-five."

"That's because you rushed life, not that I'm going to drag that up again." But she grimaced anyway. "Silver polished, crystal gleaming, and china so clean I can see myself in it and all laid out in the dining room?"

"I did that yesterday. I'm surprised you haven't already looked to see." Patsy walked behind Mam, who ambled toward the living room and the foyer.

Mam's shoulders visibly squared. "I have never been nosy, you know that."

"I have to agree, you have not." She pressed her hand to a section of rollers. "Have you heard from Lloyd? How are things in Germany?"

"Got a letter yesterday. He's doing well. Who knew he'd take to army life like he has."

"Well, I, for one, miss him."

"No more than Holly Franklin. My land, that girl is counting down the days. Literally." Once at the foyer, Mam took a brief detour to sneak a peek into the dining room. "Yes, I'd

179

say you're all set." She opened her purse and retrieved her car keys. "When will Gilbert be home?"

"Tomorrow."

"Will he stay long this time?"

Patsy blinked at her mother. "He said he will." She tried to smile. "So maybe so."

Gainesville, Florida

Maybe it would have been better if Harold had just stayed in jail that night, Billy figured.

The preacher had come to the house before Billy got home. Before he could even get Ronni back to her father's house. Before he had time to tell her parents what had occurred. Not that they hadn't already heard. News traveled fast. Bad news even faster.

Asking her father for permission to date his daughter would have to wait until another evening. Until then, he and Ronni decided on the way back, they'd keep everything as it was.

He didn't even ask to kiss her, though his heart burst with desire to do so. That would come later too. Oh, Father in heaven and shout hallelujah; that would come later.

When he arrived home that night after ten, the mood in the house was as dark as the interior. Mama sat at the kitchen table, hands clutching each other, illuminated only by the dim lighting over the stove. A sight he'd seen one too many times in his life already.

"Mama," he spoke from the darkened interior of the dining room.

"You should go on to bed now." She didn't bother to look at him.

But Billy took a seat near her instead. "Where's Daddy?"

"He went with Brother Ralph to the jailhouse." She cut her eyes toward him—he could see the whites of her eyes—but her head didn't move. "You all right?"

"Yeah. I'm okay." He looked around the room. "You want me to turn on a light?"

"No, thank you, son."

Billy reached across the table, touched his mother's hand. "Did he . . . ?"

"No. But I'm sure it's coming, sooner or later. He'll make this all my fault." Billy saw her lips break apart in a half smile. "It's been a long time since he's lost his temper. I guess we have that much to be grateful for."

"Mama . . . we can leave. You and me." He squeezed her hand. "We can find a place nearby and . . ."

"How do you suggest we live, Billy?" She sighed. "I suppose I could take in more laundry, like I used to back in Casselton."

Billy didn't say anything at first. "I don't remember that."

"You were just a baby back then. Four years old, I think. Harold was five."

Billy thought for a moment before asking, "And Patsy?"

His mother's breath visibly caught in her chest. "Patsy was thirteen." She smiled again. "She went with me to get that old washing machine. We kept it on the back porch. Lands, your father didn't hardly make anything in those days. I guess the move to Miami did us some good after all."

Billy didn't want his mother to force the conversation away from the subject of his sister. There were things he wanted to know. Needed to know. "I remember that. And I remember Patsy helping you with the laundry you took in."

Mama continued to look straight ahead. "It wouldn't do to let people know around here that I used to wash other people's clothes. Your daddy would be so mad."

181

"Mama, can't we talk about Patsy?"

She looked at him fully now. "I'd prefer not to, Billy."

"But why?" When his mother didn't answer, he added, "Why did she go away?"

Mama looked down at her hands. "Some things in life don't need to be discussed."

"But Mama, she was my sister." His felt his eyes narrow. "She *is* my sister."

"Always and forever. As she will always be my daughter." Billy heard Mama swallow hard. "I wonder sometimes . . . I think about calling . . . but that wouldn't be right."

"You know where she is?"

Mama raised her chin. "Our pastor—mine and Patsy's daddy's—he knew of this family. I only met them once . . . before I called. They lived in South Carolina. Good people. I . . . I've talked to them a few times."

"About Patsy?"

"About Patsy going there. About . . . other things. And I know if anything bad had ever happened to her, they'd call me."

"But Mama, how would they know where to find—"

Billy's words were halted when Mama suddenly grabbed his hand, still lying near hers on the table. "Tell me about your evening, Billy." She shook her head. "Not that whole debacle with your brother. Tell me about you and Veronica. Did you tell her how you feel, like you told me you'd tell her?"

In spite of the angst, Billy smiled. "Yes, ma'am. I did."

"And?"

"She feels the same way too. Mama, are you sure you don't want me to turn on a light?"

"No." Her lips pursed. "Just keep a listen out for your

daddy and the reverend coming back. And when you do, go right on to bed."

"Not unless you do, Mama. Not unless you go on to bed too."

"That won't be necessary."

As if on cue, a tap came to the back door. Billy stood so quickly his chair almost toppled over. Mama rose from her chair too, but more slowly. "It's okay, son," she said. "That'll be Mrs. Stone. She's coming over to sit with me."

Billy watched as his mother opened the door to both Mr. and Mrs. Stone.

"Hey, Billy," Mr. Stone greeted him as he stepped in. "If that's Billy. I can barely make him out over there."

"Land sakes, Bernice," Nadine Stone said almost simultaneously. "What in the world are you doing sitting in the dark?" And with that, a switch was flipped up and light filled the room. Before Billy had time to respond, Mrs. Stone had made her way past him, into the dining room, then the living room, turning on lights as she went along. "I've never seen anything like this in my life," she declared. "You'd think someone had died."

Herbert Stone had reached Billy, shook his hand, and said, "You all right there, son?"

"Yes, sir."

"We heard about what happened from Brother Ralph."

Billy frowned. "I thought I saw you at the spring fling. Over by the ringtoss."

"You did. We didn't stay long." Mr. Stone then looked at Mama, who stood motionless near the back door. "Bernice, are *you* all right?"

Mama closed the door. "Yes. I didn't realize the house was so dark." She shot her son a look that read, "Say nothing."

Mrs. Stone rejoined the group. "I'll make coffee while we wait."

Billy watched her moving about in the Liddle kitchen as though she knew it better than her own. He looked to his mother, who seemed to jerk to life. "Here, Nadine, I'll do it. You get the cups and the spoons."

"I'm . . . I'm going to head on to bed, I think," Billy said.

Mama returned to where he stood, gave him a light hug, and said, "I'll talk with you later. Sleep well."

Billy nodded at Mr. Stone, said "good night" to Mrs. Stone, and then ambled down the hallway toward his room, grateful for their presence and confused by his mother's behavior. More now than he'd ever been. Seemed to him that a woman whose oldest son had almost killed her youngest would have more of a reaction. That a woman who'd had her oldest child's name brought up for the first time in years wouldn't let all talk of her fall away without another word. And that a woman whose brutal husband was on his way home from jail with their son would be too upset to calmly prepare coffee for the neighbors.

The scent of it brewing reached his bedroom door before he had time to close it.

Nearly an hour later, he heard the front door open, close. Harold's voice saying their mother's name. Billy strained to hear his father's footsteps, but instead heard the family car's engine turn over and hum for a minute, followed by the crunching of tires rolling out of the driveway.

He furrowed his brow, raised himself in bed on his elbows, and waited. Minutes later, after a low conversation he couldn't make out but recognized as being between Harold and Mr. Stone, footsteps increased in heaviness as Harold walked down the hallway.

His bedroom door opened. Billy was still balancing himself on his elbows. He turned his head to see his brother's silhouette shadowed there. "Sorry, Bill."

Bill. He'd never been called that before. He chose not to answer.

"You mad at me?"

"Shouldn't I be?" He sat up fully. "I can still smell the beer on you."

"Yeah, well . . . I already got lectured from the old man and now from Mr. Stone. I don't need it from you."

"Go to bed then."

Harold snickered. "Think I will."

19

Billy woke the next morning to a blinding headache. He went into the Jack and Jill bathroom he shared with his brother to dig around in the medicine cabinet with his hand covering his eyes, hoping to find a bottle of Bayer.

Instead, he knocked everything into the sink and onto the countertop.

"Billy?" It was Mama's voice.

"Mama," he whispered.

She placed a hand on his shoulder. He wore pajama bottoms and a top, but the top was unbuttoned and it hung open. Sick as he felt, it was an odd moment between mother and son. He'd been modest with her since they'd moved to Gainesville.

Harold never had been. Harold didn't care how he looked in front of anyone.

"What's wrong, son?"

Billy fiddled with the buttons on his pajama top, but it was difficult with his eyes closed. "I have a bad headache. I've never had one like this before."

She rubbed his shoulder, back and forth, back and forth. "Sounds like a migraine." She kept her voice whisper soft. "And it's no wonder. Go on back to bed. I'll bring you something for it."

Minutes later his mother entered his room. She gave him a pill that she said was stronger than a Bayer. He took it along with a sip of water. He returned his head to the coolness of his pillow, keeping his eyes closed.

"I'm applying this ice pack to your forehead, Billy." He felt both the cold and the weight of the pack. The feeling it gave him was remarkable; it hurt so good. "All this stress has been too much for you, I'm sure." Mama sat on the edge of the bed. Within seconds he felt the soft stroking of her fingertips along his brow. He groaned. She hadn't done this since he'd been a boy. But he remembered it well.

"Feeling a little better?"

"That pill must work fast," he whispered.

"It's the one the doctor gives me when I have my headaches sometimes."

Billy breathed in and out of his nostrils. "I didn't know you had bad headaches, Mama."

"That's not the kind of thing a son should worry about his mama."

God love her, he thought. Somehow her devotion to him had been skewed all these years. Enough to keep a headache from him but not enough to keep them all safe from his father. He turned his jaw a little to the side. More reflex than movement. And in that moment he went from not knowing to knowing. Instinct. Bloodline instinct.

"That was it, wasn't it?"

"What?"

"That's why Patsy went away. You were protecting her from Daddy."

"Shhh, now. If you get yourself all riled up, your headache will return."

"But that's it, isn't it?"

"Yes."

He blinked to open his eyes, but her fingertips slipped over his lids and he closed them again.

"Don't open your eyes quite yet, son. Trust me. Let this pill work to ease you back to sleep. When you wake, you'll feel much better and I'll make you some soup to eat."

"Why would you send her away but not us? Not you, me, and Harold? Or just you and me?"

"You're too young to understand all this, Billy."

He continued to breathe in and out through his nostrils. Finally, he said, "I remember him whipping her."

The stroking stopped, then resumed. "He has always believed that spanking was the best discipline."

"I didn't say spanking."

She didn't answer.

"And I don't remember him ever spanking me." He kept his voice at a whisper. "Maybe once."

"No, he never spanked you. He never had to. Harold broke the rules enough for both of you."

"And you? Did you break the rules?"

"Sometimes."

Billy felt himself floating backward, as though his head had grown heavier and was falling into the abyss of his pillow. With the feeling came a memory, the sound of his father demanding to know, "Where's the girl?"

"Where's the girl." The words slipped off his tongue so slowly he wasn't even sure he'd said them.

"What?"

"That's what he said. Daddy. 'Where's the girl.' Never called her by her name, did he?"

"Only sometimes. Rarely."

No more . . . looks! The words echoed. They were his

mother's words. His mother's voice, spoken to his father. "Loooooks . . ."

"Shhh . . ."

He was drifting. Falling. Slipping away. He wouldn't fight it. Okay, Mama. I'll go back to sleep and I'll wake up feeling better. But I'll also wake up knowing. It wasn't Daddy whipping Patsy that sent her away. It was something else. Something sinister.

And Mama had loved *her* enough to keep her safe.

_____

The headaches came frequently at first, then subsided. About once every six weeks, he'd wake with a migraine, his mother would give him one of her pills, and he'd return to bed. A few hours later, he'd wake, feeling a little "hung over" as Daddy called it, but no worse for the wear.

Mama had taken him to see the doctor, who'd run a series of tests. But they came up with nothing. "He's not dying," Dr. Ciuba said matter-of-factly. "I suspect it's just growing pains."

Daddy had put it another way. "As long as you can do your work, you'll live," he said.

Daddy. A man who was managing to spend less and less time with his family. By the fall of 1958, he was practically a shadow passing along the walls of the house. Sometime Saturday afternoon—usually just before supper—his car rolled into the driveway. Then, on Sunday afternoon, after church and Sunday dinner, he took the newly packed suitcase from his wife's hand, kissed her on the cheek, and meandered out the door.

Billy had never seen his mother look so relaxed. Or perplexed.

Only once had he overheard them speaking of the way of things. It was late one October Saturday night. Billy had just returned from a date with Ronni; they'd gone to a church social, one of the few things they were allowed to do. Billy was reading *Of Mice and Men*—the report that was due on Monday—when the voices of his parents interrupted the flow of Steinbeck's words.

Why was she nagging him, Daddy wanted to know. "The bills are paid. You have the nicest roof over your head you've had in your entire adult life. I doubt Sweeny could have done this well for you."

"Don't you dare say his name," Mama said. Billy could tell her teeth were clenched. And he wondered where she had gotten her bravado. "You are not worthy to say his name."

There was a pause. Billy waited for the smack. But it didn't come.

"What?" his mother countered. "You aren't going to hit me?"

"Not. Yet."

Billy placed his book, splayed and facedown, on top of the blue chenille spread of his bed before sliding off and standing. He took only one step.

"So, I'm supposed to be happy with you here only one night a week, Ira? I thought it would get better when we moved to Gainesville. I thought you said that being so close to the home office would change things."

Another pause from his father. Another step from Billy.

He thought he heard his father chuckle.

"Are you telling me, Bernie, that you actually miss me?"

"Yes, Ira." His mother's voice was soft. Sweet. "I do miss you. I miss you very much."

But . . . how could she?

His father chuckled again. He'd had more than one drink tonight; perhaps that accounted for his good mood. Maybe.

By now Billy stood at the door, cracked it just a little so as to hear better. He felt rather than saw that he wasn't alone. He opened the door a little wider, craned his neck around the frame, and saw his brother leaning in the open doorway to his own room. Harold raised a hand as if to say hello. Billy returned the gesture. They both turned to look at the closed door across the hallway.

Had their mother just giggled?

Billy looked at Harold again. Using his thumb, Harold indicated they should both return to their rooms. Billy took two steps backward before easing the door shut.

He returned to his bed. And his book.

Work for Mr. Sikes was going well, which was good in the fall and winter of the year when cutting lawns shifted from once a week to about once every three and then once every five or six. He worked at Sikes's Seafood two nights a week— Tuesdays and Thursdays—and on Saturday afternoons. But, during softball season, if there was a game, he was given the time off. Ronni, on the other hand, worked twice a week, Monday afternoon after school and Friday nights.

Mr. Sikes was as shrewd a businessman as he was a father. Billy had, at least, figured that much out. He was also officially *not* dating Veronica Sikes.

Though Mr. Sikes had given Billy and Ronni permission to "see each other," he'd not okayed dating. "Seeing each other" meant sitting together at church on Sunday mornings and Sunday evenings. And, they were allowed to sit together or hang out together at Wednesday night youth group. Fortunately for them, Brother Ralph had a social planned for Saturday evenings, usually wrapped around sports and other such events. They were allowed that too.

They were also allowed to hold hands. They were *not* allowed to kiss.

"Holding hands," Mr. Sikes had told him, "is fine. A chaste kiss on the cheek to say good night—as long as it lasts no more than two seconds, and in my fatherly opinion, that is stretching it—is fine. Your lips on my daughter's lips is not fine. Your hand on any other part of her body other than her hand is also not fine. Are we clear?"

"Yes, sir. Of course, sir."

"And if I hear differently, Billy, I won't allow the relationship to continue. Not to mention I'll fire you from your job at the restaurant."

"No, sir. I mean, yes, sir. I mean, I understand." Billy swallowed. "Sir."

"And don't go imagining yourself like Romeo and Juliet, do you hear me?"

Billy nodded once. "Yes, sir."

"Any questions?"

Billy had thought before braving, "Exactly when *can* I kiss her, sir?"

John Sikes's eyes met his head-on. "The day she becomes your wife, if God so allows."

Billy didn't like the answer so much, but he wasn't going to argue it either. "Yes, sir."

By spring of '59, Billy was as busy as any junior in high school had ever been. Cutting the neighborhood lawns was back in, spring season was gearing up, he was working steadily at Sikes, socking away a nice little nest egg for the day he finally got to kiss Ronni, whom he was officially *not* dating, and doing well in school. Mostly A's with the occasional B.

Daddy had been consistently sticking to his Saturday afternoon to Sunday afternoon pattern but had also managed to squeeze in a Wednesday night most weeks as well. He'd mellowed somehow, Billy thought. And, as long as Harold stayed out of trouble, living at 1711 Clinton Street had become tolerable.

In fact, life as a whole wasn't so bad. Mama was happier than he'd ever seen her since he couldn't think when. Daddy hadn't hit or cursed at anyone in months. And it looked like Harold just might graduate come May.

But then Harold got arrested and sentenced to five years for breaking and entering.

And that wasn't the worst of it.

Trinity, South Carolina

Patsy stared at herself in the full-length mirror hanging behind her bedroom door. She stood before it, dressed in a white slip. Lace embraced the sweetheart bodice, the straps were spaghetti slim. The hem brushed across the bottoms of her knees.

Her hair swept past her shoulders. She scooped it up, the weight of it heavy in her hands. She then brought it over one shoulder, twisted it into a fishtail braid, and tied it off with a ribbon that had been lying on the nearby dresser.

She pressed her palms flat against her belly, turned for a side view, inhaled deeply, and jutted out her chest. After four children, her stomach was still flat. From a physical standpoint, she looked pretty much as she had the day she married Gilbert.

No wonder he couldn't keep his hands off her.

Her own dropped to her sides. Her shoulders slumped.

From somewhere in the recesses of their home, she heard one of the children call her name. No, not her name. *Mommy.*

"Coming," she whispered, knowing they wouldn't hear her. She turned back to face the mirror.

Patsy brought her hands to her face and pulled at her cheeks until the bottoms of her eyes drooped downward. She looked like something . . . scary. "Dear God, what is wrong with me," she said aloud, releasing her skin. "Why can't I make a full connect with my children?"

"Mommy?"

Six-and-a-half-year-old Pam stood on the other side of the door. The other side of the looking glass. Patsy stepped back, opened the bedroom door, and looked into the freckled face and upturned nose of her second born. "Yes, sweetheart?"

"When is Daddy coming home?"

Patsy looked at the narrow Timex at her wrist. It was nearing seven o'clock on a Friday night. "In about an hour. He promised no later than eight-fifteen."

"Will he have time to play with us?"

Patsy tapped the tip of her daughter's nose with her finger. "Doesn't he always?"

Long dark ringlets bounced around the girl's cherub face. "Not always."

Patsy placed her hands on her hips. "You're awful cute when you're honest."

Pammie, as Gilbert called her, turned her face upward and giggled. "Daddy says I'm precock-shous."

Patsy stepped over to her dressing table, opened a small jewelry box, and pulled out a single strand of pearls. Wrapping them around her neck to fasten the clip, she said, "Precocious."

Pam went to her parents' bed, jumped up on it, and crossed her ankles. "I don't even know what that means, so how can I say it?"

Patsy gave her daughter her best "what are you doing"

look. "Young lady, what is the rule about being on Mommy and Daddy's bed?"

"I'm not to be on it?"

Patsy crossed her arms. "And so then would you care to tell me why you *are* on it?"

Pam cocked her head as though she were studying the situation. "Because . . ." she said, drawing the word out, "I'm . . . *precocious*?"

Patsy lifted her hands, palm up, several times. "Up, up, up." Pam jumped off the bed, which Patsy immediately went to so she could straighten it. "Where is your brother?"

"Which one?"

Patsy sighed. "Greg. Where is Greg?"

"In his room playing."

Patsy placed her hands on her daughter's shoulders and guided her toward the door. "All right then. Go tell Greg to make sure Kenny and Georgy are ready for Daddy to come home."

"They are."

"Go . . ."

Pam turned to face her mother. "Mommy?"

"What Pam?"

"Why are you so awful tired lately?"

Patsy crossed her arms. Would she ever get this child of hers out of the bedroom so she could dress in private? "And why, pray tell, do you ask that, Miss Pamela Milstrap?"

"I heard Grandma tell Grandpa that you were awful tired lately. Are you not sleeping well, Mommy?"

Patsy pressed her index fingers to her temples. "Mommy is sleeping just fine, sweetheart. But I know a little girl who won't be able to sit down for a week if she doesn't scoot and let me get dressed."

"But, Mommy. You can get dressed with me in the bedroom. We're both girls."

"Pamela Elizabeth Milstrap."

Pam's face registered surprise. "I'm going," she said before scurrying down the narrow hallway of the oversized house Gilbert had gifted his family with.

Patsy sighed as she closed the door again. This time, she went to the end of the bed, sat upon it, and then threw herself back. The tears she had grown familiar with welled up in her eyes before sliding toward her ears, one at a time.

She pressed her palms against her belly again and wondered how much longer she could keep up the façade. Perfect wife. Perfect mother. Perfect homemaker.

Perfect because she must be. Had to be. So Gilbert would come home. Would never leave her. Or send her away.

She. Had. To. Be. Perfect.

Truth was, she stood at the edge of a precipice, looking over the edge, barely able to stand. One incorrect move and she would topple over like the Winnie the Walking Talking Doll she'd come to be.

With broken parts.

What is wrong with me?

Fluttering beneath her palm caused her to rub the satin between flesh and flesh. Another life . . . a fifth child . . . and she wasn't even sure she knew what she was doing with the four she already had.

And, just as with the previous four pregnancies, the dreams had returned. Dreams of a pea patch, and Nehi Peach soda, and a pretty but haggard woman waving good-bye from beyond a bus window. Dreams of two little boys with upturned noses and of a man with steel-gray eyes.

Even the thought of him caused her to sit up. To shudder.

196

To shake her head in defeat. She could not do this again. Not like before. Not alone.

Tonight, she decided, she would tell Gilbert.

Tonight, she would demand that things change.

Tonight, she would move away from the edge of the cliff, if only by one step.

20

Sweat dripped from the tip of Billy's nose, off his brow into his eyes, and down the front of his bare chest in rivulets. His legs and arms were clammy and his socks drenched. But, he was nearly finished with the Stones' yard; when he was done, he had only his own to do—hopefully before Daddy made it home that afternoon—with just enough time to shower, get dressed, and head over to the recreation department for the pregame warm-up.

He pushed the mower across the final stretch of green grass before shutting the motor off. It whirred to silent as Billy pulled a limp handkerchief from the back pocket of his dungarees. He wiped his face, down and around his chest, then stuffed it back into his pocket. A noise behind him caused him to look over his shoulder. Mrs. Stone was coming out with her customary glass of icy-cold lemonade.

Billy reached for the T-shirt draped over the handlebar of the mower, guided it over his head, and pushed his arms into the sleeves in time to reach for the glass and to thank his mother's best friend.

"You are more than welcome." She glanced around her. "Another fine job."

"Thank you." He took a long swallow of the refreshment. "Again."

Nadine Stone planted her fists on her hips. Today she wore a pair of fashionable black-and-white checkered shorts and white top. In spite of her age—which Billy dared not even guess—he had to admit she could pull off the look. "I need to ask you to do a favor for me, Billy, if you will."

He drained the last of the lemonade before wiping his mouth with the back of his hand and asking, "What's that, Mrs. Stone?"

"I know you still have to cut your lawn—I just talked to your mother on the phone—but Mr. Stone left some important papers on his desk and he's asked if I can bring them down to the hospital."

Billy handed Mrs. Stone the empty Tupperware glass. "I wondered where Mr. Stone was at today." He smiled. "Glad to know I'm not the only one working hard on a Saturday."

Nadine Stone returned the smile. "He's horribly behind on a project and . . . well, he just realized he forgot the file, and wouldn't you know it? I just put a pound cake in the oven. You *know* how long those take to bake. I can't turn off the oven and I can't leave. Herbert can't come home because he has a meeting in fifteen minutes."

"So, how can I help you, Mrs. Stone?"

Her hands dropped from her hips and her arms crossed in front of her. "Would you mind horribly taking the file to Mr. Stone?"

Billy looked down at himself. "Like this?" He laughed. "I'm filthy. Mama wouldn't let me be caught dead at the hospital looking like this."

She waved at him. "Of course, I know you have to shower. There's time. As far as your lawn is concerned, your mother said you can just deal with it on Monday and she'll explain it all to your daddy."

Billy nodded. "Okay, then. Sure. I'm happy to." He glanced toward his house. "I'll shower real quick and get on back over here as soon as I can."

"You are the best," she said.

Fifteen minutes later he had showered and dressed. Mama stood by the back door, ready to hand him the keys to her car. "I'll be back shortly," he said, giving her a swift kiss on the cheek.

"Drive careful," she said.

"I always do, Mama," he said as though chiding, even as he smiled.

He drove the two houses over to pick up the file, which he thought to be relatively thick for something forgotten. He walked from the Stones' front door and returned to the car, file tucked into the curve of his hand and resting against his thigh and hip. He wondered what it would be like to be a businessman like Mr. Stone. To *run* something.

As he pulled out of the driveway, it dawned on him that he actually did run something. Something besides a lawn mower. He ran a business. It didn't have a formal name and he didn't have an accountant or a secretary, but he did have a savings account and a bankbook with pages of entries, all in the black.

The thought kept him smiling as he drove to the hospital. Yeah, boy. He already *was* a businessman. And not just that; his business was booming.

He was also doing well with the man he hoped would one day be his father-in-law. The more he learned about the restaurant business, the more he liked it. Billy entered the parking lot, parked his mother's car in the first open spot he could find, pulled the key out from the ignition, and allowed his mind to travel to a future time and place.

Him and Ronni, in business together. Maybe managing Sikes's Seafood Restaurant together.

But then, where would Mr. Sikes be? Billy could hardly see the man retiring, and he couldn't imagine himself bussing tables and serving sweet iced tea and hush puppies the rest of his life either. He'd made enough money to soon buy his own car for cash and still have some in the bank. But it wasn't enough to support a wife and children.

Children . . .

He grabbed the file resting beside him on the seat, opened the car door, and stepped out onto the asphalt of the parking lot.

He'd only been to the hospital once. His friend Frank Morris had tripped over second base during practice and severely broken his right leg, which had then led to pneumonia. Billy wasn't old enough to drive then, but his mother drove him there every day possible to visit and help pass the time with card games and news from the gang. They'd walked through the double doors together, into the foyer, and had announced the patient's name to a woman sitting behind a U-shaped desk. He figured he'd do the same today. Only this time, he'd square his shoulders and give the distinguished name of Herbert Stone.

At the notion, Billy felt even more of a businessman. And he liked that.

The parking lot and hospital were separated by a two-way street. A gleaming white sidewalk stretched before the wide glass double doors, which were accessible by about a half dozen short, narrow steps. As Billy stepped from beyond the last parked car, he turned his attention to oncoming traffic, the sidewalk, and the doors.

And that was when he saw him.

Trinity, South Carolina

For a man who'd just been told his life was about to change, her husband sure looked pleased with himself.

Patsy crossed her arms and cocked her right hip. "I hardly see the humor in this, Gilbert." She gave him her best "I mean it this time" face. At least she hoped she did.

But if Gilbert was reading it, he was ignoring it. Instead of promising to change his schedule—not to mention taking some birth control responsibility—Gilbert knelt on the floor of their bedroom in front of her, wrapped his arms around her hips, and kissed the flat of her belly. "Hello there, Little One. I'm your daddy."

Patsy threw her hands up in disgust. "Ugh!"

He peered up at her, all boy and all man. Dimples and a curly mop of hair and twinkling eyes. "I know, baby doll. I know you don't want more children." His fingertips kneaded the small of her back, sending chills up her spine and down her legs.

Why did he have to know her so well? Know her and every inch of her body? All the right places to touch, all the right words to say? And why did he have to be kneeling before her?

"Then why do *you* look so happy, I wonder."

He stood, this time slipping his arms around her waist and drawing her close by rocking their hips together. "Because, Pats, I believe God decides when we have children. I believe they are his blessing."

She wiggled out of his embrace, went to the bed, and sat.

Crossing her legs, she said, "That's because you get to go on the road without them. You don't have to change their diapers, get up with them at all hours of the night, wipe up the spittle and the puke, or listen to them argue over a toy. If I hear the words 'it's mine' or 'I had it first' one more time, I think I'll scream." She drew in a deep breath and spoke on the exhale. "Not to mention that you don't have to make sure they're fed, clothed, and that they get enough sleep."

Gilbert sat next to her. He touched her again—he was always touching her—this time rubbing her arm with his fingertips. "They're your children, Pats. Your *children*. Do you expect they're going to do that on their own?" Patsy felt tears forming in the backs of her eyes as he continued. "And as for me not doing any of those things, I'm working my tail end off out there *on the road* to make sure they have food to eat, clothes to wear, and beds to sleep in." From the corner of her eye, she saw him turn his head this way and that around the room. "You have to admit, I've done a pretty good job, haven't I?"

She looked at him fully, set her jaw against the knot forming in her throat, and said, "But you're never home, Gilbert." The words came in a whisper, strained and angry. "So what difference does it make?"

His left hand swept around them to rub her belly. "Looks like I'm home enough, eh?"

She stood, blinked, and felt two anxious tears slip down her cheeks. "Oh, you are so funny. I'm practically rolling on the floor with laughter here."

Gilbert's face changed as his hands pressed the bed at both hips. She knew that look; he was no longer amused. "You need to get over yourself, Patsy. You're a woman. I'm a man. We're married. We sleep together and we make babies." He

203

stood, walked over to his chest of drawers, and picked up his watch, which he'd placed there the night before when he'd finally gotten home.

After ten o'clock. After the kids were in bed and the food had gone cold and she was too tired to talk, much less argue about another baby coming into their lives.

"So, that's it? I'm supposed to just accept that? I married you, I sleep with you, and I give you babies, is that it?" New tears welled up and were now burning, stinging.

He turned to look at her. His hands extended as though he were in defeat. "Look, Pats. I don't mean to be crude. And I certainly don't mean to be cruel. Not to you of all people. I love you like mad and you know that."

"And I love you. That hasn't changed."

"But the fact of the matter is, *this* is the way of life."

She could no longer hold back the tears. "Then why can't I . . ." Patsy dropped her face into her hands. Her hair, which she wore down, fell as a curtain between her and her husband. "Why do I struggle so?" she asked between sobs. "Rayette is a wonderful mother to her kids. Sandra makes it look like second nature. But, I feel so inadequate."

She felt Gilbert's arms come awkwardly around her. She heard the shushing sound as the warmth of his breath tickled her ear. "Come on, now, Pats. Don't you think you are being just a little hard on yourself?"

She shook her head.

"When I walk into this house, what do I see?" he asked against her temple. "A well-kept home, a beautiful woman I have the pleasure to call my wife, four perfect kids. What more is there for you to have to accomplish?"

There was no answer and she knew it. There were no real words to express how she felt. The perfection came only because she demanded it of herself. The social obligations, the family responsibilities—both in their home and at Mam and Papa's—all came with such a sense of burden. Just two months ago, when Lloyd had come home and married his girl, she'd thrown the best shower, organized the finest reception. And all the while, she felt as though she were choking.

She just couldn't figure on what.

She feared she never would.

She couldn't even figure out what caused her downward spiral to start. It had been about midway through her first pregnancy. Everything was going well. She'd not had morning sickness. She'd hardly gained weight or carried any of the other maladies she'd heard her friends complain about. Other than Gilbert being gone so much—too much—her life was, truly, perfect.

So *why*?

She raised her head, looked into her husband's eyes. "You are absolutely right, Gilbert." Patsy took in the deepest breath her lungs could hold, slowly released it, willing every muscle, every fiber, every sinew to relax with it. She wiped her cheeks dry with her fingertips. Gilbert held her so close, her wedding rings scraped across his chest. "You know," she said, "I'm sure this is all just hormones. Maybe that's my one sign of being pregnant. I'm hormonal."

He kissed the brow above both eyes, then her cheeks, the tip of her nose, and finally her lips before saying, "Have you talked to your doctor about it? I'm sure you could get something to help."

"No, but I will. I promise."

He squeezed her even more tightly into his arms. "I love you more than words, you know that, right?"

She nodded. "And I love you too. I do."

His eyes searched hers for a while before he said, "Tell you what. I'll start giving more responsibility to Terry. After all, as my assistant he should be able to take on more of the workload. He's single, so I doubt he'll mind." He winked in that old way he used to do that drove her crazy. "I'll increase his salary, so I know he won't."

"Oh, Gilbert . . . So you'll be home more?"

"Absolutely, Pats. With you and the kids here, why wouldn't I want to be?"

She sighed. "And can we *please* stop at five?"

He grinned. "I'll do everything within my power." Then he laughed a little. "We'll work it out, I promise."

She drew her arms up and around his neck before kissing him soundly. "Welcome home, baby," she muttered against his lips.

The knot in her throat had disappeared.

21

Gainesville, Florida

What was his father doing walking into Alachua County Hospital? Carrying long-stem flowers, no less?

Billy paused long enough to watch until Ira disappeared on the other side of the front doors. He jogged across the street, up the steps, and walked into the foyer to the U-shaped desk he remembered. An older woman with short gray hair and a firm line for lips sat on the other side, working a crossword puzzle with a short pencil. She looked up with a sigh. "May I help you?"

Billy looked beyond the desk and into the foyer. Collections of vinyl couches, chairs, end tables, and coffee tables topped with worn magazines met his gaze. No more than five people were scattered among them. None of them were the man he called "Daddy."

"Um . . . my father just came in." Billy raised his hand, keeping his fingers horizontal. "Tall man. Big." He tried to look as confused as he felt. "He forgot to tell me where to meet him."

The woman smiled at him as if they were in on a secret.

"Fifth floor, hon. The elevators are over that way." She pointed to the left.

"Thank you, ma'am." The file was heavy in his hand. He clutched it tighter under his fingertips.

His feet felt like lead. Something was wrong; he knew it. Anyone his father was an acquaintance of, they knew as a family, right? Unless, of course, there was someone here from his father's job. Well, of course. That was it.

He pushed the top brown button in the brass plating next to the elevators and waited for the doors to slide open. When they did, he stepped into the tiny cubicle, pressed the 5, and waited again.

The elevator was painfully slow in its ascent. There were no stops along the way, and when it finally rocked to a stop at the fifth floor, the doors opened to a small L-shaped desk. Behind it, a thin young woman dressed in a white nurse's uniform and a dark blue bib apron looked up. Her cap held three blue ribbons at the top of both sides. On the desk was a stack of metal charts, which her hands rested upon, as though attempting to keep them from sliding away. Above her was a sign with bold black lettering.

5th FLOOR
MATERNITY

"May I help you?"

Billy blinked as he read the sign. "Yeah . . . yes, ma'am." He looked from the sign to the nurse. "My father just came through here. I was supposed to meet him, but I don't know where."

Keeping her hands on the charts, she turned her attention to a piece of paper to her right. "Mr. Liddle?"

"Yes, ma'am."

"He's with his wife in room 512."

"His wife."

"Yes," she answered, beaming. "Congratulations on the birth of your little sister, by the way."

Billy's heart hammered so loudly, he couldn't hear himself respond, "Thank you."

He just stared at the woman as though he were looking through her. And perhaps he was. At that moment, he couldn't be sure of anything more than that the floor beneath him had turned to quicksand and the air around him was being sucked from the hallway.

Then the nurse pointed to her right. "It's that way," she said.

He started down the hall. Doors with numbers—502, 504, 506—swam before him as though they were riding ocean waves. When he came to 510, he slowed in his pace until he was practically walking heel to toe. At 512 he paused. The door was ajar. He could hear his father speaking, a woman answering back. She sounded young; other than that, he couldn't make out what they were saying.

He took a step closer, turned his head to see better. Daddy sat on the bed, the flowers, still clutched in his hand, lay on the other side of a woman's legs. The woman—young like he suspected and very pretty—sat upright in the hospital bed. She wore a pink . . . what did they call that thing? A peignoir, Ronni had called it after they'd seen Doris Day wearing one in a movie. It was made of material so soft and sheer he couldn't believe she dared wear it in a public building where anyone could see.

Where he could see.

Where his father could see.

"Beautiful today as always, my love," he heard the familiar baritone voice of the man he no longer recognized.

209

"Have you seen her?"

"Just did. She's the most exquisite thing I've ever encountered." And then Ira Liddle leaned over and kissed her, right on the mouth. It was a deep and passionate kiss, full of ardor. "Next to you, of course," he said when they'd broken apart.

The woman slapped at him playfully. "Oh, you," she said.

It was all Billy wanted to see. But not everything he wanted to hear. He pressed his back against the wall next to the door so his position was at a maximum for eavesdropping, especially around the dings and calls from the overhead system.

"Have you told her yet?" the woman asked.

"Now, now. What did I tell you, my sweet?"

"Not to worry."

"Then why are you asking me, pet? Surely it can't be good for a young mother."

Billy's eyes narrowed. His father sounded nothing like the man he knew him to be. The man he'd thought he'd known his whole life.

"But when?"

"Soon."

"How soon?"

There were kissing sounds. Billy ground his teeth, squeezed his eyes shut as he clutched the file for Mr. Stone against his chest. He couldn't breathe. Dared not try.

"Soon, I promise. I'll tell her everything, I'll file for divorce and I'll make an honest woman out of you. And I'll formally adopt the baby."

Billy felt the onslaught of another migraine. He pounded his head against the wall.

"What was that?" he heard his father say.

Without thinking Billy turned toward the door, pushed it with such force it bammed against the wall, and said, "It's

210

just me, old man." For a moment, he thought it was Harold's voice coming from within him.

"Billy!"

His father had stood and now started toward him. The moment's valiance was gone; Billy jerked at the sound of his name, dropped the file, and ran.

Just like he'd always done.

He barreled down the stairwell, taking two sometimes three steps at a time, holding on to the railing to keep himself from falling. When he reached the first floor landing, Billy jerked the heavy metal door open and stumbled into a small passageway. For a moment, he braced his backside against the glossy white wall, pressed his hands against his knees, and panted toward the tiles on the floor. When he'd straightened, he listened for voices, something—anything—to guide him to the front of the hospital, then thought better of it. If his father had taken the elevator, he'd be in wait for him, either in the foyer or the parking lot.

Or worse, at home.

He had to think, he told himself. Think, Billy. Think.

Billy pushed himself away from the wall, pulled the stairwell door toward him, and stepped back in. He took the stairs, this time one at a time, up to the second floor, opened the door, and just started walking, past closed office doors with nameplates that looked like wood with cream-colored lettering. He stopped when he found the one that read HERBERT STONE, ADMINISTRATOR.

Billy tapped on the door, waited for Mr. Stone to tell him to come in. When he did, Billy stepped into a tidy outer office. From beyond a secretarial desk and chair, he peered into a luxurious inner office where his family's neighbor stood on

211

the opposite side of a large desk. "Oh, there you are," the older man said. He stepped around the desk, stopped, and said, "Son, are you all right?"

Billy shook his head. "No, sir."

Mr. Stone continued toward him as Billy rested his hand along the top of an occasional chair for support. His head was pounding. "Did you bring the file?"

Billy looked at both hands. "I must have . . . I think I dropped it."

Herbert Stone guided him into the chair. "You look like you've seen a ghost."

"No, sir." Billy tried to shake his head from side to side, but the pain made it impossible.

"What then?" Mr. Stone pulled his secretary's rolling chair to Billy and sat opposite him.

Billy looked up, squinted against the office light, and said, "I just saw my father and his mistress, Mr. Stone. On the fifth floor."

"The fifth floor?" The words came as part question, part statement.

In spite of every effort he made to the contrary, he started to cry, making himself sound more like a young boy than a young man. He wrapped his head in his arms. "I don't know what to do, Mr. Stone. I don't know what to do."

And then he threw up.

22

Summer 1960

Sikes's Seafood Restaurant was buzzing with the news.

Senator John F. Kennedy had won the California Democratic Primary. "He's a shoo-in," Billy heard one of the afternoon regulars announce. Four men who came in every afternoon for a cup of coffee and a slice of Mrs. Sikes's homemade key lime pie.

Another said, "He's too young. What does he know?"

Billy shook his head and smiled as he hauled another bag of ice on the breadth of his shoulder from the truck parked out front to the freezer in the back. Why the iceman wouldn't just drive the truck around to the alley was anyone's guess. But if Mr. Sikes hadn't thought to question him, Billy sure wasn't going to.

John Sikes sat at a table near the kitchen doors, glass of iced tea sweating onto thick pine, ledger spread out before him. Billy could tell he pretended to work, but what he was really doing was listening. One day, he thought as he dropped the bag of ice into the chest freezer, that would be him.

He headed back through the dining area for the third time when Mr. Sikes stopped him. "What do you think, Billy?"

Billy turned, breathing heavily. "What do I think about what, Mr. Sikes?"

"Kennedy. What do you think?"

Billy looked from the table of coffee-drinking, pie-eating table politicians to his boss. He grinned. "I think I'm only eighteen. I've got three more years before I'm old enough to vote."

"But you have an opinion, right?"

Billy nodded. "Yes, sir, I do."

"And?"

He smiled. "Well, sir . . . Daddy didn't teach me much, but what he did teach me was to keep my thoughts on politics to myself."

John laughed. "All right then, son." He looked at his watch. "By the way, where's my daughter?"

Billy took a single step backward before answering, "She said she'd be here as soon as she was finished getting her perm down at the beauty salon. You've known her longer than I have, sir. Your guess is as good as any."

Mr. Sikes took a sip of his watered-down tea, picked up the pencil laying across the open ledger, and said, "I should have told her to take the day off."

"I'm sure she'll be here soon, sir."

"Mmm . . . How have *you* been doing, Billy? No headaches lately?"

"Just one last week, and that was the first one in a month. Doctor says I'm fine though. Says some people just get migraines from time to time."

Sikes nodded. "Let me know if you need anything."

Billy returned to the truck. It was only four-thirty in the afternoon and already he was bone weary.

214

After his parents' divorce, when there was only him and his mother left, he'd taken as much work as he could get to help them survive. Mama had gotten the house in the legal settlement, her car, and enough cash to get them by for a while. She'd been more of a bulldog than he'd ever expected, no doubt because of her friendship with Nadine Stone. Many was the time he heard the two women at the kitchen table; Mama crying and Mrs. Stone practically holding a pep rally.

Her first order of business was to sell the house. "It belongs more to the bank than to us," she told him. "We'll sell, move into someplace smaller, and save what little bit of money we'll have left over."

Mama never once talked in terms of "I." It was always "we." Her and Billy. Them against the world. Somehow they'd make it, she told him. They had each other, they had some money, enough good sense, and the good Lord to guide them.

Billy had never felt such a burden in his life.

Her second order of business was changing her last name to the name she'd shared with her first husband. She asked Billy to understand; he complied. What else was he to do?

Shortly after finding his father in a hospital bed with another woman, he'd gone to the prison where Harold resided, to tell his brother of their father's indiscretion and the half sister it had produced. Harold seemed neither shocked nor upset.

"Sounds like something the old man would do," he said.

"That it?" Billy asked from the round table with the chipped paint amongst a noisy roomful of the same. "That's all you got to say?"

"What do you want from me, Billy? You wanna hear me cry or something? Well, boo-hoo." Harold's face was as cold as his heart. "Come on the inside with me for about fifteen minutes and then tell me all your sorrows. This place makes your problems sound like a cakewalk."

The difference being, he and Mama hadn't asked for this and Harold had gotten what he deserved. "Aren't you going to ask about Mama, Harold?"

Harold leaned back in the metal chair and crossed his arms. "Sure. How is she?"

"She's hurting. She's embarrassed." Billy shrugged. "Scared a little. Mrs. Stone has been a big help to her."

Harold chewed on his lower lip before answering. "You know, Bill, Mama knew the kind of man she was marrying when she married dear old Dad. She can't tell me she didn't. When you grow up and get wise to the ways of the world, you'll see what I mean."

Billy just shook his head, the irony of his brother's words not lost on him. There wasn't anything more to say. Not really. So he stood and said, "I'll come back to see ya soon, Harold," and then walked out of the prison's social hall, knowing it would be awhile.

Since then, he and Mama had moved into the guesthouse of one of Billy's Clinton Street customers. Mama had gotten a job at the hospital in admissions, working from seven in the morning to three in the afternoon. She said she was happy, but Billy only saw evidences of stress and the hardships of life etched across her face.

Billy continued with his lawn service until Mr. Sikes increased his hours and he was forced to choose.

The smell of sweat and grass or of fish with the scent of Ronni's perfume. The choice was easy.

Somehow he'd made it through the remainder of his junior year and had kept senior year to all it was supposed to be. He and Ronni continued in their unofficial nondating capacity.

216

No kissing and minimal hand-holding. Church functions or movies and burgers with their friends. He loved her more with every passing day, but he had nothing to offer her by way of a future. Certainly not working for her father at his current salary. Even full-time now that he'd graduated.

Even with his good grades and a number of scholarships offered, college was out. He wanted a future with Ronni but felt the need to be a financial help, not a hindrance, to Mama. What he needed was a plan, but try hard as he could to come up with one, nothing surfaced.

Until the day he went to the barbershop to get his hair trimmed and everything changed.

—————

Billy liked wearing his hair a little long but not like the beatniks. He kept it slicked up, combed back, and short over his ears. To keep it from falling into his face, he headed over to Costlow's Barbershop, which was only five storefronts away from Sikes's.

He always went a half hour before his appointment; it meant having an opportunity to listen to the older men talk about their youth, the wars they'd fought, and what pleasures they found in life now. It gave Billy something to hold on to, knowing that every life has its problems and that somehow by the grace of God, people managed to rise above them.

On a particularly hot day in July 1960, with the thrill of Independence Day celebrations dancing over Gainesville, Billy listened to five men and two barbers as they spoke of "the way we used to do it back in the forties."

Billy sat in one of the chairs pushed against the storefront window and to the right side of the spinning barber's pole. Sunlight skipped across it, sending reflected shafts along the walls of the shop.

"The wife wants us to head over to Cedar Key," Larry Jones said.

"Cedar Key?" Old Mr. Bailey barked from a chair across the room. The elderly gentleman sat, legs crossed, newspaper folded in his lap as though he were reading it, which he was not. "I thought that place got wiped off the map back in . . . when was it now? . . . '50?"

"What are you talking about, Marcus?" Ben Costlow's trimming scissors stopped midsnip over Larry Jones's head as he shot a glance over his right shoulder.

"Back in '50 . . . Hurricane Easy, I think it was." Billy watched as the man pondered, eyes cast toward the ceiling, chin bobbing up and down as his mind clicked off the hurricane seasons. "Yeah, that was it. Hurricane Easy." Watered-down eyes returned to look at Mr. Jones. "Tore that little island up. Had an old army buddy who lived there. He was a fisherman. The entire fleet of fishing boats was destroyed." The man's jaw went back to bobbing. "That was their primary source of livelihood over there, don't you know."

Mr. Costlow returned to his concentrated efforts over Larry Jones's cut. "So, anyway . . . what in the world does Dee want to go over to Cedar Key for?"

Billy watched as Mr. Jones's shoulders shifted. "First of all . . . *Marcus* . . ." He shot the man on the other side of the room a know-it-all look. "The island may have suffered in nineteen hundred and fifty, but this is nineteen hundred and *sixty*—"

"I know what year it is!"

Every man in the shop guffawed. Billy looked at his knees and bit his lip to keep from laughing, afraid he would come across as disrespectful.

"That's ten years, mind you."

"And I know my math too."

The laughter continued.

"Ten years is a long time and did you ever stop to think that maybe, just maybe, they've rebuilt? Why, Dee tells me that they've even got a police force now and Ma Bell has added a phone system."

"All I know is . . . my friend told me that near 'bout ever' house was destroyed. Ever' one."

Billy cleared his throat. "Uh . . . Mr. Jones?" In the mirror, Billy watched as Larry Jones's eyes shifted to him. "What is Mrs. Jones hoping to do there, if you don't mind my asking, sir?"

"What she always does," Aaron Bennett, the second barber who'd been relaxing in his chair throughout the exchange, said. "Fish! That woman would rather hold fishing gear than ole Larry sitting there."

This time, Billy laughed with the others. But when the merriment had subsided, it got him to thinking.

Fish . . .

The local library told him everything he needed to know about Cedar Key. It had, indeed, been rendered nearly nonexistent by Hurricane Easy, but it wasn't the first time the cluster of islands off the west coast of Florida had taken a beating.

"Eighteen-forty-two," he told Ronni the following evening. They fought off insects and heat by gliding in the swing hanging at the right end of the porch. Ronni held a funeral home fan; her constant and almost violent waving of it kept both of them in the way of a breeze. "Depot Key—one of the Cedar Keys, which is now called Atsena Otie—was hit by a hurricane that raised the water level twenty-seven feet."

"Twenty-seven? Should that have destroyed it?"

"It nearly did." Billy felt himself growing as excited as he'd been when his idea first came to him. "After Florida was admitted into the Union, Cedar Key was used as a shipping port. In the mid-1800s, the town started to grow. A hotel, a general store, but then everything kinda shut down because of the war."

Ronni smiled at him. "Billy, school is *over*. Why are you giving me a history lesson?"

Billy shifted in the swing to better face her. He slapped at a mosquito lighting on his arm and killed it, then wiped away the evidence with his fingers. "Just listen. History is what brings us to where we are now, Ronni, and helps us to know where we're going. Or where we *should* go."

Ronni tilted her face toward the waving fan. "It's wicked hot out here. But if we go inside, it'll be to Travis and Mama staring at us." She grinned at him in that way she had that made him want to throw all "no kissing" rules to the wind.

He looked down at his hands and flexed his fingers. "Can I finish?"

"Please do." She giggled, he knew, at the seriousness of his tone.

"Okay . . . eighteen hundred and ninety-six. Are you with me?"

She pressed her lips together to keep from laughing further. "Yes," she finally said with a nod of her head, "eighteen hundred and ninety-six."

"Another hurricane, this one with a ten-foot tidal wave. Ten foot."

At that, Ronni sobered. "My gracious," she said. "Wonder what that would look like."

"Personally, I don't ever want to know." He took a deep breath and sighed. "Stay with me, here. There were two mills on the island of Atsena Otie. One was the Faber Pencil Factory and the other Nutters Mill."

"Nutters Mill?"

"They produced cedar slats. Both did."

"Oh. Do they still?"

"No. Both were destroyed by the hurricane in 1896. It tore apart the island and they were never rebuilt."

"So, why are we talking about it?"

"Because, what is *now* Cedar Key—just across from Atsena Otie—has become a fishing village. They have an airstrip. They have history and apparently the most amazing will to survive. *And* they've opened up their first restaurant."

Ronni narrowed her eyes. "Meaning?"

Billy wiggled in the swing again. "Meaning that I think Cedar Key is going to resurrect itself as a place for tourists to come. Fishermen. Bird-watchers. There's a wildlife refuge there, you see."

"Oh."

"I've even heard that a lot of artists—painters, writers, and that kind of thing—like to go there, just to soak up the muse."

Ronni glared at him before bursting into a song of laughter. "Soak up the muse?" She pressed her slender hand, the one not holding the fan, against her chest and forced herself to breathe normally. "Oh, Billy. You *have* been at the library reading up, haven't you?"

Billy felt himself grow warm under her amusement. "Yeah. But that's because I have a plan, Ronni."

"What plan?"

Billy reached for the hand waving the fan and said, "Turn and look at me."

Her face grew somber. "But then I can't fan us."

"I don't care about the heat anymore, Ronni. I'm pretty

much drenched out here." So then how was it, he wondered, she still managed to look so fresh. He looked at her hand resting in his and listened as she blew the pesky insects away from her face. "All right, then. You can still fan us when we sit like this, no?"

"Yes, I can." She resumed waving the funeral home fan; Jesus kneeling in the Garden of Gethsemane coming toward him, away from him, toward him, away from him. He smiled to himself. He was about to propose a life together on Cedar Key Island to this beautiful young woman he'd loved since he was a boy, and Jesus was going to be a part of it.

"What are you smiling at, Billy Liddle?"

"I'm just thinking . . . you were the one who led me to church. You were the one who showed me I can have a relationship with God. And that God was greater than any problem I had at home . . ."

Ronni pinked in the glow of the porch light. "I know . . ."

"And now I'm going to talk to you about our future, and here you are waving his picture at me."

Ronni's eyes left Billy's face long enough to glance at the fan before sweeping over to him again. "Our future?"

"Yeah." Billy reached up, traced the side of her delicate face with his fingertips. It was the most intimate he'd ever dared allow himself to be with her. "I want to marry you, Ronni. Surely you know that."

She looked at her lap, grabbed his fingers with her free hand, and brought them down to where their knees nearly touched. "I want to marry you too, Billy. But we've got to have more than that. We've got to have more than a plan. It's got to be doable. We have to see the evidence of it being successful . . ." She frowned. "Because I don't believe in 'poor and in love.'"

A bubble of laughter escaped Billy's chest. She wanted to marry him. "I don't either, Ronni. And that's why I'm going to talk to your father about opening another Sikes's in Cedar Key. The timing is perfect. We'll be in on the ground floor of what I believe will be something great. I've prayed about it, Ronni, and God hasn't given me a check in my heart that says, 'Don't do it, Billy.' All I'm getting is that this is the path I'm supposed to be on. *We're* supposed to be on." Just in case anyone was hanging out near the opened living room window, he leaned over enough so that he could speak quietly and she could still hear. "This isn't a romantic setting, I know. We're both sticky hot and fighting these nasty bugs. But here it is, Veronica Sikes. If you can love me out here in this heat, you can love me anywhere. If you can trust me enough to rattle on about the history of a place you clearly know nothing about . . ."

Her eyelashes batted. "I do trust you. And I love you, William Liddle. I'd *love* you in the middle of a garbage dump."

"And in Cedar Key?"

"Mmmhmm."

"Then, you'll marry me?"

She nodded but said nothing until, "Tomorrow, talk to Daddy. Ask him about the restaurant. Tell him what you've got in mind. If it's okay with Daddy, it's surely fine by me."

23

John Sikes listened to every word Billy spoke from the opposite side of the gun-metal gray desk in Sikes's Seafood office. His expression never fluctuated. His body didn't move. As Billy began, Mr. Sikes had leaned back in the large black chair, supported by the paneled wall behind him, rested his elbows on the arms, and brought his hands—clasped together—to his face. The index fingers rose like the steeple of a church and pressed against his lips, which were pursed.

Other than when he had given Billy the rules for dating his daughter, Billy had never seen him quite so serious.

When Billy finished saying everything he could think to say, Mr. Sikes leaned forward. The springs in the chair creaked. Even the floor seemed to moan and the walls sigh in expectation of what Ronni's father might say next. Billy just held his breath—literally—as Mr. Sikes's arms fell against the top of the desk. His head dropped between his shoulders, his eyes cast downward, and for a moment Billy worried he'd killed the man. But when he looked up again, he smiled for a millisecond, sighed out of his nostrils, and said, "Breathe, son."

Billy's whole body relaxed as he blew air from between his lips.

Their eyes met. Held. They spoke without words.

You want to marry my daughter.

I do.

You want me to invest in a restaurant.

I do.

And you want to marry my daughter.

Billy watched John Sikes's Adam's apple bob in this throat before he spoke. "I'll need time to pray about this, you understand."

Billy pressed his damp palms onto his thighs and wiped downward. "Yes, sir."

"Because this is a tall order."

"I know, sir."

"You aren't just asking me to make a large monetary investment. You're asking me to give you one of my most prized possessions."

"Yes, sir." His voice rose on the last word, dangling there.

John Sikes raises an eyebrow at him. "But?"

Billy allowed a nervous cough to escape. "I don't . . . I don't know how to say what I want to say."

The eyebrow rose again. "You don't know how to say it? Or, you don't know how to say it to me?"

Billy wiped his palms against the material of his pants again. "Yes, sir. The latter, sir."

John Sikes leaned back in his chair again, assuming the old position. "Billy, if you are going to manage a restaurant for me—and if you are going to be my son-in-law—then I suggest you get used to saying to me what's on your mind."

Billy swiped his parched lips with his equally dry tongue. He attempted to swallow but his throat didn't quite follow through. He took a deep breath. "I love her too, sir. More than my own life."

John Sikes closed his eyes. "I know you do. And you have, I can tell, managed to love her within my rules."

Billy raised his right hand. "On my honor, sir."

To which John Sikes laughed so hard, Billy thought the chair would tip out from under him.

Billy tried to meet the laughter with a smile. "Glad to know I can make you laugh, Mr. Sikes."

The older man stood, extended a hand. Billy did the same. The men shook.

"I'll let you know when I'm ready to talk about this further."

Billy shook Sikes's hand once more and said, "I look forward to it, sir."

A week passed before Ronni called Billy early one morning to tell him her father wanted to speak to the both of them. That night. And that he wanted Billy's mother there too.

"How did he sound?" Billy asked her.

Ronni paused before answering, "Like my father, I guess."

"What does that mean?" his voice squeaked around the words.

Ronni giggled. "It means he just sounds like Daddy. I can honestly say I'm not getting a read on him."

"Did you talk to your mom? What did she say?"

"She said that she doesn't know what he's going to say either. That we'll just have to wait."

Billy gripped the phone tighter in a palm that was growing damp. "But, Ronni . . . wouldn't he have talked to her about this?"

"Sure he did, Billy. But the final decision rests with him. Just like, one day—if God so allows—you'll make this decision for our girls."

Billy thought his knees would give out at the thought. "Ronni," he whispered. "I can't even think that far."

He heard her sigh, sweet and long. "I can."

He closed his eyes against the words. "I'll go talk to Mama before she leaves for work. What time tonight?"

"Can you be here at six? Mama said we'd have dinner first."

"Sure. Six. That's perfect." Billy said good-bye, told her that he loved her "more than life."

"I love you too." Then she giggled. "By this time tomorrow, Billy Liddle, we'll either be engaged or two star-crossed lovers who weren't meant to be."

At first Billy couldn't answer. Then he said, "Let's hope it's the first."

He disconnected the call and went in search of his mother, whom he found applying red lipstick to her thin, pale lips from over the bathroom sink. "Mama?"

She looked at him and smiled. "There you are. Who was that on the phone?"

"Ronni. Her parents want us to come to dinner tonight. Mr. Sikes has made a decision."

His mother smiled at him, just as he knew she would. She opened the chrome and mirrored medicine cabinet, placed her tube of lipstick on the bottom shelf, and then closed it with the slightest *click*. "I have something I want to show you," she said. She started toward him. He stepped into the tiny square hallway between their two small bedrooms and waited for her to walk past him.

He followed her into her room, where she opened the three-paneled closet door and reached for the top shelf, which she couldn't quite get to. "Let me, Mama."

Mama stood back and pointed. "That hatbox, pushed to the rear."

The hatbox made Billy think of a box of Good & Plenty. Sprinkled on the bright pink background were pairs of black gloved hands holding delicate black parasols. He grabbed the black velvet-corded handle and pulled it toward him; it was heavier than he'd anticipated. "What have you got in here, Mama? Bars of silver?"

"Just you be careful," Mama said, already reaching to take it from his hands.

When it was firmly in her hands, she took it to the already made bed and set it down carefully while Billy closed the closet door.

Mama sat, patted the mattress on the other side of the case, and said, "Sit for a minute."

He did.

He watched as she opened the hatbox, sliding the top off and placing it on the bed beside her. She removed a hat—dark brown felt with a feather and pearls—that he couldn't remember ever seeing her wear. When she'd set it on the hatbox top, she reached in again to remove—tenderly, reverently—a jewelry box as she said, "Everything in this box is dear to me, Billy. And the pieces inside this jewelry box are even more than that." She opened the box. "Now, they are only a few." She pulled a gold chain from the bottom of the case, drew it over the back of her hand. At the end rested a delicate piece. "This is called a lavalier. It belonged to my mother, your grandmother."

His mother sighed. "She was such an elegant lady. I'm sorry you never got to meet her." He watched as her lips twisted in a weak smile. "She would have just adored you." She replaced the necklace. "I always wanted . . ." Mama took a deep breath. "I wanted Patsy to have this one day . . . but . . ."

Patsy. His mother was daring to speak of her. "You know

where she is, don't you, Mama? More than what you told me that night . . . a few years ago . . . that you know people who know . . ."

His mother shrugged. "She could be anywhere." Then she reached over and patted his hand. "Perhaps . . ." Her voice rose. "Perhaps Veronica can wear it on your wedding day. Something old . . ."

He smiled but felt sad. Conversation about the past was over and it was time to move on to the future. "She'd like that, I know."

Mama pulled a small velvet box from inside the case. "This . . ." She opened it to display a stunning—even in his way of thinking—sapphire ring. "This was mine."

"Mama." Billy could barely think. "I've never seen anything like it." He looked to his mother's face; her eyes had yet to leave the brilliance of the ring. "Daddy gave this to you?"

"Goodness, no," she said, looking up. "Your father gave me the gold band I hocked after . . . well, you know."

"Yes, ma'am." He looked at the ring again, more mesmerized by its beauty than he had any right to be. "Then . . . who?"

"Patsy's father gave me this. This is another item I thought would be hers one day but . . . it was too valuable to have put it on the bus with her."

"The bus . . . Mama? What happened?"

He waited for an answer. Instead, she said, "There are nearly fifty stones in this ring, Billy." She pointed to both sides with an index finger and a short, rounded nail. "Tell Veronica she will have to be careful with these along the shoulders. She'll want to have the ring checked once a year by a good jeweler to make sure the stones aren't loose."

Billy's heart hammered. "Ronni? You're giving *me* this ring?"

Mama slipped the ring halfway down her left third finger and admired it in the overhead light. "The love I had with Patsy's father . . ." She sighed. "Was the most wonderful kind of love." She looked at him. "Like yours and Veronica's. That's why you must be the one to have it." She pulled the ring off her finger and set it back into the jewelry box. "This afternoon, go to Maxie's Department Store. Go to the fine jewelry counter and ask the salesclerk if you can purchase one of their ring boxes. You'll want that for tonight."

Billy sat up straight. "But, Mama . . . what if Mr. Sikes says no?"

To which Mama laughed. "Oh, Billy! Clearly, you jest."

Dinner that evening seemed, to Billy, to be nothing more than a meal of endless courses. But Veronica Sikes looked stunning. She wore the frilliest dress he'd seen her wear since their senior school dance—mostly white but with shiny blue satin and what he'd heard his mama call a "sweetheart neckline." The dress was strapless, which nearly drove him crazy, but she had a matching wrap draped across her shoulders and tucked into a narrow satin belt that fit snug around her tiny waist.

And she wore a single strand of pearls. When he told her how pretty they looked, he avoided adding that her skin practically shimmered beneath them.

She touched them lightly with her fingertips. "They were my grandmother's." She gave the slightest wink that only he could see. "Mama thought tonight would be a nice evening to wear them."

Maybe his mother was right, he figured as he chewed

230

methodically on the roast and potatoes served by Mrs. Sikes. Perhaps Mr. Sikes was going to say yes to his dual proposal.

When dinner was finally over and everyone had eaten the last of the key lime pie and drank the final slurp of coffee, John Sikes leaned back in his armed dining chair and said, "Well, I guess we may as well get to the real reason for this evening."

Billy glanced across the table to where Ronni sat next to her brothers. Her hands immediately went onto her lap as her shoulders squared.

Mr. Sikes continued, "Stanley and Travis . . . why don't the two of you start clearing things away in the kitchen for your mama?"

Seventeen-year-old Stanley—whom Billy had palled around with from time to time but not enough to form any real friend-ship—rolled his eyes. "Gladly." He jabbed his brother—eleven-year-old Travis—in the ribs before saying, "They're gonna talk adult and mushy in here, Trav. Let's get out while we can."

Mischievous, button-nosed Travis rubbed his side. "I wanna hear what's gonna happen to Sissy."

"Travis Trenton Sikes," Mrs. Sikes said fluidly.

The young lad hung his head. "Yes, ma'am."

After the two younger Sikes left the dining room for the kitchen, John Sikes cleared his throat and began with, "I guess you know you're both only eighteen years of age."

Billy felt his stomach tighten. His mother, God love her, reached across the six inches of space between them and placed her hand near his thigh, just enough to let him know she was there for him. "Yes, sir."

John leaned forward to rest his forearms on the edge of the long table draped with a lime-green tablecloth. "But . . . I also know the two of you have been friends since you were twelve—best friends, in fact."

231

No one responded. No one moved.

"And I also know you professed your love for each other two years ago and, Billy, you have honored my desire that my daughter remain pure and chaste for her wedding day."

"Yes, sir," he said, almost too forcefully.

Mr. Sikes visibly swallowed a smile. "You've shown maturity beyond your years, Billy, considering the unfortunate decisions of your brother and father . . ."

Billy could only blink at the reference, but he heard his mother's intake of breath.

"And you've proven to be a good citizen of this community in your youth. A good worker in my restaurant." He looked at the woman sitting to Billy's right. "And a good son."

"That he has," Mama said.

Billy glanced across the table. Ronni was staring at him and her eyes shimmered with tears.

John Sikes took a deep breath. "Billy . . . I don't know if I could have been half the man you are at eighteen, to be honest, and I was a pretty fine catch." He smiled. "Just ask my wife."

"Hear, hear." There was a long pause as Ronni's parents looked at each other from opposite ends of the table. "Go ahead, John," Mrs. Sikes finally encouraged.

"Let's start with the Cedar Key idea. I've done some research into the seaside village. I've read up on the history. Fascinating, I must say. I've made calls into renting one of the buildings along Dock Street. Put together some numbers . . ."

Billy waited, his eyes fixed on the man who held his future in his hands.

"I think it's a viable plan, Mr. Liddle."

Billy exhaled a breath he'd not been aware he was holding. "Really, sir?"

"But I also think eighteen is awfully young to take on such

a thing as management." He glanced at his wife. "Mrs. Sikes and I have discussed it. For the first year, I'll manage and you'll be my assistant manager. Can you live with that?"

Billy nearly leapt in his chair. If he was saying yes to the restaurant, then maybe . . . "Yes, sir."

"And one year should also give my daughter and her mother time to plan what I'm sure will be the wedding of the century."

Billy felt one side of his mouth rise in a grin. He looked at Ronni, who had stopped holding back her tears as she looked at her father. "Oh, Daddy," she whispered.

John Sikes winked at his daughter. "You all right with that, kitten?"

Ronni nodded in answer and her father turned his attention back to Billy. "Mr. Liddle . . . do you have something you'd like to ask my daughter?"

Billy looked at his mother. She, too, was crying. One look at Mrs. Sikes told him she had joined in as well.

"Go ahead, son," Mama said.

Billy stood, slipped his hand into his front pants pocket as he walked behind his future father-in-law, and then came to stand beside the young woman he would one day call his wife. Retrieving the small ring box from where it had been tucked all evening, strategically hidden by his suit coat, Billy knelt on one knee. He opened the box.

Ronni gasped; her hands flew to her lips.

"Veronica Sikes, will you do me the honor of being my wife?" he asked, having practiced all afternoon.

"Yes," she whispered as her slender fingers came along both sides of his face. "A thousand times, yes." She looked up at her father, and Billy did the same.

"Chaste only," he remarked.

Billy looked again to Ronni, who smiled with closed lips. Billy stretched toward them, and they met his halfway. For the first time, they sealed their love with the briefest of kisses.

It was the sweetest moment of his life.

24

Summer 1961

The wedding was set for June 24, 1961, the last Saturday of the month, and the opening of the restaurant exactly four weeks after that. For a year, Billy had worked side by side with his future father-in-law (who insisted Billy call him John) and had done his best to soak up everything he could about opening a restaurant and keeping it going. He'd put in long hours for very little pay, and John had matched him hour for hour. He'd also helped Billy purchase a 1957 Chevrolet Bel Air, black with white tail fins and wide whitewalls. It was both reliable and not so shabby to look at.

The two men rented a two bedroom, one bath cottage with bead-board interior on 5th Street that would one day be home to Mr. and Mrs. William Liddle. The men called it practical while Mrs. Sikes and Ronni declared it to be "precious." The rooms were small, but both the exterior and interior had been renovated after 1950 when Hurricane Easy had hovered over the town for nearly ten hours. The damage had been extensive but, in true Cedar Key fashion, cleanup and renovation had been sure.

During the week, as workmen clamored and hammered around them, Billy learned by doing and by listening.

"You'll never be bored, Billy," John told him one afternoon as they walked from 5th to the Dock Street location of what would soon be Sikes's Seafood Cedar Key.

"I haven't been so far, sir." While Billy had reluctantly taken to calling his mentor by his given name, *not* calling him "sir" was out of the question.

"We'll need to look at hiring soon enough. Have you made a list of employees? Hostesses, waitstaff, cooks, washers . . ."

"I went over the list you gave me." They walked along G Street—a longer route, but they enjoyed the view—the wide expanse of the Gulf of Mexico to their right and before them. The beach the locals called "the spit" was covered by a high tide. Large pelicans flew with purpose toward the east while seagulls made lazy trails overhead. Billy looked across the way to Atsena Otie, the original Cedar Key. Its narrow white beaches gleamed under the early morning sunlight. "I've made some posters for the outside of the building to let people know we're hiring soon. Whenever you give the word, I'll change the 'soon' to a date."

"Soon . . ." John said. He looked up, breathed in. "Nice day." They rounded the bend where G became 1st.

"Freedom 7 lifts off in two days," Billy noted as though the thought came to him from nowhere. He tilted his head to look at the perfect blue of the sky arched over them. "Hard to believe an American is going to travel in space."

"I told Harriett we'd come in early Friday morning so we can watch it on television with the family."

"Oh?"

The older man grinned. "Stanley and Travis don't want the rocket to take off unless their old man is there to watch it with them."

Billy smiled. "Does Ronni know? That we're coming in?"

They walked between the shadows of the small, old homes along both sides of the street. A local had told Billy that "they were floated over from Seena-Otie after that hurricane late last century. All that was left, near-bout." Every morning, when he and John walked this way, Billy felt stirred by the history surrounding him.

"I told Harriett to be sure to tell her." John cast a sideward glance toward him as they turned onto C Street. "Harriett said Veronica's dress is finished and that it fits like a dream."

Billy made a pretense of waving his hands about his ears. "Ahhhh . . . don't tell me," he said with a laugh. "I'm not supposed to know anything about the dress." The sun now blazed across the water and onto them.

John chuckled. "You're not supposed to *see* the bride in the dress. Hearing about it . . . my boy, prepare yourself. It's *all* I hear about. Veronica's dress, the bridesmaids' dresses, flowers and petit fours."

Billy raised his voice as they walked up to what would soon be their restaurant to be heard over the workmen who came even earlier than they. "Petit fours? What in the world is that?"

John Sikes slapped him on the shoulder. "You'll know soon enough . . ."

On most weeks, Billy and John drove home to Gainesville for a day or two, but on different days, always depending on what had to be done in Cedar Key. Some weeks there was no trip inland at all; a meeting with insurance and supply company reps or the need to work out licenses or food supply issues took precedence over their need to be with those they loved. Their Sunday worship time was spent at one of the churches on the island.

Most evenings while in Gainesville were spent with Ronni,

usually at the local movie theater. Together they'd giggled over *101 Dalmatians*, felt inspired by *Swiss Family Robinson* and *Exodus*, and been frightened by *Midnight Lace*. Afterward they'd meet up with friends at a nearby soda shop and then either go back to Billy's to spend time with his mother or Billy would take Ronni home. He rarely lingered; he felt he'd taken enough of the Sikes's family time, what with John pouring so much of himself into the Cedar Key venture and the efforts for the wedding.

But the early morning of May 5, both families gathered at the Stone residence with Mr. and Mrs. Stone. Mrs. Sikes had gained permission from the school to allow Stanley, a high school senior, and Travis, now a seventh grader, to stay home the first half of the day so they could watch an American's first venture into space. The school had graciously granted permission.

Mrs. Stone made a pot of aromatic coffee and Billy's mother brought both orange and grape juice. Mrs. Stone's dining room table was laid out with a variety of breakfast foods from all three households, decorated by tiny American flags flying stiff from toothpicks.

Breakfast was finished amongst a high level of excited conversation, and then everyone went into the living room to gather at the sofa, the matching chairs, the transferred dining room chairs, and the plush white carpeting. Early delays in the liftoff had everyone sitting on edge, but Walter Cronkite kept them informed. Coffee cups were drained and juice glasses sat empty on the coffee table. No one dared move from the Olympic console television set Mr. Stone had purchased just for the occasion.

A last minute delay at T-15 minutes. Billy held his breath as information about the real-time trajectory computer was

238

explained to the American public. "Fascinating stuff," he said out loud, but to no one in particular.

Finally, at just past nine-thirty, they heard what all of America, if not the world, had been waiting to hear. ". . . three . . . two . . . one . . . zero . . ." They watched as the long arm fell away gracefully. ". . . liftoff . . ." The long white bullet with the dark head seemed suspended in a puff of white smoke until it eased upward into the perfect sky, marred only by a few thick white clouds ringing the horizon.

Newscasters had already explained that they were not allowed as close as they'd like to be. To Billy, what with the black-and-white of the screen and the cameras so far away, the rocket looked more like a narrow school pencil than a ballistic missile. Further complicating the visual of the home viewer was all that smoke rising from its base.

"It's all kinda fuzzy," Travis said.

"But it's history," Herbert Stone pointed out. "And at least we can hear what's going on in the control tower and from Freedom 7."

"Oh . . . roger . . ." As if on cue, Shepard's voice, marred by static, came through the Olympic set. "Liftoff and the clock has started . . . all systems are go!"

The small group clapped and cheered as though they were a part of the onlookers, mostly men, the television now displayed. They stood with binoculars pressed against their eyes. A few held cameras that they tried to shield against the bright morning sunlight. Reporters and cameramen from various television stations appeared to be on alert for the next moment . . . and the next.

"Oxygen is go . . . cabin holding at five-point-five."

"It really does just look like a tiny dot on the television screen," Mama muttered.

From the television speakers they heard more chatter exchanged between Shepard and the control room. "All systems go," Shepard said.

"That's all systems go," came the static-covered response.

". . . switching to manual pitch . . ."

"What does that mean?" Ronni looked up at Billy from where she sat at his feet with her legs curled under her.

"Shhh!" Travis said.

Ronni scowled at her little brother. Billy leaned down and said, "It's an aeronautical term . . . something they do in the flight rotation. Pitch, yaw, roll."

Ronni looked at him as if he were the smartest man in the world. His heart flipped before he turned his attention back to the television. ". . . from the periscope . . . what a beautiful view!" Shepard gave a bird's-eye report of the state of Florida.

Travis, who had been sitting on the floor near the television, came up on his knees. "Boy, imagine that. He just said he can see where we live!"

". . . forty-five thousand feet now . . . roger . . ."

Stanley scooted to the edge of a dining room chair. "It's really something, huh, Dad? It's like all those Buck Rogers comics coming true." He glanced up at his father, who stood behind him, hands on his son's shoulders.

John Sikes laughed. "It sure is, son. It sure is." He gave his son a playful shake.

Billy glanced toward his mother, who sat on the sofa next to Nadine Stone. Her eyes moved from John and Stanley to fix on the television screen. Her lips pressed together. She seemed both in the moment and not a part of it at all. Billy knew, as only her son could know, what she was thinking. John Sikes was more than just here with his boys; he was making a memory for them. Her sons—one in prison and

240

the other sitting close by—were without a father to share this moment, much less take anything away from the experience of having had it with him.

His heart sank. He wanted to speak out loud, but he didn't dare spoil the moment. He wanted to let her know that it didn't matter to him. Not really. Not anymore. That he hardly thought of the man, and when he did it was with great relief that Ira Liddle was out of his life. He wanted her to know that his prayers daily went before his one true Father, asking that somehow both his earthly father and his brother be brought to righteousness. And he wanted to assure her that he recognized the gift God had given him in the form of John Sikes.

There was more he wanted to tell her. Something he'd held inside for a few weeks now. Something he had not even spoken to Ronni about—and he told her everything. A decision he had to make. Had to make alone. And, for now, without hearing the opinion of everyone around him.

He patted Ronni's shoulder and she smiled up at him. Together they turned their attention back to the television set. Just a little over fifteen minutes after liftoff, the capsule carrying Alan Shepard hung suspended from a helicopter over the Atlantic, making its way back to land. Again, the small audience clapped.

Nadine patted Billy's mother on the knee. "Come on, Bernie. Let's have some more coffee." She looked to Harriett Sikes sitting next to Bernice. "Harriett?"

"I'm with you. The rest of this is going to be male-oriented, I can just tell."

"Mama!" Ronni chided. "I'm interested in this."

Harriett Sikes gave her daughter a knowing look. "You, my dear, just don't want to leave Billy's side." She pointed playfully. "Or his feet."

John Sikes took a step back. "I'm going to have a little more coffee too . . ."

"I'll get it for you," his wife said. "Why don't you just sit on the sofa where it's more comfortable."

A half hour later, as Billy and John stood together at the dining table replenishing their red, white, and blue paper plates, Billy spoke quietly to his future father-in-law. "John . . ." He cleared his throat and hoped he wouldn't be heard, even over the voices coming from within the living room and the kitchen. "I need to ask you a question."

John stopped spooning fruit salad onto his plate and looked at Billy. "What is it, son?"

"Your attorney . . . Mr. Morris."

"What about him?"

"Do you think you could make an appointment with him? For me? I have some questions I'd like to ask him."

John blinked at him. "Anything I can help you with?"

"Ah . . . no." Billy forced a smile to defuse the moment. "I just have a couple of legal questions. Things to do with Mama . . . but . . ."

John glanced toward the living room and back to Billy. "Does this affect my daughter in any way?"

"Oh no, sir. Not at all." Billy raised his right hand. "On my honor."

John nodded. "All right then. I'll call him later today. If he can't fit you in this week, will that be okay?"

"Sure . . . of course. I'd just like to ask him some questions as soon as I can."

"Fine then . . . I'll call him this afternoon."

25

Trinity, South Carolina

Gilbert Milstrap sat behind a paper-strewn desk. His secretary—a middle-aged woman named Mary Ann Dexter—stood on the opposite side, fists planted on ample hips. "I don't know how in this world you expect to succeed in business with a mess such as this." She shook her head. Gilbert swallowed a smile while he wondered if she used an entire can of hair spray in the mornings before showing up promptly at eight o'clock. The woman wore her dyed honey-blonde hair like a football helmet; while her face appeared to go from left to right, her hair didn't move one iota.

Gilbert spread his hands over the clutter. "I don't know, Miss Mary Ann," he said with a smile. "Somehow I just make it work."

She leaned over and made a show of picking up files and slapping them into new stacks. "No, what you're doing is making it *into* work for me. More work, I might add. I deserve a raise if I ever deserved a raise."

Gilbert leaned into the soft leather of his executive chair. He laced his fingers together and formed a pillow out of his hands for the back of his head. "Ah, what would I do without you?"

Mary Ann straightened, one file still held firmly between the fingers of her right hand. "A question I ask myself all the time. In fact, where you'd be without me in your office and Martha in your kitchen is . . . well, I'll tell ya. You'd be working under somebody's car in your daddy's shop on the outskirts of Trinity. That's where you'd be." She added the file to the last of the now neatly formed stacks. "See how much better this is? Now you can make heads or tails out of things."

Gilbert chuckled again. "But Sergeant, I was making heads and tails before you walked in here." He leaned forward, picked up the manila file Mary Ann had just set down. "You must admit, I've turned one little service station café into quite the business venture. Let's see now . . ." He shook the file toward his secretary, who had tilted her head to the side and cocked a brow. "*This* is the file on the new location in Augusta." He returned it to the stack before holding up his hands to demonstrate his ability to count. "Gilly's Café— famous for Martha's homemade pies and out-of-this-world country-fried pork chops—is now in . . . one, Florence; two, Summerville; three, Savannah; four, Charleston; five, Columbia; six, Rock Hill; seven . . ." He eyed the file. "Augusta; and of course, eight, here in Trinity."

"You sound like a commercial."

He clapped his hands together. "I am, dear Mary Ann. I am. If I don't toot the horn, who will? Do you think the Colonel took his chicken idea from a service station to what it is today by keeping his work to himself?"

"Humph. I don't know about chicken, but I'm making a fresh pot of coffee. Want any?"

He reached for the Gilly's Café coffee mug sitting on the

desk near a shoe-box-sized phone with multiple lines. "Why not."

Mary Ann took the cup with a playful jerk. She marched toward the door separating their offices, mumbling all the way.

Gilbert decided to toy with her. "What was that, O Lady of the Unemployment Line?"

She turned. "I said between your children and your restaurants, you're practically a small country. That's what I said. *You* want to fire me now? 'Cause I know a good lawyer who'll prove I'm right."

Gilbert held back none of his laughter at the words. "Oh, Mary Ann. *You* are the mess." He wagged a finger at her. "That's what you are."

Mary Ann turned toward her office just as her office phone rang. "Maybe that's Colonel Sanders now wanting to share a billboard with ya." This time she raised both brows. "I'll be back shortly with some fresh coffee."

Gilbert blinked as she closed the door behind her. He stood, stretched, and walked toward a bookcase where framed photos in various sizes lined one shelf. Some were school photos of the kids. A few were candid shots of family outings. One was a recent Olan Mills of the whole family. He picked it up, blew away imaginary dust—as though Mary Ann would allow such a thing in his office—and looked at the menagerie. Three sons—ten-year-old Greg, six-year-old Kenny, and five-year-old George, whom everyone called Georgy, except Pammie, who called him Georgy-porgy, much to his chagrin. Pam was the oldest of the girls at nine, followed by Donna, who would be two in November and who was held by her mother.

"Pats," he said. "What happened to the sparkle, babe?" He

stared at his wife's image in the photograph. She'd managed to smile, but it hadn't reached her blue eyes. At one time, they'd shone as though the sun had burst from within them. But over the years, they'd become dark. Lifeless. In spite of all the life she'd brought into the world.

For a while, little things helped. His being home more often, time with her brother, her parents, her friends. His sister Janice had practically bent over backward for her, adding their kids to her own for outings, and Rayette called daily just to make her laugh. But lately, nothing had worked and everything had gotten worse. Her sleep patterns were off. She often woke in the middle of the night gasping for air. While the house remained spotless, she couldn't seem to find anything. And dinner was whatever Martha cooked at the Trinity café and he brought home.

After Donna's birth, Gilbert had talked to Patsy's doctor about her worsening condition. While he appreciated the good doctor's medical knowledge that "some women get a little depressed after giving birth," Gilbert felt it was something more and that his wife needed something beyond the vitamins and sleeping pills she'd been prescribed.

In the last year, he could hardly take a two-day business trip without her crying, begging him not to leave her, as though it would be forever. She'd even accused him a few times of having another woman in each of the towns where Gilly's was located. Nothing could be further from the truth, but nothing he said truly satisfied her either.

Mary Ann's voice through the phone's intercom system interrupted his thoughts. "Gil, a Walter Bonfield is on the phone for you. Line one."

The call he'd been waiting for. Gilbert returned the photo to the shelf as he said, "Thank you, Mary Ann." He walked to the desk, picked up the receiver, and punched the blinking box with LINE ONE stamped across it. "Gilbert Milstrap."

"Mr. Milstrap? Walter Bonfield here. You left a message for me about a week ago?"

"I did . . . I was . . . well, I was hoping to meet with you in person as soon as possible. At your office or . . . somewhere?"

The voice on the other end of the line chuckled. "If you're picturing Sam Spade in a dark and shadowy office located on a street in some sleazy side of town, you're way off. My life isn't film noir. I work out of my cheery little home here in Charleston. I have a wife and three kids to support. And I'm way more handsome than Humphrey Bogart ever dreamed of being."

Gilbert nodded. "I understand. So, where should we meet then?"

"Your place here in Charleston not on the table of possible places?"

Gilbert sat in his chair and scooted closer to his desk. "I'd prefer to keep this out of my business affairs."

"All right. When will you be back in Charleston?"

Gilbert flipped the pages of his desk calendar. "Next Wednesday."

"There's a place on Bay Street that serves a real good cup of coffee. We could meet about three? Four? Whatever is open for your schedule."

"Do they serve breakfast?"

"Yes, sir, they do at that. Got some real good pancakes."

"How about I buy you pancakes then Thursday morning?"

"Sounds good."

Gilbert looked frantically for a scratch piece of paper, but with everything now in neat stacks, it was impossible. He pulled the calendar to him, picked up a pencil, and wrote the name and the address of the restaurant as Bonfield gave it. "Got it," he said. "What do I need to bring? Anything in particular to make this thing go fast?"

"Anything you have. Birth records, birth dates, names—full names are best. Last known address, that kind of thing."

Gilbert sighed. "I'm afraid I don't have a lot . . . but I'll be happy to give you what I've got."

"The less you have, Mr. Milstrap, the longer it's going to take. I won't lie. That could run into some money."

Gilbert laid the pencil beside the calendar. "Money, I've got, Mr. Bonfield. It's answers I need."

Gainesville, Florida

A week after Freedom 7 made its historical launch, Billy entered Attorney Morris's office at exactly five minutes till two. He could feel sweat forming rings at the armpits of his white button-down short-sleeved shirt. But for a moment, he wished he'd brought a jacket.

Albert Morris kept an impressive office. There wasn't a stick of modern furniture like in so many businesses these days. Books filling the shelves were obvious treasures. The furniture was thick and highly polished. Tiny sofas in the sitting area of the reception room were overstuffed. Matching winged-back chairs were arranged by twos or fours within the long expanse of the room, which hummed. A glance to his left and he spotted a window air-conditioning unit.

Everything smelled like vanilla and there was no receptionist, which he found odd.

A glass-beveled door at the far right of the room opened. A young woman—not much older than Billy—stepped from beyond it and into the room. Her hair was long and blonde and it bounced in a curl just above her shoulders. She wore an orangey-colored dress tied off by a sash at her waist and shiny black heels that clicked on the hardwood floor beneath them. Halfway to him, she stopped. "May I help you?"

For a moment, Billy felt taken aback. "Ah . . . I'm here to see Mr. Morris. I'm Bil—William Liddle."

She smiled brightly. "Yes, Mr. Liddle. Have a seat." She motioned toward the nearest tiny sofa. "I think you'll find this settee is very comfortable."

Settee. He'd never heard of such. "Thank you, ma'am." He sat, but on the edge where it wasn't so comfortable after all.

"Would you like a cup of coffee while you wait? A co-cola?"

Billy wiped his palms along the knees of his best pair of church slacks. "A co-cola would be nice."

"On ice?"

"That'd be nice too."

Minutes later the pretty young woman returned with a glass filled with crushed ice and a small bottle of Coke. "Here you go," she said. "When you're done with the bottle, just return it to me."

For a crazy moment, Billy pictured the girl hauling empty cola bottles to the store for the pennies they brought. He swallowed a smile. "I'll do that."

"Mr. Morris is ready to see you now," she said. "You can bring your glass and bottle with you."

Albert Morris stood from behind his desk when Billy entered the opulent office filled with dark wood, heavy drapes, and more thick books than Billy thought possible to read. When the attorney extended his hand in formal greeting, Billy had to set the bottle and glass down but struggled to find a place. Mr. Morris looked to a table sitting next to a leather wing-back chair and said, "There's coasters right there. Help yourself."

An awkward moment later, a wet-handed Billy shook Mr. Morris's hand. They both ended up looking at their palms, then rubbed them together and laughed.

"Sit, Billy, please," Mr. Morris said, all the while returning to his own chair. "My goodness, look at you. How long has it been?"

Billy tried to smile but he wasn't sure it took. "I'm not sure, sir. Graduation, maybe?"

Morris nodded. "Probably so. Of course, we saw quite a bit of you when you and Frank were in school. Not to mention when Frank broke his leg and you visited with him nearly every day at the hospital. That was a fine thing you did, Billy. Frank's mother and I will always be grateful."

Billy busied himself pouring the Coke into the glass. It fizzled and popped, making Billy all the more thirsty. "How is Frank, Mr. Morris?"

"He's doing well. He's up at Duke, you know."

Billy took a sip of his drink; the fizz tickled his nose and the liquid stung as it went down this throat. "Yes, sir. I heard that."

"What made you decide against college, Billy? If I remember correctly, you could have had your choice."

"Um . . . yes, sir." Billy returned the glass to the coaster before shifting in the seat so he faced forward. "A lot . . . a lot had to do with Mama . . . and Daddy, of course. Which is why I've come to talk to you." He glanced around the room. "Although . . ." He wasn't sure how to finish verbalizing his thoughts.

Albert Morris glanced around the room with him. "Although?"

"Mr. Morris, I have to be honest. I need legal advice and I need help, but I'm not sure I can afford you." Billy choked out a laugh, hoping to keep everything friendly.

The attorney with the full head of short-cropped hair and thick brows arching over handsome features—even to Billy's way of thinking—leaned back in his chair and crossed his legs, allowing the ankle of one to rest on the knee of the other. "Why don't you tell me what you need, Billy. Let me decide if you can afford me."

Billy pondered long enough to collect his thoughts. "Mr. Morris, you know about my father . . ."

Albert Morris nodded. "I do."

"And you know I'm marrying Veronica Sikes next month."

Morris smiled. "My wife—and social secretary, by the way—has informed me we'll be there. Congratulations. Veronica Sikes is a fine young lady. Fine young lady."

Billy smiled too. "Yes, sir, she is that."

"Frank will be home by then too. He's planning on coming as well."

"I'm glad to hear that." Billy leaned over, rested his elbows on his knees, and cracked his knuckles. "There's something I'd like to do . . . I'm not sure if it's legally possible, but I'd like to find out."

"You've come to the right place."

Billy's throat had gone dry again. He felt a headache threatening from the base of his neck. This was going to be more difficult than he thought. He took another swallow of Coke before offering up a prayer to God that he could get through the meeting. Then he'd go home and rest. "Mr. Morris, I'd like to have my birth certificate changed."

Albert Morris blinked three times rapidly. "In what way?"

"I'd like to have my father's name removed. I'd like any and all references to his being my father eradicated."

Morris straightened in his chair. "Well, Billy, I can't say I blame you, but . . . have you spoken to your mother about this?"

"No, sir. In fact, I don't want opinions on it. I'm a grown man now and I know my own mind. I just want to do it."

Mr. Morris leaned his forearms against the desk, clasped his hands together, and said, "You understand that if you do this, you'll have no rights to his estate when he dies."

Billy shook his head. "If he owned the crown jewels, I wouldn't want anything the man had." He drained the Coke, replaced the glass, and said, "Understand, Mr. Morris. This isn't anger or vengeance talking. This is me putting Ira Liddle where he belongs in my life, which for me is nowhere. I haven't seen him since . . . since he and my mother divorced. I don't talk to him. I don't even talk about him." Billy wiped a moist palm over lips that had gone dry again. "I realize just how much of a father he was—or *wasn't*—and I want no connection to him."

"You're a godly young man from everything I know about you. Have you prayed about this, Billy?"

"Yes, sir."

"Do you feel this is God's direction?"

"Not entirely, if I'm going to be honest." Billy paused. "Mr. Morris, I don't want you to think I don't pray for the man. I do. Every day I pray for God to penetrate his heart, but . . . that doesn't mean I want any *legal* connection to him. I've got to put him behind me . . . and . . . well, you know how when we accept the Lord, we're baptized?"

"I do."

"That's an outward symbol that we're putting the past

252

behind us, that we're allowing our sins to be washed away, right?"

"Yes, it is."

"Well, this is an outward symbol that I want shed of any connection to the name Ira Liddle. Same as Mama changed her last name. I don't want to go that far; I just want to make sure Ira Liddle has no part in my future."

"Ah." Albert Morris pulled a yellow legal pad from a drawer, jotted notes with the pen he removed from the pen/pencil stand at the top of his desk, and said, "This means, of course, that Ira Liddle also can make no claims on anything you may or may not accomplish in this life."

"Yes, sir, I know."

The two men sat in silence as Morris made further notes on the pad. Billy finally dared to ask, "So, what will this cost me, Mr. Morris. Because, to be honest, I'm not making a whole lot of money right now, what with Mr. Sikes and me trying to open the restaurant in Cedar Key."

Albert Morris glanced up from his notes. "Billy," he said, the y coming out like a question. "You came to the hospital nearly every single day to visit my son."

Billy blinked. "Yes, sir."

"That was a gift, you know that? Frank was miserable during that long stay in the hospital."

Billy chuckled. "Yes, sir. I remember."

"So here's what I propose," Mr. Morris said, leaning back once again. "I propose I file all the necessary paperwork for you pro bono."

"Pro . . ."

"That means 'free of charge.' I can never truly repay you for what you did for Frank, but this will maybe put us somewhere on the same page."

Billy couldn't believe what he was hearing. He slid all the way to the end of the chair. "Oh, but Mr. Morris—"

Morris raised the pen, pointing the narrow tip toward the ceiling. "Nope. That's my offer. Take it or leave it."

Billy stood. And this time, he was first to extend his hand. "I'll take it, sir."

26

Spring 1963

There was nothing about waking up in the morning that Billy didn't like. And why not? When he opened his eyes, it was to a beautiful wife snuggled up against him, breathing in and out so sweetly he could almost feel her breath slipping around her form and entering into his own lungs. Beyond the sounds right there in his bedroom—soft breathing and creaking mattresses—were those that poured in from the outside through the opened bedroom windows. The seagulls calling to one another, the early morning boaters revving up their engines, chatting briefly about this or that, insects starting to swarm, and the breeze rustling the palm fronds.

Soon he'd shave while the coffeepot coughed and sputtered and bacon and eggs sizzled in the frying pan. He'd smile, listening to Ronni fuss over the grits as they bubbled and threatened to burn in a two-quart pot. "I just can't quite get it right," she'd say. Every morning. Never failed.

If she ever did get it right, he felt he'd almost be disappointed. She was so perfect in every other way; she needed something to make her a little less angelic and a little more human.

That morning, after breakfast and a kiss good-bye to his bride, he walked to the restaurant so Ronni could have the car. He'd come to know every line in the sidewalks and every chip in the paint of each storefront. He knew the owners' cars and the boats he could expect to see lined along 2nd Street. He had grown comfortable, even at his young age, with the rhythm of the older citizens, their morning routines, the way they talked and experienced life. And that was one thing he could easily say about Cedar Key. People here *experienced* life, they didn't just live it.

The management of Sikes's Seafood Restaurant in Cedar Key had been fully turned over to him. He hired a good staff, and business had grown. Slowly at first, then steadier. With summer on the way, he reckoned, they'd be even busier.

As he'd predicted before he'd proposed to Ronni, the last few years had shown a steady upswing in tourism and the small island's population growth. Even a few famous people had come not only to see the place where John Muir stopped on his thousand-mile walk to the gulf a hundred years before, but also to check out the Island Hotel, what with its haunted history, which Billy wasn't altogether sure he believed in.

Billy arrived on Dock Street and continued with his morning routine, saying hello to the fishermen and boaters he saw along the way, stopping to watch a few birds in flight. Once at the restaurant, he unlocked the front door, walked in, flipped on the nearby light, turned and shut the door to lock it again. He opened up the windows, allowing the salty breeze to push away the staleness of the previous night. He stood by the one at the farthest end of the restaurant, breathing it all in. Fat pelicans sat in rows along the boardwalks, each one with its beak pointed toward the sun lying low still in the east. A few gulls sat alongside them, but this was definitely the pelicans' territory.

Billy rested his hands over the thin leather belt looped through his lightweight trousers as he looked out across the dark gulf water to Atsena Otie. A single boat rocked toward it in the high tide. He smiled at the sight; maybe today he could get his friend to take him and Ronni out to the island. She enjoyed walking the trails, reaching the old graveyard, and reading the headstones. Pretty soon the hot weather would bring swarming mosquitoes, which would keep them away, so hopefully . . . today . . .

The flat of Billy's palm swept down his crisp white, short-sleeved shirt. The blue and white necktie felt cold to his touch. "Well, young man," he admonished himself. "Best get some of that paperwork done before the lunch crew comes in." He reminded himself to call the Ice House and Cedar Key Fish & Oyster Company to place his orders.

The phone rang from the office directly off the kitchen. "Coming," he said but still took his time; something he'd learned to do in the few years since he'd moved to Cedar Key. No one rushed. If anyone from the island—and only a few had a phone—was on the other end of the line, they'd know this. The ringing wouldn't stop until he answered. And if they did hang up, they'd call back.

"Sikes's Seafood," he answered. It was early still and he could just answer with a "hello," but it could be his father-in-law on the other end and he didn't want a lesson in restaurant management before lunch.

"Baby . . ."

"Hey, sweetheart. Miss me already?" He grinned. The

thought of her wanting him to come home didn't disappoint him.

"No . . . I mean, yes. I . . . Billy . . ."

Billy sat in the chair behind his desk. "What is it?" His thoughts flew to his mother. Was something wrong on the mainland? "Mama?"

"No . . . yes . . . she just called." Ronni took a deep breath. "Billy, you need to come home. Now."

Trinity, South Carolina

As soon as Patsy saw four of her children climb the steps of the school bus, she squeezed Donna's toddler fingers that were sticky from morning jam. "Come on, baby. Let's go home," she said to the pigtailed, urchin-faced child.

Donna grinned up at her, all the while dragging her little feet. "Carry me, Mommy."

"You're a big girl, you can walk."

Donna's bottom end eased toward the sidewalk stretching in front of the neighboring houses. And the whining started. Again. "Carry meeeee . . . I want you to caaaaary me . . ."

"Donna." Patsy jerked her daughter's hand in a lame attempt to get her to stand. How was it that such a little child—whom she clearly outweighed—could hold her own in this common tug-of-war? "Get up, do you hear me?"

"Uhhhhh . . ." More pulling.

Battles of will with this child were always futile. Not to mention, Patsy was just too tired to put up much of a fight. "Come on." She bent at the waist and scooped up her daughter from her armpits. When Donna had settled herself on her mother's hip, Patsy said, "Are you happy now?"

"Yes."

"Ugh . . . you are something else, do you know that?"

"I'm spoiled rotten." Truer words had never been spoken, but from such a face . . .

"You are that."

They walked a few steps in silence.

"You're clearly getting too heavy for this."

"Mommy?"

"What, baby?"

"Is Daddy going to be home today?"

"No, sweetheart. Daddy works, remember?"

Donna rocked against Patsy's hip. "But I want to see Daddy."

"Donna, stop it." She patted her daughter's bottom. "Daddy will be home for supper like always."

The child settled. "Why does Daddy go to work so early?"

Why, indeed. "Because he has a lot of work to do."

"I don't like Daddy being gone so much."

"Me either."

"Is that why you call him all the time?"

Patsy shifted Donna from one hip to the other. The driveway leading to their house was within sight. "I don't call Daddy all the time, Donna."

"Daddy says you do."

Patsy stopped. Looked at her daughter. "Did you hear Daddy say that?"

The toddler nodded. Dark pigtails bounced alongside her ears as darker eyes grew wide. Eyes that always reminded her of Billy's . . . and their mother's. "He said he's worried." She pouted, then reached up with sticky fingers and pressed her mother's lips together. "Why is Daddy worried?"

Patsy pulled away from pressing fingers and resumed walking. The sooner she could get Donna in front of the television, the sooner she could call Gilbert and give him what-for. "I'm sure you misunderstood him."

"No."

"No, what?"

"No, ma'am. I didn't. He was talking to Grandma on the phone when you were at the grocery store."

Patsy arched a brow. "Grandma B?"

"Uh-huh."

"Yes, ma'am."

"Yes, ma'am."

They turned onto the driveway, lined with yellow and white daffodils. Approached the right side of the house, where pungent honeysuckle grew on a trellis. The scent was almost too sweet for her right now. Sickeningly sweet . . .

"How do you know it was Grandma B?"

Donna shrugged and wiggled some more. "Daddy called her 'Mam.' That's what you call Grandma B, so I know."

Patsy squeezed her arms around her daughter's backside in another attempt to keep her still. "Want to watch *Captain Kangaroo*?"

"Uh-huh."

Patsy sighed. "Yes, ma'am."

"Yes, ma'am, and *The Alvin Show* too."

She put her daughter down. "Then let's scoot inside." She patted her daughter's back to encourage her to get along. It worked. Donna ran full steam toward the side door the family most commonly used.

Within minutes, Patsy was in her bedroom calling Gilbert's office. Mary Ann answered on the second ring.

"Hi, Mary Ann. Is Gilbert in his office?"

"He is." Patsy wasn't sure, but she thought she heard exasperation in the secretary's voice. "Hold please."

Patsy narrowed her eyes. She did *not* call too much. She did not.

"Hey, honey."

The back of her knees came against the unmade bed, which she plopped down upon. "Did you tell my mother that I call you too much?"

A long pause. "Who told you that?"

"That doesn't matter, Gilbert. Did you?"

"It does matter. Who told you that?"

Patsy crossed one thin leg over the other, swung it back and forth. She didn't have to answer the question. She wasn't on the defensive. She was the one with the evidence of betrayal. "Did you?"

"Patsy, I'm not playing games. Who told you that?"

"I'm not playing games either, Gilbert Milstrap. I want to know if you said it and I want to know if you feel that way. Because I don't. Feel that way. *Or* call you too much."

"How many times a day would you say you call me, Pats?" Gilbert's voice was steady and calm.

She didn't know . . . maybe twice. Three times . . . twice. "Twice."

Gilbert chuckled, but not as though he thought this was the least bit funny. "Mary Ann keeps a record of every call that comes into this office, did you know that?"

"So?"

"So . . . you call sometimes five and six times a day and, quite honestly, for no apparent reason other than to check on me or to tell me how hard you have it at the house. Donna won't stop fussing, the kids aren't doing their homework, the pickle jar won't open. But mostly to see if I'm here at the office, doing whatever I do but you *doubt* I do, and to make sure I'm coming home on time. Which I always do."

"That's not true."

Yes, it was. It was so true.

But how could she trust that he was where he said he was . . . or that he'd come home at the end of the day. And what if, one day, he met some pretty waitress at one of his cafés or a spiffy secretary at one of the supply offices he sometimes visited? Dressed to the nines, nails done, hair combed—not like hers, worn long and braided down her back—with makeup even? What if?

"It is true. And it's also a private matter and I'm at work. I've got things to do here today, Patsy, and I cannot keep spending time convincing you that I'm here or that I'm coming home or even that I love you and always will." He breathed out. "Even though I do and always will."

The side doorbell rang. "Great. Now who?"

"What is it?"

"Someone is at the door. I have to go."

"Patsy—"

"What?"

"You all right?"

"What do you think?" And with that, she hung up.

The doorbell rang again. "Coming!" she hollered, leaving the bedroom and walking down the long hallway, then into the main part of the house. From the family room, the voices of Mr. Green Jeans and Captain Kangaroo echoed from a too-loud television. "Turn that television down, Donna Sue Milstrap," Patsy said as she entered it.

Along the way she picked up toys, cradling them in her arms. Several children back she'd placed a wicker basket—narrow on the bottom and with a wide rim—at the side door, which led from the family room to the carport. It was the place where all discarded and forgotten toys went to rest.

There, she dumped the items and opened the door to find Mam standing on the other side.

"Mam, what are you doing here?"

Mam stepped in without invitation, not that she needed one. "I take it Rayette and Sandra haven't gotten here yet."

Patsy shut the door, placed a hand on her hip, and said, "Why on earth would they be here this time of day?" Or at all, for that matter.

Mam had already made it halfway to her grandchild, who sat on the floor but was scurrying to stand. "I'll let them fill you in," she said with a wave of her hand. "Come to Grandma . . . come to Grandma, you little darling."

"Grandma!" Donna ran with outstretched arms.

Patsy closed the door while the two hugged and cooed over each other. When her patience had worn thin, she said, "Mam. What are you doing here?"

Mam turned to her, Donna still wrapped in her arms, legs dangling and swinging. "I'm here to watch this adorable, wonderful, most precious child with jam all over her fingers." Mam frowned. "Really, Patsy . . ."

"Me!" Donna squirmed. "You're gonna watch me!"

Mam practically beamed. "That's right, you."

"Mam." Patsy now walked toward the two of them, frustration at the morning and everything it had held coursing within her. When within reaching distance, she pulled her daughter away from her mother. "Why would you think you need to babysit?" Donna squirmed and whined against her, all the while stretching toward her grandmother.

Mam took the child back. "Because, Patsy, Rayette and Sandra are taking you out for a little shopping and some lunch."

Captain Kangaroo ended and the theme song to *The Alvin*

263

Show began. *"This is the Alvin Show . . . the Alvin Show . . . you're positively gonna love the Alvin Show . . ."*

Donna, no longer enamored of Mam, pushed herself away. "Down, down, down . . ." She skipped back to her place on the floor in front of the television set.

Mam chuckled. "Well, I now know who comes first around here."

Patsy tapped the toes of her foot. "Mam . . ."

Mam slipped the handle of her purse from the bend in her elbow, walked over to an end table, and placed it there. "Patsy," she said firmly. "Your friends are coming to get you. Go to your room right now and put something appropriate on. You're hardly dressed for the house much less the out-of-doors."

Patsy felt herself frown. She'd walked to the bus stop and back in her pedal pushers and cotton shirt. Looking at herself, she thought she looked fine. Not dressed enough for town and lunch, but surely good enough for students and their parents. Looking back at Mam, she said, "What shall I put on then?"

Mam harrumphed. "Like you even need me to tell you. Go put on that pretty green frock Gilbert bought you not too long ago."

"Gilbert didn't buy it, Mam. I bought it."

Mam shook her head. "I thought Gil did. Doesn't matter. Just go do like I tell you before I take to ordering you about like you were a ten-year-old."

"Oh, all right." By the time she'd changed and applied a light amount of makeup, Rayette and Sandra were in her family room, chirping away like birds on a wire with Mam. Donna pitched a small fit upon realizing her mother was going somewhere without her, but Mam got the situation under control as she attempted to shoo the three younger mothers out the door.

Patsy stopped suddenly. "Wait. I left something in my room," she said.

"What?" Rayette asked. "Looks to me like you have everything."

But Patsy wagged fingers at her. "No. Really. I'll be right back."

She slipped around her friends and mother and wriggling daughter and headed back down the hallway toward the bedroom. She hadn't really forgotten anything, of course. She wanted to call Gil one more time before she left.

Just in case . . .

27

Cedar Key, Florida

Billy sat in a folding chair on the front porch of the little cottage he shared with his wife. He'd long past loosened and shed himself of the blue and white necktie. He'd pulled his shirttails out from his pants and drawn the belt from their loops. Both belt and tie were now lying at the foot of the bed. Unless, that is, Ronni had put them away.

His hand clutched a tumbler of cold iced tea. The glass was sweating; water pooled along his fingers.

For long minutes he stared ahead to the house across the street. The structure was covered by trellises, which were matted with the thick green vines of velvety blue morning glories. It appeared the house had never been painted, but the flowers of its vertical garden exuded an abundance of color.

Billy blinked. Took a deep breath. Exhaled. An occasional insect flitted around him; he'd swat and go back to staring.

Off and on during the afternoon, Ronni pushed open the squeaky screen door, taken one step out onto the porch, and asked if he were all right. He'd simply nodded. A quick look at his watch told him she was just a hair past her usual "just checking up on you" inquiry.

As though she'd read his mind, the screen door opened. "Billy?"

He didn't answer. He couldn't. Not quite yet.

This time, she stepped fully onto the porch, grabbed the folded chair propped against the front porch wall, and popped it open. She sat, crossed her legs. He glanced over at them. They were tanned and shapely.

My gosh, even in a moment like this, she stirred him.

"Billy Liddle, you listen to me," she said. Her right hand came to rest on his left arm. "We've got some decisions to make. I've called Brenda. She's already at the restaurant, getting it ready to open. She said she can handle whatever needs to be handled for as long as you need her to."

"Fine."

"But, Billy, we've got to make some decisions. Do you want to leave now to go to Gainesville or do you want to wait until tomorrow?"

Billy took a long swallow of his tea. "We should go today. Mama said the Stones were with her, but they'll need to get on soon enough and . . . I'm sure she needs me. I just . . ." His words caught around a lump in his throat.

"Just?"

"Don't know what I'm going to say to her. I've never had to deal with anything like this before."

Her warm fingertips slid up and down his arm. "I know."

He turned his head toward her. Her beauty was blurred by his tears, but she looked amazing for the middle of the afternoon just the same. "My brother is dead, Ronni," Billy said. "I woke this morning with a brother and I'll go to bed tonight without one." He blinked. A tear slipped down his cheek. "All because he couldn't just wait out his sentence."

"I know."

"He always thought he was tougher than everybody else."

"Why was that, do you think?"

Billy didn't say anything at first. Instead he watched a cluster of butterflies flitting around the lantana growing in the front yard. When they left for the neighbor's garden, Billy answered. "Ira was the same way. He bullied those weaker than him. Harold. Mama." He waited. "Patsy."

"Patsy? Who is Patsy?"

"My sister."

This time, Ronni fell silent. "Excuse me, Billy Liddle . . . did you say your *sister*?"

"Yeah."

She uncrossed her legs, left from over right. Then right over left. Billy sensed a slight stomping of her foot. "You have a sister?" The words came out half question, half statement.

"Mmmhmm. A half sister. Half brother too. I didn't know about him until . . . Mama waited to tell me about him."

Ronni gripped the sides of her chair. "I'm going to try very hard not to be upset with you right now because I know you are in mourning. But would you care to explain?"

Billy blinked, kept his focus on the house across the street. On one of the morning glories. "When I was little—*little little*—there were five of us in the house. Mama. Harold. Me. A sister named Patsy—she came from Mama's first marriage—and, of course, Ira Liddle."

"Your mother was married before?"

"Her husband died. The ring"—he looked casually toward his wife's left hand—"came from her marriage to her first husband."

"I thought . . . it was . . . *her* mother's. Why did I think that?"

Billy had to think before answering. "Maybe I told you about that other thing . . . the necklace thing."

"Mmm."

They sat in silence for a while before Ronni asked, "So, what happened to her?"

Billy rubbed his temple with the tips of his first and second fingers. He hadn't had a bad headache in quite a while, but he was surely getting one now. "Patsy turned thirteen, Ira took to looking at her too long, and Mama put her on a bus."

"Oh, my sweet Jesus." Ronni pressed her left hand against her chest. "I cannot imagine. How horrible for your mother." She edged her chair closer to his. "And no wonder it's never discussed. How painful it must have been for her." Her hand fluttered over the back of his head. "For you."

"I hardly remember her."

"You're rubbing your head. You getting one of your headaches?"

"Yeah."

Ronni stood. "I'll go get your medicine." She took a step toward the door. "Wait. You said a half brother too. What about him?"

Billy squeezed his eyes shut, rubbed his temple a little harder. "I don't know much about him, Ron. He went to live in the same place as . . . Patsy . . . only right after he was born."

Ronni said nothing. She didn't move either.

The headache was growing. "Ronni . . . my medicine."

The screen door opened, closed. He listened to her footsteps fade toward the back of the house. A moment later, they returned. The door opened. Closed. He felt his wife's presence beside him. He opened his eyes; a hand with two pills nestled in the palm was just under his chin.

"Thank you," he said.

"When you're done taking them, I'll take your tea glass back into the house."

He swallowed the pills and the lukewarm tea before handing the glass to her. "Ronni?"

"What, Billy?"

"You mad at me?"

She stared down at him. "Mad? No. Disappointed? Yes. You should have told me this before now, Billy Liddle."

Billy reached for her left hand, squeezed it in his. It was warm to the touch, but he felt a chill all the same. "Would you have thought any less of me?"

"Of course not. What kind of Christian do you take me for?"

He squeezed her hand again in answer, noticing this time that her engagement ring was no longer wrapped around the third finger. He wanted to say something, but now was not the time.

"Billy," she said softly. "Come inside and lie down. When you wake, we'll drive to Gainesville. Your mother needs you now."

Billy nodded. It was all he could do.

Trinity, South Carolina

Gilbert was poring over the monthly profit and loss forms when he heard the phone from the outside office ring. He stole a glance at his Timex. It was nearly four in the afternoon. If Mary Ann buzzed his office line, that would mean one of two things. One, Patsy was calling him again, or, two, Sandra was calling to report on her "kidnapping."

He prayed for the latter.

He got neither.

270

"Gil, Walter Bonfield is on the phone for you."

"Bonfield?" He hadn't heard from the man in months. In fact, he'd thought about hiring another private investigator. "Put him through."

"Sure thing."

Seconds later, Bonfield's voice said, "Mr. Milstrap?"

"I thought maybe you'd quit on me."

"No, sir."

"Last I heard from you, we'd hit a wall in Miami, Florida."

"Well, I think I may have something for you."

"I'm listening."

"Didn't you say your wife had a brother named Harold?"

"That's right. He's the older of the two boys." Gilbert bounced his pencil along the edge of the desk pad.

"Well, I got a call from a man I know down near Orlando. I'd asked him to keep his eyes and ears open for me."

"And?"

"And . . . he tells me that early this morning there was an attempted breakout of a prison situated over there in Raiford, Florida."

"Raiford?"

"Over in Bradford County."

"I've never heard of it." He tapped his pencil twice more. "What does this have to do with my wife's family, Mr. Bonfield?"

"A Harold Liddle was the name of the convict who tried to escape."

"And you think this could be my wife's brother?"

"I'm willing to go check on it for you. It's the best lead we've had in months." He sighed. "It'll mean a road trip, though. I've called down there to talk to the warden, but he's got his mouth shut tighter than a pickle jar."

"What about the local paper down there? Did you try to call them?"

"Of course. Of course. They're not saying a whole lot either. I know my job, Mr. Milstrap. I can get people to talk, but I gotta go down there to do it."

That much was true. Walter Bonfield had managed to get enough information out of some of the old-timers in Cassel-ton to track down Ira Liddle's business dealings. The family had moved to Miami shortly after Bernice Liddle put Patsy on a bus. In Miami, Walter had learned enough to know what life was like for the Liddle family. From what he was able to surmise, Ira Liddle had been fired for immoral behavior with some of the salesclerks and had moved his family without much to-do. And no one seemed to know where. Even the neighbors were at a loss, but they'd told Bonfield what they knew.

"That's fine. I'll wire some money to you in the morning if that works."

"Works fine for me."

"Mr. Bonfield?"

"Yes, sir."

"Harold Liddle—what's he in for?"

"You mean what *was* he in for . . ."

"He's . . . ?" Gilbert gripped the phone tighter.

"Dead. Yes-siree-bob. Shot him."

Gilbert closed his eyes and exhaled. The pages of the P&L statement ruffled beneath him. "That's too bad."

"Yes, sir. If this turns out to be your wife's brother . . . my condolences."

"Thank you." After exchanging good-byes, Gilbert re-placed the receiver. He ran the fingers of his left hand over his forehead and into the crown of thick wavy hair he constantly fought to tame. For a moment, he allowed his brow to rest in the palm of his hand while he breathed in and out through his nostrils.

This was not good. Not good at all. If *this* Harold Liddle turned out to be Patsy's brother, she'd never recover from the news. Unless, of course, there was something good to tack on to the end of it.

Bonfield had to find Billy and Bernice. He had to.

28

Summer 1963, Cedar Key, Florida

To soften the blow of what he was about to ask her, Billy went out and bought his wife a brand-new Volkswagen Ragtop Beetle. A red one. Ruby red.

As he hoped, she went crazy over it. When he drove it into their short driveway, he peered over at the cottage and waited for her face to appear at the window as it always did. Sure enough, within moments, the sheer curtains parted. Her face was quizzical. Billy had the ragtop pushed back; he stood on the red and white vinyl seat and popped through the opening for a wave.

Her mouth fell open; the curtain dropped. Seconds later, he heard the front door open along with her sandaled footsteps on the narrow planking of the porch. "Billy Liddle," she squealed.

He dropped back into the car and opened the driver's door. "Whaddaya think? Huh?" he asked, arms spread wide as he unfolded himself from the interior.

"Ohmygoodness! Ohmygoodness!"

Ronni wore her dark hair in a flip near her shoulders. It

bounced, catching the light from the early afternoon sunlight. She wore a pair of white baggie shorts and a blue and white checked top that exposed the skin between the waist of the shorts and the hem of the shirt. She looked like a schoolgirl, not a grown woman. As always, one glance at her made him crazy.

But, at least for now, he had to stay focused.

"You like?"

"Did you . . . ? Is it . . . ?" She clapped her hands together as though he'd already given her the answers she wanted to hear.

"Did I buy it?" he teased.

She stopped jumping up and down, placed her hands directly on his shoulders, and stared without a word.

"Yes, I did."

He laughed at her gasp.

"Is it ours?" She didn't wait for an answer; she squealed, threw her arms around his neck, and bent one leg at the knee as she squeezed him.

He laughed and said, "You're killing me."

Ronni released him. "I cannot believe you did this . . . can we afford it? Of course we can afford it. You'd never do anything like this unless we could, and goodness knows we could use a second car now." She darted around the car. "It's red. *Red*."

"The restaurant is doing all right," he said by way of short explanation. Billy held up the keys and jiggled them. "Wanna take her out for a test-drive?"

Without words, she answered him. In a blur, she ran past him, up the cottage steps, over the porch, and through the door. Moments later, she returned exactly as she'd left, this time with her purse dangling from the crook of her arm. "Let's go!"

She immediately slid into the driver's seat.

"Hey, I know," Billy said. "*You* drive." He handed her the keys with a chuckle before getting into the passenger's side. After he'd shut the door and Ronni hers, she threw herself toward him. Billy wrapped his arms around her waist, allowed her to kiss him, to tell him how much she loved him, that he was the best husband a girl could ever ask for.

"You better believe I am," he said with a final peck to her lips. "Now are you going to back this thing out of the driveway or am I going to take you inside?" He wiggled his eyebrows for the fun of it.

Ronni returned to her side of the car. "First we drive . . ." She cut her eyes toward him playfully. "Then you take me inside."

They took the car for a spin, driving up and over every street Cedar Key had to offer. Along 2nd Street, Ronni drove ever so slowly, making sure to stay within the speed limit. But along the more uninhabited roads where dark green foliage and colorful oleander grew thick among the rising palms, she pressed her foot against the pedal and drove like she was Steve McQueen in the *The Great St. Louis Bank Robbery*.

"Don't try to stop me," she shouted above the warm air pushing its way through the windows and the ragtop. "I just want to do this one time."

"Just don't kill me," Billy called back, holding his arms up in mock surrender to her wiles.

Ronni threw her head back and laughed.

Let her have her fun, he thought. As soon as they got home . . . as soon as he'd made love to her . . . he'd ask her to listen to his idea. To pray about it. Pray about it with him.

But for now, let her have her fun.

Trinity, South Carolina

"No!" Patsy shrieked. "No! No! No!"

She was on her knees in the bedroom she shared with her husband, bare knees against grass-green carpet that chafed and burned. It felt as though a hole were being rubbed through the bones.

Not that she cared.

Her hands were raised. Her fists shook at the man who stood over her.

Gilbert had her by her wrists, holding her up against her will. She tried to pull away from him, but his grip was firm. "Stop it," he hissed between his teeth. "The children."

Hot tears streaked down her face. Her hair, unbrushed and loose, played with the delicate skin at the small of her back.

She was dressed only in a pair of pajama bottoms and a bra. Even in her state of discontent, she knew she must look a sight. No doubt eyes red and swollen. Mascara leaving its telltale signs from her red-rimmed eyes to her jawbone.

Not that she cared. She didn't care. Couldn't. What mattered—the only thing that mattered—was that Gilbert was leaving her. Abandoning her like the others in her life had. First her father, then her mother . . . now Gil.

Gil, who dropped to his knees in front of her, wrapped her in his arms, drew her to him. "Listen to me right now," he breathed into her left ear. "Are you listening?"

"I won't . . . I won't listen. I cannot bear this, Gil." Her voice was strained. She choked on nearly every word. "You cannot do this to me . . ." She folded into his arms, but he wouldn't let her slide to the floor as she wished. To lie there, to curl into a ball, to roll under the bed and never come out again.

"I am not doing *anything* to you, Pats. I'm simply going

to open another Gilly's. You've got to trust me on this. It's for us. For the kids. For our family."

She jerked in his arms, reminding herself of the way Donna acted when she didn't get her way. If it worked for their youngest, surely acting like a toddler in the throes of a tantrum would work for her.

"Stop it." He squeezed harder.

"Let me go, you monster. Let me go so I can lay right here and die and then you can be rid of me!" Patsy knew she was out of control; she just didn't care.

"Pats! The children . . ."

As though on cue, twelve-year-old Greg stuck his head around the door that had been previously closed but not locked. "Daddy . . ."

Patsy could hear the fear in her son's voice. She knew it well, this sound of fear. It had been with her nearly her whole life. She'd kept it stifled. Pushed down. She'd done everything she could to live above it. To be the good daughter, the good foster child, the good wife and mother.

But now fear had won.

"Not now, son." Gil tightened his hold around her.

"But, Daddy," their oldest whispered. "Georgy and Donna are crying . . . what do I do?"

Patsy jerked her face toward her son's.

Yes, there it was. There was the fear. Etched all over his face. Mouth gaping. Eyes wide.

"Get out!" she bellowed. "Do you want to see your mother like this? Does that make you happy too?" Her stomach rolled. Her heart hurt. Why was she doing this? Why was she saying these things to her firstborn?

Gilbert's hold on her became almost suffocating.

"You're killing me," she said. "You're killing me and I

know that's what you want. Then you can do whatever you want. Have *whomever* . . ."

"Greg," she heard her husband say. "Call Dr. Haven. Tell him I need him to make a house call quick."

"Yes sir, Daddy."

Patsy heard the door close, felt herself being lifted up. Her feet dangled at the floor until she stood flat upon them. Gilbert dipped, his arm slid under her knees, and he scooped her up, laid her on the unmade bed.

"Daddy?"

Pammie. First one, then another.

"Pammie, get Daddy a blouse from Mommy's closet."

"Daddy?"

"Pammie, be a big girl now and do like Daddy tells you. Then I want you to go sit with Greg."

So that was the way it was to be? Greg calling the doctor. Pammie getting her dressed. And what would Gilbert do between now and when the doctor came? Sit on her? And once Dr. Haven arrived? Then what? What would he tell his old friend? That his wife had gone mad? Would they put her away? Give her shock therapy? Lock her away for the rest of her life?

Patsy thrashed about, trying to free herself. Even as Pam helped Gil dress her—first in a shirt for the sake of decency, and then in house slippers—she fought them until there was nothing left to fight with. "I'm okay," she finally whispered, though it didn't seem to matter. "I'm okay," she said again.

Gil, sitting next to her, fell over her prone body. Arms wrapped her in a warm embrace. Sobs racked his body. "I love you," he told her. "I love you so much. I just don't know what to do to make you better . . . to make you believe me . . ."

She arched her back. "What's wrong with me, Gil?" she whispered. "I don't know what's wrong with me . . ."

He shook his head. "I don't know, baby. But I'm not leaving you, I promise. I'm right here with you." Then he spoke prayers into her ears, pleadings to God, until Dr. Haven sauntered in, black bag in hand.

Cedar Key, Florida

"You want to do *what*?" The words were nearly lost in the hum of the oscillating fan atop the chest of drawers.

Billy lay on his side, next to Ronni, who lay on her back beside him. Most of her body was under the crisp white sheet of their bed; both arms rested outside the cover. Her dark hair fanned against the pillowcase and the green in her eyes appeared intense in the afternoon sunlight that snuck between the slats of the venetian blinds at the window. Occasionally enough of a breeze forced them to billow inward then clank against the sill.

Billy ran his fingertips up and down his wife's bare arm. Between their lovemaking and this gentle display of his ardor—not to mention the new car—he hoped . . .

"Ronni . . . my mother is getting worse by the day. I haven't said anything because I haven't wanted to burden you with it. Especially not since Harold's . . . funeral . . . and the shame that whole thing has brought back to her and to me."

Her left hand reached for his stroking one. "Stop . . ." Then, as if to soften the word, she said, "It's starting to tickle."

Billy brought her hand to his lips and kissed each knuckle. "Thing is, baby, I got to come back here. To Cedar Key. No one here knows about anything that happened all the way over in Bradford County or even my connection to a man named Ira Liddle. And even if they did, the folks here aren't the kind to care."

"That's true."

"But Mama's had to stay in it." He looked beyond her, to the milk glass lamp on the bedside table and the white leather Bible beneath it. "Ronni . . ." He brought his eyes back to hers. "Mrs. Stone called the other day. She told me Mama is hardly coming out of the house. She's cut her hours at the hospital in half and has declined all social invitations. She didn't even attend Easter services or go to the Fourth of July picnic at the park."

Her hair made a crunching sound against the linen pillowcase as she turned to look at him more fully. "My goodness, Billy. Not even?"

"Mmm-mmm." Billy rested his forehead against her shoulder, tanned from living on the island but still silky soft. He caught a whiff of Arpège and, on instinct, kissed the skin beneath her lips. "I'm worried about her, Ron. I'm all she has."

Veronica remained quiet beside him; he knew better than to disturb her. She liked to mull things over. Pray about them before she spoke. He had never minded her doing that and he wasn't going to start minding it now.

Finally, she shifted beside him, brought a hand to his face, drawing him to look at her. "Billy." She closed her eyes. Thick black liner arching at her lash line seemed to wink at him. When her eyes opened, green eyes shimmered beneath tears. "You're not all she has."

He started to say something. To argue. To say that yes, he knew she had her friends, and her faith. But that Mama's faith wasn't as strong as theirs. She'd managed to hang on during the years of abuse. She had lived through losing two children to hardship and decision, and the shame caused by Ira Liddle, and by Harold, who—no matter what—had still been her son. But Mama wasn't strong like them, and Mrs. Stone's concern had him more than worried.

Before he could speak, his wife pressed a finger to his lips. "She has me too. I'm her daughter-in-law and I love her."

"And she has friends and her faith, I know—"

"More than that, Billy Liddle." Veronica turned on her side to face him. Her hand rested on his hip as naturally as butter melted on warm toast. "I wanted to wait to tell you. I'd planned a romantic dinner the next time you had the night shift off."

"Tell me what?"

"That she's going to have a grandchild too."

"Veronica Jean Liddle."

She only nodded.

"Are you sure?"

She nodded again. "I'm nearly three months."

Billy brushed wayward hair away from her face. "Why didn't you tell me?"

"You've been so busy lately and—between your work at the restaurant, the civic things you've managed to get involved in, and the Fourth of July preparations—I wanted to wait for the right time."

He rolled to his back. "My goodness, girl. You sure know how to top my gift of the VW out there."

She giggled. "Billy."

He looked at her.

"Let's get your mother here as soon as possible. Maybe a future with a little one to hold will bring life to her living again. You know, like Naomi in the Bible."

Billy could only stare at his wife. This incredible gift of God he'd been blessed with. First as a friend. Then as a girlfriend. A fiancée. Finally a wife. Now, the mother of his child. A son or a daughter . . .

He reached under the sheet and placed his hand along the flat of her belly. "I love you," he said.

"I love you more."

29

Fall 1963, Charleston, South Carolina

It wasn't so bad, really.

Being in the hospital.

The nurses were nice. Most of the time. Except when they weren't.

Sometimes Gabrielle, one of the younger ones—the one typically assigned to her—made Patsy laugh. And Patsy was learning that she loved laughing. A lot. When it came.

Another thing she had started to appreciate was not feeling guilty for her lack of meal preparation. Breakfast, lunch, dinner. It was all planned out and cooked and served, without her even having to wash a dish afterward. And, she liked having her laundry done for her except when they dried her underwear. That was frustrating. Made her feel out of control. Would it hurt them so much to just let them air-dry in her room?

Still, in the three months since she'd been admitted, Patsy had found peace here. She wasn't ready to discuss the details of her life, but she no longer flinched at the doctor's probing. Clearly, it gave the man something to do.

But she wasn't talking. Not really. Not yet. Oh, they wanted her to, all right. But that also made her frustrated. She'd stormed out of many a session. Took her awhile, but she eventually went back and said she was sorry.

Sometimes she actually was.

When she'd first arrived, they said she had a "flat affect." She didn't know what in the world *that* meant, so Gabrielle explained it to her one day while they were taking a walk. "It means, Miz Milstrap, that you don't show much emotion."

Patsy hadn't commented. To say anything might mean showing she *did* have feelings, which were mostly sadness and loneliness. And the sense that something was missing. In spite of all the people around her and the activities they kept her busy with. There was something . . . it was out there.

She had a dream one night that whatever that something was, she had her finger on it. She couldn't see it; she could only feel it. It was right there, close enough to grab hold of and identify. But, in doing so, she knew if she did, it—whatever it was—would expose *her*. The revelation of looking into a mirror and not liking what you see. And so, in her dream, she ran from it. Fast and furious. When she woke, she was covered in sweat. So much so, she had to change her nightgown and bed linens in the dark of night.

For the most part, her days were spent in games, arts and crafts, seeing her doctor, going to group, and tending her own little garden. In August, she'd had the prettiest gaillardias of anyone at the center. They grew thick in colors of burnt red and gold, and wine red. She had some nice cosmos too. She would have loved to plant some impatiens, but there wasn't enough shade in her plot of earth.

Saturdays were too long, but she enjoyed Sunday afternoons. After services, family members came to visit. Gil always came. Sometimes he brought the older children, but Patsy liked it better when he didn't. They just seemed ill at ease or too active, which only made her nervous the rest of the day. Besides, she liked having Gilbert all to herself. To wrap her arms around. To hold on to. If only for a few hours and even if it meant dealing with the unquiet feeling, which told her that when he left at the end of visitation, he would never come back.

Mam and Papa had come with him once or twice. More than that, actually. Those were the difficult visits. Mam was always dabbing at her eyes, trying so hard not to cry. Papa just kept calling her sugar plum, telling her it was all going to be okay.

She knew that. If there was anything at all she knew, it was that. Everything would be okay.

She just didn't know how.

"God knows," Gabrielle once told her. "He knows the path, and he's laid the bricks. You just have to be the one to walk down it, is all." Then she raised a hand toward the ceiling, right there in the recreation hall where they were sitting, drinking glasses of iced tea together, pretending to watch *The Secret Storm*. "Miz Milstrap, he loves you more than you even love your own children. He loves you more than you love yourself."

This was a topic Gabby managed to bring up at least once in her typical seven-to-three shift. That warm autumn afternoon was no exception. Gabrielle sat on the upturned end of a metal bucket at one of the far corners of the backyard gardens. Patsy was on her knees, tending. While Gabrielle talked, Patsy shifted her attention from the rich soil and her blooming snapdragons to the woman's white uniform. It was starched purely stiff and she kept the hem of it tucked under the knees, which were pressed together. Her white stockings looked gray against the honey-and-chocolate color of her skin; her feet stuck out on either side of the bucket, Patsy supposed to keep her from toppling over.

"I know all that, Gabby," Patsy said. She craned her neck to look around her nurse. "And I also know you are going to have a dirty hind end, what with it sitting on the end of that pail."

Gabrielle only laughed. "I can live with it if you can."

Patsy pulled the floral gardening gloves from her hands, tossed them to the green lawn along with her trowel. She fell back on her backside and adjusted her Bermuda shorts. Keeping her feet together, she spread her knees and then wrapped them with her arms, linking her fingers. "Tell me something, Gabby. What made you decide to be a nurse for the nuts?"

Gabrielle shook a finger at her. "First of all, you are not nuts. You're just tired and sad about something deep, is all. You've got a lot going on in that mind of yours, and it all needs to be sorted out. Which is why you're here and I have a job, praise Jesus."

Patsy shook her head. "Maybe so." She looked at the Keds that had become so dirty she was no longer allowed to bring them inside the hospital halls. She squinted at the woman pretty enough to work as a movie double for Ruby Dee. "So then, what made you decide to work *here*?"

Gabrielle shrugged. "I had a hard time finding work in most places. I'm not an aide, and that's what they wanted to hire me for. I'm a nurse. And . . . you know how it sometimes is here in South Carolina."

"Mmm. I know." Patsy moistened her dry lips with her tongue. Darned ole pills they had her on made her mouth so dry and lips downright crackly. "Did I ever tell you about Martha?"

Gabrielle rubbed her dark lips together before saying, "I take it she was a Negro woman like me?"

Patsy dropped her shoulders. "Why ever would you ask that? And, yes, she is. But she's more than just some Negro woman. She works for my husband as his head cook at the Trinity location. You know my husband is the owner of Gilly's . . ."

"You've mentioned it a few dozen times."

Patsy unfolded herself and stood. She dusted the dirt from her knees and the back of her shorts before bending to retrieve the gloves and trowel. "Did I ever tell you about how we met?"

Gabrielle stood. She kicked at the pail; it fell onto its side and she reached for the handle. "No, I don't believe you did."

"Well, you sure don't sound too interested."

"I'm only interested in what you *want* to tell me."

Patsy paused. Her eyes danced over the colors in the garden. Beth Reeves, her roommate, was hard at work, weeding around her pansies. Beth's nurse—a white one named Janie—stood behind her, arms folded, head turned upward toward the sky. Clearly bored. No doubt wondering what the rest of the free world was doing while she was keeping watch over a nut patient.

"Well?" Gabby said. "Are we going back in or are you just going to stand here and stare?"

"I'm thinking."

"About?"

"Whether or not to tell you how I met Gil."

"Well, Miz Milstrap," she said with a chuckle. "This isn't like you're President Kennedy and you've got to decide whether or not to go to war against the Cubans."

287

"I just don't want you to think I'm breaking down and talking. If you think I'm ready to talk, you'll tell the doctor and then he'll really start asking questions."

Gabrielle pretended to pick at a piece of lint on her uniform, not that she fooled Patsy. "What you say to me, stays with me."

"Mmmhmm . . ."

"You want I should go inside and clock out? 'Bout that time anyway. Nearly two-thirty so I need to get you back inside."

The two women walked across the enclosed lawn, traversed the lush landscape dotted with other members of the staff and patients, toward the back of the hospital. "I was thirteen years old," Patsy began, even against her better judgment, "and my mama had put me on a bus."

"How come?"

Patsy inhaled deeply. "She didn't want me anymore."

Gabby patted her between her shoulder blades. "I can't imagine that . . ."

They reached the door. Gabby pulled a key out of her pocket, unlocked it, and then pulled the door open for the two of them. "Kick your shoes off, Miz Milstrap, and put them in your cubby."

"Like I have to be told . . . and I dearly wish you would stop calling me Miz Milstrap. Call me Patsy."

Toe against heel, Patsy removed her shoes. Gabrielle giggled and said, "Can't. Against the rules." Then, as if to quickly change the subject, "My gracious, those shoes have had it. You ought to tell your husband to bring you some new ones."

With her house slippers on, Patsy and her nurse proceeded down the long, unadorned hallway leading to the single elevator that would take them back to the fourth floor. Their feet echoed atop highly polished terrazzo.

"So? Are you going to tell me?" Gabrielle probed.

"Tell you what?"

They reached the elevator. Gabrielle pressed the up button. "Why your mother put you on a bus."

"I told you. She didn't want me anymore."

"And I told you, I don't believe you." She dropped her head back; dark eyes watched the lighted numbers overhead as the elevator came toward the first floor.

"Believe what you will. She put me on a bus one day without any warning and sent me to live with Mam and Papa. You've met them."

"Good folk."

"They are that. If Mama was going to send me away, at least it was to people like them."

The elevator door opened, stopping her from saying anything else. Gabrielle extended her right arm. "After you."

Patsy stepped inside, followed by her nurse-friend.

"Push four, please."

Patsy jutted her finger against the round 4 button. "When your daughter becomes a liability, you have to send her away, you know. And then, just to make sure you don't have to deal with her, you move and leave no forwarding address. Yep, that'll fix her."

Gabrielle crossed her arms. "Miz Milstrap, let me ask you a question. Have you spent any *real* time thinking about what happened with your mama from her perspective?"

Patsy put her hands on her hips. "Maybe. And maybe I don't want to talk about it."

The elevator jolted to a stop and the doors slid open, revealing a wide hallway. Orange and green vinyl sofas stretched along both sides, interspersed with walnut tables topped by tall, beige lamps designed with gold sunbursts front and center. Two or three neatly stacked magazines lay before each lamp, recent ones on top.

At the end of the hall stood wooden double doors. Thick and locked.

Without another word, Patsy walked toward them, waited for Gabrielle to push the button that rang the nurses' desk, and then listened for the buzz indicating the doors would open.

"By the way, Miz Milstrap," Gabrielle said as the doors closed behind them, "you've got kitchen duty this evening."

Patsy stopped. They were near her room anyway, but this was clearly news. "What does that mean?"

"It means you've been here three months today and you get kitchen duty. Pretty simple, you go down to the cafeteria about thirty minutes before supper. Miz Linder, who runs the kitchen, will give you your duties. Probably folding napkins to start."

Patsy jerked her head toward her room door. "Then I'll go wash my hands and get ready."

Gabby nodded. "I'll go turn in my report to the head nurse."

Patsy felt her heart hammer, but only for a beat or two. "You won't talk much about me, will you?"

"Miz Milstrap," she answered with a shake of her head. "I've got you and four other patients. You think all I want to do is talk about you? Besides, I told you, whatever you say to me is between us. I leave the deep stuff to the doctor."

"Mmmhmm."

Gabrielle winked. "Go on now. And I'll see you tomorrow."

―――――――――――

The following day was an especially good day because she received a letter from Lloyd, who'd been stationed at Fort Stewart, Georgia, for the past two years. He and Holly were expecting their first child; his letter was filled mostly with how it felt, knowing he'd be a father for the first time.

"Holly is doing just great," he penned.

I, on the other hand, am a nervous wreck. Isn't there a rule about not raising your hands over your head? I came home from work the other day, and there she was, standing on a step stool, arms way over her head, getting a dish off the top shelf of a cabinet.

Patsy giggled at the thought.

I wonder sometimes . . . if I cannot get her off the step stool (what kind of husband am I?), how I'm going to be a good father. And, with the unrest going on over there in Vietnam, I wonder if I'll get called to leave for locations unknown. Leaving Holly here, alone, is not something I'm altogether keen on. But, if my country needs me . . .

  I am grateful for the way I was brought up, though, Patsy. Mam's and Papa's examples were of godly parenting. I know I learned a lot from them, probably more than I realize. When this baby is born—what do you think? A boy? A girl?—I believe my parenting skills will come naturally because they have been ingrained in me my whole life.

  Not much news other than this. Prayed for rain all summer and now praying it'll stop before the fall crops are all washed up. Georgia farmers and their families are flocking to the churches nearly every night. It's something to see.

                              Your loving brother,
                              Lloyd Buchwald

Sitting atop her made bed, Patsy read and reread the letter. She clutched it to her heart and fought tears as she read it one more time. Each time, her eyes stopped on one line in particular.

Leaving Holly here . . .

"Don't leave her, Lloyd," Patsy spoke to the page of legal-sized notepaper. "You should never leave your wife. Even if war calls. Don't you dare."

She decided to write him her thoughts on the subject. She went to the small desk made of fabricated blond wood, pulled a sheet of paper from it, and went to the nurses' desk to ask for a pen. Silly, she thought, returning to the room, that they weren't allowed to have pen or pencil in their rooms. But those were the rules.

"Dearest Lloyd," she began . . .

```
I received your letter just this morning and al-
ready I have read it at least five times.
    I am doing fine here. In spite of where I am. I
can't imagine what Gil is saying to folks as to
why I'm not home right now. Does he tell them I
am in a loony bin? Or does he say I've gone away
to tend to a great-aunt or something? You know
how people do things like that. Girls get preg-
nant before they are supposed to and they go live
with a family member "just for this school year."
Somebody goes a little bonkers and suddenly a
relative no one has ever even heard of gets sick
and needs some TLC.
    Well, enough of that. I want you to listen to
me because I am your big sister, and even being
here under the watchful eyes of loads of doctors
and nurses, I still have enough of my faculties
```

to glean a little wisdom and pass it along to my
baby brother.

Lloyd, no matter what, don't you leave Holly
alone. It's a terrible thing, being left alone.
I know. Gil has done it nearly since the day we
married. Always to better our family, I know,
but alone is alone. Let the army fight wherever it
wants to fight, but without you. Soldiers they've
got, but Holly only has one husband.

Even before marrying Gil, I was alone . . .

Patsy sucked in her breath and felt hot tears form behind her
eyes. She blinked hard; they spilled down her cheeks. A small
box of tissues was at her bedside table; she went to it, pulled
one, then another out, wiped her eyes and blew her nose.

My whole life.
There's so much you don't know . . .

So much no one knew, not even Gil.
The tears started again. Patsy pulled more tissues. Wiped.
Blew.

. . . things we've really never discussed. Maybe
if I'd talked to someone before now, I wouldn't
be here, in this place. But that's okay too.
Really, it is. Just know you were the lucky one
because you had both a mother and father your
whole life. I'm not bitter or anything. I love
you too much for that.

Don't leave Holly, Lloyd. Don't leave your
children either. I'm sure this one is the first of
many.

I love you too,
Patsy

She tri-folded the paper, slipped it into a letter-sized en-velope, addressed it. Odd, she thought, her legs felt weak as dishwater when she walked her correspondence to the nurses' desk, along with the borrowed pen, and asked that it be mailed as soon as possible.

"Will do, Mrs. Milstrap," the desk's receptionist told her. "It'll go out first thing tomorrow morning."

"Thank you," Patsy said. She looked down at her hands. They shook. She took a few deep breaths, exhaled, until both the quivering of her hands left and the strength in her legs returned.

"You all right?" the receptionist asked.

Patsy smiled. Or at least she tried. She could feel how crooked it looked. "I'm fine as frog's hair all things consid-ered." She took a stab at smiling again. This time, it felt like it looked real nice.

With that, she walked back to her room, grateful her room-mate was elsewhere. Patsy didn't know where. Didn't hon-estly care. She was just glad to be able to lay herself down the length of her bed, swallow back the tears that begged to come, and—only for now—be alone.

30

Sundays were never easy. Much as he loved his wife, for Gilbert, they always came with a sense of dread.

Patsy was tapping a red checker up and down on its game board when Gilbert walked into the recreation room. He gave her his best smile; she returned it with a frown. A scowl, if the truth be told.

She wore a housedress of some orangey color with cream woven through it. Looked like sherbet to him; tasty, but he hadn't come there to eat. Her hair was in a single plait, straight down the back of her head and then thrown over one shoulder. For a split second he thought of the way it looked down, waving across her back or covering one eye as she worked on a project with one of their children.

Of course, that had been awhile back.

For now, she looked madder than a wet hen; he prepared himself for the onslaught of words sure to come from her just as soon as she made it across the room to where he stood, framed by the door.

"Where have you been?" she hissed. "You're so late I almost went back to my room."

Gilbert glanced around, looking to see who may be

listening in to their usual greeting. A few of the patients and their visitors gave a cursory look but turned back just as quickly to what they were doing. He gave them a nervous grin as he took his wife by the arms, turned her around, and said, "I'm five minutes late."

She swung back to face him, wrenching herself free of his hold. "Five, my great-aunt Martha. You're ten if you're a minute."

He forced a smile. "Okay. Ten." He looked over at the checkerboard table. Oh, happy diversion, he thought, as though he were Shakespeare writing a play. "Were you waiting to play a game with me?"

Her eyes met his and held them for long seconds until she said, "Sure."

He followed her to the table, sat across from her. "I guess I'll be black," he said.

"What does *that* mean?"

He picked up a game piece and waved it at her.

"Oh."

He realized then she still held the checker he'd seen her with when he'd come in. "You be red." He hoped she got his double meaning. She *should* be ashamed of herself, acting up so.

"Ha-ha."

Good. She got it.

"You go first."

She slid a checker from one square to another. He did the same.

"Why were you so late?" she asked, making her next move.

Gilbert placed the tip of his index finger on a checker, held it there. He pursed his lips as though he were trying to think it through. "It's Sunday."

"I know that. Move already."

He moved. "I have five kids to get ready for church, Pats. Then church. Then I follow your mother and daddy to their house so we can eat and then I jump in the car and head over here. Sometimes there's traffic and—call me crazy—I just can't figure out how to get that Ford of mine to fly."

Patsy blinked at him, looked down at the board, and jumped one of his pieces. "Call *you* crazy . . ."

He chuckled. "Ah, good. There's my girl." He had a jump, but he didn't make it.

"Gil . . . it's just that . . . I worry when you don't show up right away."

He reached across the red and black squares for her hand, which she willingly gave. "You have nothing to worry about, Pats. I'm here for the long haul. I'm here until we get this all worked out."

He watched her chest heave up, back down. Up again. "And after that? What will you do? Leave me?"

He shook his head. "Never." She didn't answer, and when the tears had backed away from spilling, he released her hand and said, "Your move."

She looked at the board. "I don't want to play anymore."

"But you're winning."

"Only because you are letting me."

She stood and he stood with her. "What do you want to do then?"

She shrugged, but even in doing so, said, "Want to see my garden?"

"Sure."

They walked out of the recreation room, down the hall to the locked doors where one of the staff stood ready to open the door for them. On Sundays, staff members took on posts all over the hospital to assure "no escape."

No words were spoken until they reached the outside. Gil looked at his wife; in spite of where she was and what she'd been through, he couldn't help but notice the glow of her skin, the twinkle of her eye. "Look how pretty you look," he said.

She gave him "the look" that said "I believe not a single word of your flattery."

"Seriously." He craned his neck to look closer at her. "You're not wearing makeup, are you?"

"No."

"You've spent some time outside then. You have a nice rosy tan on your face."

"I like being in my garden." She stopped and pointed.

They were at the edge of a colorful display of flowers he knew nothing about. "Nice, hon." She beamed under his praise. "I never knew you had this in you."

Her arms folded across her chest. Overhead, birds called to each other. The murmuring of other patients in the garden swirled around them as what little bit of city traffic existed on a Sunday filtered over the high brick wall. "I take care of the flowers at home." Her voice was almost argumentative. Or maybe a little hurt. Probably because he'd never really noticed.

"Yes, well, I've had to hire someone to take care of the yard since . . . since . . . well. You know."

"You had no idea just how much I did around the house, did you?" She actually smiled at him.

"I do now." He touched the tip of her nose with his finger. "You know, I kind of like this 'no makeup' look you have going. The natural Patsy."

"I never wore that much, Gil. Pressed powder and some-times lipstick and a little mascara."

Something else he'd never really noticed. So much. Had

he really been so consumed with his work? Had he not seen, really seen, the role of wife and mother—to all his offspring—she had been?

"How are my children?" she asked when he'd said nothing.

"Good. Ready for their mama to come home."

Patsy looked at her feet, shuffled them, and said, "Maybe by Christmas, you think?"

"What has the doctor said? Anything?"

"Only that if I'd talk about the things that have hurt me in my past, I'd get to go home sooner. He says I bottle things up, and the bottle finally got too full."

"Do you?"

Patsy shrugged. Kicked at a small pebble with the toe of her sandal.

Gilbert followed her action with his eyes. It was then he noticed a weed sneaking between two flower stems near the garden's front edge. He reached down, plucked it from the ground, and handed it to Patsy. "You've got a weed growing in your garden, you get it out. Right?"

She nodded.

"Same with hurtful memories." He paused. Waited for her to say something. When she didn't, he added, "You want to know what I think?"

She cocked a half grin at him, squinting one eye against the bright sunlight. "If I say no, will you tell me anyway?"

"Probably."

"Then go ahead."

"I think," he said, taking her by the hand and turning around so they could walk the length of the garden, "that your fear of my leaving you goes all the way back to the day your mother put you on the bus for Trinity."

Patsy stopped, narrowed her eyes at him.

"Maybe even further back. All the way to your daddy—your real daddy—dying."

She took a step away from him. He reached for her hand, slipped fingers around her wrist. She tugged, but he held firm. "Let me go."

"I just want you to remember, Pats. I was on that bus too."

She jerked hard enough to release herself. "So, what of it?"

The anger had returned. Maybe he should have just kept his big mouth shut. "I'm just trying to say, Patsy, that even though that bus took you away from your mother, it brought you to me."

Her lips twisted. Her breathing became labored. Before he could say anything more, she turned and ran toward the door leading to the hall, which led to the elevators, which led to the fourth floor.

"Pats!" He took a step after her, then stopped. The struggle he'd grown accustomed to fought its way from his stomach to his chest. If he ran after her, she'd only grow angrier. If he didn't, she'd think he, too, had abandoned her. Still, he was tired now. He wouldn't leave her. He wouldn't. But sometimes—times like this—he felt like a fool.

A begging fool.

———————

The following day, while at work, Gilbert received a call from Dr. Jennings. Patsy had been fairly upset, he said, since the visit from the day before, and he wanted to know what had transpired between the two of them.

"Do you want the play-by-play or just the part at the very end?"

"Can you bring those two somewhere in the middle?"

Gilbert cleared his throat. He felt a little like a schoolboy, in trouble with the teacher, called in by the principal. "To start with, she was upset about my being a few minutes late. So, we went over the whole 'I'm not leaving you' talk. Again."

"Your wife's insecurities, Mr. Milstrap, are at the core of her issues. I wish you'd try to take on a more sympathetic tone."

Gilbert drummed his fingers over a manila file marked "Spartanburg, South Carolina" as he eyed the thick black lettering in Mary Ann's penmanship. With any luck, and in spite of the recent downturn in his personal life, he still might be able to pull off opening a new Gilly's there. "Dr. Jennings, let me remind you of how far *I've* had to come with all this. I bust my behind to take care of my family—my kids—and run a successful business. A very successful business, I might add."

"What does that have to do with your wife, Mr. Milstrap?"

"Everything. I am barely hanging on here, Doctor. I'm getting to the hospital every Sunday. I'm sending her cards like you said to. I'm encouraging her family and friends to do the same. I try to stay positive. But, quite frankly, I'm not seeing a whole lot of progress here."

"What is it you're looking for, Mr. Milstrap?"

"My wife at home, that's what I'm looking for."

"At what price?"

Gilbert felt his temper flare. "Don't you dare talk to me about price, Dr. Jennings."

A pause followed. The good doctor obviously had no retort. And why should he? He wasn't paying the price Gilbert had been paying. What did he know about crawling into bed at night, so bone weary you barely knew your own name but still keenly aware that the warm body that *should* be in the bed next to you, wasn't. What did he know of not hearing her voice, seeing her smile—really smile, not that fake thing she'd been doing lately—hearing her laugh? And what could he understand about being a man like Gilbert Milstrap? No diplomas on his wall, just hard-earned knowledge for a self-made man who somehow snagged the prettiest little girl in the world. And now . . . he was losing her . . . to something way beyond his control. Death would have been one thing; this was something altogether different.

"Look, Doc, what do you think is the outcome here? Do you think you'll ever get to the real reason my wife can't seem to connect to me anymore? To our children? I mean, I know she loves me. Loves them. So, what's the problem? You've told me if I think about bringing her home, I could face another breakdown, this one worse than the last. But, quite honestly, I'm not sure you are doing her any good at all."

"May I speak?"

"Please."

"Her nurse has reported that she is starting to talk. To her. She's not saying anything in group and she certainly is close-mouthed in private sessions. But, if she is starting to open up with Gabrielle, then this may be the opening we'd hoped for. Although, I admit, your wife's nurse can be pretty close-mouthed herself."

"So then . . . what are your plans?"

"We are still at the wait and see, Mr. Milstrap. If your wife doesn't *want* to talk about what happened to her as a child—and I do believe whatever happened with her mother is at the core of this—then I cannot force her. To even try would be futile."

Gilbert tapped the 1812 Overture on the file. "And you still think this is a simple case of abandonment issues?"

"There's no such thing as 'simple' when it comes to this kind of trauma. But, yes. I think that, even with the medication we have her on, the best thing she can do is talk."

A tap brought Gilbert's attention to the door. It opened just enough for Mary Ann to stick her head through. "Thought you might want to know that Mr. Bonfield is on line two."

Gilbert opened his mouth, but nothing came out.

Dr. Jennings said, "Mr. Milstrap?"

"Ah . . . hold on."

Mary Ann's eyes were wide, like a child's holding the secret of where the cookie jar had been hidden. "He says it's important."

"Dr. Jennings, I have a very important call I have to take. Can I call you back?"

Gilbert felt the tension from across the miles and the line. "No need. I think we've said all we need to say for now."

"I'm sorry. I have to go." He pushed the line two button. "Bonfield?"

"Glad you were in, Gilbert."

"Do you have something?" He opened the narrow top drawer on the right side of the desk, pulled out a steno pad. He flipped open the rigid tan cover along with a few pages of scribbled notes from a call he'd taken from Greg's science teacher.

But that was another story . . .

"I believe I do."

"Go ahead." He picked up a pen. "I'm ready."

"It took some digging. I found a man named Liddle, William. Lived in Gainesville, Florida, at one time with an Ira Liddle, Bernice Liddle, and our deceased criminal, Harold Liddle."

"That's him."

"Hold on now. Problem is . . . well, first let me tell you . . . when I called down there for his birth certificate records, a sweet little thing named Sheila answered, gave me all the information I could have asked for."

"I thought you were a family man, Mr. Bonfield."

"I am. But when a gal is sweet, I use all my *sweets* for the cause."

Gil tapped the pen against the wide-lined paper. "All right. I guess I'm not here to be your conscience."

"My conscience appreciates that. So, here's the thing. According to the birth certificate records, this Billy Liddle is *not* the son of Ira Liddle."

"Who *is* he the son of?"

"Well, he appears to be fatherless. Which, by the way, is why I've had a little trouble finding him. I was trying to trail a boy whose father was Ira Liddle. But, like I said, this particular call led me to Sheila."

"Who was sweet."

"Boy howdy."

Gilbert scribbled a few notes. "So then . . . what about William Liddle, son of Ira Liddle?"

"Doesn't seem to exist."

Gil rubbed his forehead. "Do you think . . . maybe Billy— my wife's brother—may have died? Maybe her mother had another son, named him the same thing?"

"Crazier things have happened. Hard to say."

Gilbert wrote WHAT HAPPENED TO IRA LIDDLE before asking.

"Well, I did a little tracking before I called. The only Ira Liddle who fits your profile lives in Macon, Georgia. Unmarried. No kids to speak of. Office supply salesman." He paused. "But he *does* fit the profile. Approximate age. Occupation. All that."

Gilbert wasn't sure what question to ask next. He had a million of them. "So what about the Billy Liddle you found?"

"He's a married man. Lives in Cedar Key, Florida, with

a wife, Veronica Sikes Liddle. Running a restaurant called Sikes's Seafood. Now, to be completely honest, the age of *this* Billy is right on target with what you told me. From what I can put together, he's your man, with the exception of the whole Ira Liddle connection. If you want, I can drive down there and look for myself. I hear Cedar Key is a right nice place. Wouldn't mind seeing it."

Gilbert wrote CEDAR KEY. FLORIDA KEYS? "Is that near Key West?"

"No. It's in the panhandle."

"Cedar Key . . . I've never heard of it."

"Take a trip to your local library. Look it up. Fascinating place."

Gilbert wrote a few more notes before asking, "Sikes, did you say?"

"Sikes, yeah. Sikes's Seafood."

"And the wife is Veronica Sikes Liddle?"

"Yessir."

"Hmm . . . okay. Anything else?"

"That's it for now. You going to head down there and see?"

Gilbert didn't answer. He wasn't sure. Certainly not now. School hadn't been in session very long. The kids needed him at home. Of course, he could leave them with his parents. Or Patsy's. Patsy sure wasn't ready to leave for a trip of any kind.

And what if it turned out . . . this *wasn't* her brother.

"Mr. Bonfield?"

"Yessir."

"One more thing—what about Bernice Liddle?"

31

December 1963, Charleston, South Carolina

"Funny thing about feeling sad," Patsy said to Gabrielle, "sometimes you don't mind it so much."

"I cannot imagine." Gabrielle sat across from Patsy at one of the folding game tables in the holiday-decorated recreational room. She held a puzzle piece loosely between two slender fingers of her right hand, twirling it as though it were a baton. "I like being happy."

"Maybe you don't have anything to be sad about." She looked across a room where sunlight poured through a wall of double-plated glass windows, across vinyl couches where patients either sat or slept. Hospital staff worked or sat idly by their assigned patients. The opening organ music for *Search for Tomorrow* blared from the lone television set. Today's episode, the announcer informed, was being "brought to you by . . . Camay . . . keeping a soft complexion is as easy as washing your face . . . with . . . *Camay*!"

Patsy mouthed the words of the commercial; Gabby laughed at her. "I'd say someone around here has seen one

306

too many episodes of *Search for Tomorrow*. That's what I'd say."

"I've always used Camay." Patsy patted her cheeks with the fingertips of both hands. "Can't you tell?"

"Have you now?"

"Well, since I moved in with Mam and Papa." Patsy looked down to the puzzle. "Are you ever going to put that puzzle piece where it belongs or do I need to do it for you?"

Gabrielle handed her the thin piece of cardboard. "By all means. I can't seem to find where it goes."

Patsy snapped the piece into place within the Augie Doggie brightly colored puzzle. A juvenile game to play but something to do, she reckoned. Better than group, that was for sure. And, she knew, if she kept talking while "playing," Gabby was all hers and not off with one of her other few patients.

"What did you use before you moved to Trinity?"

"Mother bought whatever was on sale." Patsy reached for another piece, this one mostly brownish-orange. She waved it at Gabrielle. "Has to be part of Doggie Daddy's body."

"Or Augie's."

"No, we pretty much have Augie in place here."

"Augie, my son, my son." Gabrielle did her best impersonation of the adult cartoon dachshund who loved, doted on, and carefully led his rambunctious son, Augie.

"What, dear old Dad?" Patsy shot back before setting another piece of the puzzle into place.

"You were saying about the soap your mother bought, Augie, my son?"

Patsy frowned. As if she didn't know the tactics of her nurse. As if they hadn't been together long enough already. "Only that her husband, Ira Liddle, didn't allow her much money for things like special soaps." She shook her head.

"Not that my mother didn't have things." *Like the cupid lipstick holder still waiting for you at Mam's.*

"Like?"

Patsy told her about the lipstick holder, about it being the unaccepted gift and the letter she refused to read on her wedding day.

"Does Mam still have it?"

"I guess so. In all these years, we've never really talked about it. One thing about Mam, she knows when to push and when to back away." Patsy picked up another puzzle piece and handed it to Gabrielle. "Your turn."

Gabrielle studied the piece before placing it where it belonged. "Tell me again about your brothers."

"Harold and Billy . . ." Patsy's gaze drifted to the outside. The sun was shining but the world still appeared cold. Trees and bushes had lost their leaves and blooms. To the east, thick low-lying gray clouds had begun to form. Was it going to snow?

"Mmmhmm."

"Harold would be . . ." Patsy calculated for a moment, "twenty-two by now. Goodness. Twenty-two . . . no . . ." She shook her head. Could it have been that long ago? Could they be that old? Then again, her own oldest was nearly thirteen. "No, wait. Billy will be twenty-two next month and Harold is a year older." Patsy felt tears forming. "I wonder if . . ."

"If?"

She shook her head again. "It's nothing."

"Now, don't do that, Miz Milstrap."

Patsy concentrated on the puzzle. There were only a few more pieces to fit together, but these were the most difficult. They were all of Daddy Doggie's body—large and all one color—and difficult to place. She picked up another piece, rolled it between her fingers as Gabrielle had earlier. "I wonder if they even remember me."

"They were how old?"

"Four and five."

Gabrielle pointed to an empty place in the puzzle board. "Goes here."

Patsy pushed it into place. "Thank you."

"I'd say it depends. If your mother and Mr. Liddle talked about you—"

"They wouldn't have."

"You sure about that?"

"Very sure." Patsy felt her stomach knot in places that were uncomfortable and familiar.

"Then I'd say probably not."

Patsy closed her eyes, willing herself not to cry. Not one tear, not one tear. Once they started, she knew, they'd never cease. Besides, she had enough of all this for one day. Now, it was time to be done with the talking and the puzzle. Time for Gabby to go to another patient. She was fine. *Going* to be fine . . .

"Which, of course, may be a good thing," Gabrielle continued, interrupting Patsy's thoughts.

Patsy's eyes flew open, meeting the almond-shaped chocolate eyes head-on. "How can you say that?"

"Because if they remembered you, they'd hurt at the loss of you. Would you want that for them?"

"No. Never. I loved them both dearly." With a weak smile, she reached for another puzzle piece. It popped into place. From across the room, the closing commercial for *Search for Tomorrow* played; this one for Dash detergent. Less suds. Cleaner clothes.

"Still do, in my way of thinking."

"Of course I do. I tried to find them once, did I ever tell you that?"

"No."

"Before my wedding. Papa took me. But they were gone. No one knew where."

"Your mama too?"

"The whole family. Mr. Liddle had packed Mama up and she'd just gone with him without so much as a 'tell Patsy where I've gone' to neighbor or friend."

Gabrielle remained quiet.

"Nothing to say about that?"

"I think that's just awful, but I don't know your mama, so it's impossible for me to say why she did what she did. Your brothers are innocents though."

"They were then, at least. They're all grown up now."

"What do you think they're like? Based on when they were young'uns."

Patsy smiled. "Harold was always into something. Rambunctious." Like her own Donna. "He was the one I'd have to pull down out of the trees before Mama or his daddy found out he'd been climbing when they'd clearly told him not to. He was the one who'd find a snake in the yard and bring it inside to scare Mama or me with."

Gabrielle laughed lightly. "I had one just like that. Name is Norris."

"Norris. I like that name."

"What about the other one? Billy."

Patsy felt one side of her mouth go up in a half smile. "Sweet Billy. He was always under my feet or Mama's. He'd rather stay inside with us, but Mama always shooed him out to be with Harold. Or, maybe, to keep Harold straight, now that I think about it, being a mother myself."

"We mamas have to stay one step ahead."

"With Harold, you had to stay two or three steps ahead."

Gabrielle looked at the puzzle. "You've only got three more pieces to go. I think you can do this on your own."

Patsy picked up the first piece. She was feeling much better, just in having talked about her brothers. Even if she missed them, remembering them this way did her a world of good. Maybe there was something to this *talking* thing after all.

"My brother Norris . . . Mama always said she had to get up way earlier than him to stay ahead of him."

"Yep. Sounds like Harold." She shrugged. "He's probably a preacher now." And wouldn't that just be something? "You know, how kids often grow up to be the opposite of what you think they'll be. And Billy's probably . . . my goodness, I guess Billy's in school or something. He wasn't reading when I left, but he seemed to me like he'd be pretty studious."

"Well, Augie, my son, my son . . ."

"What, Daddy Doggie?" Patsy was down to two pieces of the puzzle. She picked up one in each hand, waved them at Gabrielle in triumph.

"If the good Lord wills it—and I'll pray he does—you'll find your brothers and your mother one day, and all will be understood. That's the thing about the Father's love—and I don't mean Daddy Doggie's. Our heavenly Father doesn't always run things the way we think he should, but when we come to him as the adored children we are, he listens and he moves. In his timing, of course, but he *will* move. You mark my words. Before this life is over, you'll know what happened to your kin."

Patsy pushed the last two pieces down, listened as they snapped into place. "Done."

311

Patsy had "taken on work" in the cafeteria. It was her job to keep supplies filled. Ketchup and other condiments. Soaps for washing dishes. Cleaners for wiping down tables and chairs in the dining hall, work areas in the kitchen. Paper products, of course. It wasn't a difficult task, but it gave her something to keep her mind occupied and made her feel like she was doing something productive in the midst of feeling anything but. Plus, Gabby said it showed she was getting better all the way around.

As the year came to an end—and what an awful time the country had experienced just a month before—Patsy struggled between feelings of homesickness and fear that she would never, ever leave this place. There was a certain level of security in that, of course. She could hide away here. She could be a wife when Gilbert came, a mother when the children came, a daughter when Mam and Papa came. The rest of the time, she only had to worry about being Patsy.

She was no one's daughter to keep busy—Patsy, I need you to do *this*; Patsy, I need you to do *that*, like she had been as a child with Mama. Or anyone's big sister who had to keep up with the boys. She wasn't a stepdaughter to be ogled and beaten and demeaned. She wasn't the thrownaway child who suddenly took up residence—no matter how good the Buchwalds had been to her, she was still and always would be the rescued teenager who came into their family late in life. She wasn't someone's wife or someone's mother. She didn't have to try to keep up to make sure they loved her, adored her, wouldn't leave her. Here, she knew they'd watch out for her. Over her.

Still, it was Christmas. She'd missed Thanksgiving sitting around Mam's table. Missed it to the very core of her being.

312

All those years of fretting about the children. Were they being too loud? Too active? Mam always said "let the children be children, Patsy," but she'd worried nonetheless. This year, she wished she'd been less anxious and more appreciative during those past years. After all, it was *Thanks*giving.

Now, it was Christmas. More than anything, Patsy wanted to be home with her family. She wanted to inhale the scent of the evergreen tree. Vanilla poured into the cake batter. Peppermints jutting out from between the cherub lips of her children. She wanted to be a part of writing letters to Santa, shopping with Mam for whatever trinket or toy those letters requested, wrapping gifts with Gilbert on Christmas Eve after sipping nutmeg-sprinkled eggnog with Gilbert's family. Standing around the piano while Janice played. Singing carols.

Always before, she'd wasted the moments. She'd not realized what she had. She'd only been focused on what she *could* lose. And now she'd lost it all. And she desperately wanted it back, she decided as she checked off her kitchen checklist sheet of necessary products. The question was, really, what did she need to do to get it? Group participation? Talk to the doctor about her feelings? She didn't like the idea of either.

Patsy pulled an order form from a filing cabinet drawer full of such items and set about to filling it out. She took it to one of the dining room tables—this month covered in red and green plastic "tablecloths"—sat in a chair, and began writing in the rectangular boxes. She paused long enough to look at one of the many Christmas trees decorating the hospital. As she did, from the overhead sound system, Elvis sang "I'll Be Home for Christmas."

She knew then what she had to do. She'd just tell Gilbert she wanted to come home. Plain and simple. If he argued with her—or if the doctor argued—she'd tell them it would only be for the holidays. She'd come back.

And maybe she would. Maybe she wouldn't.

She'd miss Gabrielle, but they could write letters or Patsy could come to Charleston with Gil every once in a while when he drove over for business. She'd shirk the social demands of the day and she'd visit with her Negro friend, and the rest of the world could scream and holler all they wanted! She didn't care.

She would join forces with the others like her who'd embraced people of other colors. She'd join that man—what was his name, King?—and she'd make a difference. Her and Gabby.

Movement from across the dining hall caught her attention. Gilbert stood between Gabrielle and Dr. Jennings. All three wore somber faces. Gil's most of all. Patsy's eyes darted back and forth between the three of them, waiting for one of them to make the first step. To walk toward her. To say something.

Anything. No matter the words; just let her know everything was all right.

But it wasn't. No. Something was wrong.

Something was bad wrong.

32

"What is it?"

The three who'd come to get her had now taken her to Dr. Jennings's office. No matter how many times she'd begged—"tell me, just tell me"—they'd not said a word until they got to the tasteful but sparsely decorated physician's office. Patsy sat in one of three sand-colored chairs. Her hands gripped the wooden armrests while her back pressed against fabric that felt as though it could dig into her flesh and leave a scar.

Dr. Jennings chose not to sit in his chair but to perch against the edge of the desk's front. He cleared his throat several times, removed the round specs that made him look like Harry Truman, and wiped them on a handkerchief he removed from the suit coat pocket beneath his white lab coat.

"I'll ask this one final time," Patsy said. She heard both strength and fear in her voice. She wondered which one the doctor would pick up on. "What's happened?" She looked to Gilbert. "Is it one of my children?"

His hand immediately came over hers. "No," he said. "The kids are fine."

Her thoughts ran to Lloyd, in service to his country. "Lloyd?"

"Lloyd is fine."

Out of the corner of her eye, she saw Gabrielle cross one leg over the other. Patsy looked to her nurse-friend, hoping for some sign in the woman's eyes. Hope. Despair. Either one; it was better than not knowing. But Gabby's eyes were closed and her lips fluttered about in what Patsy supposed was a prayer.

When Dr. Jennings had returned his glasses to his face and his handkerchief to his pocket, he cleared his throat a final time. "Mrs. Milstrap."

Patsy looked at him.

"Mrs. Milstrap, your husband came here today with stressful news. I wanted him to bring you here to tell you and to let you know that if you feel you need anything, all you need to do is ask."

Patsy turned her attention to Gilbert. If her eyes were reading as she'd hoped, he knew there was no more time for stalling.

"Hon," he said, "it's Papa."

Patsy drew in a breath. "No . . . What? No . . . is he . . . ?"

Gilbert nodded. "I'm afraid so. He had a brain aneurysm during the night. Mam called Doc and they managed to get him to the hospital. But he died shortly after. Doc said there's never really much hope with these kinds of things."

Patsy allowed the tears to come, a guttural scream to slice through her throat. She felt Gabrielle's arms around her. Gilbert's. She heard Dr. Jennings call for another nurse . . . demand two cc's of something . . . *No!*

She broke free of the love of her husband and her friend. Looked toward Dr. Jennings standing on the other side of the desk now, shiny black phone gripped in his hand. "I'm fine," she screamed. "I'm fiiiiiiine!" She bent at the waist, bellowing toward him. "My father is dead; am I not supposed to *feel* anything? Why would you even *think* to take that away from me?"

"Hold on," Dr. Jennings spoke into the phone. Then: "Cancel the order." He returned the handset to the receiver. "Mrs. Milstrap, you have spoken correctly. You should feel something. Do you want to talk about it?"

"No, I don't want to talk about it. Sometimes you don't want to talk about anything; you just want to feel. Didn't they teach you that in medical school?" Gilbert stood beside her now; she grabbed hold of his shoulders. "How is Mam?" Before he could answer, she added, "I need to get to Mam. And Lloyd. Has anyone told Lloyd?"

"Mam is all right, sweetheart."

"Don't lie to me, Gil. For heaven's sake don't lie. She's been married to the man nearly her whole life and you tell me she's fine?"

"I didn't say 'fine,' I said she is all right. And she is. Mam has the strength of a hundred men; you know that."

"It surely hasn't hit her yet," Gabrielle said from beside her. Patsy returned to her seat. As if on cue, the others did the same. Mam had the strength Patsy wished she possessed. Even in all these years, it hadn't rubbed off on her much. Maybe a little. Maybe just enough to . . . She looked at Gilbert. "I'm going home."

He, in turn, looked from her to the doctor. "Doc?"

Dr. Jennings sat in his office chair, pulled it and himself toward the desk. "I don't know if—"

"I wasn't giving you a request, Dr. Jennings," Patsy said. For a fleeting moment she felt herself sitting in the car with her mother. Begging. Asking for the possible and being told it was impossible. *All she had to do was get on the bus with me. We would have made it just fine.* "I've been here long enough to know how things work. And I'm going home. Let's face it; if I'd opened up by now, I'd be home already anyway. But I haven't wanted to open up. Believe me, if I'd wanted to, I would have."

"Pats . . ."

"No, Gilbert. My father has died. The man I've trusted and loved and depended on since I was thirteen years old. The only true father I've ever known. Mam needs me. Lloyd will need me. My children will need me. And I *want* to be there, Gil. I *need* to be there."

Gilbert looked at the doctor. "Doc?"

"Mr. and Mrs. Milstrap . . . I really don't think . . . Mrs. Milstrap, I don't think you are as ready for this as you believe yourself to be. You are pulling on a supernatural emotion that says 'I am needed therefore I am strong,' but in your case, that's just not true. You've suppressed important feelings for a long time now. If the dam decides to break while you are with your family—"

Patsy squared her shoulders. "If the dam breaks, then I *should* be with my family, don't you think? Dr. Jennings, I'm going home and you can't stop me."

"That's true. I can't." He threw his hands up slightly, looked to Gilbert, and said, "I'll have the papers drawn up within the hour. You can take your wife home within the next two."

The room seemed to whirl around Patsy. Fear and elation spun with it. Again, she gripped the armrests. She was going home. Home. Good or bad, no turning back now.

Patsy turned toward Gabrielle. "I feel like Dorothy leaving Oz and the scarecrow. You, I'll miss most of all."

Gabrielle blinked back tears. She turned to Dr. Jennings.

"I have an idea, if I may suggest it, Dr. Jennings. Why don't I go home with Mr. and Mrs. Milstrap. I can be of service to the family, I'm sure of it. And, if Mrs. Milstrap needs me, I'm there for her. She and I have come to trust each other." Her eyes turned to Patsy. "Haven't we?"

"Oh no, Gabby . . ." Patsy placed her white hands on top of Gabrielle's black ones. "I mean, yes. Yes, we have. But I can't allow you to leave your family."

Gabby's hands encircled Patsy's. "It won't be forever, Miz Milstrap." She turned her face toward the doctor again. "If Miz Milstrap does all right, I can come back alone. But if she needs to return . . ." She faced Patsy again. "*If* she needs to return, she promises she'll be honest about that."

For a long minute, Patsy didn't blink. Everything the woman said made sense. And, to be honest, there was a part of her that needed Gabby still. Just as she'd needed her mother all those years ago. If only her mother would have come with her . . . and now, here was Gabby, saying she'd do what her mother had been unable—or unwilling—to do.

Patsy nodded. "All right."

"Promise?"

"Yes, I can do that." She peered over her shoulder. "Gil?"

"I'd sure love to have you home again, Pats."

Patsy released Gabrielle's hands. Stood. Reached for her husband's. "Then take me home, Gilbert. Take me to Mam." She pressed her lips together. "Mam needs me."

———

It wasn't as easy as she'd thought it would be.

First, there was the noise level inside her home. Five children don't come quietly into any room. They march, each one to their own tune, singing their own song. Greg and Pam did their best to keep the three youngest quiet for her, but they

319

weren't overly successful. Besides, even Patsy could see they needed their own space and time to grieve. They'd known Papa the longest of all the grandchildren.

Then there were family and friends. They all came to offer their condolences, but upon seeing her, they froze. It was as if she were a freak in a circus. Mam had seemed relieved to see her, and Lloyd too, of course. But everyone else had appeared at a loss for words.

The morning of the afternoon funeral, with the family gathered at Mam's, Patsy looked around and realized her oldest children were unaccounted for.

"Have you seen Greg and Pammie?" she asked Gil.

"Mmm . . ." He looked around the living room, where he'd taken refuge with Lloyd and a few others. "No, actually, I haven't. Not for a while."

"Do you need me to look for them, sis?" Lloyd was already halfway out of his chair.

She held a hand up. "No. That's okay. I'll find them."

Patsy went into the kitchen, where Gabby was labeling dishes of food from friends and members of the church. "Never seen so much food in my life, have you?"

"No. Gabby, have you seen Greg or Pam?"

"They walked out the back door there about five minutes ago. I hollered after them but they just kept walking. Mr. Milstrap told me how your son and your papa always went fishing on the weekends. It's going to be hard on the boy."

"Hard on us all. Papa was really something." Patsy walked to the back door, opened it, and said, "Gabby, if anyone needs me, I'm going out to the workshop. I bet that's where I'll find them."

"Sounds good."

As she suspected, Patsy found her children inside the

floral shop. Before opening the door, she peered through the multiple-paned window and watched them, standing there in their Sunday best. They weren't speaking. They just stood, staring. When she opened the door, they turned toward her.

"Mama," Pam said, then rushed toward her and wrapped her arms around her waist.

Patsy kissed the top of her head before closing the door behind her. She took a few steps and turned to gaze at a room all too familiar. Unpainted workbenches formed the shape of an *L* along two walls. Scattered about were containers of ribbon in a variety of colors, baskets in various shapes and sizes, stacks of standard brick foam, wire, and cutters. A plastic vase full of card holders looked as if it might tip over, supported only by a heart-shaped foam wreath hanging from a pegboard. Patsy righted it, inhaled, and then looked at her children. "Smells like Papa in here."

"Cigars and aftershave and flowers," Greg noted. He kicked at the tile floor with the heel of his shoe.

Patsy's heart ripped in two. She'd seen so many emotions on her son's face, but this one was new. "You're going to miss him a lot, I know. I will too."

"Yeah, well." Greg shoved his hands into the pockets of his dress pants. He stared at the floor he continued to kick, but his eyes cut toward her. "I guess it's to be expected. People leaving you and all."

"Gregory . . ." The name was spoken as though it had pushed its way from Patsy's lungs.

Pam shot past their mother and to her brother. Fists planted on her hips, she said, "Greg, you promised."

Greg's face flushed, his eyes seemed to catch fire as they met his sister's. "I don't care." Then he looked at Patsy. "What'd you come back here for anyhow?"

It seemed to Patsy her heart stopped. It must have stopped. Surely, torn as it was, it couldn't keep beating. "Gregory, my father has died."

Pam swung around. Oddly, Patsy became aware of how mature her daughter appeared to her just then, dressed in a dark blue A-shaped frock, dark socks drawn nearly to her knees, black Mary Janes shining under the overhead light. Pam's hair—thick and dark—fell to her shoulders where it curled upward and was kept away from her face by tiny barrettes clipped at her temples. When had she grown up so? "We know that, Mommy."

Mommy? When was the last time Pam had called her that?

Patsy noticed tears in her daughter's eyes. "But will you leave us again?"

"She'll leave," Greg answered, already taking steps toward the door. "Not that she was ever really here to begin with."

"Greggy!" Pam pleaded in vain; her brother was already out the door.

Patsy stared behind him, saying nothing. Hardly breathing.

"I'm sorry, Mama, it's just that . . ."

Through a fog Patsy made her way to her father's work stool. She brushed her hand along the seat, scattering dust and debris as she did. The dust caught in a stream of light coming from the window. It danced and twirled and then hung suspended. The debris fell to the floor at her feet. Somehow, she managed to sit, to grab hold of the edge of the work counter. The scent in the room made her feel as though she'd throw up. She took in a deep breath, willed herself not to. Her little girl was still in the room.

"It's okay," Patsy whispered. "Believe me, it's okay."

Pammie came to her, laid a tiny, gentle hand on top of her quivering one. Patsy noticed a small birthstone ring—an amethyst encircling her third finger. She nodded toward it. "When did you get this?"

"Daddy gave it to me." Her eyes caught her mother's. "For being so brave."

"When was that?"

"After you left."

"After I left." She swallowed. "I remember how you helped Daddy . . . that night . . ."

Pam shrugged. "It wasn't that, Mama. It was after that. Taking care of things. Helping with supper and getting the little ones ready for school and bedtime and . . . well, you know."

Patsy cupped her daughter's cheek in the palm of her hand. "You are very brave, my Pammie."

Pam smiled weakly. "I've missed you, Mommy."

Patsy gathered her daughter into her arms; both wept without care. "I missed you too. So very much."

"And you won't leave us again, will you?"

How could it be, Patsy wondered, that she'd done the very thing to her children she'd been angry at her mother for doing to her? Abandonment only bred anger. Confusion. And a strange sense of betrayal that one may not ever be able to get past. No matter how hard they tried. She'd lost her mother, her brothers, and now . . . her son. Her firstborn.

"Will you?" Pam asked again, and Patsy could hear the trepidation rising to a near panic.

Patsy squeezed her daughter and cried harder still. And wished, with all her might, she knew the answer.

33

With the funeral and Christmas behind them, Gilbert knew it was time to make his move. To do what he needed to do. To save himself. His children. His wife, most of all.

As soon as he stepped into his office that morning in late January, and after Mary Ann had brought him a cup of coffee, he asked her to get Walter Bonfield on the phone.

Mary Ann gave him a look of apprehension as she reached for the heavy coat he'd pulled his arms free of and thrown over one of the office chairs. "Everything all right?" she asked, walking the coat to his coatrack and hanging it on one of the hooks.

Gilbert took a sip of his coffee. It was hot and strong; he winced as it slipped down his throat. "It will be."

Mary Ann left his office and he went to his desk. A minute later, his phone buzzed. "Walter Bonfield is on line one."

Gilbert picked up the handset. "Mr. Bonfield, I'm glad I caught you this morning."

"Anything new I can help you with?"

"Yes. I've decided I want you to go down to Cedar Key. Tell me what you can on this Billy Liddle."

"Something happen?"

"Instinct, Mr. Bonfield. My gut tells me this Billy Liddle is my wife's brother." Heaven knew, he hoped he was right. "See what you can find out for me, will you? Snoop without being obvious."

"I can head down there . . ." Gilbert listened to what sounded like paper being flipped. Perhaps pages from a calendar. He didn't know. He didn't care. He just wanted Bonfield in Cedar Key as soon as possible. "Two weeks."

"Two weeks? You don't have anything sooner?"

"I'm sorry. I'm on another case right now that has me pretty tied up."

Gilbert started to take another sip of coffee, but remembering how hot it was, blew into the cup instead. Two weeks felt like a long time, but maybe it was God's timing. Bonfield had other clients, and their need for his services could very well be just as important. He took a sip, closed his eyes, and swallowed. "I see. Okay, then. Two weeks. I should hear something from you in two and a half?"

"Absolutely."

"Talk to you then."

Gilbert ended the call, looked up to the door between his office and Mary Ann's, and waited for her appearance. As if on cue, she opened the door and walked in, her own coffee cup in hand. "Dish," she said.

Gilbert watched as his secretary—and often his big-sisterly confidant—lowered herself into one of the chairs opposite his desk. Telltale signs of a recently eaten donut lay on the front of her dress. He pointed, not wanting to state the obvious. Mary Ann looked down, said, "Oh," brushed the crumbs away, and returned her attention to him.

"Ah . . . so the thing is . . ." He ran his fingers through his hair. He'd gotten a haircut the day before; it managed to

325

tame the curls, but only a little. "We're still plugging along, but Patsy is . . ."

"Still sad?"

"Gosh yes." Gilbert placed the mug on the desk, linked the fingers of his hands, and said, "I wish you could have seen her that day, Mary Ann."

"What day?"

"On the bus. When she was a kid and I was some upstart airman thinking I was all dashing and dandy."

"Dandy? Now there's a word I haven't heard in . . . thirty years."

Gilbert forced a chuckle. "She was scared witless. I remember wondering about where she was going. Then she told me, she was coming here to Trinity. We ate dinner in this dive behind a bus stop. Food was good—not as good as what you get at Gilly's—and while we ate she told me she was moving here to live with people she didn't even know. Didn't tell me why—not until later, that is—just that Lloyd Buchwald was her brother and she'd never even met him."

"As a mother, I just cannot imagine what it must have meant to her mama to have put her on a bus and send her off like that."

"I know. As a father, I feel the same way. But things were different back then, Mary Ann. You and me . . . we've never been faced with desperation. Not really."

Mary Ann didn't say anything for a moment. Then, "When did you find yourself in love with her?"

This time, Gilbert's faint laughter was for real. "Oh my. I came home from the service, for good, and Janice told me that Miss Grace's school was having their annual dance that night and I should go." Gil gave Mary Ann his cheesiest grin. Unlocked his fingers. "Local hero and all."

"Mmmhmm," she said. "I remember."

Gil shook his head. "I didn't have a thought in my head about going there and meeting anyone special. In all honesty, I was going to make an appearance and then go meet some of the guys for a more, shall we say, grown-up party."

"Mmmhmm."

"But then . . ." Gilbert paused. Allowed himself to remember the way she'd looked that evening. "She was dressed in this pinky-peachy colored"—Gilbert waved his hand about himself—"dressy thing."

This time, Mary Ann laughed. "A formal."

"Yeah. Okay. But it wasn't just the way she looked—which was pretty and not so much like a little girl anymore—it was the whole package. The way she carried herself. The way she . . ." Gil felt himself blush. "Smelled."

"And you were a goner."

"One hundred percent. I knew she was too young and I knew Papa Buchwald would have my hind end if I did anything inappropriate. So, I set my sights on being respectable, building a business, a life . . . and eventually, adding a wife."

"And you were happy."

Gilbert's breathing slowed. Oh yes. He'd been happy. "You know, Mary Ann, when we say those vows—for better, for worse—we don't really think about the worse, do we?"

Mary Ann shook her head slowly. "I married a man who stood on both feet and promised me the moon. But six months after our wedding, a car accident left me with someone sitting in a wheelchair the rest of his life. Many a time he's told me to leave and make a better life for myself. And every time I remind him, 'Hon, that's not the vow I took.'"

Gilbert peered toward the single window in the room, and beyond to the town outside his office walls. Life goes on, he thought, no matter what happens inside a marriage, life goes on. He looked back to Mary Ann. "And I daresay, when you look at Tom, what you see is the man standing before you."

She blinked. Took a sip of coffee. Blinked again. "Most times, you're right, I do."

"And when I look at Patsy, I still see that scared little girl, and then the young woman she became. Full of chatter and laughter and . . ."

"What?"

Gil swallowed past the lump in his throat. "She has my heart, Mary Ann. She thinks I'll eventually be like the others and be gone, but . . ."

Mary Ann shook her head. Not a strand of hair moved, but one thin brow cocked upward. "I've never seen anything so pathetic in my life as her weeping over her daddy's grave like she did. I told Tom when we got home that it just made me want to cry myself." She took a sip of her coffee. "I know she's still hurting over losing him and will for a long, long time. But I have to ask, how are the kids taking all this?"

Gilbert finished his coffee as well before he answered. "The younger ones don't really have a grasp on the fact that their papa isn't coming back. Ever. Pammie and Greg understand better, of course. Pammie is so happy her mama's home, she seems to be making the best of it. But Greg . . . Papa and he were buddies."

"They were that."

"And to make matters worse, Greg's pretty mad with Pats. They hardly even speak. And when Greg does talk to his mother, it's with such . . . disrespect, such contempt. Patsy seems to be . . . I don't know . . . *allowing* it. Letting him get away with it? Maybe because she feels guilty for having left him in the first place? I don't know. What I do know is that there's a level of tension in the house you could cut with a sword. Never mind the knife."

"Well, I'm not his father, but if my brother or I ever talked to our mother with disrespect, we'd have been taken out to the woodshed."

Gilbert shook his head. "My daddy would have done the same. But I can't. Not this time. Maybe when he was younger, but he's thirteen now. And while I have told him to shape up or suffer the consequences, I also understand his feelings."

Mary Ann took a long sip of her coffee before gripping the mug with both hands. "Boss, I wish I could say I have the answer for you. I don't. In our day, we weren't allowed to have feelings." She shot him a cautious smile. "What about that Negro woman . . ."

"Gabby."

"Is she still helping you out?"

Gilbert nodded. She had been such a godsend. *Gabrielle.* She told him once that her name meant "heroine of God." And she was that. But he couldn't ask her to stay forever and he wasn't ready to send his wife back to the hospital either. Didn't seem to be the answer. Hadn't really helped before. Why would it start helping now?

Gilbert slapped his hand onto his desk. "Mary Ann, we've been down memory lane long enough and we've got work to do."

She saluted him as she stood. "Yes sir! I'll get right to it."

She was halfway across the room when he stopped her. "Oh and Mary Ann . . . in about two weeks or so, I'm going to hear from Bonfield again. Be sure I get the call, no matter where I am."

"Will do."

Two and a half weeks. If he could make it that long. And

surely he could. As a businessman, he knew just how productive two and a half weeks could be. *If* the positive remained the focus. Two and a half weeks could also tear down a plan. Shred it into thin slices of nothing.

With the door closed behind Mary Ann, Gilbert bowed his head. "Lord," he said, "you created a whole world in seven days. I'm giving you double and a half that time. Just as I trust what you did that first week, I'll trust even more in what you'll do with this time."

His chest heaved. He felt tears coming—something he wasn't all that accustomed to—and he let them form and spill over. "Because I love her, Lord. And I know you love her more, although sometimes that's hard to imagine." *She's my girl*, he prayed silently.

She's mine too, his heart heard in response.

Exactly two and a half weeks later, the call came. Gilbert ended the call, pushed the button on his office phone for another line, and placed a call to Dr. Jennings. He left a message with his secretary, then returned to his work and waited for a call that would not come for another three hours.

He told Dr. Jennings what he knew and how he'd obtained the information. Why he'd waited so long to share it. He hadn't been sure, not completely sure anyway. Now he was as sure as a man could get. And he believed, truly believed, that this one trip—if what he believed to be true was indeed true—could bring his wife to understand her past, live in her present, and actually *have* a future.

"You could be wrong and this could backfire," Dr. Jennings told him after a long pause.

"But if I don't try," Gil said, "the situation stays the same."

"That's true."

"I'd ask Gabby to stay with the kids, but she needs some time with her family."

"She's resigned from the hospital, did she tell you that?"

She hadn't.

"I talked to her husband the other day. When school is out, he's going to look for work over there in Trinity. He's willing to move the family just so she can stay there."

Without hesitation, Gilbert added, "Tell him he has a job with me the minute he gets here."

They spoke awhile longer. Dr. Jennings concluded the call by saying that if he were needed, he'd only be a phone call away. That he wished them both the best.

Gilbert ended the call satisfied. He'd talk to Gabby that night. Tell her to go home and be with her own family for a change. Inform her that her husband had a job when they moved. Then he'd call Janice, see if the kids could stay with her and Marvin and their kids for a few days.

After that, he'd tell Patsy his plan. Tell her that an arts festival was about to happen down there in Cedar Key and that one of his employees had told him about it. Once he had her convinced, he'd call the woman who owned the cottage Bonfield told him about and request information.

He jotted notes on a piece of paper. Everything he needed to remember.

And it hit him. There was still one thing he hadn't told Dr. Jennings.

Gilbert reached for the phone, then replaced it. No, he decided. Best that he not say anything at all about what Bonfield had told him. Best to just let things happen.

Patsy would know everything in time. And, somehow, they'd get through it.

Together.

34

Spring 1964, Cedar Key, Florida

Patsy looked out the front of the Ford Falcon Futura. A town—a little harbor town—was coming into view. Fishermen on a dock. Weathered hands pulling crab baskets from the water and into a boat. The scent of the marsh washed over her.

In spite of its pungency, she liked it.

"Are you hungry, Patsy? I'm ravenous."

She looked at her husband again, nodded. "Yes. A little."

The dimple on his cheek returned. "See there?" Gilbert said. "Another good sign." The car slowed as they entered the city limits. "Let's get to the cottage, settle in, clean up, and find this place Walter told me about."

"Sikes's?"

"Sikes's Seafood. I'll bet the food is about as fresh as anything you can get on the coastline."

Patsy inhaled deeply. She liked a good fried shrimp. And deviled crab. She hadn't had that in ages. That with a baked potato . . .

The cottage was everything it had been touted to be. The cottony-white walls, the dark, rich furniture, the white eyelet curtains and bed linens, and the polished hardwood floors helped Patsy begin to relax. To feel that maybe her life was going to be okay. Even if only for a week.

A week in Cedar Key.

Patsy unpacked while Gilbert showered. When he was done, she took a quick bath, worked the tangles out of her hair, then brushed it until it shone. She worked it into a long braid that snaked over her shoulder, and slipped into a knee-length mint-green A-line skirt with matching sleeveless blouse. She wore no jewelry, no makeup. Only coral-colored lipstick.

The way Gilbert liked it.

"Will you put the top up on the car?" she asked as they stepped from the front porch of the cottage. "It took forever to get the rats out of my hair."

Her husband slipped an arm around her waist. "Anything for my lady."

She sighed as he opened the car door for her. Allowed her to get in gracefully. Closed it. She watched him sprint around the front to his side.

He is trying so hard.

Already a line was forming at the front door of the restaurant. Patsy glanced at her watch. Five o'clock. She thought they would have been early enough. Maybe the food really was that good.

She waited at the end of the line while Gilbert gave the restaurant's hostess their name. He returned a minute later. "Fifteen minutes. That's not bad."

Over the fifteen minutes, she found herself drinking in the

sights and sounds of Cedar Key. Already she liked it here. It called to her, like an old friend, and made her feel as though she'd been here before.

Seagulls soared overhead. Patsy craned her neck to watch them, then lowered her chin to view them through the glass walls of the restaurant as they dove into the rhythmic waves below.

They inched closer to the inside of the restaurant. Gilbert slapped his flat stomach. "I smell good ole fried seafood. I think I'll have shrimp. What about you?"

She strained to make the decision. "Deviled crab."

He wrapped his arm around her waist again and squeezed. "Somehow I knew you'd say that."

"You know me well."

"Since you were no more than a pup."

"Milstrap, party of two?" the hostess, a young woman of about twenty-five and pretty as a blonde Breck Girl, called over the heads of the few hopeful patrons left standing in front of them.

Gilbert raised his hand. "That's us."

They entered the restaurant, Patsy behind the hostess, Gilbert behind her. Sikes's Seafood was all wood and glass. The walls sported lifesavers and nets with shells caught between the yarn. Large mounted fish. Stuffed replicas of tropical birds perched on beachwood. It was typical tropical, and to add to the setting, the Beach Boys sang "Surfin' USA" from a jukebox.

The hostess stopped short before turning toward a man in dress casual attire. "Oh, I'm sorry," she said to Patsy and Gilbert. "Just a minute please while I ask my boss a question." She returned her attention to the man. "Mr. Liddle?"

At the sound of the name, Patsy felt the air suck into her

lungs before she heard the intake of her breath. Gilbert's hands gripped her forearms.

The man stopped. Turned toward them. Smiled briefly. "Yes, Brenda . . ."

"Billy?" The name slipped out of her mouth as though she'd been speaking it her whole life and not just in part.

He blinked at her while Gilbert continued to squeeze her arms, supporting her.

"Are you Billy Liddle? William Watson Liddle?"

He blinked again. "I am . . . I'm afraid . . ."

"Patsy." If she tried to say another word, she'd die right there in front of the other diners, as the Four Seasons declared "Big Girls Don't Cry."

Patsy. The name pulsed through his body as he looked at the woman before him.

Of course . . . those eyes. She hadn't grown much taller. Everything else had changed with age. But if memory served, and if he could trust his mother's treasured photos, this was Patsy.

The man standing behind his sister had a firm grip on her shoulders. His right hand released its hold long enough to extend in a handshake. "I'm Gilbert Milstrap. Patsy's husband."

"How'd you . . . I . . ." Billy glanced around the room. People were eating without notice or care. And a full house at that, so early in the evening.

He looked to his hostess. "Brenda, please take Mr. and Mrs. Milstrap to the private dining room." Throbbing shot from one temple, across his forehead, to the other.

"But, Mr. Liddle, it's been reserved—"

Billy waved an impatient hand. "Just do it, Bren. And then call whomever and tell them a family situation has come up and the room is being used tonight. They can have the room free of charge either later tonight or tomorrow." His breathing was erratic. The migraine would be in full swing if he didn't get to his medicine.

"And call my wife." He looked from his hostess to his sister. "I'll be with you in a moment." Just long enough to take his pill. "Be sure to order some sweet iced tea. We make the best here." He paused. Stared at his sister. This really was his sister. Patsy. "This is amazing."

Brenda did as he asked, leading the way to the back of the restaurant where a large room jutted over the water. He watched as the three wove their way between square tables. His gaze went to the glass overlooking the gulf. The evening light—even muted this time of day with the sun to the west of Dock Street—still had a piercing quality. Without a word to anyone else, he made his way to his office, opened a desk drawer, and grabbed the prescription bottle kept there. He opened it, shook two pills into the cup of his hand, and swallowed them with a swig of iced tea he always kept close by.

Brenda opened his office door. "Hey, boss . . ."

"Hi." He waved her in, told her to shut the door. When she stood on the other side of his desk, he asked, "Did you get Ronni?"

"She's on her way." She looked toward the open drawer. "Are you getting—"

"Yeah."

"They've sure been worse since—"

"I know." Billy swallowed. "Listen, Bren . . . what you heard out there . . ."

She took the humble folding chair in front of his desk, sat, and crossed her legs. "I'm not going to tell anyone or say

336

anything to the other staff. You know me better than that. But, seriously. Is that really your sister in there?"

Billy took another swallow of tea, considered, then drained it. "Yeah."

"My goodness. Like a long lost?"

He closed his eyes and nodded; the headache was lessening, but it wasn't leaving. "Listen, did you get them some tea?"

"I did. And two orders of shrimp cocktail, though I doubt they'll be eating. She's crying all over her husband's shoulder in there. I don't know if I ever heard anything quite like it."

The office door swung open; Ronni rushed in like a gust of gulf breeze off the coastline. "Is it true?"

Brenda stood. "I'll leave you two alone." She took a step, then looked to Billy. "What should I do about . . . *them*?"

Ronni had made it to his side. She stood next to him, cradled his head against her abdomen. "Tell them we'll be right in," she answered, as though she'd been expecting this since the day he'd told her about Patsy and Lloyd.

Billy breathed in the scent of her. He'd be all right now. "I can't believe it, Ron . . ."

"God has answered your prayers, baby." Joy leapt in her voice.

He closed his eyes, sighed. "I can't believe it," he said again.

She patted his shoulder. "Come on. Introduce me to my sister-in-law."

It was too awkward and too emotionally draining for Patsy to stay at the restaurant. She whispered to Gilbert even before her brother and his wife walked into the private dining hall that she really wanted to get out of there. When Billy and Veronica finally came in, Gilbert stood, shook hands with

Billy again, then with Veronica, and suggested that they'd do best to talk at a later date. Maybe tomorrow.

Veronica seemed to take right over at that moment. To be so young—and clearly she was not much older than a teenager—she certainly had a manner about her for taking charge. Patsy, too weak to even stand when they'd come in, sat idly by and allowed it. Even though this was *her* brother and *her* world that had been tilted not twenty minutes earlier. She just couldn't . . .

"I say we go to our place," Veronica said. Patsy glanced up through wet lashes. The dark-haired beauty looked at her husband—Patsy's baby brother—with wide eyes that implored him to go along with her. "Billy?"

Billy only nodded, raised a hand as though he didn't know what else to do, then let it drop. He was obviously just as taken aback as Patsy. The only one who seemed to be nonplussed was her husband, and by now, she'd figured he knew they'd find a Billy Liddle in Cedar Key all along. She'd deal with him on that matter later.

Patsy and Gilbert drove behind Billy and Veronica, neither one of them speaking. Patsy sensed her husband wanted to say something. Perhaps even gloat a little. He'd always been so sure of himself; was he this time? Or had he thought this completely through at all? What if, God forbid, things had not gone well. *This* Billy Liddle had not been *her* Billy Liddle. Then what?

While they drove along the narrow streets, Patsy took in what she could of the island. It was nearly dark, but she made out what she could. Many of the buildings were old, some obviously refurbished, others brand-new. She liked what she saw. Everything seemed quaint. It spoke of a simpler time. Kind people. Backyard folk, Gabby would call them.

338

Within a few short minutes, they pulled up to a small cottage that reminded Patsy of the one she and Gilbert had rented for the week. Veronica practically leapt out of the VW bug in front of them—it was as cute as she—and ran around to the driver's side, waiting for her husband to open his door. Patsy almost giggled at the girl's enthusiasm, but she was too worn out already. And for the life of her, she just couldn't believe that the man getting out of the car was her brother.

"Ready?" Gilbert asked from the driver's seat.

She nodded, opened her own door, and got out.

Within minutes, the four sat across from one another at the kitchen table. Veronica had poured more iced tea for them. Patsy wasn't thirsty necessarily, but holding the glass gave her something to do with her hands. Gilbert, on the other hand, sat beside her and gulped every bit of his down. Before he could put the glass back to the table, Billy said, "Let me top that off for you," while Veronica cut four slices of pound cake. It looked good and smelled even better—butter and vanilla wafted from the plates—but Patsy hadn't really had dinner. And feared if she ate the sweet dessert on an empty stomach, she'd be sick before morning came.

Patsy cleared her throat, asked if she could use the bathroom. Veronica immediately showed her the way.

Patsy closed the door to the small room and braced her hands on both sides of the sink.

Breathe, she told herself. Again. Again. She closed her eyes and willed the room to stop spinning.

Steadying herself took longer than she'd liked, but finally the spin digressed to a wobble. She opened her eyes. Rubbed her fingertips under their red rims. Clearly, she'd aged decades in the last year.

She'd do best to splash cold water on her face, she decided, before returning to the others. Eyes closed and water dripping from her chin, she fished around for the hand towel hanging from the round plastic handle on the wall, dried her face, and then looked back into the mirror.

There were the eyes again. Just like Billy's. So much like his. Not the same color but . . . so close. Except that Billy's held something she didn't quite have. A peace perhaps. But from where?

It had to be the lifestyle then. No . . . Billy'd had it just as difficult as she, even more so. Yes, their mother had cruelly sent her away, but Billy had been stuck with the likes of Ira Liddle.

A knock on the door caused her to blink rapidly.

"Pats, you all right, hon?"

"Yes. Just a moment and I'll be right there."

She listened as Gilbert's footsteps faded toward the kitchen. Patsy ran her palms over her hair, squared her shoulders, and gave a nod. The time had come. She had to go back into that kitchen and ask her brother the question that had been on her mind all evening.

And nearly all her life.

On her way back, Patsy's eyes scanned the living room for framed photographs—anything, some whatnot perhaps—that spoke of the life she'd known before Trinity. Though Veronica decorated with bric-a-brac and framed photos, only one caught her attention; she walked over to it, picked it up, and studied it. It was an obviously impromptu snapshot of her mother standing at a kitchen sink—not one Patsy was familiar with—drying dishes stacked in the drainer. She wore a typical housedress and high heel pump shoes and a floral bib apron with rickrack trim. She was so pretty. Beaten down by life as she was, her beauty was second to none.

She took the photo into the kitchen with her and asked Billy the question weighing heaviest upon her. "Where is my mother?"

His eyes clouded over. "Come, sit down."

Gilbert stood. The look on his face said he already knew the answer.

Patsy lowered herself to her seat, held the photograph to her heart.

"She died," he said. "Last year. Just days after Christmas."

The words echoed through the long and old tunnel between her mind and her heart. She was too late. Only by months. But too late.

Patsy stared at Billy as Gil and Veronica remained silent. There was so much more she wanted to know but couldn't seem to ask. How had she died? Where had she been all these years? Had Mama ever mentioned her? Called her name on her deathbed?

First one, then another, then another . . . little by little they all leave you, Patsy.

"Um . . ." her brother finally said, "I hate to tell you this, but Harold . . . Harold is also dead. He . . . he was in prison . . ." He waved a hand. "Long story and I'll explain it all later but . . . he tried to escape in an uprising and . . . he was shot."

Patsy continued to stare. *First one . . . then another . . .*

"You probably don't want to know about Daddy." He snorted. "I hardly want to talk about him. He and Mama divorced back years ago when I was sixteen. Far as I know, he's remarried, got a little girl who was born before Mama and him ever even divorced."

Gilbert cleared his throat from beside her, startling her. Patsy looked at him, waited for him to speak. "I hired a private detective . . . if you're wondering. That's how I found you." He ran his fingers up and down the glass of tea. "He found a man named Ira Liddle in Macon. Fits the description of your father, but . . . this man never remarried."

The two men stared at each other. Veronica tapped her short and groomed fingernails against the white Formica of the tabletop. Patsy glanced from one to the other, then back down to the photo she still held in her hand.

"I'm sorry about Harold," she whispered, looking back to her brother.

Billy nodded. "Harold made his choices. In the end, we all get to make our choices. It took me awhile to come to grips with it, but I've got a good wife and a father-in-law who listens and then doles out the best advice I've ever heard." He paused. "And, I've got a good Lord who listens too. I don't know where I'd be if I didn't have him."

"Amen," Patsy said, though she thought she sounded more like Mam or Gabby than what she was feeling in her heart. She patted Gilbert's hand. "I think I'm too tired to keep talking. Can we go home now?"

"Sure," her husband said, offering a weak smile.

They left with a promise to return the following day. Gilbert, always the businessman, asked if morning or afternoon was better. Billy chuckled and said, "Cedar Key doesn't hold to time. We'll catch each other, I promise."

On their way out, Patsy returned the picture to the end table where she'd found it. She gave it one last glance, then forced a brave smile to her face. "Thank you for your hospitality," she said to her new sister-in-law. "Maybe tomorrow I'll feel like that cake."

"I'll save it for you," she said. "And hold you to it."

She and Billy said an awkward good-bye at the door. She wanted—oh, how she wanted—to throw her arms around him and never let him go. But she couldn't. Not just yet.

Maybe tomorrow when she saw him.

Yes, tomorrow. She'd feel more like talking then.

35

Darkness still cloaked the sky the next morning when Patsy rose, dressed quietly, and wrote Gilbert a note, leaving it on her pillow. She found a flashlight by the back door and used it to light the way back to where they'd been the night before—across from Dock Street and the restaurant where she hadn't gotten her deviled crab but had found her brother. The thought made her smile, in spite of all that had happened in the last twelve hours of her life.

She and Gilbert hadn't talked at all during the short drive to their cottage, and little more than that after going inside. One thing she could say for her husband, he knew her well. When to approach her and when to leave her alone. Last night had been a time for the latter.

Today, as she walked in predawn darkness, she knew the time had come for her and God to have a little talk. Just the two of them. And there was no better place than the marina she'd spotted the night before.

She'd also noticed a few benches. Odd that she had, she now thought, keeping her eyes on her feet and her feet within the beam streaming from the flashlight. These were unfamiliar streets. Long and narrow, with very few street lamps. Foliage

344

grew thick and tall on both sides, crowding the houses and cottages like the one she and Gilbert had rented.

Nothing on the island seemed to be stirring. Just her and a breeze strong enough to make her happy she'd worn a sweater. Lights winked in some of the houses, but she saw no one outside. She shivered with a sense of both adventure and fear.

The area around the marina was better lit. For that she was grateful. She turned off the flashlight and slowed her pace. After picking the bench along the sidewalk near the water's edge, she slid onto it. Looked around. Behind her, boats rocked, water lapping at their hulls. In front and to the right side of her, a sliver of the quarter moon's reflection danced atop a multitude of ripples and waves. A solitary bird gave its throaty call. She listened for an answer. One never came. For all she knew, she and this lone, unseen bird were the only two awake and stirring about.

So she sat on the bench in the dark and waited.

Which was fine with her. She needed this time to herself. To think. In quiet. To figure out how she was feeling about this sudden upset . . . or completion . . . in her life. If it was completion. After all, it had only been one brother standing in the restaurant, just yards from where she sat now. Only Billy. Harold was dead.

And her mother was dead. *Dead*. There would be no surprise reunion with Mama. No seeing her. Touching her. She'd never have the chance to ask any of the questions she'd always thought she might. Never have the chance to present the "whys" and "why nots." Every chance was gone.

Mama was dead and Daddy was dead and Harold was dead and Papa was dead . . . But she and Billy were very much alive and well. She and Billy and Lloyd.

She'd hadn't told Billy about Lloyd. She should. Maybe today when they saw each other again. Today.

As if in slow motion, the sky along the horizon changed color. From the darkest gray to a hazy shade of blue. The sun was coming up, just as it always had and always would.

But the temperature was still slow in rising. In spite of the sweater (and the slacks that went with them), she hadn't fully anticipated how chilly even a spring morning before sunrise could be. She pulled her feet to the bench and hugged her knees to her chest. She took in a deep breath, planted her chin between her knees, and waited as the blue changed to orange over a thin line of red. She thought to pray, but words weren't yet forming. Maybe they weren't supposed to, she decided. Maybe this moment was just about her and God and sitting quiet.

Clouds she'd not noticed before now hovered above the changing colors. Below, resting on the water, a sliver of land stretched its arms wide. She wondered what it was. A piece of the mainland? An island?

"That's Dog Island."

Patsy gasped, dropped her feet, and swung around. Billy stood mere feet behind her on the street. "How'd you know . . ."

"What you were wondering? I wondered the same thing first time I came here. Wondered it about all the keys around here you haven't yet seen."

Patsy shifted to the right and patted the bench beside her. Billy took the cue and sat. He smelled of shaving cream and aftershave. Not the little-boy-after-a-night-of-sleeping smell she remembered. She brought her feet up again and this time lay her cheek against her knee. "Actually, I meant, how did you know I was here."

346

Billy scooted up, shimmied out of his thick jacket. "Oh. I didn't." He draped it around her shoulders, tucked it behind and around her. "There you go." He crossed his arms and slid back on the bench. "I was on my way to work. I usually walk this way, though not typically so early."

"I took you away from your work last night, I suppose." Billy's face glowed in the morning sunlight. Patsy looked out over the water, toward the strip of land that was Dog Island, and watched the sun peek an eye open. As if on cue, a variety of birds came, seemingly from nowhere. "I can't remember when I last saw the sun come up."

"I see it all the time. Not every morning, of course. But this is really one of the things I love most about living here."

"Sure is a quiet place. A lot like Trinity. Only smaller, if I can even imagine myself saying that." The sun had made it halfway up. "If *anyone* can believe that a place could be smaller than Trinity."

Billy laughed beside her. "I don't remember anything but big places. Miami. Gainesville."

Patsy looked at her brother's handsome face again, his features bringing back so many memories of their mother. "You don't remember Casselton?"

"Only snippets. I remember a little about the house." He seemed to study the water. "It was a two-story house."

"That's right."

"And fields in the back with a vegetable garden."

"Yes." A breeze came from the gulf, rustled the palm fronds and the thick branches of the oleander. Patsy tilted her face into it, her own thoughts now filled with memories of coming in from that field, bushels of vegetables balanced on a hip. On instinct she reached for her hair falling down her back, and pulled it over one shoulder, twisting it as she did.

347

Billy stole a glimpse at her as his eyes shifted downward. "I remember the night you left." His lips drew thin. "He was a raving madman that night."

Patsy didn't have to ask who *he* was.

"I remember hearing them fight. Harold slept through it, mostly." He coughed a sad chuckle. "I was scared out of my mind."

Patsy tilted her head to see him better. "Why?"

He groaned. "Ahhhh . . . Daddy . . . all he wanted was to know where you were and . . ."

"And Mama?"

"All she wanted to do was to protect you. I remember hearing her say that she'd sent you somewhere where he couldn't get to you. 'No more whippings . . . no more looks,' she told him."

Where he couldn't get to her . . .

Billy shook his head as though relieving himself of another memory. "The place we lived in Miami was a matchbox," he said.

"Wait," Patsy said. She wanted to know more.

"It had an indoor bathroom, but it was so small," he continued. His way, she supposed, of letting her know he wasn't altogether ready.

Patsy nodded in acquiescence. "How long did you live there?" The sun now sat on the water like a giant yellow-gold ball, bobbing up and down, waiting for a child to come rescue it. And maybe play with it.

"Until I was twelve."

The sun hovered just over the skyline. She thought of her own Greg—now just a little older than Billy had been when going to Gainesville—and how difficult it would be if they just up and moved. "That's a hard age to move." An even harder age to have your mother up and send you away . . . not that thirteen would be any better.

"Not really. I didn't have many friends in Miami. Mama was never happy there. Harold, he was really the only one who got . . . upset."

Patsy looked at him. "What?"

Billy shrugged. "I was just thinking . . . remembering. He and Daddy had such a fight. Mama and me, we sat in the kitchen. At the table. And when it got really bad, Mama told me to leave."

"Did you?"

He grimaced. "Yeah. Always. With every fight."

Patsy fought the urge to wrap her arms around him and pull him close. He wasn't a little boy who needed protecting anymore. He was a grown man. Married. Running a business.

"Only once did I stand up to the old man." He looked at her.

She didn't speak, willing him, this time, to go on. She had to know. As much as she could take and as much as he could give. For now.

"The day I found out about Daddy's affair. And the baby."

"I wonder whatever happened to that woman and the little girl . . ."

"Maybe some things we don't need to know."

Patsy let the words sink in, wondering what he meant, exactly, by them. "Were you and Harold close as you grew older? You were nearly inseparable when you were little boys."

"At times. As we grew older it became pretty apparent how different we were. Ronni says we're like Esau and Jacob from the Old Testament. One was the father's son and one was the mother's."

Patsy smiled at him, straightened her legs, and dropped

her feet to the ground. She pulled the jacket from around her shoulders, laid it across her lap. "You being Jacob?" She flipped her hair over her shoulder.

"Yeah. Not that Harold was really Daddy's. He just . . . he fought back. He never let Daddy get the best of him. Of course, in the end, I suppose Daddy won. He turned Harold mean." He looked at her, searching her face, it seemed. "You wear your hair long for religious reasons?"

Patsy laughed. "Oh goodness, no. Back on my wedding night, Gil asked me not to cut it. So, other than a trim, I never have."

"That's some husband you have. He sure went the extra mile to find me. And to get you here."

Patsy sighed. "And to be honest with you, I haven't even thanked him." She smiled to lessen her own guilt. "But I will. It's just that . . . I . . . I haven't handled all this . . . my life story . . . so well, I'm afraid."

Billy leaned forward, cracked his knuckles, rested his elbows on his knees. "Look . . . I don't know how much you want to know—"

"Everything. Tell me everything. Whatever you can say for now and save the rest for later. But just . . . tell me. I'm ready. I think."

Patsy watched as the words seemed to swirl around in her baby brother's head. "Mama . . . after Daddy left . . . she had a time of it. There was a neighbor, Mrs. Stone, who sort of came in and demanded that Mama be strong. Get a job. Change her name. We got a new place. Small. It was just the two of us; Harold was already in prison. She always seemed like she was doing all right, but deep down, I knew she wasn't. She was pretending, just like she'd done . . . all my life, anyway. I tried to get her to move to Cedar Key with

Ronni and me, but she said no. Young lovers didn't need a mother or a mother-in-law hanging around, she said."

Patsy laughed at the thought. "I've been lucky in that. Gil's mother has hardly bothered me at all. Just been there when I needed her and left me alone when I didn't."

"Same here. Ronni comes from good people. I couldn't ask for better. And . . . well, they led me to the Lord, so for that I'll always be grateful." Billy sighed. "Anyway . . . Mama stayed on in Gainesville after the wedding, but after Harold got killed, I really put in for her to come here. Then we found out Ronni was expecting . . ."

"Expecting?"

Billy closed his eyes. Nodded. "Yeah. The baby didn't make it past four months, but . . . doctor says that's not so uncommon."

"That's true." This word of acknowledgment and comfort from the woman who never miscarried but just kept getting pregnant. Regret shot through her spirit. She'd never really appreciated her children. Always complaining, more with each new pregnancy. And here was this sweet woman who would never have the chance to hold her first in her arms. Patsy ached to hold all five of hers right then and there.

"Ronni was devastated, and, for Mama—who'd *just* moved in—I guess it was the final straw. A few months later, we found her in bed one morning. Sleeping." Tears formed in his eyes and he swiped at them. "Or at least we thought so."

"Sleeping, as my friend Gabby would say, with Jesus."

Billy nodded.

"Did she . . . did she ever . . . talk about me?"

Billy didn't answer at first. Patsy supposed he was weighing his words again before saying anything. "Yeah. Not a lot. But she kept your picture. For a long time she kept it hidden away from Daddy, but I knew where it was." He looked at her. "She never would say why she sent you away though. I asked when . . ." He shook his head. "Well, more than once."

"And?"

"She wanted to try to call you but she didn't want to interfere, I think. And sometimes, if I brought up trying to find you, she'd get so upset I'd just let it drop."

The words caught Patsy unguarded. She'd never even considered . . . "I don't . . . I don't know what to say. I thought . . ."

"That she'd forgotten you?"

Patsy could only nod. Her head was beginning to ache. She rubbed her fingertips hard against her forehead.

"Do you get headaches?"

She looked at him. "Sometimes. Not too often."

"I do. Really bad ones. Ronni thinks it's all the memories I keep locked up."

Ronni, Patsy decided, was someone she wanted to get to know better. Her wisdom came from somewhere deeper than Patsy had ever dared go. "Do you?"

"Yeah. I guess I'm a lot like Mama in that way. I didn't even tell Ronni about you and Lloyd until after Harold died." He looked at his watch. "I gotta get to the restaurant." He smiled at her. "But . . . you're here for the arts festival, right? You'll be here this weekend?"

She nodded.

"Good. I want . . . I want to spend as much time together as we can." He stood and she handed him his jacket.

"Thanks for this. It was colder than I anticipated."

Billy looked around them, up high and over the water where several seagulls and pelicans flapped their wings lazily across the high tide. "It's going to be a nice day though. I can tell already." He winked at her still sitting on the bench.

She was almost too afraid to move. "All right then. Come to Sikes for dinner? On the house."

Patsy nodded.

He started to walk away.

She called his name. "Billy."

He stopped. Looked over his shoulder at her.

"Is she . . . is Mama buried here?"

He nodded. "Ask anybody where the cemetery is. They'll tell you. She's not too far inside. Look to your left, all the way to the back. You'll see a picket fence around a grave . . . she's near there."

"Thanks."

"You going?"

Patsy nodded. "Yeah. There's things I want to say."

36

Within an hour of Billy leaving her alone on the bench, a steady stream of fishermen left the dock in boats they'd brought around from the marina. Earlier, flocks of birds had come to the shoreline on a tiny stretch of beach where they remained. Occasionally something startled them. First one, and then the entire flock stretched their wings, rose into the sky, encircled the water, and then settled again on the white sand. Gray pelicans—some with dark heads, others capped in creamy white—had also arrived and perched atop the wooden side slats of the docks. A few craned their necks to look over their homeland while the rest tucked in their bills, closed their eyes, and basked in the morning sunlight.

Every so often someone walked past where Patsy sat. The greeting was always the same. "Good morning," they'd say.

"Good morning," she'd reply.

"Nice out today."

"It is."

And then they were gone. Friendly, but no need to stop, she supposed.

The weather had grown warmer. Patsy peeled away her pink sweater, leaving only the matching shell underneath.

The sun felt good on her skin. In fact, *she* felt good, in spite of her circumstances. There was just something about the water . . . something healing. It called to the most wounded of souls, hers included. She felt pleased with herself for having dared to leave the cottage, to walk to the marina alone, to sit and reflect. To think about where she'd been. Where she was. Where she was going from here.

Her watch told her it was now nine o'clock. A sense of relief washed over her that Gilbert had not come to find or check on her. Oh, how she loved the man. He'd clearly gone to great expense to find her brother. To bring her here. Not to mention the money he must have spent keeping her in Charleston. The only good thing she could say about being there—other than it had enabled her to keep her distance— was that she'd met Gabby.

A smile pulled itself across her face. Gabby. What would she think of all this? From what Patsy could tell so far, Veronica, whose strength and faith came through in nearly everything she said and did, and Gabby would get along just fine. They'd talk about God and Jesus and prayer and miracles; she could just hear them now.

God.

"Where were you in this story, I wonder," she dared to say aloud. "Were you there when my father died? When Mama married Mr. Liddle? When he beat her? Beat me?" *Looked at me with those eyes.* Her smile had slipped to a frown. "Were you there when Mama practically shoved me onto that bus?"

Remember, Pats. I was on that bus too.

She allowed herself to imagine that she hadn't gotten on the bus. That she'd managed, somehow, to convince Mama that she should stay. How would life have been for her? Growing up helping Mama. Watching Billy and Harold reach adulthood.

Maybe Harold wouldn't have turned out so bad, had she been there to help.

Wisps of hair tickled her cheeks. She brushed the long mane with her fingertips, twisted it as they ran the length, and held it in a fist when she'd reached the end. She stretched her legs.

He would have raped me. The thought came from nowhere, it seemed. *Mama couldn't have protected me, and no amount of helping would have made the difference there.*

No. Mama couldn't help.

But she had, hadn't she? She'd put her on the bus.

Hush now, child. Yes, I know. Yes, I see. Why do you think I'm letting you go?

"Mama . . ." The name slipped from her lips before she had time to stop it. Patsy looked around. Only the pelicans, joined now by a few gulls, were witness to this moment. The wind picked up. She released her hair and let the breeze have its way with the long dark strands.

Her hair. She'd grown it for Gilbert.

Oh, the things we do for the ones we love.

The things we do. Like finding brothers. Or sending us *to* brothers.

Lloyd. She smiled again. She couldn't wait to tell Lloyd about finding Billy. He'd never known him, of course. But they were brothers. Half brothers. Then again, she and Billy were half siblings. Not that it mattered. Blood was blood and they would all love each other. Have family reunions. Maybe this Christmas . . . if that scuffle in Southeast Asia didn't interfere . . .

She stood. Arched her back and stretched her arms toward heaven. Turned. Looked out across the marina to a small wooden house at the end of a boardwalk jutting several hundred feet into the gulf water.

"That's the Thomas house."

She whirled around to find Veronica standing nearby wearing pedal pushers and a white cotton blouse and rather smart sandals. A small cream patent purse dangled from her right hand.

"I didn't hear you."

Her sister-in-law smiled. "I know. Billy says I walk lighter than a feather flits." She smiled broadly. "I just talked to him on the phone. He said you were still sitting down here." When Patsy said nothing, she continued. "He was worried."

"How'd he know I was still here?"

Veronica pointed toward Dock Street; Patsy followed the direction of her finger. "He can see you from the office window of the restaurant."

Patsy raised her hand and waved, imagined her brother waving back. "That's sweet of him to worry." She took a few steps toward her sister-in-law. "I was just going back to the cottage and then later on to the cemetery."

"I can take you to where Billy's mama—I'm sorry, your mama—is buried if you like."

Patsy shook her head. "That's nice, but I want to go alone." She shrugged. "Well, I may have Gilbert take me, but . . . I will need directions though."

"It's out a ways, but easy enough to find." Veronica pulled the purse to the crook of her arm and allowed it to rest there. "Can we sit down for a minute? I've got something for you."

"What is it?" Patsy asked, not moving.

Veronica tilted her head and smiled. "It's not bad."

Patsy returned to the bench; Veronica sat beside her. She opened the purse and retrieved a small white box.

"I asked Billy if it was okay . . . I haven't worn it in a while." She extended the box toward Patsy. "Or at least, it seems like a long time . . . well, he and I both thought it was a good idea you should have it."

Patsy took the box, opened it. Resting on a bed of pressed cotton was a ring encrusted with sapphires and diamonds. "Mama's ring," she breathed out, retrieving it from its safe-keeping. "I'd almost forgotten about this."

"*Your* father—not Billy's—gave it to her. So, in my way of thinking, it's rightfully yours, not mine."

Patsy looked at the younger woman. "I remember Mama telling me all about it. It originally belonged to my great-grandmother. This is quite old, you know."

"And beautiful."

Patsy returned it to the box. "Did Billy propose to you with this?"

Veronica nodded. "Your mama didn't think . . ." Her green eyes grew large, reminding Patsy of an intuitive cat's. "Well, I don't know what she thought . . . but, it's mine and I want you to have it and so does Billy. And that's that."

Patsy clutched the box in her fist. "Thank you."

Veronica snapped the purse closed. "You're welcome."

Patsy's insides went to war; she wanted to say something about the baby, to tell her she was sorry for her loss. Part of her even felt like Gabby, wanting to say something encouraging, like "I'm sure there will be more," but that seemed hollow in a way. Instead she said, "I'm sorry for your loss."

"My loss?"

"Were you and my mother close?"

Veronica shrugged. "Yes and no. I mean, she was always so nice, but . . . something about Miss Bernice . . . she never let anyone too close. I guess Billy was as close to her as anyone. From what I can tell and what I remember, Harold was more their daddy's boy and Billy just always stood close by her."

She shook her head. "Still, there was something missing in Miss Bernice. Even after Mr. Liddle left. Whatever it was he took away from her, she just never really got it back."

Instinctively, Patsy knew that part of what was taken was her. But hearing it and knowing it didn't fit with what she'd believed for so long. Or, at least, what she thought she believed. "I'm glad she and Billy were close," she said for lack of anything else to say. Too much and she'd start to weep. Maybe break down completely. Maybe enough to need to go back to Charleston, which she had no intention of doing. "And I'm sorry Mama . . ." Patsy gave a half smile. "There were times when . . . when Mr. Liddle was on the road—he was a traveling salesman, you know—"

"I know."

"Well, he was on the road from Monday morning until Saturday afternoons usually. Sometimes Fridays but mostly Saturdays. And Mama . . . she was a totally different person during the week than she was come Friday. Thursday night it would usually start. She'd get all nervous. Mondays she was still wound a little tight. But Tuesdays, Wednesdays, and Thursdays she could be a lot of fun. At least that's the way I remember her." A motorized fishing boat passed nearby them, interrupting Patsy as it made its way toward Dog Island. She raked her teeth over her bottom lip. "I wonder if Billy remembers any of that."

Veronica patted her hand, the one holding the ring box. "Well, you'll have plenty of time to ask him and maybe even to reminisce. I just know we're all going to be close. I can feel it."

Patsy couldn't help but marvel. "Are you always so sure about things?"

"What do you mean?"

"For such a young woman, you just seem so sure about yourself and everything around you."

Patsy thought she saw Veronica blush. "I guess maybe I am."

And then Patsy laughed. Hard. It felt good. Veronica laughed with her.

"Hey, can I give you a lift back to the cottage?"

Patsy stood. "You know, that would be nice."

Patsy found Gilbert sitting on the front porch of the cottage with a cup of coffee in one hand and a small book in the other. He wore a white cotton T-shirt and a pair of khaki slacks, no belt and no shoes. She kept her eyes on him, watching her getting out of the Volkswagen and saying good-bye to Veronica.

"Amazing," she said from the bottom step, looking up at him. "I didn't know you cared to read." She turned to wave good-bye to Veronica then looked back at Gilbert. "By the way, dinner at the restaurant tonight is on Billy."

He closed the book, dropped it to the gray-painted slats of the porch. "That's right nice." He smiled at her. "Nah, something told me you didn't want my company down at the water."

She took the three steps to the porch. "Oh? Why's that?" She tossed her sweater over the nearest arm of the green and white glider running the full length of the short porch. Then she joined it. It slid back and forth with her weight; she steadied it with her feet.

He shrugged. "If you'd wanted me to come with you, I figure you woulda woke me up."

"Does that bother you? That I didn't ask?"

Gilbert shook his head. He hadn't combed his hair yet; the

curls fell like a mop along his forehead. "No. You take whatever time you need. That's one of the reasons we're here."

She crossed her legs. "So, you hired a private detective, did you?"

"Mad at me?" he said by way of answering the question affirmatively.

She paused long enough to cause his brow to rise, then said, "Maybe. Did you know for sure about Billy when we got here?"

"No. I had every reason to believe, but . . . no. At the very least I figured we'd get a nice vacation out of our time here." He looked around. "It's nice here, isn't it?"

"Don't change the subject, Gilbert Milstrap."

He pointed at her. "You're already changing," he said with a wicked grin. "I can see that clear from over here."

"In what way?"

He waggled a finger at her. "Can't quite put my finger on it, but it's there, all right. Tell you what else. I don't know what I would have done if I'd been wrong about Billy. I'm just glad I wasn't." He tilted his chin. "Sorry about your mama though. I sure was hoping . . ."

"Don't be sorry, Gil. What you did . . . well, I believe it's the nicest thing anyone has ever done for me." She remembered the box in her hand. "Except maybe for this." She held the box between her fingers and wiggled it at him.

"What's that?"

"My mother's engagement ring. It's worth a fortune so we need to put it somewhere safe."

Gilbert set the coffee mug next to the book, then joined her on the glider. He took the box from her fingers, opened it, whistled low, and said, "My gracious alive, girl."

"Like I said . . ."

He closed the box, placed it next to him, then rested against the back of the glider, bringing one arm around her and drawing her close. Patsy dropped her head to his chest and listened to the thump-thump of his heart. She pressed her palm against the shirt. Inhaled. It smelled of her husband and the sunshine the tee had been hung out to dry in. She closed her eyes, her heart feeling heavy and light all at the same time. This place really was like a balm. And she really was blessed.

"Hon." Gilbert's voice pulled her back to the porch. She sat up, wiped the drool from one side of her mouth, then gasped at the small wet circle formed on her husband's tee.

"Oh. How long did I sleep?"

"A few minutes, I guess." He pulled the wet part of the shirt from his chest. "I was telling you . . . I wanted you to know . . ."

Patsy looked from the white tee held by strong fingers to the gentle eyes of the man who'd brought her here, in more ways than one. They shimmered with moisture. "Gil?"

The tears spilled down his cheeks. "I love you so much . . ." he wept. "I'm sorry. I told myself I wasn't going to do this . . ."

Patsy slipped her arms around his neck, pulled him close to her as he brought her closer to him. Chest to breasts; for a moment she thought she felt their hearts beat as one. "Oh, Gil. I love you too. I do . . . and I'm the one who's sorry. Sorry for all I have put you through these years. I know you thought I was just slap crazy, but I couldn't seem to control my fears. I'm not saying my fears are miraculously gone, but . . . somehow I think things will start to get better now."

He squeezed. "I've been thinking. Not just this morning. For weeks. Months even. And I want you to know that I understand, Pats." He pushed her away from him so that they looked into each other's eyes. "Well, maybe I don't understand fully. But I realize you've lost so much in your life and that you are afraid you'll lose me too." He took a breath. "But nothing has changed for me. I'm still here for you. Always."

Patsy placed her hands on both sides of his face. "On the way from the marina, I was thinking that, yes, I have lost a lot. But, you were right, Gil. *You* were also on that bus. And it brought me to Trinity. To Mam. To Papa. To Lloyd. To Rayette and Sandra and, my gosh, really such a good life. And, I guess you could say that eventually that bus led me to Greg and Pam. And Kenny and George and Donna." She made a show of saying the last three names.

"But first, to me."

Patsy kissed him soundly on the lips. "To you." She kissed him again and again and again. "You, you, you." Her arms slipped around his shoulders once more.

"Careful," he whispered in her ear. "You may not know this, but there's a man over there standing in his yard, pretending to water his flowers, but most definitely watching us."

She nuzzled his neck. "Let him get his own girl."

Gilbert stopped the car just inside the gates of the cemetery. He shut off the engine before turning to her. "Are you sure you want to do this alone?"

Patsy nodded.

He draped his arm over the steering wheel, looked out the windshield. She did the same. Just past a cluster of graves, the grasses of the marsh waved against the afternoon sun. Beyond the marsh, she spied fishing huts.

"Patsy."

She looked at her husband.

"I have something for you. Stay right here."

Gilbert left the car, walked to the back, opened the trunk, closed it, and returned to his seat. He carried with him an oblong box and an envelope. "What in the world . . ."

"Mam wanted me to bring this. She said . . ." He took a deep breath. "Mam said to tell you that it's time."

Patsy took the offering, knowing full well what was inside without so much as opening it. "The cupid lipstick holder."

"Want to tell me about it?"

She shook her head. "Not just yet." But she pulled it from the box, ran her hand over its ornate brass structure, then set it on the seat between them. She picked up the envelope, opened the car door, and said, "I'll be back shortly."

"Take your time," she heard him say.

A narrow path snaked between a few of the grave markers and up a slight incline. Patsy walked it, allowed her eyes to glance over the headstones and monuments. Some were still shiny in their newness. Others, sectioned off by wrought-iron fences, were old, moss-laden. Shadows from massive live oaks, dripping with Spanish moss that shimmied in the breeze, danced over the cement and brick and—interestingly—oyster shells marking final resting places. Palm fronds in tans and browns and greens rustled. The smell of salt and fish wafted across the cemetery. She saw a wooden fence up on the hill towered by a wooden cross; a boundary to a single grave. Just as Billy said it would be. She walked toward it, reading names engraved in stone until she came to the one she sought.

Bernice Elizabeth Sweeny
1916–1963
Beloved Mother

Elizabeth? Had she known that? It was the middle name Patsy had given to her firstborn daughter. Perhaps somewhere, in the recesses of her memory, she'd remembered. "Hey." She swallowed hard. "Hey, Mama."

Patsy looked down to the envelope in her hand. Across the front, her name was written in penmanship she'd all but forgotten but now found familiar again. "To My Daughter," it read, "On Her Wedding Day."

Patsy sighed, slipped her fingers under the back flap, and released the seal, tearing the paper as she did. She pulled two pieces of paper folded together from inside, opened them. Even after all these years, the scent of her mother reached her nostrils.

Coty.

For a moment, Patsy was back in the car, inhaling her mother's fragrance, begging her not to put her on the bus.

"I'll stay away from him . . ." She opened her eyes, realizing she'd just whispered to the grave at her feet.

Don't make this harder than it is . . .

She nodded, wiped tears from her cheeks, wishing she hadn't already started to cry, grateful at the same time that she had. Her fingers opened the tri-folded paper. Tucked inside was an old photograph. Patsy held it up and close. It was of her mother on her own wedding day, the one when she'd married Patsy's father. She'd been so very young, so beautiful. Her lips held a deep Cupid's bow and were painted what appeared in the sepia finish to be red. Her dress was elegant; the veil wrapped the crown of her head then spilled to the floor with her gown's train. A single strand of pearls dipped at the base of her swanlike throat, and a massive cluster of flowers was clasped in her hands.

Patsy slipped the photograph behind the letter and read. "Dearest Patsy," it began.

Patsy took a deep breath. This was it. The words of her

mother's heart she'd put off reading for too many years. Words Mama believed Patsy would have read on her wedding day. The day her life started anew.

Patsy swiped tears blurring her vision. When the writing became clear again, she continued.

I have pondered for days what I would say to you here in these few lines. I have wondered if I could even go through with the writing of them. Or putting this piece of paper into an envelope, the envelope into that tiny piece of luggage sitting across the room from me right now. Waiting.

Oh, Patsy! How I would that this were all so different. I don't know how much you will remember. The good, oh please let it be so! And not the bad. I pray to the good Lord above that you will never recall how life was for a while for you and me. That you will only remember the happy moments we spent with your father. Above all, that you will know I made my decision to marry Ira Liddle not fully knowing what kind of man he was, only that he could provide for you and me when we needed it so desperately.

I am sorry, Patsy, for what I put you through these past few years. I make excuses, but that is all they are. Just know I never did anything thinking it would hurt you. Nor would I ever, even after today is but a bitter memory.

This afternoon, you will arrive home from school. The boys will be at Mrs. Dabbs's house. You will get off the bus, unaware of what I am planning to do. And you will question me, I know you will. We will cry. But, no matter how much you beg—and you will—I will put you on the bus and send you to Mr. and Mrs. Buchwald. Because

I have to, Patsy. For your own safety, even if, every day, I die a little bit more.

I trust the Buchwalds, Patsy. I have trusted them. They will hold two of the most precious possessions. I pray you will be blessed by them as I have been.

Sweet Patsy, I have asked Mrs. Buchwald to give you this cupid lipstick holder on your wedding day. I saw you holding it that day I asked you to help me get ready for Mr. Liddle's return, and I know you find it pretty. I want you to have it now, with all my love.

Patsy, what this cupid holds is for outer beauty. Promise me, your mother—for I will always be your mother—that you will never depend on physical beauty but always the loveliness that comes from within. I know you will do that for me.

One final thing because the time is almost here that you will be home—promise that you will remember me with kindness. That you will know what I have done is for your own good. And that while I cannot go with you, Patsy . . . I cannot . . . I am with you in a deeper way. Today, as you stand before God and the man I pray will be as good to you as your father was to me, I will be close enough in spirit to hear the words of forever you speak to your young man.

I have prayed already and will continue to pray that death will not part you any time soon. Not for a good long time. That you will be blessed with happiness and health and beautiful children whom I will gather on my knee and hold, even if only in my heart.

I love you, Patsy. Never forget that. I will love you until the day I die.

Have a happy day, my child. And a happier life.

```
Don't let anything come between you and that.
Life is too precious to waste. Live it to its
fullest. My Patsy. My child.

                    Yours,
                    Mama
```

Patsy swallowed. *For your own safety.* She read the words again through a veil of unbridled tears. Patsy gasped. "You didn't give me away," she whispered. "You made sure I . . ." The remainder of the words wouldn't come. Nor did they need to. Patsy knew now that her mother had made a most grievous of choices, but the right one for Patsy. While she'd never understand it all, she at least understood this much. Her mother had loved her. Very much.

She wiped her eyes, started to fold the paper, but stopped short. A line near the bottom begged that it be read once more. And so she did.

"Life is too precious to waste," Mama had written. "Live it to its fullest."

Patsy looked from the paper to the car where Gilbert sat waiting, just like he always had. Waited for her in the diner at the bus stop. Waited for her to grow up enough to declare his intentions. Waited to marry her. Then waited for her to get to this moment, right here in the cemetery of a town she'd never heard of until just a few days ago. He'd picked her up when she'd fallen and held her up when she couldn't stand.

He'd been brave enough to bring her here and strong enough to let her walk from the car to the grave alone.

Patsy folded the letter, slipped it and the photo back into the envelope, then took a final look at the slab where her mother's name was carved. "I'll live life to its fullest, Mama," she said. And then she smiled. "I promise."

37

2012, Cedar Key, Florida

Patsy Milstrap liked getting up early in the mornings. She enjoyed the feel of the house when it was still cool enough for her to need a thin housecoat and a warm pair of socks. She liked the sense of calm when only a small table lamp lit the way from her bedroom to the kitchen, where a single night-light shed only the tiniest glow along her spotless countertops.

Every morning was the same, really. She rose in the dark, poured herself a glass of iced tea, then went out on the bal-cony of the house she and Gilbert had vacationed in and she had retired to, to wait for sunrise. The evening before, the television weatherman told her what time the sun would rise the following day. That morning, the previous night's broadcast said 6:34. A look at her watch told her it was now 6:15. She had a few minutes. Maybe more. The weatherman was never exactly right.

She took a sip of tea. She was seventy-eight years old now; next week she'd be seventy-nine. Another year older. And, she figured, another year closer to seeing Jesus face-to-face. Not

369

that she was sick. Goodness, she felt just fine. A little tired, maybe. But at near seventy-nine, she should be.

She smiled. Funny how when you're young you think you'll never get old, and then you start to get old and you fear getting older. And then, you're older and you find yourself ready to see Jesus. "When you're ready, I'm ready," she spoke out loud. "I'm not rushing you, but I wouldn't mind being with the one I've worshiped for so long now." The one who had taken her sad rags and turned them into a dancing frock. Like the one she'd worn to the formal, the night Gil had come home from the service. Peach taffeta.

Patsy chuckled. She had probably looked like a big ole bowl of frilly sherbet. But she'd been young, and when you're young you can pull things like that off.

Mama. I'll see you too. You and Daddy and Mam and Papa.

Not to mention Rayette, who'd died just a few years back, so suddenly, with a massive stroke. No one had seen that coming any more than when Papa had passed away.

Oh, and Gabby. My, how she'd missed her over the years. They'd made quite an impression on Trinity and Charleston and everywhere in between. Almost gotten themselves in a world of trouble a few times, but God had protected them both.

And of course, her beloved Gilbert. Oh, after six long years apart, wouldn't he be pleased to see her! She wondered if the good Lord would allow her darling to greet her at the pearly gates instead of Saint Peter, and if he would let them slip off somewhere private for a welcome-home kiss.

The rushes, thick along the marsh, swayed in the early morning breeze. The wind caught in the fronds of the palm trees, and they rustled like a baby's toy. Patsy's eyes darted from one to the other and then back to the horizon. Life around her was stark and black against the sweet lavender of the sky. She noticed the way the clouds had formed, like pink sand the Almighty himself had swept with one hand across the heavens.

Patsy sipped on her tea. "Oh, Lord God," she spoke softly. "You are the Creator of all things beautiful and good. I thank you now for this day and all that it holds. May you keep me safe in the palm of your hand until that time you call me home."

She thought then of her children, Gregory and Pamela, who'd also be waiting for her entry through heaven's gates along with their daddy. Finally, she'd hear their voices again, after so long of not . . . Not since 1976. It's a terrible thing for a parent to bury a child. But to bury two at one time, young lives snuffed out by what some called unfortunate and others called an accident. She just called it "heartache." But she'd gotten through it, grateful she and her firstborn had managed over the years to meet somewhere in the middle. Even if it wasn't all the way, it was better than it had been back in '63 and the few years after.

She closed her eyes. The gulls were waking; they called to each other. Some cawing, some laughing. Or so it seemed. She wondered what they found so amusing this early in the day. Perhaps, she reasoned, they were simply saying hello to their Maker as she just had.

We each pray in our own way, Pats.

The fingers of her left hand drummed the arm of her chair, but they stopped at what she thought she'd heard. Gilbert's voice. She opened her eyes; the sky had grown lighter. The dark curtain of night was being pulled from the wings. She sighed as she waited.

A motorboat from somewhere close by buzzed along the

water's edge. It always reminded her of Gilbert's old electric razor, which was preferable to allowing her mind to liken it to the sound of the engine of the boat where her oldest had played. And died.

The sound was faint, then loud, then grew faint again. A fisherman, off to work. He'd soon be followed by another, she knew. And then another.

All of this around her, this was the way of morning in Cedar Key.

Patsy breathed in deeply. Her chest grew tight in memory, recalling the day Gilbert brought her to the island for the first time. How sad she had been. How lovingly he'd treated her. How gentle and kind. Bringing her here to see Billy, not that he'd known for certain. But loving her as he did, he was willing to chance it. Anything, anything at all, for his Patsy.

But that was Gilbert! He'd taken care of her from the moment they'd met on the bus to Trinity. Treated her with the kindness of an older brother, then a young man in love, then a husband—a lover and a friend, a provider and confidant, and sometimes the source of her aggravation, all at once.

My, my. She needed to call her new friend Kimberly Granger today. Make sure she was doing all right, expecting as she was. That girl wasn't a spring chicken; having babies could be difficult enough on a woman's body. Miss Kim was forty-two. Praise God in good health though.

Oh and Billy. She really must call him today as well. He and Veronica were supposed to see the cardiologist—a three-month follow-up to his recent stent surgery—and Patsy wanted to make sure he was all right. How she wished they'd come back to Cedar Key to live and not just to visit like they sometimes did. Then again, living and being so close to a big hospital like he was over there in Gainesville . . . well, that was a good thing. And they were close to Veronica's brothers and their families. Family was so important. She knew, what with hers scattered here and yon. Just like Billy and Veronica's children. Now, why didn't young'uns stay close to their parents when they grew up these days? That's what she wanted to know.

Her fingers drummed the chair's arm again, fast at first, then leisurely. They slowed with her breathing.

My goodness, but wasn't she ready for a nap. And so early in the morning too.

She wondered how come.

Her eyes closed again, this time feeling as though it was without any effort from her at all. They burned a little, like she hadn't slept well the night before when she knew good and well she had.

She breathed in salt air and marshland. So, what would it hurt if she took a little nap? She'd miss the sunrise. That was okay. There'd be another one tomorrow, and the day after that . . . and the day after . . .

Patsy's body swayed on a big seat in a long bus. She opened her eyes; the world went by in a blur of dark and light greens intermingled with dark browns. And cypress trees with fat bases jutting up from flat-as-glass swamp water.

Old fear washed over her. Where was she going? Who'd be there to meet her when she arrived?

Someone sat next to her; she looked to find her mother, her beloved mother, dressed as she'd been that awful day. Hat, gloves, lipstick.

"Mama?"

Mama turned slowly to gaze at her. "Why, Patsy. Look at you, all grown up. How old are you now?"

"I'll be seventy-nine next week."

"Clearly not . . ."

"Mama, what are you doing on this bus? Did you decide to come with me?"

Mama smiled. "Oh no, child. I've already gone this route; no need for me to go again. I just wanted to let you know now, while I can, that I was there in my heart."

"Where?"

"On the bus that took you to Trinity. And on the day you graduated from school. And the day you married. That first time you held a tiny life in your arms . . ."

"You were there?"

"Oh yes." She pointed to her chest. "In here I was." As her hand came down, the other pulled the hem of her glove away to reveal the old watch Patsy had not seen since 1946. "Darling, do you have a mirror and a comb?"

Patsy looked to her lap. There was the small embroidered purse, the one she took with her to school that day. The one she clung to as though it were a life preserver and she were sinking in a vat of water. "I think there's one in here."

Mama smiled. "Make sure your hair is combed before you arrive." She leaned to the right and looked straight up the aisle. "Looks like we're almost there."

Patsy opened the purse and pulled out the comb and mirror. She turned back to her mother, but the seat was empty. Her mother was gone.

Patsy brought the mirror up to her face. Her eyes grew large. Gone were the lines and wrinkles, the eyes that had lost some of their vibrancy. Looking back at her now was the young face of a thirteen-year-old girl. The girl she had once been. She blinked, touched her fingertips to the bone just under the right eye sockets. She pulled the skin down; it sprang back with youthful zeal. "My, my . . ."

She looked out the window again. The world had grown dark, and she was becoming tired. How was it she'd felt energized one moment and so worn out the next?

Then, as though she held some great knowledge, she said to herself, "Such is the way of dreams."

She put the mirror and comb away, leaned her head against the window, and allowed the rocking of the bus to lull her back to sleep. A few of her muscles twitched as the blanket of rest fell over her. It felt good. And warm. Everything was going to be all right. This time. She knew it. Because Papa was waiting for her at the bus stop. And Mam and Lloyd at home. In Trinity.

Someone shook her shoulder.

"Sleepyhead . . . hey, you."

She blinked. Wiped her fingertips across still-moist eyelashes. "Where . . ."

"Hey there."

She looked to the seat beside her. And there he was, her Gilbert, looking so dashing in his airman's uniform, cap tucked under his arm. He was smiling, a single dimple buried deep within the flesh of his right cheek.

"Hey, little sister," he said, his voice sounding like it belonged to an angel coming to take her home. "Hungry?"

Slow Moon Rising

Anise
July 2000

Some memories come with distinction. Exactness. Moments I can recall with precision as to what I was wearing. Where I was standing. The music playing on the radio.

What I was thinking.

The day I met Ross Claybourne—*Dr.* Ross Claybourne—is no exception. The memory is clear.

I had put in a full day at the Calla Lily, my newly named floral shop. Up until two years before, when my mother died, the shop had been known as Kelly's Floral Shop, appropriately named for the woman who'd opened it, Gertrude Kelly.

"Gertie" she'd been called by family and friends.

Not by my brother and me, of course. We'd called her "Mom."

And Dad . . . Well, in the beginning he'd also called her

Gertie. But soon after my tenth birthday, I suppose he called her "the plantiff." After that, "your mother."

But that's another story. And a sad one. I tend to stay away from sad stories.

I was making floral margaritas for the Stockford wedding reception, ten to be exact. I'd filled the plastic margarita glasses with wax crystals, covered the wide opening with a circular piece of cardboard, and then hot-glued a mat of duckweed, which I topped with golden-yellow preserved gardenias and freeze-dried orange rose petals.

I placed them in a carrying container, along with yards of white and peach netting, which would be used to form a cloud at their bases. I reached for the on/off knob of the radio. Faith Hill's song "Breathe" wafted from its small speakers, a song expressive of passion. Something I'd never really known.

The phone rang.

I finished the task of switching off the radio before turning toward the old wooden countertop where the phone rested, the black rotary phone my mother had installed in the mid-seventies and I'd not been able to part with.

"The Calla Lily," I said. "This is Anise."

"Oh good, Anise. I caught you. I was afraid you had already headed out to the church for the wedding." My caller was Lisa MacNeil, co-owner of the Harbour Inn, one of the oldest bed-and-breakfast inns of New England. She was also my best friend.

I sighed appropriately, knowing Lisa would understand. "I'm nearly loaded up. One last box to carry out to the van. Cheryl is already there, so . . ."

"Are you planning to stay once you get everything set up?" Panic rose in Lisa's voice.

"Goodness no. You know me and weddings." I allowed a giggle to escape my throat. Forced but effective.

"Can I burden you to bring a fresh arrangement for the front hall sometime later today?"

"What happened to the one I brought yesterday?"

Now it was Lisa's turn to sigh. "An unsupervised child just *had* to inspect it."

This time my giggle was real. "I think I have something here that will suffice. I'll be there around . . . five?" I reached for a pad and pencil to make myself a note.

"Perfect. Dinner afterward with Derrick and me? At the inn, on us?"

I paused. Saturday evenings were nearly always spent with my brother Jon and his wife—and my assistant—Cheryl and their family. My *not* being there would hardly be a tragedy. And, since I'd sometimes rather spend an evening with Lisa and Derrick, I decided to take her up on it. "Sounds good," I said. "I could use some Lisa and Derrick time."

"See you when you get here."

I delivered the remainder of the flowers and other arrangements to the Chapel of Saint Mark and found Cheryl already busy at work. I watched her with amazement. What she'd managed to accomplish in the short time she'd been there was nothing short of miraculous. Already the reception hall looked ready for the one hundred guests who would celebrate in just a few hours, though I knew we had a few touches left to arrange.

As soon as Cheryl spotted me, she met me at the first table I'd come to, which had been set up as a place for staging our boxes and containers. "Before I forget," I said, "I have to go out to the inn this afternoon to replace the front hall arrangement. Lisa has asked me to stay for dinner. I hope that's not an inconvenience."

Cheryl—a tall, willowy redhead—pretended to pout, but I knew her better than to take it to heart. "Well, I can't say I blame you. Although little Aleya will be devastated."

"Tell her I'll see her tomorrow and I'll bring her a lollypop."

Cheryl brightened. "Well, with news like that, I can guarantee you she'll get over the devastation."

We reached into the box with the floral margaritas simultaneously; our chatter was complete and work about to begin.

A few hours later, my Land Rover rambled toward the seashore and the inn. The windows were down; a cross breeze of thick air ruffled my recently ordered L.L. Bean linen cropped pants and a long-sleeved linen tunic. Though the summer sun warmed our eastern Maine town during the day, I tended to get cold in the evenings when the wind blew in from our surrounding hillsides, skipping across Seaside Point's shoreline. Because the inn was only a stone's throw from both, I slid a long, narrow scarf around my neck as soon as I pulled into the personnel parking area behind the grand inn.

The back of Harbour Inn rose majestically before me. Still early in the evening, faint light poured from nearly every one of the twenty windows stretched across the second and third floors. The first-floor windows were dark, save those of the inn's restaurant against the right corner.

I slipped out of my car, closing the door quietly behind me. Such peace as what was felt in the gentle rustling of the shrubs, the lapping of water, and the salty-sweet air should not, in my opinion, be disturbed. I opened the back door, pulled the container holding the front hall arrangement—a summer collection of apricots and greens—toward me, and closed the door with a click. With the vase held tight against my body, I mounted the seventeen steps leading to the wide porch. A quick glance upward showed that the porch lights—though few—had already been turned on in anticipation of night's fall.

Lisa purposefully kept the lighting muted. Too much, she said, deterred from the romantic feel of sitting in the rockers in the evening, listening to the quiet sounds of the sea, the music from the restaurant.

With it still being before sunset, the flap-flap of the American flag—proudly displayed at the left side of the inn—greeted me. I watched it as I climbed, paying no attention to where I was going. And why should I? I'd gone up these steps a thousand times or more. I knew each one. Just how high to step. Just when I had reached the landing.

But this evening's ascent was complicated by one of the inn's guests coming down. Rather quickly. Looking out toward the harbor rather than to where he was going. We crashed into each other without warning; the vase slipped from my grip, falling to the step at my feet, then tumbling to all those behind me.

I turned and watched as though in slow motion as it shattered. The small amount of water I'd placed in the bottom splashed against the white boards while colors of green and apricot sprayed the brick landing. Dizziness washed over me; a strong arm wrapped around my waist while a hand gripped an upper arm.

"Are you all right?"

"Oh no!"

Our words were spoken together; mine but a whisper, his a deep baritone. I looked from the disaster below to celestial blue eyes slightly crinkled and etched by laugh lines. "I . . ."

I righted myself, gripping the clean-white board railing to my right. My assailant's hands fell away. Just as easily, they returned to slip under my left elbow, to guide me the remaining two steps to the landing.

"I am *so* sorry," the man said, though rumblings of laughter echoed within the words.

I shook my head as I studied him. An older man. Well built. His hair neatly trimmed and receding. Clear skin. Handsome to a fault and with an easy smile, nearly irresistible. Nearly. "You don't sound sorry."

Peals of laughter escaped him. He pressed a hand against his chest as he said, "No, really. Really. I am." He looked toward the busted vase and dying flowers. "That could have been a real accident."

I planted my hands firmly on my waist; the linen tunic billowed like a puffy cloud. "That *was* an accident. What could have possibly made it more real?"

The man took a breath before extending his hand. In frustration, I stepped backward, nearly losing my balance again. Instead of shaking the man's hand, I reached for it in desperation, lest I topple and lie among the tossed flowers. I felt it jerk, my body slam against his—rock solid and smelling of expensive aftershave—my arms lock around his neck as he took several steps backward.

Just then, Lisa barreled out a back door. "What in the world?"

Now it was my turn to laugh . . . so hard, I had to find one of the rockers to sit, the man not far behind me. Together we rocked and hooted—I still have no idea why—while Lisa stood at the top step, looking to the ground, shaking her head. When we finally sobered and I had wiped the tears from my cheeks, Lisa turned to us and said, "I take it you've met."

The man stood. I noticed his attire now. Pressed slacks. Blue dress shirt, unbuttoned at the neck and cuffs, which were rolled to the elbows. Casual confidence exuded from every pore of his being, even as he, again, extended his hand. "Ross Claybourne," he said. "Nice to bump into you. Twice."

I laughed again, this time more subdued. I slipped my hand into his. It was warm. Soft for a man's. "Anise Kelly."

Lisa joined us, pointing toward the railing and the scene below. "I take it that was the floral arrangement for the front hall."

I leaned back, crossing my legs. "I'm afraid so."

Ross Claybourne shook his head. "My fault entirely. If you'll let Lisa here know about the cost to replace it, I'll be more than happy to pay."

"Don't be silly," I said. "I wasn't watching where I was going either." I stood. "Lisa, I'll run back to the shop, get another arrangement, and be back within forty-five minutes."

Lisa waved her hands toward us. The overhead light shimmered within her dark blonde curls—cut short and framing her face—as they bounced in the fair breeze. "No, no. Just come in and we'll have dinner. What's one more night without a centerpiece?" She looked to the man standing nearby. "Dr. Claybourne, were you planning to go out for dinner or will you join us in the restaurant tonight?"

His gaze slid to the harbor, then to the hills, before resting on the two of us. "I hadn't really decided yet. I just thought to get some fresh air first." He nodded at me. "Nice to meet you, Mrs. Kelly."

I swallowed. "Miss Kelly."

A blush rose from the color of his shirt to his cheeks. "I apologize. Miss Kelly." He nodded at Lisa. "Enjoy your dinner, ladies," he said, then skipped down the stairs, stopping halfway. By now Lisa and I had stepped to the railing and peered down. His attention returned to us. "I'm more than happy to pick up the damage. The least I can do."

"Don't you dare, Dr. Claybourne," Lisa said. "We have staff for that and you're here for a much-needed break, remember?"

Even from where I stood, I could see the whisper of a cloud as it filled his eyes. Not entirely obscuring their blue brilliance but enough to tell me the man's heart was wounded.

Derrick and Lisa filled me in on Dr. Claybourne's story over steamed garden vegetables and halibut, broiled and seasoned to perfection by Derrick—a master chef. We dined in their private quarters of the inn: a sitting room, kitchen with eating area, bedroom and bath beautifully decorated in seaside blues and greens, yellows and reds.

"He's a widower," Lisa said.

I stabbed a piece of cauliflower with a silver fork. "Recent?"

Derrick, a handsome, fortysomething man with a remarkable full head of sandy blond hair, stuck the pad of his thumb to his lips to gather some of the seasoning of the fish. "Last year. He came here to get away for a while. To heal, if a man can heal after losing his wife of thirty-five years." He pointed an index finger first at me, then at Lisa. "Don't you two go cooking up anything for him, you hear me?"

Lisa gave him her best "get over yourself" look. "First, Mr. MacNeil, your words would have a much better chance of warning us if there were not such a delightful twinkle in your eye."

Derrick rolled his green eyes in protest.

"Second," Lisa continued. "Just how is it that you know so much about Dr. Claybourne."

Derrick took a long sip of his iced tea. "I have no idea what you mean," he said after a deep swallow.

"You most assuredly do. You know exactly how long the man was married."

Derrick's hands shot up as though he were being held at gunpoint. "Can I help it if he told me himself?"

Lisa's eyes—a matching shade of green to her husband's—narrowed. "What else did he tell you? Spill, Derrick Mac-Neil, or you may find yourself sleeping on that sofa in there tonight."

I could only smile at their banter, fully aware of where it was all heading. My sweet friend had always wanted for me what she and Derrick possessed, a loving marriage. Completion in each other. Their love was second only to their devotion to God, in spite of the years of prayer for a baby that never came.

I was not far behind them, however. Only my prayers had been for someone to love me. The way Derrick loved Lisa. The way my brother Jon loved Cheryl. The way our father loved . . .

Derrick chuckled; my thoughts were interrupted. "His wife's name was Joan, they have four daughters—all but one grown—and Joan died of cancer."

I blinked. "What kind of cancer?"

He shook his head. "He didn't say."

Lisa's shoulders dropped. "How sad. For him and for the girls. One still left at home, did you say?"

Derrick nodded. "Yes. But I didn't get her name. Her social. Or anything on the other girls. Sorry, ladies." He grinned as he picked up knife and fork and cut his thick slice of tomato into bite-size portions. "Oh," he added, popping a piece into his mouth with his fingers. "One he did mention. She's a doctor, like him."

"What kind of doctor?" I asked.

Lisa stood, made her way over to the L-shaped kitchenette. "Pediatrician. I'm going to put on some hot water for tea. Anise?"

"Do you have any of the herbal raspberry like you had the last time I was here?"

Lisa stared at me as if I had three heads. "Of course."

I smiled at her. "Then, yes."

"Is Dr. Claybourne's daughter a pediatrician as well?" Lisa removed the stainless steel teakettle from a back burner and set about filling it with water.

"I think so," Derrick said from beside me. "He said they were in practice together."

I shrugged. "Well, then, that would make sense," I said, as though I knew what I was talking about. I wiped my mouth with the rose-colored linen napkin that had rested in my lap, laid it beside my plate, and stood. "Let me get the tea set ready," I said to Lisa.

"You know where it is."

Indeed I did. I also knew how special it was to her. It had been a gift from her mother-in-law on her wedding day, passed down two generations. Creamy white bone china from England with a spray of yellow daffodils and green ivy. I also knew how it must pain her that she had no one to pass it along to.

"Are you going to services in the morning?" Lisa asked after I'd arranged the tea set on a carrying tray.

"It's a Sunday, isn't it?" I asked with a smile.

She leaned in and whispered, "Good, because Dr. Claybourne asked to go with us."

"I heard that," Derrick said.

All I could do was laugh.

Acknowledgments

Before I begin my ramblings about how much I love Cedar Key and the gratitude I have for those who took part in the writing of this book, I must first tell you how difficult *Waiting for Sunrise* was to write.

A few years ago, I wrote an article for Crosswalk.com about loving those who have mental illnesses and the boundaries we are forced to set. My email account was flooded with responses by folks within the church body who have suffered in silence because of the taboo we've placed on mental illness.

Mental illness doesn't always make itself known by wild ramblings, matted hair, bugged eyes, and frothing at the mouth. It comes in all forms and knows no social or economic boundary. It doesn't even care about your religious background, and it surely doesn't care about what you think you know about it. Mental illness can come from places in our bodies that simply are not fully connected or formed *or* it can come from unresolved issues from our past.

In the course of my own life and the lives of my beloved family members, I have learned much about abandonment,

387

post-traumatic stress disorder, Axis I and Axis II psychoses, etc. When I outlined this book, I knew how a form of mental illness would affect Patsy's story but had no idea how it would play a role in my personal life while I was writing it. This made the writing all the more difficult, but it is something I now feel a passion for as I've never before felt. And, I believe there should be no more stigma around mental illness than, say, diabetes.

On another related note, however, what we knew in the sixties about mental illness or dysfunction is a far cry from what we know today. Our methods of treatment are so much more advanced. It was not altogether uncommon in the sixties for those with inability to cope to go away for a while to hospitals and institutions (not that it was *ever* discussed publicly). Some patients were dealt with more severely than others, by use of medication and shock therapy. Praise God some of those treatments no longer exist.

Please know, my reader, that when it came to Patsy's abandonment issues, I went as deep into her psyche as I could . . . for now. So, bear with me as you read.

Now, on to other things! I've said it before and I'll say it again: Cedar Key is definitely one of my most favorite places in the world to roost. It is, for me, a tropical paradise. From the moment I arrive and long after I leave, the sweetest peace falls over me. Rest and respite: this is what Cedar Key is all about.

As Billy says to Veronica, there's a lot of history in Cedar Key. I feared I may not have gotten it *all* right when it comes to Cedar Key in the fifties and sixties. But God blessed me; just after book 1 in this series, *Chasing Sunsets*, was released, "old-timers" from Cedar Key notified me. They loved knowing I'd used their home as a romantic setting for the novel, and they were willing to share their memories.

388

So allow me to start there. Thank you to Annette Haven, who gave me fantastic information. And to Beverly Goode (Edna Brown), who has shared with me so many fond memories of growing up on the island and, better still, who has become my friend. A thank-you to her brother, Henry Brown, who in his eighties has a sharp memory. Henry was the mayor of Cedar Key in years past as well as the owner of the Cedar Key Fish & Oyster Company (mentioned in chapter 26).

A huge thank-you to Captain Doug and to his lovely wife Barbara of Tidewater Tours. Somehow the "thank-you" to these two was left off in the last book's acknowledgments, and quite frankly I cannot imagine having written the book without them! I have taken many tours with Captain Doug and enjoyed every one to the fullest. He is a font of information and knowledge.

Thank you, Karlene Duke, for sitting one afternoon and talking with me about being a young teenager in the late 1940s. What fun (and I enjoyed the cake and coffee and view from your lovely home)!

Thank you to Lena Nelson Dooley, Connie Stevens, Fred St. Laurent, and Ed Vandemark, for sharing with me about that day in May when an American astronaut went into space for the first time. And thank you, Loyd Boldman, for explaining to me what was being said by NASA on the YouTube tapes.

Thank you, Mark Hancock, for explaining to me about abandonment issues and syndromes. Not to mention just listening to me ramble on about *my* problems, never mind Patsy's!

Thank you to my Cedar Key traveling buddies: Robi Lipscomb, Cheryl Moss, and Janice Elsheimer. Thank you to my friends Cynthia Schnerger, Gayle Scheff, and Rene Forehand, who read pieces of the work. Thank you (HUGE "Thank you!") to Shellie Arnold, who read the whole thing and kept making me dig deeper into my feelings. Ouch.

Thank you to the Jerry B. Jenkins Christian Writers Guild Word Weavers Orlando chapter and to our novel group for the critiques and praises. You also make me work harder than I knew I could.

Another huge thank-you to Jan Powell, who gave me a place to write in her Tampa home, undisturbed, so I could get back on track with my word count.

Thank you to my readers and fans. You are why I write and who I write to.

Thank you again and again to my agent Jonathan Clements (you da man, L'il Bro), to the whole Baker Publishing Group family, to my editors at Revell, Vicki Crumpton and Kristin Kornoelje (whom I met for the first time in—ta-da!—Cedar Key)! Thank you to my family, who puts up with me while I'm writing—most especially to the most wonderful of all huggy-hubbies, Dennis.

Always and always, *Thank you, Lord Jesus, that you will never leave me nor forsake me and that you show me, time and again, how even the rotten details of my life are clay in your hands.*

For further clarification within the book, to my knowledge, there is no Mercy Street Baptist Church or Alachua County Hospital in Gainesville, Florida.

Eva Marie Everson is the author of over twenty-five titles and is the Southern fiction author for Revell. These titles include *Chasing Sunsets, Things Left Unspoken* and *This Fine Life*. She is the coauthor of the multiple-award-winning *Reflections of God's Holy Land: A Personal Journey Through Israel* (with Miriam Feinberg Vamosh) and, of course, the Potluck Club and the Potluck Catering Club series with Linda Evans Shepherd. Eva Marie taught Old Testament theology for six years at Life Training Center and continues to teach in a home group setting. She speaks to women's groups and at churches across the nation and internationally. In 2009 she joined forces with Israel Ministry of Tourism to help organize and lead a group of journalists on a unique travel experience through the Holy Land. She is a mentor with Christian Writers Guild and the first president of Word Weavers, a successful writers critique group that began in Orlando and has since become the Jerry B. Jenkins Christian Writers Guild Word Weavers. She serves on its national leadership team. Eva Marie speaks at writers conferences across the country. In 2011 she served as an adjunct professor at Taylor University in Upton, IN. Eva Marie and her husband Dennis enjoy living "life on the lake" in Central Florida, are owned by two dogs, and are blessed to be the grandparents of the five best grandkids in the world. Eva Marie considers a trip to Cedar Key the perfect respite.

Meet Eva Marie Everson at
www.EvaMarieEversonAuthor.com

• • •

Connect with her on her blog
My Southern Voice

**www.evamarieeversonssouthernvoice.
blogspot.com**

• • •

Find her on
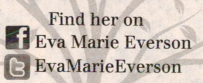 Eva Marie Everson
EvaMarieEverson

Sometimes you get a *second* chance at your *first love*

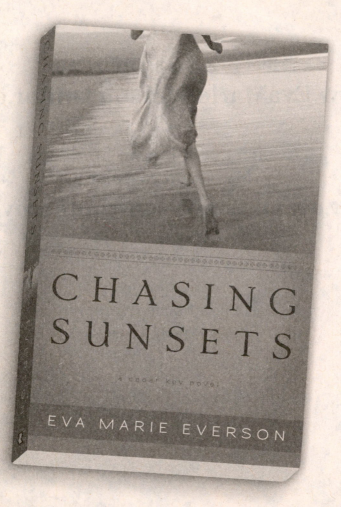

In this perfect summer novel, a woman at a crossroads returns to the family summer home on Cedar Key island looking to reinvent herself and learn to love again.

Revell
a division of Baker Publishing Group
www.RevellBooks.com

Available Wherever Books Are Sold

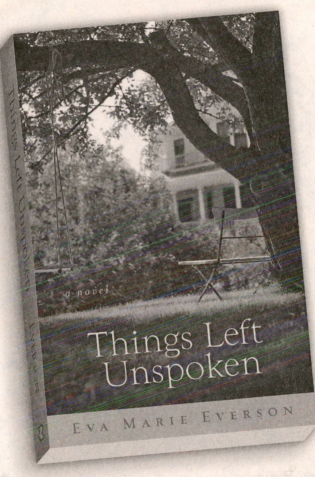

A New Novel by Bestselling Author
ANN H. GABHART
Will Capture Your Heart

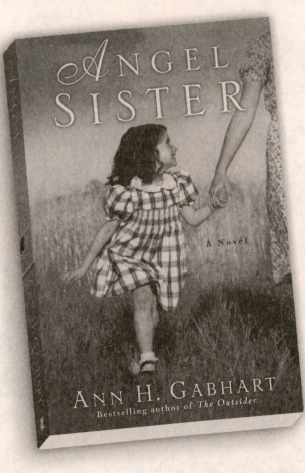

In this richly textured novel, award-winning author Ann H. Gabhart
reveals the power of true love, the freedom of forgiveness, and the
strength to persevere through troubled times.

Revell
a division of Baker Publishing Group
www.RevellBooks.com

Available Wherever Books Are Sold

"Dan Walsh's books grab your heart and don't let you go until the last page. I look forward to reading every novel Dan writes."

—Dr. Gary Smalley, *bestselling author and speaker on family relationships*

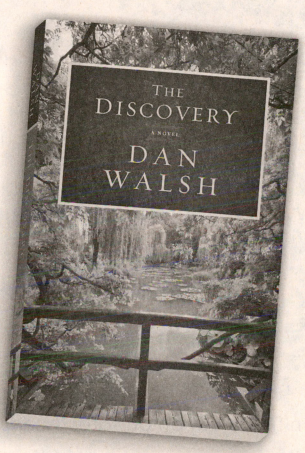

Laced with suspense and intrigue, *The Discovery* is a richly woven novel that explores the incredible sacrifices that must be made to forge the love of a lifetime.

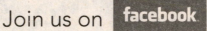